Wherein Victory Seems Unlikely for Our Heroes . . .

Eliza reunited her pounamu pistols with each other and then tapped Wellington on the forehead. "I think we can sort out your journal issues later—say, when we are safely back in the Archives?"

"Ah yes, good point." Wellington adjusted his collar and straightened slightly. "So it is your pair of pistols against all those guards and a madman?"

"Looks to be about the size of it."

"And we have no Ministry backup, and no escape plan whatsoever?"

"Let me think on that . . ." she said, pulling back the pistols' hammers. "No, none of those to speak of."

"So we're going to have to stop Havelock alone then, while trying to escape with our lives and any hard intelligence we can gather?"

"Yes, Books."

"Do you have a plan?"

"Working on one," she replied brightly. "Be a dear and get the door, will you? My hands are full."

PHOENIX RISING

A MINISTRY OF PECULIAR OCCURRENCES NOVEL

PIP BALLANTINE &
TEE MORRIS

HARPER Voyager
An Imprint of HarperCollins*Publishers*

This is a work of fiction. Names, characters, places, and incidents are products of the author's imagination or are used fictitiously and are not to be construed as real. Any resemblance to actual events, locales, organizations, or persons, living or dead, is entirely coincidental.

HARPER Voyager
An Imprint of HarperCollins*Publishers*
10 East 53rd Street
New York, New York 10022-5299

Cover art by Dominick Finelle
ISBN 978-0-06-204976-6
www.harpervoyagerbooks.com

First Harper Voyager mass market printing: May 2011

Printed in the U.S.A.

10 9 8 7 6 5 4 3 2 1

To Jared Axelrod and J.R. Blackwell, two of the most creative people we know—thank you for being the gateway drug into this amazing world called Steampunk.

ACKNOWLEDGEMENTS

Like many accomplishments in life, this book comes as an unexpected one. In our wildest dreams, we did not picture this idea to reach your hands, gentle reader, but nevertheless here our inaugural endeavour finds itself. By no means, though, did this ripping good yarn reach you solely thanks to us. We are in excellent company, and people must be thanked for making what we thought improbable into an adventure from the past that never was.

Thank you to our agent, Laurie McLean, for seeing the potential in the idea and then passionately standing behind Agents Books & Braun through it all to see them to the end of the mission. Thank you, Diana Gill, editor at Harper Voyager, for passionately fighting for the Ministry. If it were not for your belief, this adventure would have been merely an idea, not a book; and thank you for frank and upfront expectations, good conversations, and terrific dim sum. To Will, for being presented an incredible challenge and rising to it, and working with us to make the magic happen. Thank you to J. Daniel Sawyer, P.C. Haring, Gary Snook, Paolo Tosolini, and the Twitter Hive Mind, for Italian translations, steampunk resources, first draft impressions, and support and inspiration to push on and see things through.

And thank you, gentle reader, for giving Books and Braun a go. We hope you enjoy the ride.

PHOENIX RISING

CHAPTER ONE

Wherein Our Intrepid Heroes Meet for the First Time and Start Off with a Bang!

Wellington Thornhill Books, Esquire, had never heard an explosion that close before. Considering the ringing in his ears, he would most likely never hear another one like it again.

Splinters, both of the wooden and metal variety, pelted his face, but he was far too distracted to notice anything painful. Perhaps they were from the cell door; perhaps they were from the contraption which held him fast. Was the engineer responsible for this torture device still where he was before the explosion? What of the guards? Time slowed, seeming to creep and flow as in the languid dreams of a deep sleep.

Two strange pops rang in his ears through the hum the explosion had left in its wake. He still could see nothing, but was grateful that he had been kidnapped by a gentleman—one that had seen fit not to strip him of his clothes before shackling him to the wall. Only a complete cad would practice such ungentlemanly behaviour. His clothing had served him well as a minimal shield from the debris, but as his wrists were bound over his head, all he could do was turn his head, screw his eyes shut, and hope for the best.

Creeping through the hum in his ears was another sound—the undulating blaring of klaxons alerting the complex to the intrusion. Considering the very liberal amount of dynamite used on his cell door, he assumed this was a full-on assault from the Ministry. He felt a swell of pride. It felt good to be so appreciated.

A lady emerged from the smoke and debris—though her improper fashions indicated she was unworthy of the title. She was wearing pinstripe breeches tucked neatly into boots that stopped just above the knee. More disturbing than the fact this "lady" was wearing trousers were the sticks of dynamite strapped around her thighs. The boots also had several sheaths for throwing knives. The bodice she was wearing was a black leather device, which not only served to lift the petite woman's bosom up but also provided a secure surface for the baldric she wore across it. All this was accented with an impressive, fur coat that flowed around her like a cape.

The stillness she engendered in the moment seemed odd to Wellington. Her gaze fixed on him, and there was no relief in her expression. She looked to be sizing him up.

Her pistols finally lowered as she spoke. Wellington's ears had cleared enough that her voice was discernable. "You Books?" she asked, sheathing her weapons.

Wellington coughed and spluttered before managing a choked, "Yes."

"Jolly good then—I'd hate to have come all this way for nothing." She applied a queer-looking key to the restraints holding his wrists. Wellington was relieved to hear the metallic ring of iron snapping open and again as she freed his ankles. She knocked away from him the array of needles that had almost turned him into a human pincushion. A few quick, hard blinks, and Wellington observed his interrogator on his face, the remains of the door protruding from his back. There was a touch of poetry that, in falling to the ground, his tray of blades, needles, and other vile instruments had toppled on top of him, decorating his corpse with the tools of his trade. Close by his tormentor's body were two guards, freshly shot.

A deceptively delicate hand grabbed a handful of waistcoat. "Introductions later. Running now," she said, yanking him off the wall.

Wellington would have liked a chance to examine this Angel of Destruction more closely, but she was correct in that they had to get away—and, from the sound of distant voices adding to the clamor of the klaxons, rather quickly. While he felt exhilarated to step out of his prison cell, the dim lighting and smooth stone surfaces enveloping him only served as a reminder that he was deep within the stronghold of the House of Usher. As he followed his savior into the torchlit passageways, Wellington still struggled to ascertain how this secret society of ne'er-do-wells was able to deduce his position within the equally secretive Ministry of Peculiar Occurrences.

Presently unable to write anything down, Wellington made a mental note nonetheless to inform the Director they had a serious breach of security somewhere. After the third left into another identical stone corridor, into another row of prison cells, he wondered if he would live to share his deductions with anyone.

"Do you know which way you are going?" he asked, his voice cracking slightly.

"Yes, we're going"—she paused at a junction, her head whipping to either side—"this way." Her hand on his jacket once again jerked him firmly after her.

They came upon another junction, identical to the other four they had already taken, when she immediately scooted back into the passageway and shoved him hard into the curve of its stone wall. On feeling the back of his skull kiss rock again, Wellington realised with horror he was being managed! *This would not stand*, he thought, *even in such outrageous circumstances.*

"Wellington Thornhill Books, Esquire," he blurted, sticking out his hand. "Pleasure to meet you, Agent . . ."

One hand slapped across his mouth as the other one drew one of the earlier-sheathed pistols. A regiment of foot soldiers ran by them, but her cold, hard gaze kept him as still as she had been in his cell.

After a few seconds, she tore her palm away and glared at him.

"Introductions?" she whispered sharply, "Are you mad?"

Wellington stared at her, and repeated, "Wellington Thornhill Books, Esquire and Chief Archivist at the Ministry of Peculiar Occurrences. And you are?"

She let out an exasperated sigh. "Eliza D. Braun, Field Agent." Her eyes darted behind him, and the gunshot echoed through the crypt. Wellington turned to see the foot soldier crumple to the ground, still clutching his rifle. She smiled slightly. "Currently saving your arse for the Ministry. Come on!"

Wellington tried to will his heart to pump faster, his lungs to take more air so that he could run a little bit longer. The world began to dissolve, picked apart by a fatal rainstorm that fell around them both.

Agent Braun reached behind her to remove a small cannon strapped on her back. "Just stay on this path, Books. I'll be right behind you!"

The gunfire managed to strike only rock and earth. Then came three heavy detonations. They were hardly enough to cause a cave-in, but the cave did an ample service in amplifying and containing their individual shocks. Wellington, through the next volley of heavy fire, kept running forward. Had the bullets stopped? He could no longer hear the soldiers or their rifle fire. Darkness enveloped him for an instant, and then he saw a light ahead of them, pouring in an open peephole set in a cast-iron door. It was blinding white, more brilliant than anything he had seen before in his life. His hands pressed against the hatch, and he felt its chill. This was it: the way out!

The sound of something heavy dragging across the dirt snapped him back to the reality colder and harder than the outside world. They were still trapped inside the fortress, and Field Agent Eliza D. Braun was making a barricade for each of them; placing barrels right in front of the locked door.

They settled in between these, resting their backs against the wall. Wellington looked across the corridor at her.

"What are you doing?" he finally asked, the klaxons still distant but the sounds of soldiers growing louder.

"Thinking." She began loading bullets into her pistols, the imposing cannon she was wielding earlier now lying by her feet. Satisfied she had enough, she snapped them shut and gripped the pistols firmly, framing her rather sweet face with the two weapons.

Wellington crooked an eyebrow. "Thinking?"

A bullet ricocheted not two inches from her head. "Yes," she replied calmly, "I always think better when I am being shot at."

Agent Braun leaned out, spraying the space before them with bullets that either found their mark or served to keep Usher's henchmen at bay. Wellington's eyes darted from one side to theother, catching only a shadow of a helmet or a rifle barrel.

"Wouldn't you think better if you used that?" he asked, motioning to the cannon.

"Katherina there is an experimental model from the Armory," Agent Braun said, considering the impressive gun. "I'll have to tell them three shots just isn't enough!"

Blasted clankertons. Wellington managed not to let the swear escape him.

She came from the top of their barricade on this volley, finishing off what was left in both pistols. Braun leaned back against the wall, her satisfied grin fading the longer she looked at him.

"Books," she snapped, "where's the bloody rifle?"

"What rifle?"

Through her gritted teeth she replied, "The rifle the soldier I shot in the corridor was carrying!"

"Oh, was I supposed to pick it up?"

Her deep breath was interrupted by more bullets tearing into the earth. She snapped both pistols open and reloaded them. Agent Braun considered Wellington for a moment. One of the pistols twirled in her grip, and then she tossed it to him, handle first.

The weapon bounced in Wellington's hands like it was fresh from the forge. He immediately cast it back to her. Barrel first.

"Bloody hell," she gasped, making certain it was pointed away from her.

"Madam, I am an Archivist for a reason!"

"I need another gun, Books! What bloody good is a *librarian* down here at present?"

"*Archivist!*" he retorted.

The howl from outside made Eliza's head snap up, as she leaned to the left to let out another volley of gunfire. He peered into the blinding white of the world outside. Freedom. It was theirs, merely a single turn of a handle and they were—

"Don't!" Agent Braun snapped, causing Wellington to start. "Just keep away from the door, Books."

"Whatever are you on about?" Why weren't they having this conversation elsewhere, say, the other side of this door? "We're almost—"

"Dead, that's what we are," she stated, so final and certain that Wellington furrowed his brow. "The door is a deathtrap. Look at the lock."

The mechanism appeared as a thick metal box the size of a man's fist, a *large* man's fist. Two cast iron coils came from the door frame and ran into the dial-decorated cube with four metallic tentacles reaching upward and disappearing into the stone ceiling above them.

He adjusted his spectacles on the tip of his nose to get a closer look at the numbers within the dials. He knew there were bullets still biting at the rock walls, and even a few struck above his head, the sparks lighting their little alcove for a moment. These bullets, though, were far less important than this puzzle.

From the corner of his eye, he saw Agent Braun extending her leg.

His throat grew dry. "What are you doing?"

"The door's armed to blow, right?" She grasped a stick of dynamite. "I'm going to help it along."

The woman was quite mad, and he was going to have to treat her as such. "But the rest of your team is on their way," Wellington said as calmly as the situation allowed.

"The Ministry remains rather underfunded by the Crown, Books, and I was given the choice of either backup or more dynamite." She held up the stick. "I went with what I could trust."

Bullets ate away at the barrels shielding them. One or two planks buckled. Their makeshift barricade would not last much longer.

"Throw it," he shouted over the gunfire.

"What?"

"Throw it!" he insisted. "I can solve this lock."

She cocked her head, her eyes narrowing just before another spray of bullets danced along the walls—one even ripped through her chemise sleeve.

"Trust me. I can do this, I just need a moment to—"

Agent Braun grabbed from her baldric what appeared to be a lapel pin comprised of clockwork gears and cogs, fractionally larger than his thumbnail. She pierced the top of the stick and flipped an unseen switch on the tiny device in one smooth motion.

She had a good arm, but even so the explosion rang Wellington's head like a bell in Westminster Cathedral. Small bits of rock rained down on them for a few seconds and then the shock subsided.

Dimly he discerned her muttering, "Bugger." Her eyes shifted back to him as she started to pull from other holsters pistols varying in size and caliber. "Right, you've got your moment, Books. Solve the lock."

Braun continued to produce sidearm upon sidearm from her shoulder baldric. This was where they would make their stand apparently, and it was up to Wellington Books to make sure it was not their last.

There was not much light to work with, but some compound inside the cast-iron box gave the numbers a phosphorescent glow. He looked at the range of numbers, letters, and symbols on the dials, twenty-one by quick count, all of them appearing random. If they were in seven sets of three or three sets of seven, this would be a simple cipher; but he needed a key. A simple key. It had to be simple for those here to use regularly.

Devilishly clever, he thought to himself. He admired its chaos, its non-sequential anarchy which, one could argue, reflected what the House of Usher—

"You said you could solve it!" Braun was firing into the dust and debris—so obviously someone had survived. "Time is a bit of a luxury here, mate!"

A key. That was what he needed for this puzzle—something that would make sense of the dials. Wellington glanced up to the small window looking out to freedom, even if the freedom consisted of a vast wasteland of ice. That certainly explained her coat. A veil of snow obscured his vista, and the howl of the wind intensified. He needed to know more. Where the hell were they?

Yes, it was a rather silly question but it did matter. "Agent Braun—where exactly are you from, may I ask?"

Braun shot him an incredulous look. "Beg your pardon?"

"Where are you from, Agent Braun? I can tell by your dialect that you are not from any district of England—"

"Well, I'm not a Pom!" she spat before unleashing a volley of bullets. Books glanced over his shoulder to see the shadows stir and then grow still, but only for a moment as the dark moved again, this time shooting as they advanced.

"It would be jolly nice," she shouted over the gunfire she shared with the oncoming soldiers, "if you'd do something useful!"

"Where—are—you—" Wellington insisted.

"New Zealand!" she shouted as she sheathed both spent pistols and then picked up two more from the ground, "More precisely, Wellington, if you must know!"

It made perfect sense. Send in a specialist—one familiar with the region.

"Where is our pickup to take place?"

"Just outside!" she shouted, firing off three rounds. "Airship is going to swing by the fortress and pick us up!"

"And did you give them coordinates?"

"Why bother?" she scoffed before shooting again. "This is the only dark fortress within sight of Mount Erebus. Would be hard to miss!"

Wellington quickly turned back to the door and began muttering to himself. Geographic location. Height. Summit elevation. Yes, he was certain. This was what he did, after all, for Queen and Country. And then finally, his fingers began turning dials.

He had dialed the final entry—"E"—into the lock when he heard a pair of dull thuds behind him. Wellington looked over his shoulder to see his Angel from the Colonies pick up the last two pistols, the ones she had been brandishing when she first appeared in his cell. Beautiful things, they were: the barrels were of gleaming brass and their handles appeared to be ivory inlaid with a deep green stone. Others might have mistaken the decoration for jade, but Wellington recognised they were the sacred stone of New Zealand—*pounamu*. Before she grasped them completely, he noted the design: a Hei-Hei, a powerful good-luck symbol. The wearer of this tiki was considered clear thinking, clever, and dedicated to a cause, their greatest strength being character.

"What's with the smile, Books?"

Yes, he was smiling at her. Fancy that.

"I thought it would be nice to catch an airship," Wellington said proudly. "No need to keep the hired help waiting."

The latch came down with a quick groan and sharp thud. Agent Braun blinked at the sudden light flooding their corridor. The wind was colder and sharper than he could have expected, but it was an exhilarating feeling.

"How did you—"

Wellington motioned to the dials, now clear in the blinding white of this continent's eternal winter. The lock display read 77°31'48" S, 167°10'12" E.

"Bloody hell, Books," Braun shook her head, replacing the cannon she referred to as Katerina back into her back holster. "Did you just pull those numbers out of your arse?"

"Madam, this is what I do. I am an—"

A bullet struck the open door, showering them with sparks. Eliza answered the shot with three of her own. "I got it the first time—you're an archivist! Move it!" She slapped a pair of tinted goggles into his stomach. "You'll need these or you won't see a bloody thing. Lucky for you I carry a spare."

The climate had a sobering effect. Needles of cold tore through his suit pants and shoes. Agent Eliza Braun and her entirely unfeminine garb, however, made easy work of the snow.

"You didn't happen to bring a spare *coat* with you, Agent Braun?"

Eliza didn't reply. At first. "Sorry, mate. I needed to travel light."

Travel light? A small arsenal of handguns, throwing knives, sticks of dynamite, and that small cannon strapped to her back was traveling *light*?

Wellington's discomfort dissipated at the sight of the airship rumbling towards them, a rope ladder dangling from the bottom of its cabin. He spared a glance behind them to see the fortress's massive main doors opening like some great maw, expelling soldiers properly attired for the weather and armoured transports rumbling alongside them. Atop the stronghold's battlements, massive cannons were coming to bear.

Wellington shook his head, looking up at the airship. "They'll shoot us down before we can—"

Her grin was both wide and unsettling as she snaked her arm into the rope ladder. "Just hold on to me, Welly!"

Welly?

Agent Braun pulled his arms tight around her waist. She then fired up at the airship, her bullet striking close to what appeared to be a purposefully painted bullseye. With the ring of a distant *clunk*, they were both hoisted through the cold, the speed of their ascent quite knocking the remaining breath out of Books. The ride upward suddenly stopped, and Wellington felt himself slip free. He scrambled to avoid falling to his death, latching onto what was immediately at hand.

It was only when Braun called out "Lads, pull me in quick, or this bookworm is going to ruin my favorite bodice!" that Wellington realised what he was hanging onto. He was caught between etiquette and death for quite the longest moment of a rather extraordinary day.

A sudden heave from the crewmembers, and Wellington was finally able to free his grip. The redness in his cheeks would take far longer to subside however. The only hint of cold now was the floor they remained sprawled across. In Wellington's ears came a low rumbling sound. Engines. Propellers. The airship was now listing sharply.

He looked up to see Agent Braun looking out of a porthole. The bodice appeared to be stretched a bit, but it was still intact. For some reason, Wellington took relief in that. Groaning, he picked himself up from the floor of the hold and joined her at the window.

"That was quite invigorating." She pulled out the two vanity pistols and chuckled. "Between them, four bullets left. You know how to show a lady to a good time."

"One moment, Agent Braun," Wellington said, trying to regain something of his composure. "You said you chose ordnance over additional Ministry-sponsored personnel. So where are these explosives?!"

"Where I left them, naturally."

The stronghold's centre erupted as Mount Erebus would

have done in its heyday. The cannons threatening to pluck them from the chilly heavens instead toppled back as plumes of fire and black smoke bellowed upward. Wellington could make out enemy soldiers attempting to flee, but a second explosion rocked the fortress. Another gout of fire tossed debris in all directions; and then in what appeared to be the opening of Satan's Dominion itself, the fortress vanished in a ball of orange fire and pitch-black smoke. Their airship listed again, only to right itself moments later. Through the porthole, they both could see the icy landscape of Antarctica scarred by darkness, destruction, and death.

Wellington looked at Agent Braun as if for the first time. "Good Lord, woman. You are an idiot!"

CHAPTER TWO

In Which Our Plucky Pepperpot Eliza D. Braun Must Pay the Piper for Her Feats of Derring-Do!

Eliza D. Braun hated to be wrong, yet she would not be accused of being a coward either. She reached the low line of warehouse buildings right on the edge of the River Thames and crossed over the street as quickly as possible. *The anticipation is the worst of it*, she told herself. Her conscience was something that she thought she'd been rid of years ago, yet events of the last week had proven that assumption a mistake.

The no-nonsense sharp lettering above the open doorway of the warehouse at the beginning of the row proclaimed, "Miggins Antiquities: Finest Imports from the Empire." Carts piled high rolled through the large door that led to the unpacking and storage warehouse, while workers and customers used the smaller entrance to the showroom and offices. Eliza tugged her long tweed, masculine coat around her against a strange, sudden chill, and went in via the latter entrance.

As always the smell of musty old artefacts hit her first. She shook her head and sneezed like a cat. By God, it was always dusty down here on the ground floor. Thank goodness it was not where she had her office. This was merely the front for the Ministry, but why imports? Why not a perfumery or a boutique?

Or a bakery. *That* would have been *heavenly.*

She nodded to those workers who had no choice but to slave away down here. However, with their noses buried in ledgers and correspondences they didn't even notice. They never did. Perhaps *that* was the reason for the chosen front.

A short flight of stairs led to agents' offices, and Eliza felt she could breathe again, finally free of the reek of old, dead things. The office behind the oak door was utilitarian but pleasant enough. Twelve leather-topped desks were laid out in the block pattern, and as always Eliza's eye was drawn to the only one that was not piled with papers. She had yet to accept Harrison's handsome face would no longer be there to welcome her. Never again.

Closing the door quietly behind her she made for her own desk, attempting not to disturb her fellow agents. Currently there were only two of the team in—the rest conducting their business in the field, where she wished she were right now. This was only where the painful paperwork was conducted. All of them avoided it as best they could. Agent Hill, from the dominion of Canada, was busy scribbling furiously in his ledger determined to get out of the office as soon as possible, but her colleague from Australia, Agent Campbell, leaned back in his chair and smiled at her.

Not today, please, not today, she thought to herself.

Her prayer went unanswered. "Gidday, Liza."

Bruce was not an unattractive man: tall, dark haired, with green eyes, just in fact the kind of male she went for. It was his unfortunate attempts at humour that stole away any possibility of a clandestine romance, and showed Bruce for what his true nature dictated. He was, without a doubt, a right git.

"Rough night out with the flock was it?"

Ah yes, the sheep jokes. Only iron willpower stopped

her from kicking his chair out from under him. "Agent Campbell"—she leaned down and fixed him with her blue gaze—"you have no idea of the fun I have when you are not looking."

His perfectly white teeth flashed in a face that was still tanned from the brighter sun of the Southern Hemisphere. He held up two tickets, wriggling them for emphasis in front of Eliza's eyes. "How about some fun *with* me then? Box seats to the latest play at the St. James Theatre. Thought we could have dinner after . . . or maybe breakfast. You know—seeing as we are southern cousins and all."

It was just like Bruce to try and use the closeness of Australia and New Zealand for his own ends, only moments after bringing up the sheep jokes. The only thing they shared, in truth, was being looked down on as "Colonials" by the Britons.

Hardly enough to push her into his loving-for-the-moment embrace. "I would rather get into a boxing ring with one of your kangaroos than wake up next to you, Bruce. I thought I had explained this clearly a number of times." She strode past him and took off her coat and hung it on the polished rack. She knew full well that Bruce was looking at her rear end appreciatively—it was the one negative of dressing in masculine pants, shirt, and vest. However, the freedom of movement it allowed her was worth it. Truthfully displaying her assets was something she was never shy about.

He waited until she had sat down at her desk before announcing, "The Fat Man upstairs wants to see you."

"You mean Doctor Sound?" Eliza shot in sharp reply.

Agent Campbell waved his hand, "You call him what you like—he's 'Fat Man' to me. Blimmin' stuck-up toff." He pulled out a slip of paper and slapped it down in front of her. Eliza recognised Shillingworth's precise handwriting proclaiming:

9 o'clock sharp. Please be prompt.

Eliza cleared her throat, stood up, and pulled out the pocket watch from her vest. "Probably wants to congratulate me on my last mission."

It was 9:03. *Damn.*

Bruce's snort of disbelief still managed to reach her ears as she sprinted across the office. The lift to the other floors was concealed behind oak paneling at the end of the corridor. Eliza slipped through the secret entranceway, inserted the tiny clockwork locket from around her neck into the keyhole, and punched the call button. While she stood in the tiny antechamber, the sound of motors and gears humming low, her mind raced.

The director of the Ministry only commented on missions for two reasons: if they had been exceptionally smooth and successful, or if they had been a total disaster. Eliza's previous missions were always successful but never smooth—this was not the first time she'd been called up to the Director's office.

After taking a long breath she stepped into the lift, closed the outer gate, and set the Chadburn to "Director's Office." The short ride seemed to go on for an age. This top floor was the sole domain of Doctor Basil Sound, head of the Ministry of Peculiar Occurrences. It opened into a small waiting room, with the razor-sharp Miss Shillingworth guarding the doorway to his office. The white-blonde-haired young woman took her duties as a secretary very seriously and with the efficiency of a woman twice her age. At the moment of Eliza's appointment, though, she was struggling to shove armfuls of brown folders into the chute that would deposit them to the Archives. Her stern ice-chip eyes darted to Eliza, but apart from that she did not acknowledge the agent's existence. The only sound in the office was that of air hissing loud and hard. Eliza's gaze shot over to the network of pneumatic tubes, all labeled a variety of locations—House of Parliament, House of Lords, Ministry of War, and many, many more. She took a covert glance at the new arrival. This cylinder, courtesy of the Thames Pneumatic Dispatch, had come from Buckingham Palace. Perhaps, a reprieve from Her Majesty?

"*Doctor Sound*," Eliza could hear Queen Vic say in her recently arrived proclamation, "*upon hearing of your scheduled reprimand of Agent Eliza D. Braun, We are not amused*."

Shillingworth let out an exasperated sigh as files tumbled to the floor. While Eliza enjoyed seeing the cool secretary in such a pickle, she wasn't about to wait for her say-so.

Eliza made sure her dark russet hair was still tucked neatly into a braid, and then strode to the door while her bravery held. She caught a brief glimpse of Shillingworth looking up from the floor. Eliza thought she heard the secretary call out to her, but too late. Refusing to keep the Director waiting, the agent shoved the door open.

The Turkish carpet of the Director's lavish office muffled much of the ambiance of East End's docklands. Thick draperies at the windows did a remarkably efficient job of shutting out the comings and goings on the river as well, giving this private chamber a heaviness that would have passed for silence on any other day at the Ministry.

It appeared to Eliza, though, that this was not "any other day" as the office's décor seemed to pronounce the argument between Doctor Sound and a tall, imposing man opposite of his desk.

"—while the Queen remains uncertain on this matter," continued the tower of a man, his index finger tapping against Sound's desk. "I assure you I do not."

A strange expression danced on Doctor Sound's face—one that Eliza had never seen. True anger.

Eliza's jaw snapped shut on her half-prepared explanation.

She would have much rather been back in Antarctica with the smell of gunpowder, earth, and sweat in her nostrils than here witnessing this. So intense was their discussion they hadn't noticed her enter, and Eliza was sure she was about to find out something extremely interesting about her superior.

That was until Shillingworth burst in. The cracks in her icy demeanor were perfectly visible as she actually yanked on Eliza's arm. "I am sorry, Doctor Sound, she just barged in without asking."

The Director turned in their direction, his portly figure surprising agile. "Agent Braun, I trust you have an explanation for bursting into my office?" His voice was mild, but she couldn't mistake its dark undertone.

Eliza's stomach clenched. "The note said promptly at nine. I was running a bit late this morning."

Doctor Sound glanced to the other side of his office and nodded. "Ah, yes, I did say nine o'clock, didn—"

"You must be Agent Eliza D. Braun, our operative we *inherited* from the South Pacific office," the tall man interjected, his voice coated with a film of civility that sent goose flesh along Eliza's arms. "How appropriate . . . since we were just talking about you." Unlike the Director, this man was strikingly handsome, with strong hawklike features and a salt-and-pepper beard. As he strode towards her, she noticed he was dressed better than Sound as well.

Though her mind was whirling, Eliza tilted her head and held out her hand. "You have me at a disadvantage, sir. I don't believe we have been introduced."

He smiled at that, before bowing and taking her fingertips, "Peter Lawson, Duke of Sussex."

The name was familiar—even to Eliza. "Private Secretary to Her Majesty, the Queen. We are indeed honoured." She smiled, and hoped this would prove to Doctor Sound that she knew exactly how to manage the peerage. Maybe he would forget those past incidents.

His grin was unsettling—the grin of someone who knew something she didn't. Suddenly his handsomeness made less of an impression on her. Suddenly she disliked him. Intensely.

He could read her discomfort and enjoyed it—that much was obvious as he turned back to the Director. "I trust you will take my advice, Basil." And then with that, he spun on his heel and left the office.

For a moment Doctor Sound, Eliza, and Miss Shillingworth stood there, awkward in the sudden silence. The rhythmic *tick tock* of the clock over the mantel only added to the mood. Finally, with a sigh Doctor Sound took a seat at his massive desk.

"Thank you, Miss Shillingworth," he began. "Please, Agent Braun," and he motioned to a chair in front of his desk.

Eliza swallowed hard and crossed the office to settle in what would have been, perhaps on any other call to the Director's office, a very comfortable chair. However, the chair was warm. It was still holding on to the Duke of Sussex. That thought made her skin crawl. Eliza hoped Doctor Sound didn't notice her squirm.

The stack of ledgers and folders before the Doctor would have made any lesser man give up in despair. Doctor Sound, Eliza remained most assured, was not a lesser man. He took off his glasses and fixed her with a sharp grey gaze. She felt as effectively pinned as a butterfly in the British Museum. "Agent Braun, as you may guess, you have put me in a rather sticky position."

Eliza wanted to enquire what exactly one of the highest-ranked officials was doing in the Director's office, and enquire why he was so miffed. However, she could guess the answer to the second question.

Unfortunately, the seat in front of Doctor Sound was a perch she was very familiar with, and that familiarity gave her a kind of badly placed courage. "I know what you are going to say, Doctor Sound . . ."

"Really?" He folded his hands before him. "Then, please, enlighten me."

"I know I made some snap decisions in the field without proper clearance." The words tumbled out of her mouth.

The Doctor held up his hand. "Is that what field agents are calling insubordination these days—snap decisions?" He readjusted his glasses and pulled two fistfuls of folders towards him. "Let us review some of your other 'snap decisions,' shall we?"

When he opened them Eliza felt all hope fade. On the front was her name, and she knew very well what was inside. She sat very still and waited for the axe to fall. The glint Eliza had seen in Sussex's eye haunted her.

"Let me see—the wanton destruction by explosion of the Duke of Pembroke's country estate . . ."

"His butler was using it as a base for—" She stopped mid-sentence when he raised his gaze once more.

"The same fate you meted out to the Embassy of Prussia." He licked one finger and flicked over another page. "That was quite the diplomatic mess."

"The agent I was following was largely responsible—"

One lift of his eyes and her protestations died on her lips. Eliza shifted slightly in her seat as he went on. "And then there is Operation Darkwater." By the gods, she had hoped he wouldn't bring that one up, though it was natural he would. "The destruction of Nemo's base and the loss of his *Nautilus* blueprints must stand, by far, as the worst of your 'snap decisions.'"

She didn't even try to explain that one. Instead, Eliza held her breath. Would they cut her allowances with the Armory again, or maybe demote her to junior Field Agent?

The Doctor pushed back the folders and thrummed his fingers. "In light of all those occurrences, though, your disregard of the orders concerning Agent Wellington Books is particularly disturbing."

Eliza swallowed hard. Ever since their mad escape she had been aware that trouble would follow. So she came back as she always did, with heat. "Agent Books is one of ours, Doctor, one of the Ministry. And when I saw him there I simply couldn't execute him, as my orders indicated."

"And what made you think you had the right to ignore them? How can you be sure that Agent Books has not been compromised? As Chief Archivist he is privy to all the Ministry's secrets."

"It was a feeling, Doctor. An instinct. The same instinct

that keeps me alive in the field, something that I wonder if you can truly grasp spending all your time here!"

She gently caught her bottom lip under her teeth. Her temper. There was nothing she could do to take those words back, but she hated being questioned for her actions in the field. She was one of the Ministry's best. Her methods might be unorthodox and final, but they always produced results.

Doctor Sound continued to study her, his expression impassive.

"I looked down at Books and just had the feeling he hadn't broken. And as he was one of ours, I made a judgment call, as is my right in the field. We have never lost—" She swallowed those words, and tried again. "We have never executed one of our own. I was certainly not going to be the first to do so." She then allowed herself a smirk. In for a penny. "Besides, it was far more of a challenge to get him out alive."

"And this roguish behaviour, Agent Braun, is exactly what troubles me. The Ministry of Peculiar Occurrences is far more than simply acting on one's impulses in the name of the Queen. The best way to defeat the shadows of menace and evil is to become a shadow yourself. We protect the Empire in secret, a detail you seem to overlook . . . often. You could take a lesson from your predecessors, and perhaps develop a lesser reliance on black powder and dynamite."

"But I *like* black powder and dynamite." She was aware she sounded like a child with her favorite toy taken away but that was what she was reduced to.

One corner of Doctor Sound's mouth jerked, and she hoped he was repressing a smile—but it was terminally fleeting. "Due to your mission history and your penchant for 'snap decisions,' disciplinary action is unfortunately warranted."

Eliza's mind raced over the options. Maybe the good Doctor was going to reassign her to the Ministry's Far Eastern outpost—that wouldn't be much of a punishment really. His next few words, however, came as a surprise.

"But first," Doctor Sound rose from his chair. "I think a different perspective is needed. If you please," he said, motioning to the door

For a second Eliza wondered if she had misheard or missed the punishment altogether. "A . . . different perspective, Doctor?"

"Indeed." He closed her folders and dropped them into his "Out" tray. "Between this morning's appointments and your own words, I believe I do need a change of scenery."

"Very well, Doctor. Exactly where—?" Eliza began to ask, her head still spinning with the Director's sudden change in demeanor.

"No need to grab a parasol, Agent Braun," he chuckled, "We're staying close to home."

"Very good then, Doctor."

Her mind was reeling, trying to ascertain exactly what disciplinary action he had in mind for her. She tried to calm her breathing. They passed Miss Shillingworth, now back at her desk, and every trace of her earlier predicament absent. The waiting area was, as it always appeared to be whenever Eliza visited, immaculate.

"Capital job, Shillingworth," chortled Doctor Sound.

The secretary blinked. Compliments from the Director, Eliza perceived, seemed to be out of the ordinary.

"We will be just a few moments," he said, reaching into his coat pocket and producing a small folded piece of paper. "Tend to this, and please ask any appointments, expected or otherwise, to call on me after lunch. There's a good lass."

Shillingworth nodded and placed the envelope at the centre of her frighteningly tidy desk.

Doctor Sound turned back to Eliza, and smiled warmly as he gestured to the lift. "After you, Agent Braun."

Eliza felt the goose flesh return with a vengeance underneath her clothing.

CHAPTER THREE

Where Our Dashing Hero of History and Cataloguing Is Finally Granted a Proper Introduction to Miss Eliza D. Braun

Drip . . .

Drip . . .

Drip . . .

Wellington glanced up from his wide desk, his eyes staring into the shadows of where the sound originated. Once upon a time, that metronome had been a harsh reminder of the deplorable conditions here. The constant, low rumble of the boilers didn't concern him because those devices were doing their job: they kept the moisture contained. Some pipes and smaller chambers, however, could not help but sweat. Add to that the stresses of the mighty and powerful Thames on the opposite side of the wall and you were bound to get damp of some kind.

This challenge he had willingly taken on. He could only complain so much.

Drip . . .

Drip . . .

Drip . . .

A strategy, he had told himself early on, when accepting this position in the Ministry of Peculiar Occurrences. *Have a strategy in obtaining what you want. Be decisive in the battles you undertake.* That military training of his really was coming to use in everyday life. With the Archives in such a state that the term "disarray" would have been considered a compliment, Wellington rose to the challenge and kept his grumblings to himself. Quietly, he surmised the problems, prioritized solutions, and then implemented them. The ones he knew would require Doctor Sound's immediate attention—such as the need for a dehumidifier in order to keep the Archives' moisture under some degree of control—were reserved for those meetings when it was the two of them, alone; and Wellington would have his rapt attention.

Those meetings were few and far between one another.

Drip . . .

Drip . . .

Drip . . .

The dripping that echoed throughout the vast collection of notes and artifacts from the field had become the pounding of a war drum. The Archives were his responsibility, his charge for Queen and Country. Each drip mocked him. Each drop challenged him. And even with his own efforts back home to assemble a dehumidifier adequate for the dank, cavernous space underneath the Ministry's office, the problem persisted. His own failures and ongoing challenges were both continuously brought to the forefront of his mind every day as he toiled at his desk.

Drip . . .

Drip . . .

Drip . . .

Now, following his ordeal, each drip was a sound as sweet as Johann Sebastian Bach's "Violin Concerto No. 2 in E Minor."

He allowed his eyes to wander around the Archives, following the various pipes, pulleys, and shelves of discoveries, eventually having his gaze end at the analytical engine's interface. His smile widened a bit, purely a vain, narcissistic reaction to his practically Shelly-esque creation that had confounded those arrogant shlockworks of the Ministry. And why shouldn't Wellington take pride in this diamond hidden within the Archives' rough? It improved efficiency down here a thousandfold, and had involved absolutely no input from the clankertons in Research and Design.

He slid out his desk's small extension and followed the various sequences down to the one he knew would be there, the one that would fit his mood. His fingers pushed against characters both numeric and alphabetical, coaxing from the metallic monster a series of clicks, whirs, and steambursts. The machine took Wellington's keystrokes, calculated, and finally followed the programmed command.

The silence was only for a moment, and then came the long, languid notes from the analytical engine's horn. Johann Sebastian Bach. "Violin Concerto No. 2." In E. The Adagio. Just what he needed.

If the recording were to be playing at home, it would sound slightly tinny in its playback. Here, in the Archives, the acoustics gave the music a delightful resonance. Not the same as being there in concert, but most assuredly close to the experience. Wellington breathed deeply, and when his eyes opened once more, he found himself staring at the open pages of his journal.

I am home. I am back in my haven, he had only just written. *And yet, I feel as if the worst is yet to come.*

Wellington swallowed hard. He had no idea what he could have done to deserve such attention as the House of Usher had bestowed upon him. The lengths at which they had gone to spirit him away from Mother England to the farthest reaches of the Empire were impressive, if not humbling.

He nodded, dipped his pen into the inkwell and added, *Perhaps this is merely the anxiety most feel upon returning from a battle. They are surprised to see the next morning's light, returning to their lands a hero. In secret, they expect their days to end abruptly. It is living the old Arabian parable of a merchant seeing Death in the streets.*

Had he returned a hero? Perhaps, an unsung one. After all, he had held his tongue—no secrets of the Ministry had been divulged. True, they hadn't begun the interrogation process, but there had been some tense moments. Very tense. Not that he would have admitted it to anyone in the Ministry, but maybe a few tears had leaked out.

Luckily, anyone who might have revealed such an embarrassment had been lost in ash, fire, and snow. Thank God.

The analytical engine clicked and whirred again, now following the protocol cards that Wellington had associated with this command. It kept with the composer, but instead searched out for another musical refrain to play. This time, the analytical engine chose "Concerto for Violin, Oboe, and Strings in D Minor." He shuddered at the shrill cries of the featured woodwind. Normally, he enjoyed the oboe, but this was not a morning for such. He punched the randomizer key, offset from the interface's array, and the analytical engine immediately searched again, this time producing the slower-paced "Violin Concerto No. 1 in A Minor." Wellington gave a slight huff of relief, returned to his journal, and jotted in the margin.

[NOTE: Review the sequence cards and protocols of the difference engine's musical selections. Attempt to program "mood" as a variable alongside composer.]

Before he could return his thoughts to his brief imprisonment, the large, heavy door clanked open, expelling a low noise that cut through Bach's soothing melodies. Wellington placed the thin ribbon of silk between the gutter of his journal, gently closed it, and pressed with his fingernail the six keys that locked his thoughts within its supple leather cover. By the time his journal reached the safety of his desk drawer, the two figures had descended two of the four storeys. He could just make out the larger man's chuckling to the smaller figure trailing behind him. From the man's gait, it could only be the Director, Doctor Basil Sound.

Here it comes, Wellington.

Should he prepare a spot of tea for him and his assistant? Or would that appear ostentatious? How many other department heads did so on surprise inspections, unless it were to soften a pending hammer blow or butter up the Director in order to gain something? Then again, apart from his own department and the clankertons, how many other departments were there in the Ministry, really?

One storey remaining . . .

Wellington yanked out the concealed blotter again, followed his fingers down to the desired sequence, and then punched it into the difference engine. With his thumb depressing the "3" key, a quick burst of steam drowned out the concerto for an instant and then the device clicked and purred while No. 1 in A Minor continued to play uninterrupted.

"I say, Wellington, you are full of surprises." Doctor Sound beamed, and immediately the Archivist was on the defensive. "I should have known you had also provided this difference engine of yours a library of music." He allowed his hand to float in time with the music. "Johann Sebastian Bach, I do believe. One of my favorites. 'Violin Concerto No. 1 in A Major.' "

Wellington cleared his throat, "Minor, sir."

Doctor Sound's conducting stopped. His wiggled his fingers as he glanced over his shoulder and then back to Wellington. "Ah, yes. Quite." He then quickly turned behind him to motion to the second figure lurking in the shadows. "Now come along, it's not like we are strangers here."

His back suddenly wrenched upward at the sight of his Angel of Destruction, Field Agent Eliza D. Braun, who seemed preoccupied at the vastness of her surroundings.

"Agent Braun!" Wellington brushed off his hands and extended one towards the striking field agent. "I can now properly thank you for saving my life."

Her heard turned quickly to look at him and the look of awe vanished. "Yes. Not bad for an idiot, eh, Agent Books?" The bitter edge was obvious in her voice.

So, she hadn't forgotten.

Now it was Wellington's turn to fidget. "Ah, yes, well . . . words uttered in the heat of the moment. I do apologize if you took them as a slight to your character."

Her eyebrows rose. "And pray, how else was I supposed to take them?"

"Now, now, Agent Braun," Doctor Sound chided. "Our boy Wellington here was out of sorts. I mean, how would you feel if you were entering in a pub one moment with high hopes and expectations for an evening of fine dining and companionship, only to awaken mere moments later in the hands of our most formidable opponents, bound for Antarctica?"

Bach's concerto concluded there. Wellington depressed the "Stop" key, leaving only the constant dripping to interrupt the heavy solitude.

"Sounds like you have a leak somewhere, Books." Braun shattered the quiet. "You should have that seen to."

Wellington opened his mouth as if to reply, only to have his words kept at bay by Doctor Sound. "Agent Books, as a token of gratitude to Agent Braun here, would you mind giving us a brief tour of the Archives?"

"Yes, Director. Agent Braun, follow me, if you please." The Archivist forced a smile and motioned with his hand towards rows of gaslight lanterns that extended into the darkness. He felt a muscle twitch in his jaw, just for a moment. Wellington eventually did break the silence; and even to his ears, his words sounded rehearsed. "Welcome to the Archives. In this section of the Ministry, we catalogue all case notes and related artifacts. Obviously, some years are more busy than others, but at the end of this walk resides the beginning, the very foundations of the Ministry."

He looked over to Agent Braun, who craned her neck to stare up at the shelves.

"There must be hundreds of case files in here," she finally managed.

"Thousands," Wellington corrected. "We are in need of a

space this massive, not so much for the case journals as for the collected evidence accompanying them."

"But . . . why?"

Pushing back the sudden headache, Wellington returned the civil smile to his face and motioned to Agent Braun. "If I do recall, a previous case of yours took you to the Caribbean?"

"Yes, Agent Hill and I were called to the Bahamas to investigate the disappearance of Lord and Lady Gosswich. They were last seen in the vicinity—"

"—of the area known by sailors as the Devil's Triangle, yes I know. And do you recall a small relic that served you and Agent Hill rather admirably in the field?"

Agent Braun's eyes flickered, and the sudden childlike wonder in her face softened his posture. "Oh yes! Clever device, that was. If I recall, it was a pyramid with something fastened at its summit."

Urging them to follow, Wellington continued deeper into the shelves. He whispered aloud the years until finally coming to a plaque illuminated by twin gaslight globes:

1872

Wellington stopped at the terminal, an interface much like the analytical engine by his desk, centered underneath the plaque. Slowly, deliberately, Wellington began pressing keys. The tiny window above the keypad revealed letters he selected, each character illuminated by a soft amber glow:

"And," Wellington said, pressing one final key, his smile wide, "enter."

Drip . . .

Drip . . .

Drip . . .

Nothing happened.

Doctor Sound lightly cleared his throat and motioned to the display screen:

DEVLIS TRIAGNLE

"Oh, dash it all!" Wellington swore as he cleared the entry and typed again, even slower this time.

DEVILS TRIANGLE

"And," Wellington said again, "enter."

This time, the "Enter" key brought to life the pulley system above them, adding a *clickity-clack-click-clack* drone underneath the drips. The pulley system eventually surrendered as a winch lowered from above their heads a small basket containing a portfolio and a chestnut box the size of an ostrich egg. Wellington took the box from the suspended tray and removed its lid, revealing a pair of identical devices.

"Gate Keys. Obtained in 1872, when the Ministry followed the path of the two-hundred-eighty-two-ton brigantine *Mary Celeste*."

"You mean, we had been to the Devil's Triangle before?" asked Agent Braun.

"The *Mary Celeste*'s crew, Ministry agents discovered, had been spirited away to an underground base in the Atlantic. These devices, used in the proper conditions, created *aethergates* that—I do believe you and Agent Hill used for Lord and Lady Gosswich's escape—connect two points in time and space, granting the users quick passage from Point A to Point B."

"Hold on," Agent Braun interjected. "I remember Agent Hill going on about these gadgets. He said these came from—"

"Atlantis, yes, Agent Braun. The 1872 case took place there. The House of Usher had seized control of the underground—or to be more accurate, underwater—base many decades ago and were pulling both sailing vessels and airships to the murky depths."

"And this was in 1872?"

"Quite." Wellington retrieved the bound volume and

flipped to the end pages. "The site was, indeed, the city of Fortuna Prime, what the Ministry research team of 1872 deduced was the capital city of Atlantis. The House of Usher had held that outpost for nearly fifty years, as far as we—the Ministry, to be precise—were to ascertain; but the lead investigator on this case theorized—if you give me a moment . . ." And Wellington's voice trailed off as he flipped to earlier pages, his fingertips selecting tabs marking various key points of the investigation. "Yes, here, Agent Heathcliffe Durham believes the House of Usher held the outpost for a much longer period, possibly dating back to Columbus' first crossing. He recommended that further investi—"

"Thank you, Agent Books," Doctor Sound interrupted. "I do believe you have illuminated our colonial pepperpot here quite adequately."

Agent Braun's lips moved as if to say something, but the words caught in her throat. Only for a moment. "Director, if we have access to these resources, why are we not using them more often in the field?"

"Because these resources, as you would believe them to be, Agent Braun, still remain unknown to us." Doctor Sound replaced the lid on to the chestnut box. "I allowed access to the Gate Keys as this was a return trip for us in the Ministry to the Triangle. Whenever we do tap into these resources, we do so with great caution and responsibility. Unlike some agents in this organisation, Agent Brandon Hill exudes infallible traits of control, trust, and reason." He paused, his eyes remaining fixed on Agent Braun. A few moments later, he continued. "We investigate the odd, the peculiar, and the unknown; and that investigation continues when time allows here in the Archives. Does it not, Books?"

"Naturally," Wellington said, turning to the interface and returning the case back to its shelf with the push of a key.

"Tell me again, if you please," Agent Braun began, "exactly how far back do these Archives go?"

Doctor Sound waved an admonishing finger, "Have you never been down here for research?"

Before she could answer, Wellington chimed in with, "No, Director."

Both Braun and Sound turned to him.

"I believe," Wellington said, thankful for the shadows of the Archives, "I would have remembered Agent Braun visiting here."

"Director, if you recall, my former partner tended to be old-fashioned. I'm sure he would have found this place unsuitable for a lady of my delicate disposition."

The tiny "*Yelp!*" escaping Wellington's lips caused both of them to start.

Clearing his throat, the Archivist motioned deeper into the chambers. "You asked, Agent Braun, about how far back the Archives go. If you please?"

They continued to the far wall where the shelves' plaque, like the others, caught the gaslight:

1840

"The very beginning," Doctor Sound murmured, his own pride evident.

"Yes, Director," Wellington added. "The Ministry's first year. These were extraordinary steps to walk in, I assure you."

His smile dimmed slightly at Braun's furrowed brow.

"Do you not see?" He motioned at the massive shelves towering around them. "We are standing in the very origins of the Ministry. Before you, I, and even Doctor Sound here winked into existence, brave souls began what would become—"

"My job, Books," Braun retorted, her own enthusiasm notably lacking. She then turned on Doctor Sound, her back now the only visible thing to Wellington. "This is all well and good, Director, but I fail to understand how a tour of the Ministry's basement will make me a better agent in the field."

Doctor Sound went to speak; but it was Wellington's

voice, now carrying an entirely different tenor from before, that answered. "We learn from the past."

Braun smirked. "Really? I thought history was written by the victors."

"That may very well be, but what I do down here is carry on the work and preserve the voices of those who lived it. And it is their case work, their expertise, that serves the next generation in the field, and in many cases brings the next generation home to Mother England safely."

"So far, Books, I have managed to come home quite safely—as you've seen—by living in the now, and not lingering in the then."

His eyes narrowed. While he tolerated the disdain of his "fellow" agents, he did not appreciate being so abused in his own den.

And she's a colonial to boot, hissed the cold voice in his mind. *I do believe this savage needs a reminder of her betters.*

Wellington stepped back, his heart hammering in his chest. *No*, he thought quickly. *Not here. Not! Here!*

"Agent Braun," he began, "allow me to demonstrate how important it is that we preserve each case. And allow me, if you will, to pull from your own past."

She snorted. "Oh, this should be grand fun."

"I remember one of your earlier cases here at the Ministry took you to India, or was it Egypt? A death on the Nile or some sort of business?"

"Actually, yes, Books. 1892. And it was *several* deaths on the Nile. One of those slow cruises for the upper crust, and the clientele were having a tough time staying alive on this one boat. I remember it being quite the initiation as the bodies of the dead all bled sand."

"I remember filing away this case. Took you how long to resolve?"

"Five weeks." Braun shuddered. "I still remember the monumental sunburn I brought back with me."

Wellington glanced at Doctor Sound who seemed to be

enjoying the repartee between him and Agent Braun. Something about the Director's smile unnerved him.

"Five weeks, and I do recall in your report that several times you and your partner were somewhat challenged, if not stonewalled?"

Braun's jaw twitched. "Get to the point, Books."

"The culprit was not so much a person as it was—"

"The Amulet of Set, what our local contacts told us had been unearthed in an excavation. This amulet was harnessing the power of this God of Evil, and Set was also fond of the sandstorms. Turns out the owner of the boat clued in on this amulet's secrets and started lashing out at the aristocrats that had him ferrying people along a desert's sole river."

"A necklace of dark magic, you say?" He crossed between them and rested his fingertips on the shelves' filing terminal, muttering to himself, "Let's see now, 1840, and if memory serves—"

"The agent's name was Atkins," Doctor Sound interjected. "Case reference number 18400217UKNL."

Wellington looked at the Director for a moment, and then over to Braun. She merely shrugged.

His fingers depressed the keys of the case number into the interface, its final key starting the *clickity-clack-click-clack* melody above them, once again. As it did back in 1872, a winch lowered from above their heads an identical basket containing a small portfolio resting atop a thin, wide chestnut box.

"Case 18400217UKNL investigated by Agent Peter Atkins," Wellington read from the portfolio's cover, "This was a case that dealt with a series of random misfortunes and, eventually, deaths centered around relatives of Parliament."

"A rather dark piece of business," Sound added.

Wellington looked up from the portfolio in his hands. "Sir, this case is over fifty years old. How could you recoll—"

"I can read too, old boy," the Director quipped. "And my memory, as you see, is quite infallible."

He felt a heat rise in his skin. "Yes, of course, Director." Wellington started flipping through the worn, weathered pages of this case report. "But you see, Agent Braun, had you reached out to the Archives, you would have discovered yourself in a similar predicament and saved yourself a great deal of—"

"Oye, Welly," her voice barked, causing him to start, "did you know this was in here?"

Wellington and Doctor Sound turned to Braun who now rested the chestnut box along her forearm. The soft glow coming from the gemstones seemed to dance in the agent's eyes, and the wider she smiled the brighter the glow became. Her fingers gently stroked the blood-red gems that brightened at her feather-touch. They both heard her sigh of admiration and wonder reverberate around them.

Quickly following the *snap* of the portfolio's closing came the *snap* of the jewelry box's lid. If Wellington had taken a fingertip or two of the colonial's, then so be it.

"And there is your first lesson, Agent Braun, in handling that which no one understands!" bit Wellington, not even bothering to keep his voice calm. "This," he said, motioning to the necklace case, "was the instigator of the crimes. Agent Atkins was able to trace the perpetrator's source of dark magic to this heirloom, the Necklace of le Fay."

"Le Fay?" Braun snorted. "As in Morgane le Fay? The Saucy Trollop from Avalon, Morgane le Fay?!" Her laugh cut through him. "Oh come off it, mate. There was no such person!"

"Perhaps, Agent Braun, you should get down to the Archives more often," Wellington huffed just before replacing the necklace back into the basket. With a few keystrokes and *clickety-clacks*, the items disappeared into the darkness above them, back into their rightful place within the stacks. "I'm sure in the field an assignment ends once you file the final report, but if you ever were curious as to what happened to your spoils of war and battle, they end up here in the Ministry Archives. Here, items are catalogued, sorted, and stored until that operation arises wherein you will need logistics. And while there may be more things in heaven and Earth than are dreamt of in your philosophy, Agent Braun, I assure you there are things far more wondrous-strange here in the Archives."

Braun chuckled. "All right then, if we can't play with your toys here in the basement, Welly, why not this?" she quipped, rapping a knuckle against the Archives' access terminal. "Why are the agents not granted this resource? This difference engine, connected to these remote terminals in such a fashion—*fantastic*! How is this powered?" she asked.

Wellington patted the brick wall beside him. "You know of the Thames?"

"Unlimited power." Her eyebrows shot up. "Those tinkers are so bloody clever."

Now he *really* didn't like her. "I beg your pardon?"

"Research and Design. Their imagination knows no boundaries, does it?"

Wellington felt a sudden twinge in his neck.

"Field Agent Braun," he began, his voice quivering lightly, "firstly, this is not a difference engine. It can do a bit more than mathematics. This is an analytical engine, based off Babbage's original schematics with a few enhancements of my own. Second, I am well aware your ilk rarely visit my Archives, and that you tap into this Ministry *resource* only when and if the need arises. The last resort, I believe one of your colleagues referred to me as. So you would have not known that this analytical engine and its connected terminals are devices of *my* design and implementation, apart from the fact that, unlike many of the prototypes fabricated by Research and Design, it *works*."

"Well now," piped in Doctor Sound, "it seems this rather overdue visit to *your* Archives is serving several plagues of the Ministry."

The Director's timing was impeccable as his words fell on the final stanza of Bach's concerto.

Drip . . .

Drip . . .

Drip . . .

"I'm sorry," Wellington said, his voice seeming quite loud to himself. "Plagues?"

"Yes, Agent Books—plagues." Even in the glow of gaslight, Wellington could see the growing tint of red in the Director's cheeks. "I thought giving you a bit of latitude down here, what with Research and Design rejecting your applications to work with them, would keep you passionate about your placement. It seems that it has. All too well."

Wellington swallowed. "Sir?"

"Yes, it is true that *your* Archives provide perhaps the most valuable of assets to the Ministry, and the work you have done in *your* Archives has been nothing short of spectacular." From behind the spectacles on his nose, Doctor Sound's eyes went chillingly dark. "But make no mistake—these are not *your* Archives."

Wellington's knees buckled slightly, but his dizziness soon cleared on hearing what Sound said next.

"And as I said in my office, Agent Braun, your mission history of 'snap decisions' begs for disciplinary action, so I am assigning you a new partner." Sound, apparently as pleased as punch with himself, glanced at Wellington. "Or would you be more of a mentor?"

No. The Director could not be—

"Are you serious?" Her voice echoed around them. "The Archives?!"

Sound motioned around him. "Lovely orientation for your reassignment, don't you think?" He leaned close into her. Wellington thought the only reason Braun didn't punch him in the nose was due to the fact she was in shock. "I think a little time down here, out of the limelight, will teach you a valuable lesson."

"And exactly what lesson is that?" Braun asked, her face still reflecting her horror at the Director's decision.

"Humility, Agent Braun," Sound added in a light chortle. "I feel you need to find out that there is more to being a Ministry agent than ordnance and action. More than chaos and destruction." And then his expression changed. Abruptly. The faint mirth that was there faded as his eyes took in, seemingly for the first time, the decades of casework surrounding them. The Director was still speaking to Braun but not looking at her. His voice was distant. "For they are the domain of those we stand against."

With a slight jerk he came back to himself, and Doctor Sound returned to peering over the top of his glasses at her. "And there it is. I have arranged for your desk contents to be moved down here."

Braun looked at Wellington, shook her head, and then returned her attention to the Director. "May I ask how long this 'reassignment' will last?"

"Indefinitely," he returned without hesitation. "Time in the Archives will give you a different point of view and teach a valuable lesson. And there is no need to be so glum. Books is down here. He's one of ours, remember?"

Now it was Wellington's turn to furrow his brow. Whatever did Sound mean by that?

"And as for you"—Sound turned his undivided attention to him—"you need to learn that there are not two agencies within the Ministry. We are a single unit, a collection of gears and cogs that work together in order to preserve the peace in extraordinary circumstances. You need to rise above your petty differences and perceived rifts, and remember that we are united under the same creed."

Petty differences? Perceived rifts?! By Jove, what did he mean?

"You need interaction with your fellow agents; and particularly in light of your recent dilemma, we will need someone ready to pick up the mantle in case something unfortunate were to befall upon you."

He took a step back and beamed. "I don't believe I could have written such a delightful pairing." Sticking his thumbs into the shallow pockets of his vest, the Director rapped his fingers lightly against his belly. "Good luck, Agents Books and Braun. I do believe this is the start of something special." He then turned and walked back through the years of Ministry history. "No need to show me the way out. I know my way down here."

Wellington was adrift in a void. And there he remained with Agent Eliza D. Braun, in silence.

Well, not complete silence.

Drip . . .

Drip . . .

Drip . . .

"By God, that drip is annoying!" Braun snapped suddenly. "Where is that coming from?!"

From his desk, Wellington heard a single bell chime. The analytical engine had finished brewing the tea.

CHAPTER FOUR

Where Our Dashing Hero of History and Cataloguing Undertakes the Taming and Training of This Shrew!

Wellington glanced up from his desk, his eyes narrowing on the woman sitting opposite him. It had been a week. Only one week.

168 hours.

10,080 minutes.

604,800 seconds.

And Wellington Thornhill Books, Esquire, had felt every one of those seconds. Even during the weekend.

He had no idea what he could have done to deserve such a punishment. He stared at the words jotted down in his journal only hours ago. *And yet with all my accomplishments and accolades, I find myself asking repeatedly 'If I am so bloody brilliant, how in the name of God on high do I continue to find myself here? With her?*

Very simple, his inner voice chided. *You were captured. You're lucky she wasn't sent to kill you right on the spot out of worry you had been compromised.*

He dismissed the thought immediately. Wellington knew

his value in the Ministry. No one could do what he did. Any replacement would take years to reach his clerical adeptness. No, he was indispensable.

Wasn't he?

A tension rippled up along his spine to stop at the base of his skull: the omen of a splitting headache.

Braun did not even bother to look at him, and Wellington was fully aware of his "over-the-spectacles" stare's reputation: it was legendary in its ability to part the aether with a chill rivaling the place where he had been kept prisoner. Shaking his head, Wellington closed his journal concealed within the gutter of the ledger, tapped in its code to lock it tight, set it back in its place on the shelf next to his desk, and continued with his own cross-referencing, this time with a set of small clay vases just checked in by Agent Hill. His memoirs reminded him of how he wanted to bring up to Doctor Sound, once more, the deplorable condition of the Archives. Wellington had been promised improvements months ago, and still there seemed to be no steps in remedying the situation. He understood there was no other place for the Archives, and he accepted that the facility needed power; and what better power supply than the Thames?

However it was criminal so many rare antiquities and irreplaceable documents were kept in a basement with a moisture quotient rivaling Welsh summers.

Then he noticed it: the constant droning of the Ministry generators. That was all he heard. There was no other sound accompanying it. Nothing. Only the low rumble of their shared power source.

"What happened to the dripping?" he asked, his voice now sounding too loud for the Archives.

"Well, thank God! He lives!" Braun scoffed. "I thought I was the only one consumed by the boredom of this hole!"

Wellington stared at her for a moment. Every slight against the Archives, he felt, was a slight against him. Perhaps he shouldn't expect a field agent to be sensitive to that. "Agent Braun, do you not notice that? The drip is—"

"Gone. Yes. I mended that damnable leak my third day here. It was working under my skin a bit."

"After only two days?" he asked incredulously.

"Books, when you are interrogated, you achieve a sort of Zen state, knowing you are about to be tortured. That way, your threshold for pain is far higher." She motioned around her. "Walking into your place of work and being subject to a torture that you have control to end at any time? That is control I intend to take full advantage of!"

The clearing of his throat made his head shake a bit. Wellington swallowed, the grating causing his mouth to twitch. "I know this has been an adjustment for you, what with your familiarity with a more exciting vocation, but I think you are doing this office a true disservice. I do not find my assignment within the Ministry boring, but quite rewarding. Without me—" He looked up from his ledger and attempted a warm, welcoming smile. "Without *us*, the Ministry would not be able to function."

Braun let out an explosive breath and produced from one of her vest pockets what appeared to be a length of polished bone. In the shadows of the Archives, he could not make out any details. She gave the shaft a quick flick, and the blade extended with a sharp *shickt*.

"Really?" Braun asked, then casually tossed the stiletto at the desk. Between two of the vases that were neatly arranged between them, the blade struck hard, causing Wellington to jump. "I thought things were sent down here to be catalogued, stored . . ." *Thunk* went the knife, ". . . and then forgotten about."

"Agent Braun," Wellington said, watching her repeat the throw again. As the blade was doing more damage on her side of the great desk, it was no matter to him. Still her accuracy was unnerving. "Did you conveniently forget my tour only a week ago? Where do you think field agents acquire their logistics before an assignment? We are the backbone of the Ministry." He motioned around him, but the *thunk* of knife striking desktop told him she was not catching his enthusiasm. "When peculiar occurrences occur, we are charged with the responsibility—"

Thunk.

"—of recording for history the bizarre finds behind said peculiar occurrence."

Thunk.

"And when field agents need to know the hows, the whys, and the what-ifs of a new mystery—"

Thunk.

"—we are called upon to arm them with what may help them solve whatever evil secret or minion of darkness has been unearthed—"

Thunk.

"*Agent Braun!*" Wellington snapped. "Would you *please* stop doing that?"

Braun sighed as she leaned back in her chair and propped her feet upon the desk's edge. "Look, Welly, I'm sorry if I'm not swept up in the passion you nurture in being the Ministry's Librarian—"

"Archivist."

"—But I did not sail to the other side of the world to number, file, and sort so others could go where the real action is. This job is about the case, about the mystery. If I stay down here for too long," she groaned, stretching her arms high, "I'm worried my skills are going to—"

With her arms still over her head, Braun threw the knife. The blade struck the desk with a hard *thunk*, but this time the hilt rapped the vase closest to it. The pottery's shattering seemed far too loud for something so small.

Wellington remained motionless, his eyes watching the shards scatter across both their desks, some of them still moving from the impact.

"See what I mean, Welly?" Braun said, sitting upright in her chair. With a grumble, she snatched a nearby brush and dustpan, sweeping up the mess as she spoke. "Normally, I would never miss; but one week in this dungeon is already cocking up my eyesight." The remains clattered and tinkled as they struck the bottom of the dustbin. "At least it's a clean dungeon. I'll give you that, mate. You really do a yeoman's job down here. I just don't know if I'm cut out for this."

Wellington pinched the bridge of his nose, pushing his spectacles high up on his forehead. He had to remember to breathe.

The question, had it not been so absurd coming from her, would have made him laugh. "You all right, Welly?"

"I'll be fine," he said through clenched teeth. "It was . . ." and his words trailed off as he motioned to where the vase had once sat.

She looked at the spot where the vase had been, her brow rising. "Oh. Um . . . oh dear . . . was it valuable?"

"Agent Hill was on assignment in the Americas. South America to be precise. He had discovered an underground network combing the jungles for these jars. When placed in a specific order, these jars were to have formed a map."

"Oh really? How clever!" Braun perked up, intrigued. "Where to?"

Wellington closed the main ledger in front of him. "The Lost City of El Dorado."

She nodded slowly. "Ah. And all the vases need to be . . . intact . . . and not in . . ." Braun looked between the dustbin and the empty spot on the desk, continuing to nod her head as she did so. "That's . . . well . . . sorry, Welly."

A stinging sensation suddenly captured Wellington's attention. He looked down to see his fingers were clenched into tight fists, his knuckles quite white. Splaying his fingers, he felt the tingle subside and the comforting warmth of circulation return to his hands.

His eyes hopped from his hands to his secured journal to the deposed field agent sitting across from him. These past seven days had each been a colossal disaster. Had it not been for the analytical engine, Eliza D. Braun could have taken the Archives back to the way he had found it more than four years ago. She was not certain if she could not catalog, or was just making the choice to ignore him and not catalog anything properly. She seemed to operate on a work ethic that if there was an empty space on a shelf, that would serve admirably for an artifact. If he wasn't repeating himself once again in methodologies of proper cataloguing, he found himself double-checking his difference engine. On Day Five, she had somehow managed to overload it with commands, something he knew he had cautioned her about several times prior.

He did notice, though, whenever Agent Campbell paid a visit, her skills would sharpen and her efficiency on the job was nothing less than spectacular. He never thought he would wish this, but secretly he hoped the Australian operative would pay more visits.

Eliza Braun's repeat failures, and her subtle insubordination towards him, was a mnemonic of how dreadful his fortune with the fairer sex had been of late. Before being sentenced to servitude with his one-time-savior-now-harbinger-of-destruction, there was the unfortunate series of events that had landed him in Antarctica. Unlike his fellow agent, the lady who had spent a day having tea with him more than a month ago had been just that: a proper lady. A striking beauty, and Wellington thought himself lucky they happened to make eye contact from across the tearoom. It would have been a delight to have a chum or even a workmate to chat about the next course of action. Perhaps they would have provided some insight, or even a warning. Instead, he blundered on his own ineptitude into an afternoon in the park with an exotic Italian beauty. Such piercing green eyes. He should have noticed more than her eyes and the rather attractive bosom, now that he thought about it. What proper lady would suggest going to a pub so late in the day, offering to pay for the first round of drinks? The first round being the last he would remember.

Now, sitting across from him was his comeuppance. Had he taken just a moment—a single, precious moment—to consider his "luck" in catching the eye of an Italian Venus, his domain at the Ministry would not have been sullied by this colonial harpy.

Patience, Wellington, he told himself. *Doctor Sound did this for a reason, and it must be good.* He looked at her in silence, repeating the thought as a mantra.

"What?" Braun barked as he continued to stare at her.

There has to be a reason, he assured himself. That, or the old man was losing his grip.

"I think," Wellington finally said, punching a sequence into the analytical engine. "We are in need of a change."

Eliza motioned to the remaining vases. "You're not putting them in the basket with the notes?"

"I'll tend to the jars later. Perhaps I can retrace the destination from memory. Wellington stared at where the last jar once was and his shoulders fell. "Perhaps."

He pushed "Enter" on the analytical engine . . . and nothing happened.

"Welly," Eliza said, catching her bottom lip in her teeth for a moment, "There is no 's' in El Dorado. Nor is there an 'o' in City."

He looked at the display:

LOST COTY OF EL DORSDO

"Oh, dash it all!" he huffed, beginning the sequence again.

"I would think," Eliza began, her head tilting to one side as she watched him type, "being an Archivist for one, and seeing as you built this bloody thing, typing would be a skill of yours."

"You would think," Wellington grumbled, his index finger smashing each key as he continued, "but I did not pursue the fine art of typing at university or elsewhere. So. I. Am. Self." And finally, with one last look at the display, Wellington hit the final key, punctuating it by stating, "Taught."

As the pulley system whirred into action, he motioned to the shadows behind Braun.

"Now then, if you would follow me, please."

The stiletto collapsed with a quick *click-click* and Braun was on her feet, following him deeper into the more recent case files of the Archives. Wellington felt a pang of hope, of optimism, that maybe his unexpected apprentice would grow to appreciate his hallowed ground. When he took this position, the cataloging was far from perfect, and Wellington shouldered the challenge as Atlas did with the world itself. How nice it would be if he could share this accomplishment with—

Behind him, Eliza Braun let out a hard exhale, expressing not very elegantly her dissatisfaction.

Well, she did manage to find and fix that rather annoying leak. Maybe that was a first step of sorts.

Reaching the black brick marking the end of the Archives, Wellington turned to his left toward a small stairwell.

"Oye, Welly!"

He turned back to Braun. She seemed more curious about the cast-iron door at the opposite end of the corridor.

"What's this?" She motioned to the secured hatch.

"That is restricted access. Director's eyes only."

She turned back to him, and the crooked eyebrow made his stomach tighten. "Really? You mean, there's even a part of your domain you are barred from?"

"Your presence here drives home the fact that this is hardly my domain." He took in a deep breath and glanced down the small staircase. Taking the spare lantern from the hook above him, Wellington beckoned to Braun. "Now instead of preoccupying yourself with where we are not allowed access, why not focus your pent-up zeal towards where we can go and where we are needed?"

Wellington turned back to the stone stairwell reaching even further down into the Archives, assured his charge would soon follow. The rough stone underfoot curved slightly, ending before a maw that surrendered nothing to the meager light cast from his small lantern. He reached into his pocket to find the matchbox, which he pushed open with a free finger. A few shakes later, the stick was in his palm.

"How are you managing?" she asked from behind him.

"I'm . . . managing . . ." He was now attempting to close the box while still cupping the free match and juggling the lantern. He had done this before. Many times. What was wrong with him today?

Braun gave a slight huff and clicked her tongue. "Oh for heaven's sake, Welly, I'm your assistant. The least you could do is give me something to assist you with!"

This would take some getting used to. "Ah, yes, of course, Agent Braun. If you would please hold the lantern?"

The lamp's side opened with a tiny creak, and from its flame the match sizzled to light. Wellington cupped the match and dropped it into a small reservoir at the top of the doorframe. A trail of fire ran along the top of the room's stone molding, casting its glow on brightly polished brass reflectors curving above it. Now the once black void was a warm gold room of brick, boxes, and half-empty shelves.

Braun smiled at the lighting device, giving a slight chuckle. "Oh this is very clever."

"Yes, it is, but once a week, we will need to polish the brass, just to make sure we have adequate illumination. And then there is all the oil that sits in the gutter. Sometimes, being clever has its costs."

"I suppose." Braun brushed her hands together and looked at the various boxes, ledgers, and piles of paper stacked before them. "So, what are we looking at here, Books?"

"You described the Archives as the place where things are 'catalogued, stored, and forgotten.' While I will still insist the Ministry could not function without our services, this is the part of the Archives that is most deserving of your eloquent description."

"What?" Since their time together, this was the first time

Braun seemed genuinely surprised. "These are 'forgotten' cases?"

He sniffed, wishing he could deny her abrupt judgement. "For the lack of a better word, yes. These are cases the Ministry either lacks the resources to follow any longer, or considers at a dead end."

Braun whispered, her eyes hopping from ledger to ledger, box to box. "How many of these forgotten cases are there?"

"I've never summoned up the courage to count them all, but I assure you, it's in the hundreds. We are talking of a ministry of Her Majesty's government that spans over half a century." Wellington sighed. "And I have added five from this month alone. I want to believe not all of these cases are 'forgotten.' Merely postponed." He gave a chortle as he hung his lantern on a hook. "I am trying to come up with a name for this collection. I keep returning to 'Cases of the Unknown.' " He approached a stack of papers that reached from the floor, past his waist. "Or perhaps 'Files of the Unexplained.' "

"Files of the Unexplained, from the Ministry of Peculiar Occurrences." Braun pursed her lips, and then shook her head. "Doesn't quite roll off the tongue, Books."

"No, it doesn't. Perhaps Dead End Cases, but that is about as promising as 'Forgotten.' "

Braun reached into the crate in front of Wellington and started pulling out files. "So, our job here is to do what with these exactly?"

He swiftly relieved her inexperienced hands of the open ledger and returned it to the crate. "We begin with the year first."

For a moment, Braun didn't move. Then her furrowed brow relaxed as it dawned on her. "Oh, come off it, Welly . . ."

"We organise them. First it is by block of years, then the specific year, then date, and finally by investigating officer's last name."

"You mean, we have all these outstanding cases," Braun

pulled the ledger she had been reading once more out of its crate, "and all we're going to do is organise them?"

"And this organisation will go a touch faster if you avoid thumbing through the evidence boxes," Wellington quipped, once more relieving Braun of the book.

"You mean to tell me you, a libra—" Wellington raised an eyebrow at her. "—an *Archivist*, are not the least bit curious about why these cases are down here?" Braun looked around and snorted. "Why are they down here to begin with, and not up in Assignments?"

"Because Assignments is for active cases. As these cases are dead enders, they would not fair well in the sunlight. I happened to find this alcove, and recommended to Doctor Sound we use it for the unsolved cases on account of its dryness and lack of light."

"So Doctor Sound knows the extent of how many cases are remaining open, and he's leaving them as such?"

Wellington slid the box to Braun and motioned over to the only bookcase that was not empty. "This goes on the bookcase marked 1891, under 'T' if you please."

The wood crate jerked out of his grasp and was thumped down on the indicated space. Wellington gave himself a silent accolade and hoisted the next box up to the thick table.

"So many cases," Eliza muttered. "I wonder if the lads know . . ."

"And if they did, Miss Braun, how would that help the Ministry?" Wellington retorted, taking a different tactic with the former field agent. Doctor Sound had told him this was an indefinite assignment for Braun, so perhaps distancing herself from "the lads" was in order. "The Ministry is a small, clandestine organisation with limited resources on call, in order to preserve our secrecy. No matter the superlative talents, abilities, or means we do make the most of at our disposal, some cases will simply not end in resolution. It is a fact, a fact we must come to terms with. And in the Archives, we must make certain the facts remain preserved until such a time when the Ministry can return their full attention to them."

Braun opened one of the ledgers from the new box, searching for a year. The book snapped shut. "Welly, being in the Ministry, even down here in Archives, you had to pass Field Agent training."

The strange knot he had felt in his stomach on seeing Braun contemplate the Archives' Restricted Access returned. "What of it?"

"So, you have the basics under your belt. With me working the details, we're fully capable."

She couldn't possibly be serious. "Fully capable of . . . ?"

"Oh, come off it, Books, you know where I'm going with this." She gave a wry grin and shrugged. "Why don't *we* take on these cases?"

She was serious.

"Because that is not our job, Miss Braun," Wellington stated. "We have our orders and our responsibilities to the Ministry, and those orders and responsibilities do not include investigating these cases. Insubordination out in the field brought you to the Archives. Where do you think insubordination in the Archives leads you?"

Braun straightened up to her full height. Perhaps it was the amber luminescence of the alcove or Wellington's hunched posture over the evidence box, but the image of Eliza D. Braun took him aback. Her eyes narrowed with some sort of survivalist's glare, as if silently promising Wellington she would—without hesitation—remove any threat to her position, no matter what that position was, in the Ministry.

For the first time since her arrival, Wellington actually felt afraid.

"I am merely suggesting," he continued after the awkward moment passed, "you reconsider whatever it is you are considering, because I believe if you did not care so much about your standing here in the Ministry, you would have told Doctor Sound to 'shove off' on being assigned here."

He closed the ledger in his hands and swallowed, hoping the peculiar fear would abate. It didn't. "Second, Miss Braun, I do not wish to partake in any such behaviour that would complicate or jeopardise *my* position here."

Returning his attention back inside the ledger he held, Books' eye fell on the date: May 7, 1893. *Hmm, a recent case*, he thought. His eye swept through the handwriting for a Case Primary. These notes were difficult to manoeuvre though, as the agent's handwriting seemed more like wild scrawlings and scribblings. The agent had been in a hurry, and from the frantic script he was determined to get the idea out of his mind before it were to slip away.

A clamor caused him to start, a tiny yelp echoing in the chamber. Wellington was now looking at Eliza Braun standing before him, her hands still holding on to a crate she had apparently lifted off the table. What remained of the box's bottom now covered parts of the table and Braun's feet; papers, ledgers, and pieces of evidence now strewn out before them.

"Chaos and mayhem comes naturally to you, don't they, Miss Braun?" he seethed.

She tossed the frame aside. "I was only trying to move it a bit closer, Welly. These two crates are—sorry, *were*—labeled with the same year. There are enough notes here to cover an entire quarter's worth of cases, but according to these boxes, it's all the same one."

Braun's eyes narrowed slightly as she reached for a volume lying across her foot. Wellington's attention returned back to his own ledger. He took in the scent of aging paper, worn leather, and the chamber's illumination, and the medley of scents cleared his mind. He flipped the pages forward, the handwriting growing less and less intelligible.

At least, it was unintelligible to him. The sound of fluttering pages tore his attention away from his open book. It seemed Agent Braun was managing quite well with the calligraphy. She was tearing through the tome, her hands tempting the pages to rip themselves free of the volume's binding. She was not even trying to conceal her expression. From the way the light was suddenly catching her eyes she knew this handwriting intimately.

His eyes then switched from Braun's odd expression to a pendant swaying from a chain intertwined in her fingers.

"Miss Braun?" Her head shot up from the book's pages. "You recognise this handwriting?"

It may have been a trick of light but Wellington thought Braun did, in fact, shiver for a moment. She blinked her eyes tightly, and then with a deep breath her voice filled the chamber even though she spoke just above a whisper.

"The Case Primary here was Agent Harrison Thorne. My former partner."

Wellington's head tipped to one side. "*Former* partner?" He considered her words for a moment before asking. "You mean, you blew him up?"

"Actually no," she said, letting the jibe slide off her. "Harry is residing in Bedlam now."

"You drove him mad?" Wellington said. "Why am I not surprised, Miss Braun?"

Again, she looked at him in that menacing manner. "You are on very dangerous ground, Books."

He took a step back and returned his ledger to the table.

"This was a case he had undertaken on his own. Doctor Sound had ordered us off it in March. That's March of 1893." She closed the ledger and motioned to the corner behind Wellington. "Fetch us a proper box, there's a good fellow."

Wellington raised an eyebrow, but crossed the chamber to replace the former crate. As he returned to the review table, Braun continued. "The trail just ended for us. Well, for him. I was new to the Ministry and he had already been on this case for a time. His partner before me, Arlington I think his name was, had been working it with him initially. Workers were disappearing for spells, and then reappearing in . . . in the most horrific of manners."

"How did I not hear of this case?"

"Because this was being covered by three teams at one time. Three different factories. Three gruesome sets of murders. Thorne was convinced they were interconnected, so he combined case notes. And that was why I replaced Arlington. From what Agent Thorne told me, Agent Arlington could not stomach it any longer.

"At one factory, workers were disappearing for weeks on end and then reappearing with their bodies drained of blood. At another, workers were disappearing and reappearing with their bones absent. The third, the corpses were skinned. Like prize bucks."

"Ah." Wellington swallowed, focusing his over-active imagination on something other than his morning's breakfast and the gruesome tale Braun spun.

"After a few weeks, following my arrival, Doctor Sound insisted we cease the case. Thorne agreed officially. Unofficially, he kept the case open."

"I see," Wellington replied softly. "Never made any further progress, did he?"

"A few leads," Braun said, her eyes turning to the pendant in her hand. "All of them just . . . ending. As if the person he was following never existed."

Wellington's brow furrowed as he tried nonchalantly to get a look at the pendant. He could make out on one side of it a crescent shape, perhaps a waxing moon. Braun seemed to be lost in a memory of Agent Thorne, and was paying no mind to him or to the fact that she was turning the pendant over in her open palm. The opposite side of the charm was the image of a cat's head.

Her voice returned, still soft but managing to fill the heavy quiet. "I tried to tell him that he was getting a bit obsessive, but with Harry it was all about solving the mystery. This one was his great white whale, and he would not let it be. When he was gone for a full twenty-four hours, we traced his ring back to his apartments. It seemed apparent that he was determined to work completely in shadow, even forgoing the safeguard of his Ministry signet. I convinced Doctor Sound that Harry . . . Agent Thorne that is, enjoyed his moments of solitude, and perhaps that was what he needed at the time. Now, I wish I had not been so convincing.

"After a week, the agents available in town started the manhunt for him." Her face twisted in disgust. "Campbell found him, stark raving mad in one of the side gutters of the West End. Sound refused to let me see him. Those two simply whisked him off to Bedlam, and cleaned out his desk while I was forced to take leave. I returned to the Ministry with my partner reduced to a memory. Apparently, my memory exclusively, seeing as how Sound took measures to keep Thorne out of conversations and reports."

The pendant disappeared in her fist. Braun quickly scanned the other dossiers scattered across the tabletop, finding what appeared to be the oldest of the ledgers. "I think this ledger marked the beginning of the case: the first murder where a worker was found floating in the Thames. If we were to—"

"Eliza."

That grabbed her attention. Wellington knew it would. "Your intentions are noble, but they are not your responsibility. Not anymore. I did not know Thorne, but if he served here at the Queen's Pleasure it meant he was of an exceptional class of man, a class that understands the importance of duty. Your duty is to the Ministry, not to the obsession of a fellow agent." The softness melted from her face, but this time Wellington was ready for it. "The Ministry has given you this charge, Miss Braun, and if you wish to continue to serve at the Ministry you will want to focus on answering this charge. If you do not, there is no re-assignment."

Braun went to speak, no doubt to protest. She stopped herself and then gave a tiny nod. Perhaps the last warning had sunk in. "You're right, Agent Books. You're absolutely right. Thorne would want me to fulfill my duty." The ledger closed in her hands. "Do we need to order the books themselves, or merely put them in a single crate?"

An excellent question. One he hadn't considered. "Well, as there is so much to this particular case, it would be a good thing to try and arrange the ledgers with oldest at the far left, most recent to the right."

"Spine up?"

"Yes, spine up." Wellington sighed. "Perhaps we can return to this crate at a later time and actually mark the spines accordingly."

"Well then," Braun resigned. "For the Ministry, let's get to it."

He watched her for a moment gather up a stack of ledgers, and open their covers, searching for a date. Within a few minutes, she had three stacks of books started, the first ledgers of each of the three cases. Braun then did something unexpected. She started singing. It was a delightful melody, lacking words but still managing to lighten the heaviness of her task. Wellington made a mental notation to himself that this was, perhaps, a defense mechanism of hers, allowing her to delve into the details of an agent she was so familiar with. Braun continued to sing the ditty as she stacked the books by chronological order, by case. She appeared to be in a rhythm now.

"Agent Braun?" he asked.

"Yes, Welly?"

The nickname would be addressed another time. But for now . . . "Thank you. For mending the leak."

"Not a jot," she said pleasantly. With that, she returned to her sorting, the soft singing resuming once again.

Perhaps the worst was over. Perhaps she would actually make a fine assistant.

CHAPTER FIVE

Wherein Our Dashing Archivist Tangles with Our Beloved Colonial Pepperpot in the Waning Hours of Morning

The scrawling of Books' pen was louder than usual. Granted, one expects there to be a hard scritching sound whenever a quill is put to paper and notations are recorded. This particular morning though, Wellington noticed the sound of his pen carving light impressions into the ledger open before him was like a spike digging through his head. He felt a knot between his brow, and realised just how distracted he was by it. But why? This was not an unaccustomed noise. In fact, he found the sounds of the Archives, from the *scritch-scritch* of pen against parchment to the ever-present hum of the generator comforting, more so than the sounds of his own house. The writing, on this particular morning, drove the unseen spike deep into his skull. Deeper and deeper with every note, integer, and letter formed by his hand. But why?

"Morning, Welly," the voice echoed from the top of the stone staircase.

Then it came to him. His assistant, Eliza D. Braun, was late. Again.

He looked up at the clock suspended on the wall next to their shared desk. Seven minutes shy of eleven. "Only barely," he whispered to himself. Then he shot back. "Cutting it close to afternoon, don't you think, Miss Braun?"

"Oh yes, Welly, well, you see I was on my way to the office when the neighbour, a sweet young slip of a girl, invited me for an early tea. As she is my neighbour and tends to my cat when I am out in the field—"

"When you *were* in the field, you mean?"

"Welly, she has been very sweet and understanding on taking care of Scheherazade. The least I could do was to join her. This was the first time I really had to sit down and get to know my neighbour a little better."

Braun's face appeared imploring to him, as if she was silently asking, "*Well what would you do if you were in my place, Welly?*"

This was the midpoint of Week Two together in the Archives, and he felt himself grasping the shreds of his patience. At this rate, Wellington would be marching into Doctor Sound's office, demanding to know for exactly how long he was going to be punished with this woman's presence in his Archives.

Yes, *his* Archives. Perhaps Doctor Sound didn't care for that proclamation, but if it weren't for his sole efforts down here . . .

"Books, are you all right?" Braun asked him as she took a seat at her side of the desk. "You look as if you're about to yell at me for something."

"Did you break anything on your way here?"

"No."

"Then I'm not going to yell at you." He placed his pen against the paper as if to resume his notations, paused and then yanked the spectacles off his face. "Miss Braun, this is yet another morning you have completely disregarded the time. Yesterday, it was a matter of recovering and returning field gear from your domicile to the Ministry. On prior mornings, you claimed it was your inability to adjust your morning routine accordingly."

Braun nodded, clearing her throat. "Yes, well, I told you on that first day this job was going to take some getting used to, what with the Archives running on such a rigid schedule. An advantage of being a field agent was a certain latitude in morning hours and routines."

"Rather too much latitude, if you ask me."

"Or simply a thank-you gift from the Crown saying, 'We certainly do appreciate you get shot at and risking life and limb for the throne. Sleep in, if you like. Cheers!'? Apart from the travel and the rather clever contraptions we get, there are very few benefits in being a field agent."

"Perhaps." He considered her for a few ticks of the clock, and then relented. "All right, Miss Braun, I will grant you this last week, but Monday morning next, eight o'clock sharp, I want you at your desk, busy working in the Renaissance."

"Henry the Seventh?"

"Eighth." Wellington said, continuing through the slight groan that Braun made. "We uncovered some new evidence on a recent case relating to Anne Boleyn."

"Really?" she asked. "And what is that exactly? That she *was* a witch and had, in fact, put King Henry under a spell?"

He looked up at her. "As a matter of fact, yes. We came across a relic insinuating as such."

"What exactly?"

"It's in front of you," Wellington said, motioning to a large book nearly covering a third of her desk.

Braun gave a whistle as she ran her hand across its immense, ornate cover. "And this is to go into the Archives? For storage?" She hefted the tome up on its edge, impressed by its unexpected weight. "It's heavy. Beautiful, but heavy. What about this book condemns poor Anne as a witch?"

"That book," Wellington said while adding to his current case's notations, "is *The Book of the Dead*."

"Beg your pardon?"

"*The Book of the Dead*—as in Ancient Egypt. As in the spell book used by the high priests of the City of the Dead. Along with blessings, prayers, and ceremonies, there are some rather powerful spells there."

"Really? Like what?" Braun asked with a wry grin, "Like Anne Boleyn was Cleopatra or something?"

She continued to laugh while contemplating the massive book until making eye contact with Wellington. He continued to stare at her, his face half lit by the lamp beside him.

"Over the millennia, *The Book of the Dead* has been compiled, revised, and bound. With each binding, the previous versions have been destroyed. Yes, there are some fragments left, but that one is a rogue copy. The first page was tested and confirmed to be of a papyrus dating back to Cleopatra's realm. The latter pages and some of the intermittent replacements were on a parchment used in King Henry's court. Apparently, this rogue copy was found in the Tower."

Gingerly, now having an idea of how old some of the pages within its binding were, Braun lowered the ancient text flat, and then opened her own ledger. She clicked her tongue while flipping through its pages, giving a soft "Ah!" on finding the grid she had created following Wellington's specifications.

"Let's see now . . . Item?" Braun looked at the book for a moment, then uttered as she wrote, "*The . . . Book . . . of . . . the . . . Dead.* Origins?" She looked at it again, then at Wellington who was watching her. The patience he was concerned about was now slipping fast, as she spoke while writing, "Eeee . . . gypyt. Quantity?" Eyes up, then back to her ledger. "One. Description?" Wellington took a deep breath, struggling to keep from erupting into a frenzy as she muttered, "Big . . . black . . . aaaand . . . dead." She then punched into the engine's main interface:

ANNE BOLEYN

Eliza pressed two more keys, and the pulley system lowered to her side of the desk where she hefted the large book into its basket. *The Book of the Dead* was hoisted above them after she pressed another key. Watching it disappear, Eliza gave a nod and returned to her open ledger. She gave the item catalogue a single check, smiled proudly, and then closed the ledger.

"Right then, time for lunch."

Had he been drinking tea, he would have sprayed it across the desk. "But you just got here!" Wellington insisted.

Braun stood from the desk as she checked the fob at the end of her bodice's chain. "Oh, Welly, hush! I think you will agree the sign of a civilised society is a regular dining schedule."

"Weren't you just tardy on account of a late tea?"

With a heavy sigh, she rolled her eyes and clicked her tongue, in a manner hauntingly similar to his own mannerism. "No, had you been paying attention you would have heard me say my neighbor invited me for an early tea, and as ladies do, we got to talking. I needed to get to know her better and she is a delightful girl. Husband is an upstanding man in business. They were talking about having a child, so perhaps it is good I am no longer in the field, what with my ca—"

"Miss Braun!" Wellington snapped. "You just arrived. And it is rather early, don't you think, for a luncheon?"

"This is also part of the challenges in adjusting to your more regimented schedule, Welly. I was endeavouring to be on time today so I took in an early breakfast. Then I had the early tea, and now I am hungry once more. So you will have to excuse me. I will not work across from a gentleman with my stomach growling." Again, she checked her watch and grimaced. "Right then, toodle pip and all that. See you in an hour. Perhaps."

With a rustle of skirts, Braun disappeared into the shadows of the Archives and then re-emerged as a bright cutout of light colours against the dark wall supporting the stone staircase.

Wellington, his fingers drumming against the desk, watched her ascend. This woman had some amazing gall. To show up for her assignment only to leave for a midday meal after ten minutes of work? Disgraceful! How could this insubordinate harridan be one of the most outstanding field agents of the Ministry? Her results must be truly astounding.

Wellington sniffed, and returned his attention to cataloguing the El Dorado vases . . . minus one. That was when he sneezed.

Wellington, while removing his handkerchief, sniffed again. And again, he sneezed, this time properly. His nose was starting to clog up a bit, but not before he identified the culprit: lilacs.

Wait a moment, he thought. *Agent Braun was wearing . . . a dress?*

The door at the top of stairs closed quietly, and he felt his back straighten. He gave another sneeze, and simmered at his end of the desk as he blew into his handkerchief.

Wellington now knew where his patience came to an abrupt end—wherever Miss Eliza D. Braun was headed.

He walked around to the back of the engine and cast a nervous glance to the hatch Eliza had just secured. Wellington counted silently, and assured himself no one would be surprising him with a visit. Why would today be any different?

The hidden terminal unfolded from its concealment and hissed to life, its display slowly going from onyx to dull amber. Wellington wriggled his fingers, feeling a hint of excitement at hearing his knuckles lightly cracking. His fingers then danced across the keyboard, but his eyes remained on the display:

ACCESS ETS

His eyes went back to the heavy iron door four storeys above. If anyone were to walk into the Archives now . . .

As the analytical engine would do when preparing tea, it gave a single chime that brought his attention back to the tiny interface.

ETS ACTIVE. AGENT?

He knew this was crossing a line somewhere, but had she not done the same just scant moments ago? His eyes narrowed on the monitor as he typed:

ELIZA D. BRAUN

He could hear the pipes in his engine shudder, and its own internal hum swelled as it sent out its signal. It searched, drawing more and more power to do so with each ping it sent.

The display flickered for a moment, and then—materializing through the aether—came a reply.

AGENT LOCATED.

NEXT COMMAND?

Next command? Providing him a hiding place after confronting Agent Braun? That sounded quite appealing. Instead, he typed:

SEND TO TRACKER.

This would take a few minutes. That would give him enough time to get his coat and bowler. For this little venture, he didn't think his walking stick would be a necessity.

CHAPTER SIX

In Which Our Lovely Miss Eliza Braun Dares the Halls of Bedlam and Tries Her Best To Make Amends to a Ghost from Her Past

For the second time in two weeks, Eliza D. Braun faced the possibility she was a right coward. Standing at the entrance to Bethlehem Royal Hospital, commonly known as Bedlam, she found her feet unwilling to carry her any farther. Looking up, the ornate gate could have been mistaken for some grand country estate—if you could ignore the writhing figures of madness above the ironwork. And from the outside it looked tidy and innocent enough, but the place was redolent with lost possibilities. It was in short, the kind of place that any sane person would avoid.

The locket in her hand felt as weighty as lead, and yet she couldn't merely ignore its message. For three days she had come here and been turned away by the nurses. He was always too ill, too lost in madness for them to let her see him.

Usually that sort of obstacle would only have fired her desire to break in—most likely with the assistance of dynamite—but this was different. Eliza was afraid to face Harrison Thorne. He'd been her partner in the Ministry and in idle moments she'd entertained the idea of his being something more. That was in the past now, and it still stung.

But it was this or find a way to be happy rotting away with Wellington Books in the Archives. It was simply not acceptable.

Tilting her chin upward at a defiant angle, Eliza set off up the path. She joined a thin trail of other visitors: mothers herding reluctant children, teary-eyed parents, and grey-faced lovers.

Not many really, for the size of the hospital; and Eliza grew suddenly aware this was about more than the locket. People's lives dried up and blew away in places like this. They had them in New Zealand too, and she knew from familial experience what to expect. That was half the problem. If she paused and allowed herself to recollect, she would see her brother Herbert's face, dirty, strained, mad, the last time she had visited him. She would then hear the wails, the screams; and she would remember how her beloved elder brother could no longer recognise her.

It was easy for Eliza to imagine that they would take one look at her and lock her up—just like him.

She shook her head. That was ridiculous. She was as sane as the next agent—so long as the next agent wasn't Harry. She had to raise a gloved hand to her mouth and stifle a light giggle at that. He would have appreciated the dark humour.

At least the Harry she remembered.

Bethlehem presented a surprisingly clean face at first, though the decorator certainly had a sense of the macabre. Tortured sculptures of Melancholy and Raving Madness stood to each side of the atrium, providing instant soberness to any fool who might try to smuggle in hope. They were more than art. These twisted, inspired visions were designed to serve as warnings to those who dared to enter the Hospital.

The competent nurse who had seen her before smiled widely on seeing Eliza approach the front window. "Miss

Braun"—her starched cap bobbed in atop her curly hair—"I am so glad you came in. Mr. Thorne is actually lucid today, so you can see him."

Eliza tried to smile back, though her stomach did a little, uncomfortable dance. "Thank you. I will need to see him in private."

The nurse's mouth pursed a little, and so Eliza slid her Ministry credentials across the counter. The response was most satisfactory.

She did feel compelled, however, to cast nervous glances along the corridors. Naturally no one from the Ministry was watching her; but that assurance did not alter the risk she was taking. Not by a jot. If Doctor Sound ever found out about her using Ministry credentials for preferential treatment, she wouldn't have to worry about rotting down in the Archives. That she knew was for certain.

The nurse called over a male warden. "Thomas here will take you up and stay just outside the door."

That said it all. *Gods, Harry!* Her hand tightened on the strange shape of the locket.

With a nod of thanks to the nurse, Eliza followed the silent, hunch-shouldered guard to the men's wing. The stories of Bedlam were legendary—legendary and horrific, so Eliza was relieved to find things had obviously changed. True, there were locked doors that her guardian ushered her through, but they led to large airy galleries with rooms running off them. These were the "curable" men's quarters, where inmates sat in small groups mending clothing, painting small figurines, and doing other menial tasks. One large gap-toothed man looked up from his tiny toy soldier at Eliza as she passed, and grinned.

"Pretty lady," he called in a singsong voice. He then giggled and added, "Pretty lady go boom."

With a start of alarm she stopped mid-stride and turned back, but the patient was once more at his task, any interest in her he might have shown now gone. Unnerved, Eliza hurried on, catching up with her guide.

A huge geared door stood before them, a veritable edifice of brass and cogs that suggested something on the other side was well worth keeping locked down. Thomas put his thick hand on a space in the doorjamb. Clockwork whirred and chugged, and the brass contracted around his palm with a bang that made Eliza jump. After a second the door rattled, and she took a step back as the door slid on tracks back into the wall.

This then must be the incurables ward, she thought, a chill passing through her as she crossed the threshold.

The difference was immediately obvious. The smell hit her in the face like a brick, and she paused to catch her breath quickly through her mouth.

Try as they might, the caretakers of Bedlam couldn't keep the rank odor of bodily function from permeating the air. This was the Bedlam that knew no visitors, the Bedlam no one could stomach. This was the Bedlam best forgotten, unless you were a regular patron of the "show of Bethlehem." Her warden led the way down the row of locked doors, and Eliza tried to shut out the wails and screams of those around them, but even her training was useless in this environment.

As she continued deeper into Bedlam, it haunted her that this place had more than one agent from the Ministry confined within its walls. Eliza promised herself a stiff drink once she got home.

Halfway down Thomas unlocked a cell and waited. Eliza paused at the door. "Thank you," she told him, and then looking into his eyes realised they were in fact a soft brown, filled with unexpected compassion.

"I'll wait outside, miss." His voice was light like a lad's, strange to hear out of such a hulking brute of a body.

With a nod, Eliza entered, the cell door softly, gently closing behind her.

Harrison Thorne was huddled in the corner, his face averted. All she saw was his head of shaggy golden blond hair and her breath jammed in her throat. It seemed perhaps nothing had changed.

Then the man she once knew as her partner and friend looked over his shoulder, and the ruin of it was all too apparent.

Eliza squeezed shut her eyes, recalling Harrison as he had been: tall, full of energy and enthusiasm, a damn fine card player, and hard to resist kissing. When she opened them again, it was to the reality she had been avoiding for so long.

He'd gone missing for a whole week before the Ministry had found him and whisked him to Bedlam. This was the first time Eliza had seen him.

"Harrison?" Her voice sounded foreign to her. Hollow. Overwhelmed with sorrow. Why had she not defied the Ministry, as she had before, and just come to see him? She knew the answer—fear. Fear of this.

Harrison's eyes, which had been hazel green, remained, but they were darting, constantly shifting to the corners of the room. They had let his beard grow wild and woolly—probably because he was incessantly moving and impossible to shave. He had his long, strong fingers in his mouth, and they were bloody where he had been chewing them. Without thinking, Eliza stumbled over and wrapped her arms around him. Highly unprofessional, but there was no one around to take note of it. *I'm sorry, Harry*, her embrace told him, or at least she hoped it did. *I'm so sorry, Harry.*

Gods, Harrison was so thin his bones poked her, and he'd been the epitome of strapping masculinity only a mere eight months ago. He let her hold him for only a second, and then jerked away, his wild beard scratching against her cheek. The Harrison she'd known had always been most particular about everything, especially his appearance. He'd always kept a carefully waxed moustache and well-starched collar. "*The clothes may make the man*," he'd once told her in response to her jibes about his incessant vanity, "*but a touch of dashing with a good peppering of debonair serves you well in the field, Lizzie.*" When he winked at her, as he did in this memory, it reminded her of her femininity. It reminded her of how much Harry took advantage of his God-granted assets. *"People open their doors, hearts, and minds for princes before paupers. Try to remember that, dear Lizzie."*

That Harrison would have been horrified at his present state.

The stranger leaned back in the corner and began examining the ceiling intently. He made a curious mewling noise in his throat, like a lost kitten. It was nearly imperceptible, at first, but grew in volume when Harrison began to rock back and forth. Eliza found herself comforting him as she would a small animal. If this was his best, Eliza had no desire to see what his worst was.

"Harry?" She whispered, stroking his hand. "It's Lizzie." She had always hated the variations of her name, but when he had called her that it seemed to lose its sting. "Gods, Harry, don't you remember me?"

At the catch in her voice her former partner frowned slightly. "Lizzie . . . Lizzie?" He looked to be trying very hard to remember scattered details.

Desperate, she pressed her lips to the back of his hand, something she'd never dared before. His flesh was rough and scarred, but still his.

Harrison touched her hair, his gesture hesitant and soft. "Lizzie. I knew a Lizzie. Such a pretty girl. I could have kissed her in Paris, you know."

Eliza looked up and smiled.

"I had many chances to kiss her, that Pretty Lizzie," he told her, his tenor mimicking a child's telling a grown-up of their latest achievement. "There was Uganda. There was Casablanca. Oh yes, I had many, many chances, but Paris . . . yes, Paris. And I think Pretty Lizzie would have let me kiss her."

"Would she now?" An invisible hand choked her. She was swallowing back sobs, and talking somehow helped her keep the emotional tide back. "So, why didn't you, you rogue?"

He shook his head violently. The child had been caught.

"Wouldn't be right. Wouldn't be right. She was special, Pretty Lizzie. She was pretty, but special. Not like the others. She was very, very, very special."

Eliza took in a deep breath, hoping her smile brought him a hint of peace. "Yes, Harry, I think Lizzie would have let you kiss her."

"But I didn't and the chance passed," Harrison whispered with a little sigh. It was as he said: the moment was gone for both of them.

But perhaps there could still be justice if not love. Perhaps their loss could still have meaning.

With extreme care, Eliza turned over his hand, and gently slid the locket she had found in the Archives into his palm. "Harrison, do you remember this?"

It wasn't her imagination, he did shoot her a look out of his watering eyes, so she went on hurriedly. "Remember, those people that died—the ones you wouldn't give up on?"

His voice was a croak, forced past chapped lips. "Bone, skin, and blood!"

Eliza pressed her hands over his, stilling them before they could reach his mouth. "Yes, it was awful. The Ministry may have given up on those cases, but not you."

"Bone . . . skin . . . blood." Harrison shook his head, jerking away from her, repeating the three horrific facts of those cases, which had haunted him then and, so it would seem, in his current state of madness.

He was falling back into whatever fractured thoughts had brought him to Bedlam. Eliza touched her forehead to his, trying to bring him back to her.

Ever so gently, she turned her head towards the locket. He followed suit. "You found this on the last victim, Harrison," she whispered, tracing the outline of the strange locket, its odd asymmetrical shape, its queer etchings of the cat staring up at them both. "Remember? You found it and you wouldn't give up."

"Did I?" His voice was faint, but in it she heard an echo of her old friend.

A tear leaked out of the corner of her eye—a weak, foolish tear. "Did you leave this for me? Did you leave it in the files for me to find?"

His mouth worked a couple of times, "You . . . you . . . see her, right, Lizzie?"

Eliza sat back on her heels. "*Her*, Harrison?" A quick scan of the room showed they were quite alone.

Harrison laughed, short and bitter—something that she had never heard pass his lips. It echoed in the room, and his head lolled alarmingly. Eliza might have, if it was anyone else, slapped him or at least given him a damn good shake.

"Please, Harrison—I don't understand. What are you talking about?" She had to be stronger than this. "Whom are you talking about?"

He stroked her hair again, a heartbreaking look of loss on his broken face. It made her think of Paris and the night trip on the Seine, one of their last missions. Her heart had been racing back then, and it had nothing to do with dynamite. Had she missed the signs because of those foolish feelings? Had her partner been teetering on the edge of sanity for months and had she been too cow-eyed to notice?

Eliza clenched her eyes shut for a moment. She was used to action, not interrogation. That had been Harrison's forte. In the last few months of their partnership though, he had developed an obsession over those cases. Bodies drained of blood, flayed down the muscle, and some mysteriously with not one solid bone left in them. The corpses, at least the ones discovered, Harry was convinced were connected, yet no connections could be made. With no plausible explanation in sight and other situations carrying the House of Usher's signature cropping up, the Ministry had dropped the cases, much to Harrison's dismay.

But he had kept this locket, a single clue. Her partner had been such a stickler for protocol and rules, except for when it came to what he referred to as the Rag and Bone Murders.

"Yes, I found her."

"I'm sorry, Harry." She whispered, pressing her hand

against the roughness of his cheek. "If I had only taken more notice of what you were doing—"

"Don't cry, Lizzie." His voice was heavy with sorrow. "I've found her"—his hands cupped her chin but his eyes weren't on her—"and now you have too."

Following his gaze Eliza saw Harrison was holding the locket up to the light by its chain and spinning it. Eliza blinked, tilting her head to one side. When spun at speed the odd shape and engravings suddenly transformed into something she would never have spotted. It was still a cat—but on spinning the pendant, the cat smiled back at them.

The Cheshire Cat, made famous in the writings of Lewis Carroll.

"I see her, Harrison, I do see her," she whispered, a dizziness seeming to creep over her, "but what does it mean?"

Abruptly he stopped the spinning effect and pressed the locket into her hand. "We're all mad here. I'm mad. You're mad." The singsong voice he said this in sent a chill scampering up her spine. Harry then began to frantically itch and shake, muttering his words over and over again.

His moans were like a beaten child, and Eliza's efforts to soothe him were slapped away. Her fear welled up into her throat on Harrison's feverish scratching at the nape of his neck. Gods, she'd broken him again, and returned him to the chapter of his life that remained painful. *No, Harry, I will not leave you this way*, she swore in silence, stilling his hands as best she could.

It was during this struggle she found a raised scar hidden behind his left ear.

"You didn't have that before," she hissed, feeling her fear and pity surrender to anger, a thankful respite from her sorrow.

"It's all right, Harrison," Eliza growled, squeezing him tight, even if it was only for a minute. Striding to the door, she pounded hard against its cold metallic surface. The orderly had only opened it slightly before Eliza yanked him into the cell. "What have you done to him?"

Thomas struggled to keep up with her, his balance restored once she released him and pointed out Harrison's scar. The fallen agent was wailing up a storm, beating at his head.

For a second Eliza didn't quite hear the warden's protestations. "That was one of the wounds he had on him when he arrived, miss."

Harrison then erupted into a frenzy, and Thomas suddenly wrapped Eliza in his arms pulling her out of the way. She probably would have kicked the orderly's teeth in, had her former partner not howled *"LIZZIE!"*

His voice caught, and his face contorted into a silent scream. The moment passed, and Harry's voice trembled as he looked at her. "Remember Lizzie, we are all mice in the maze. So it doesn't matter where you go as long as you get somewhere. You're sure to do it if you keep walking long enough. And when you get there, you have a place to rest, to eat, to drink." He then popped up on his feet and threw his arms into the air, and screamed, "TO LIVE!"

The ramblings came to her if they were some pronouncement from on high, but she recognised it. Some small sane part of Harrison was trying to drive the point home. All the air went out of her, and she allowed herself to be hustled out of the cell. *Yes*, she thought, her eyes fixed on Harrison, *I understand.*

Thomas secured the cell, Harrison's screams still audible despite the door's thickness, and then propped himself against the wall. He looked tired. "Mister Thorne's gone now, Miss. You won't get anything sensible out of him now."

"I'm sorry about mistaking that wound," Eliza whispered, looking down at the locket. "I just assumed . . ."

Thomas' retort came in silently motioning the way they had come, and escorting her back towards the main atrium. Passing through the Gallery, the wizened man she had seen earlier in the gallery was waiting, his eyes gleaming. "Booooooooom!" he whispered with a wink.

It was almost too much, and Eliza quickened her step after

the orderly. On reaching the entrance, Thomas stomped off with no politeness or pleasantry. Taking note of both their expressions, the nurse wisely chose not to ask questions.

Eliza now left Bedlam as she had arrived but feeling considerably more shaken. She hadn't even been able to say goodbye to Harrison—not that he would have noticed.

As she walked down the path towards the gate, she took the odd locket and put it around her neck to serve as a challenge to those who ripped her partner and friend from her. It lay chill against her chest and she pressed her hand against it, as if to memorise the feel of it.

Her racing heart had not quite returned to normal when she looked up to see a familiar figure. Standing beneath the statue of Madness was Wellington Books, as dapper and well turned out as Harrison had once been. All his outfit needed was a walking stick, and he would have turned a few of the ladies' eyes in his direction.

"So." He spoke dryly, his words sobering. "How is the luncheon in Bedlam, Miss Braun?"

INTERLUDE

Where the Agent of the Outback Makes New Friends in High Stations

Agent Bruce Campbell was happy in a variety of places: hanging off a cliff face in Bengal, fighting off belligerent Sherpas in Nepal, or even swimming amongst the deadly great whites in his own Australian waters. And he was adroit at any number of activities; shooting, chasing beautiful women, and mixing the perfect after dinner aperitif.

What he was not happy doing was drinking tea with a Privy Counsellor in the midst of the finery at the Grosvenor Hotel. Glancing out of the corner of his eye, Bruce realised that the people surrounding them were mostly ladies of fashion. He shifted in his seat. Dammit, he recognised some of them—even with their clothes on. As long as they weren't with their husbands, he had a fighting chance of getting out of here and into more friendly settings like, say, a gunfight.

That was, if the man opposite of him would allow it.

Peter Lawson, Duke of Sussex, needed no card, no introduction—Bruce knew very well who he was, but not quite how to address him. So instead he sat still and waited for the Privy Counsellor to speak.

Sussex leaned back in his seat, replaced the cigarillo carefully between his lips, and fixed Bruce with a gaze that he recognised from a hundred different predators. The agent knew how to cope with such looks when locked in a stare-down. Flash a devil-may-care smile, wink if time allowed, and then deliver his world-renowned (at least as far as he was concerned) "Thunder from Down Under" blow that left many a jaw shattered and opposing agents on the floor.

This time, the look was coming from someone with the ear of Her Majesty the Queen. A bureaucrat. And he was in a tearoom.

Bruce did the only thing that came naturally—he froze.

The sound of the dumbwaiter rattling up from the centre of the table was a welcome relief in the middle of this tense moment. Bruce swallowed—he would have much rather had a beer than tea. With the poms however, it was always bloody tea.

Sussex stubbed out his cigarillo, leaned forward, and took the pot off the brass multi-tiered plates, one of which kept the liquid at just the right temperature.

"Another bloody McTighe device," Bruce muttered, leaning away from it.

"Not a fan of the Scotsman then?" Sussex carefully poured two cups. "What a pity. He is the nation's foremost inventor."

The Australian shook his head, "When his gizmos don't kill people."

"Progress has a price. Civilisation must move forward." The Duke glanced around the room, taking in the quiet chatter of the ladies, and smiled. "And sometimes we do have to thin the herd a little."

Sussex reminded Bruce of nothing more than a crocodile. He'd dealt with plenty of those in his younger days in the wilds of Queensland, and was confident this one would be no different. He might lurk under water, but now he was ready to strike.

"So tell me, Agent Campbell, your position at the Ministry? Do you find satisfaction in your role defending the Empire?"

Finally, they were coming down to the heart of the matter.

"Doing my part, Your Grace, to defend good Queen Vic," he answered with a shrug of his massive shoulders. For a few moments, they exchanged no words; and Bruce wondered in a panic what he needed do. Help himself to a tea? Grab one of those frighteningly dainty sandwiches.

It was when he caught the eye of the table next to them, the looks of shock and condemnation clear on the patrons' faces, that it dawned on him. His voice apparently carried beyond the table.

"I see," Sussex said, still stirring his tea. "Well, I'm sure Queen *Vic* appreciates your efforts—efforts that I will assume do not include diplomatic negotiations?"

Bruce cleared his throat, squirmed in his seat, and took a chance to reach for a cup. "Well, I'm not the talker when partnered with other agents. I'm more of the . . . ah . . ."

"The muscle."

He saw that one coming. Bruce was more than fists and guns. He knew that. He was just more *comfortable* with the fists and guns than the diplomatic aspects of the Ministry. Bruce also knew that, and preferred it that way.

"Nothing wrong with being a man of deeds, not words. I assure you, there are members of Parliament who would prefer to hold open debate in the local pubs as opposed to the House of Lords. Strike a man on the floor, and it is an outrage. Strike the same man at the Prospect of Whitby and it is fair sport." Sussex smiled, and Bruce felt the desperate need for a water closet. "You have a place in this world, Agent Campbell, but I must wonder if it is at the Ministry."

Bruce furrowed his brow as he leaned forward. "I don't think I follow you, Your Grace."

The Duke spread some clotted cream on his scones with the precision of an artist. He raised his eyes and smiled at the agent. "It is not common knowledge amongst your fellows yet, but I would be surprised if the organisation sees the year out."

Bruce blinked. "Bloody hell!" he whispered as he brought the cup to his lips, pinkie extended. He had learned some things in London.

The ladies around him shot him a second round of horrified glances, but this time he was too shocked to care.

"Yes, I am sure it comes as quite a surprise to you." Sussex devoured his scone, and then dabbed at the corners of his mouth with a linen napkin. "I know you have become used to a certain lifestyle—as have your children."

His children? Bruce sat up a little taller, the one hand lowering the cup gingerly while the other clenched in a white-knuckled fist under the table.

"I understand you have quite a number. Some with your darling wife"—the Duke tilted his head, that crocodilian smile flicking over his lips—"some not."

Despite the coolness of the tearoom, Bruce felt a thin line of sweat break out on the back of his neck. He found his intimidation of Sussex quickly waning. This pom was treading on matters that were not his concern. "With all due respect to your title and position within Her Majesty's council, Your Grace, get to the damn point." he hissed under his breath.

"The point, my dear colonial, is that you should spend less time at the boxing matches and more at the card tables," he purred, helping himself to a salmon sandwich. "When the deck gets shuffled, it's nice to have made friends with the dealer earlier."

Bruce heard Sussex, but his attention was divided. In his mind, he was preoccupied with financial sums, imagining what his wife Grace would say, and seeing the many shining faces of his children.

"I've played my fair share of hands," he replied cautiously. "Which way are you cutting the cards?"

"Sound is proving most ineffective with this . . . this organisation of his." Sussex went on, "The Ministry has always been less of a representation of the Crown and more of his private agenda. I feel—as does Her Majesty—that its time has passed, and the formation of a new entity would be entirely in the Empire's best interests. Something more dedicated to clandestine operations that concern both internal strife as well as international dangers. 'British Intelligence' has a lovely ring to it, do you not think?" With the sandwich, he merely nibbled at it, his eyes no longer regarding Bruce but seeming to lose themselves in a grand painting covering the tearoom's far wall. "Regardless of what we call this new branch of the government, it will fall on me to populate it with the brightest minds, the most valuable resources."

The croc had its teeth in him now, and Bruce could feel it dragging him down. Surely there was only one way to make this less painful—let the bloody thing have its way. If he had to guess who had the more power between Sussex and the Fat Man, his bet was on the Privy Counsellor.

Bruce sighed, "And what would I need to do to get into this new department?"

Sussex's eyebrows raised, his eyes looking above him as if he were searching for the answer to be floating in the aether above him. "Oh, let me see, a branch of Her Majesty's government specialising in intelligence gathering and clandestine operations requires an individual of strength, cunning, resourcefulness . . ." His gaze then locked on to Bruce. ". . . and loyalty." He leaned forward, his face hardening, the veneer of gentility disappearing completely. "I think you are more than the sum of your parts, my dear colonial; and while it may seem I am strong-arming you into roguish behaviour, I assure you the final choice is yours.

"Help me bring down Sound and the Ministry. Serve as my eyes and ears on the inside. I assure you that your actions for the betterment of the Empire will not go without proper compensation."

Only by tightening his jaw did Bruce avoid spitting out another crass comment. He thought of the friends and colleagues he had in the Ministry, and even the Director himself—who had been nothing but kindly to him. He wouldn't call them "mates" like his friends back home, but they were individuals that relied on him to cover their backs. Even that loudmouth tart, Braun, he wanted beside him in a fight. She was a crack shot, handled explosives as if she were in a kitchen cooking up breakfast, and nastier than a Gurkha in a bar fight. This was a betrayal of trust at the highest level. A point of absolutely no return.

Then he thought of Grace and the children. He owed them more.

Sussex, seeing his pause, smiled thinly. "If your conscience is bothering you, Agent Campbell, then please remember we are all on the same side. Your ultimate loyalty must lie with Her Majesty after all, mustn't it?"

Bruce looked at the finery, the luxuries of the upper crust displayed all around them. It was so beautiful, so perfect, and yet it was so hollow. But it was the place he, and his family had to live in. He'd been at the bottom of the barrel before in his life—he wasn't going back there ever again.

"Tell me what you need, mate. I'd hate to let ol' Queen Vic down after all."

Sussex's smile was chilling and humourless. It was how things would be from now on.

CHAPTER SEVEN

In Which Our Intrepid Heroes Call a Truce and Rise to the Challenge of Revels and Mirth!

Since his colleague simply started rather than replying, Books asked, "Is the gruel here as good as the papers claim it to be?"

Braun raised her eyebrow. "Oh, the slop here is par excellence. They could tidy up the place a bit though. Better have a discussion with the management about it." She pursed her lips together, considering him for a few seconds. "Keeping secrets from me, Books?"

He straightened up slightly on that. "Whatever do you mean, Miss Braun?"

"For an Archivist who seems to rarely leave the Ministry dungeons, you were able to track me without fail. How'd you manage that?"

Wellington shook his head and reached into his coat pocket. "The same way you found me bound for Antarctica."

To the cursory glance of a passerby, the device he held in his hand would have appeared as a compass, but this compass rang with a tiny, single chime. The needle that one would assume pointed north instead pointed at Eliza. Underneath the needle was a tiny map of their current city block, and of its two inset lights, the green one blinked cheerfully.

Eliza looked down at her ring. "The Emergency Tracking System."

"Amazing possibilities wireless telegraphy offers, wouldn't you agree, Miss Braun?" he quipped, before shutting the tracker's domed lid with a quick *snap*.

The silence they shared, save for the clamour of London bustling around them, could have well been a shouting match. Eliza's anger at being followed and at getting caught—and by an Archivist no less—was evident. Wellington in turn however did not let his displeasure at being betrayed show. His thumb absently rubbed the Ministry's coat of arms etched into the tracker's cover. They were still part of Her Majesty's government, and both bound to that service. In that much, they were equals. He needed to consider her well-being as a fellow agent.

"How is he?" Even Wellington was surprised by how calm his question sounded.

Braun adjusted her hat. "As if you really give a toss about Harry? He was merely another name lost in your precious Archives until a few days ago."

"Yes," he replied. "And I suppose this is simply your weekly visit to see him?"

She took a step closer. "Don't, Books."

"The posturing is trite, Miss Braun, and I would advise the same to you: don't think you can hoodwink me without a thought. As you have noted, I am a resourceful gent." He looked down at her. "I do not appreciate such deception, especially from a colleague."

Braun tightened the shawl around her shoulders and shivered as she cast a final glance towards Bedlam. "I'm done here." She gave Wellington another perusal, and then asked, "Did you plan to spend the rest of the day standing here, or were we to head back to the office?"

He shook his head lightly, pushed his spectacles up the

bridge of his nose, and offered her his arm. "Come along, Miss Braun."

"If you please, Books," she snapped, brushing his offer aside, "when we return to the office, address me by my proper title." Eliza glanced around her and whispered, "Agent." With a curt nod, she added, "Don't think I've not noticed that little tactic of yours."

"A tactic which apparently is not working, Miss Braun—seeing as you have decided to take this matter into your hands. On Ministry time, no less."

"Yes," she rolled her eyes as they started walking, "because as we know, the Archives will fall into ruin if I miss a few days of cataloguing."

Wellington grinned a bit, but cast the idle thought aside. "You have a duty to the Ministry; and as we are both well aware of, you do wish to keep your position there. I can say I have seen what you do in the field, and regardless of your liberal application of dynamite you are a . . . valuable asset to the Ministry. It would truly be a loss to not have you within the ranks."

Their walking ceased. Braun looked into Wellington's eyes and then nodded. "It hurt to admit that, didn't it?"

"Far more than you can fathom, yes, but I do believe it. Completely." He motioned ahead, and their walk resumed. "So consider what I am doing to be for your own good."

"Remember what was once said about the road to hell and good intentions, Books," she quipped.

"Perhaps, Miss Braun, but let us also agree your failure is a failure on my part as well. I have been given the responsibility to acclimate you to the inner workings of the Archives, and so far you have not spent a full day there."

Braun took objection to this assessment. "Hold on a moment! I have accomplished a few things."

"Yes, you have destroyed one irreplaceable vase, miscatalogued several items between the Stone and Bronze Ages . . ."

She muttered, "The green makes things look more stony than brassy."

". . . And you have entered in the inventory one book. Have I missed anything?"

Eliza rapped his arm and beamed. "I fixed the leak."

"Your position at the Ministry is Archivist, not Plumber."

"All right, so I am not going so elegantly into my new service, what of it?" She gave a shrug, her hands imploring as she continued. "Books, you saw what I love to do first-hand. Do you expect me to give that up so easily?"

"Yes I do, Miss Braun," Wellington stated. "As a field agent, you were expected to follow orders and, from what I saw firsthand, you did just that and it saved my life. So yes, I expect you to do as you did back in Antarctica, and follow orders."

They continued in silence, Braun's face now blushing brightly. The last thing he wanted or needed to do in order to build a rapport was to embarrass her, but what were his options? It ate away at her, he could see, as she attempted to tell him something several times, failing to do so when her mouth opened.

Finally she let out a disgusted sigh and tapped him on the arm again. "Come on, Welly," she said, ignoring the silent "*Ow!*" he made. She appeared to be undeterred in her next bold question. "Where is your sense of adventure?"

"Well," he winced, continuing to rub his arm, "if I did have your definition for a sense of adventure, do you think I would take such an assignment as Archivist at a place called the Ministry of Peculiar Occurrences?"

Braun went to answer, but paused.

With a nod that spoke a silent "Exactly," he went on. "For me, the excitement is in the mystery, in researching something I am unaware of on that particular morning. The artifacts your lot bring back from various missions all have stories to tell. I've been quite content going beyond what the field agents accomplish. In many ways, a case cannot be closed before it is truly solved."

"And that, my dear Agent Books," stated Braun, her eyebrow crooked sharply as she spoke to him, "is where you contradict yourself. You say you love a good mystery and yet down in the depths of the Archives are cases which have stumped the field agents and even the old man upstairs."

"Miss Braun," Wellington said, looking at her over his spectacles, "I doubt if Doctor Sound would appreciate such a moniker as 'old man.' "

"The point is you are an agent of the Ministry. Regardless." She stopped him in the middle of the sidewalk, catching him in the chest with a single finger. "You had to go through the same training, the same evaluations, the same rigours; and here you are, taking great pride in your involvement yet trying to remain as far from the field as possible, surrounded by the mystery you tell me you are so attracted to."

"Miss Braun—" he began.

"And if we are to be working together, as partners," she said, gingerly placing her hand flat against his chest. "*Eliza.*"

"Miss Braun," he said, removing her hand, "I find it most intriguing you speak of contradictions only a moment before calling me your partner. A partnership is based on many things, but at its core is trust. You must admit that we are off to a bad start in that department, aren't we?"

Braun looked away for a moment, and then conceded, "That was before I knew if I could trust you."

"And what makes you think you can trust me now?"

"Because if you were truly all rules and regulations as you carry yourself, you wouldn't have been waiting for me at the entrance of Bedlam. You would have been waiting for me in Doctor Sound's office. With Doctor Sound debriefed on my behaviour over the past week, I have no doubt."

A single finger went up to contradict her, but no voice came out. In fact, he felt quite exposed in that moment. Granted, reporting this to Doctor Sound may have relieved him and his Archives of her permanently, but instead he had chosen to deal with her himself.

She was right.

He did not dare examine the why in that judgement call. A judgement call he hoped he would not regret.

"So there is a spirit of adventure in you?" Eliza proclaimed with an amount of satisfaction—so much satisfaction that passersby cast worried glances their way. "I knew it."

"That will do, Miss Braun," replied Wellington, straightening his waistcoat and then proceeding back to the office as he spoke to her. "I am trying to nurture a relationship between us, a healthy, *working* relationship, mind you. And it would have accomplished nothing—"

"Welly?" Braun called out to him.

He stopped, and then looked around him. Wellington was talking to open air, nothing more. He turned around to see Braun still at the street corner, pointing in a different direction from where they were headed initially.

"And what is in tha—" Wellington then heard the oncoming rumble of a carriage. He sprinted back to the street corner, back to the damned contrary woman.

"This way, Welly," she said.

"But the Ministry isn't that way," he insisted. "In fact, I do not even require the tracker to tell me that this is most certainly *not* the way back to the Ministry!"

"Yes, but I have a more efficient route, if you would follow me." And with a slight laugh, Braun spoke over her shoulder. "Besides, I think your spirit of adventure needs a bit more exercising."

Wellington looked back up the street anxiously, back the way he had been heading. He *knew* this way was the shortest distance between the Ministry and Bedlam. So did the tracker. Exactly what Eliza Braun was up to and where she was headed was a mystery, and he knew what the mystery pertained to. She had already proven to be something of a woman who insisted on having her way in a situation, whether her way was proper or not.

Then again, she was a talented field agent and could very

well know of several alleyways that could get them back to the office faster than his preferred route. He had, inadvertently, gained her respect—for the time being—by showing up to Bedlam alone. It was a start, and he needed to build on this sliver of trust earned.

Therein was the mystery: what was Agent Eliza D. Braun up to?

"Eliza!" Wellington marched up to her in wide strides, a skeptical look fixed hard in his features. "I honestly do not recall any clever shortcut from this area which can get us back to the docks. As you have placed a bit of assurance in me, now I need a bit in return. We are headed back to the Ministry, yes?"

"Eventually," she said, her smile far too wicked for his liking.

"Now, Miss Braun, we really should be getting back to the Archives. I think this love of mystery and pursuit of adventure has enjoyed plenty of exercising for—"

Wellington suddenly found himself spun around and shoved against the side of the nearest building. Eliza was clasping tight onto the lapels of his frock-coat, and holding him still by virtue of the fact she was pressed against his whole length. One of her legs was jammed between his, giving the suggestion that damage to his nether regions could be in the offing if he moved.

"Bugger the exercise, Books." Her words came out as a hiss on his face. Her lips were scant inches from his. "I'm tired of playing gentle with you. You could have been a librarian—"

"Archi—"

Her grip tightened on his coat, and now her leg was starting to move slowly up and down along the inside of his thigh. "*—librarian* anywhere, but instead you chose a career in the Ministry. So now you're in the Ministry. Wonderful. Now, how about the rest of you?"

Wellington dare not look down, but he could nevertheless feel the rise and fall of her breasts against his chest. His blood was rushing to all sorts of inappropriate places, and he found himself breathing faster. Yes, she was using her feminine wiles on him, he knew that; but Wellington also knew with the right application of effort on her part, this slightly arousing and highly delightful position he found himself in could easily turn painful.

"Go on, Welly," Eliza cooed, "tell your new partner how long it's been."

He wanted to give her that "cold archivist's stare" of his, but that would have meant looking down towards the heaving bosoms. His voice was a half-octave higher as he stammered, "That's a rather personal question, don't you think, Miss Braun?"

Eliza continued as if she didn't notice a thing. "When was the last time you felt your heart race, your blood flow, or simply found yourself completely reliant on your wits to see yourself to the next morning? When was the last time you *lived*?"

Eliza's warmth against him was so distracting that he was struck dumb.

Her lips, as soft-looking as warm velvet, parted as she whispered, "When was the last time you did that, Welly? Really *felt* alive?"

He swallowed hard, trying to ignore the smell of lilacs that emanated from her skin. For reasons that currently escaped him, his earlier allergic reaction to her scent failed him now. Damnation. "The day I joined a complete stranger for tea. She was a beautiful woman, Miss Braun. Eyes like emeralds. Skin like silk. Quite striking."

"And?"

"The following week I woke up in the hold of an airship, en route to Antarctica."

Braun nodded. "Well then, that explains quite a bit now, doesn't it?"

"What? That the last time I followed the lead of a beautiful woman, it was a poor choice?"

Her devious smile softened a bit, then Braun reached

up and lightly flicked the end of his nose. "It's all the time you spent in the Archives. Alone. You need to know how to think fast so you don't end up in the situation I met you in. You, my dear colleague in cataloging, sorting, and shelving, need to remember what it means to *live*."

Abruptly she released him, stepping back, withdrawing her heady warmth. Wellington had to take a moment to regain the shreds of his composure. When he looked up he realised she was actually beckoning him to follow her. "Come on, Welly. Let's go have some fun."

He could still smell her perfume, and Wellington found it conjured mixed emotions. One of those mixed emotions was ruin. He knew there was no way he could convince her to return to the Archives. Not now. What was more, the whiff of perfume had quite derailed his own logical process. Perhaps that was the reason, and the longer he caught a whiff of her scent or felt her warmth, he never would. For some reason Wellington Thornhill Books found he could not muster the wherewithal to deny her anything.

Best not to let her know that.

CHAPTER EIGHT

In Which Our Daring Agents of the Ministry Share a Quiet Drink and Discover a Hidden Clue

Eliza wondered if Wellington's façade was starting to show the odd crack or two. He'd allowed himself to be ushered into a cab and driven north towards Fleet Street with never a comment passing his lips—though he couldn't have failed to notice that they were venturing into the city proper. This wasn't a quick pop down to the local establishment. They were crammed up against each other in the narrow confines of the hansom cab, and Eliza only just managed to avoid taking his arm in a tight embrace. It would have been priceless to see the expression such an action would have engendered, but she would not dare further intimacy. Rubbing up against him had been utterly inappropriate, and somehow dangerous at the same time. Eliza always enjoyed the thrill of shocking the opposite sex. It was part of her nature that had amused Harry a great deal. Pushing manners to teeter on the precipice was where she found an equal euphoria to that of demolitions and covert operations, and Wellington sometimes resembled a pom caricature—full-of-fuss-and-feathers. Watching him squirm did blunt the serrated edge of her punishment slightly.

The danger, though, came from one undeniable fact that Wellington Books, while still a bit stuffy, was hardly unpleasant in his carriage and demeanor. Her antics in the alleyway had also heated her skin and even teased her most intimate of places. Had it been *that* long since she'd pressed against an attractive man? As Wellington preoccupied himself with where they were heading, Eliza closed her eyes and pushed back the lingering sensations. Perhaps seeing Harry had unearthed old spirits.

Her inappropriate enjoyment she would keep to herself. Yes, that would be best.

Eliza glanced over her shoulder and loosed a wink at Wellington, receiving a crooked eyebrow in response. There was another danger, at least nagging in the back of her brain, in having the inexperienced Books along for this particular adventure. His world was a world of parchments, relics, and statistics. However, this was her lead, and some wicked part of her enjoyed the fact that she had the very proper Archivist along for the ride—all unknowing, opening his idealistic eyes to the real world behind his ancient baubles. Having him in plain sight was also much better than having him crop up at some inopportune time.

She afforded him a smile. Eliza had not considered the ETS, and Books had been resourceful enough to get his hands on a tracker. Out of the corner of her blue eyes, Eliza watched him, silently cataloguing her own question concerning that little feat. *More than you appear, aren't you, Agent Books? I shall have to find out one day how deep that rabbit hole goes.*

They reached Fleet Street, and Eliza rapped on the roof to tell the driver that this was far enough. After paying him through the hatch in the roof, she led Books out onto the pavement. She couldn't resist taking him by the arm and leading him down the little alley to their detour from the Archives: Ye Olde Cheshire Cheese. The little cheery sign above the door caused Books to stop and actually cock his head. It was so like a confused spaniel that Eliza had to stifle a laugh.

"A very interesting and literary choice of pub, Miss Braun," he commented.

Ah, so he was going to display his vaunted intellect and make her look like a complete fool once again. Well, time to turn that one on its head. "Oh you mean Dickens and Johnson—or perhaps the Poet Laureate himself, Mr. Tennyson? Yes, I believe they have all imbibed here. Why Books—not frightened off by a few wordsmiths, are you?"

He raised an eyebrow. "Certainly not. Miss Braun. This is merely not the type of place I would have thought you frequented."

Eliza knew the comment had not meant to be cruel, but she bristled nonetheless. "Contrary to popular belief not all of us colonials are without culture, but perhaps tonight I will show you something that we are good at: Drinking." *This is it*, she decided, *I am going to humble this dusty man, blow out a few of his cobwebs. He's not that old. Time he remembers it.*

Another little part of her mind whispered, *And wouldn't it be fun to find out what lies underneath the veneer?*

The inside of the Cheese was deep brown wood paneling, smoke, and suddenly hushed conversation. Its occupants were, as in most pubs in the respectable areas of London, all male. Eliza was used to the eyes of men being on her—sometimes with lust, sometimes with disapproval—sometimes with both. Yes, today it was most definitely both.

"Miss Braun," Wellington whispered at her back, "Perhaps this isn't a good choice of drinking establishment. These are all journalists, not used to the company of a lady . . ."

Eliza's jaw tightened, and by the gods she wished for dynamite and a knife. In lieu of that she took off her shawl, displaying her other arsenal, the one that got her into as much trouble as the aforementioned physical weapons. She was rewarded with an indrawn breath from Wellington as he caught sight of her sharply drawn-in corset.

"Good God, Miss Braun, did you wear that in Bedlam?"

He only wrenched with difficulty his gaze from her curving bosom.

Eliza laughed. For such an analytical man he really was sadly lacking in a clue. "I do know better than to taunt the mad with what they cannot have. I kept my shawl there."

"Yet everyone else is fair game?"

Her reply was a wicked-through-and-through grin. Books was a man of letters, fully capable of drawing his own conclusion.

"Now," Eliza went on firmly, while looking around for just the right spot to sit. "You get the drinks in, I'll find us a table." She made for one in the corner, providing the best view of the room, including the door.

"Miss." The gruff voice of the publican behind the bar cut through the near deathly silence. "I think you'll be wanting that one." He gestured to a large round table by the fire, set away from the rest of the patrons. A small lidded box served as a modest centrepiece for its leather top.

While its location sated the agent in her, Eliza's pub patron frowned a little at the table's isolation. She went to protest when she noticed the barkeep's eyes were on her bosom. It was not a leer or any sort of lust-filled gaze. Her fingertips itched and she only just stopped herself from touching Harry's locket.

"This will, indeed, do nicely," she said with as much lightness as she could muster.

Wellington snorted, his eyes looking from table to table. Finally accepting his evening at the Cheshire Cheese, he asked, "What can I get you then, Miss Braun?"

"Beer. Lots and lots of beer."

The newspapermen, some dressed rather shabbily, some in the height of fashion, followed her progress to the table, their eyes never leaving her generous cleavage. Harry would have called what she was doing foolhardy, but attention was her intent. The time for sensible, subtle action had passed long ago.

With the publican's recommendation, the brazen tactic

led her to this particular table for a reason. A sweep of her eyes assured her that Books was struggling to be noticed by the barmaid, while her boss continued cleaning glasses and staring at the newcomers as surreptitiously as he could out of the corner of his eye. Eliza took her seat, and ran her fingers along the lid of the table's centerpiece. No lock. A hint of dust that she rubbed between her thumb and forefinger. Inside the box was a set of playing cards. The pattern on the set's back was not one she was familiar with. Was it a falcon, or an eagle?

"A Phoenix," Books had made his return more rapidly than Eliza would have thought possible. He was carrying a pint literally overflowing with good dark stout and a chipped glass of something resembling white wine—either that or vinegar. He placed them carefully down on the table and took a seat next to her. "Not one of the usual designs for playing cards."

So now he was a connoisseur of the deck? *Really—let's see how well you know your stuff!* Eliza hid her examination of the deck beneath a bit of flourish. The one-handed Charlier cut, where the top cards were adroitly folded beneath the bottom ones, caused Books' eyebrow to rise a good inch. It was childish, but Eliza smiled.

"Quite familiar with cards then?" Books quipped, "I shall have to remember that."

"You try spending months on a ship from New Zealand with no other entertainment. A lovely American taught me a thing . . ." She grinned at the memory, ". . . or two." The cards paused in her hands, and then she chuckled. "No, three."

A quick movement of her fingers, and she laid the line of cards in a ribbon spread, then flicked them back and forth, letting the faces of the cards flip up and then back a few times.

"A pity one is missing," Books observed, and she had to stop her flourish to realise he was right. "The Queen of Hearts," the Archivist went on, seemingly unaware of her sudden stillness.

"Nice catch, Welly," she said, taking a good long drink to steady herself.

The din of arguing journalists and camaraderie continued around Eliza but she was a statue. She stared at the fifty-one cards splayed out, her mind racing at what this meant. The pendant and Harry's ramblings of "mice in a maze" made sense, but when he said, *"I've found her, and now you have too . . ."* she thought was in reference to the Cheshire Cat. Was he referring to the Queen of Hearts? She needed time to figure it out.

Her deductive reasoning came to a quick halt on looking up at Books. He was tracing the base of his wineglass. He looked as she pictured herself in the Archives. "Why aren't you drinking, Welly?" Was her company that despicable to him?

Books cleared his throat and looked a little shamefaced. "Did you not hear me the previous times I've mentioned it? This," he said, motioning to the activity around him, "is how I got into trouble last time."

Eliza smiled into her beer. "Go on—tell me about her—this vixen that got you with a simple honey-trap."

The Archivist shifted uncomfortably in his chair. "I would rather forget her." Yet he appeared unable to do that, at least for now. He made no effort to mask how unsettled it made him. Finally Wellington took a sip of his wine. His face went very pale, before he carefully put down the glass. "Another problem, the barkeep is mixing his bathwater with the wine."

Choking back a laugh, Eliza gestured for the barmaid to bring them another pint of stout.

"If you must know," he grumbled, "she was forward, quite like yourself; but her gift of conversation astounded me. I felt as if we could really talk about anything."

"What did you talk about?"

"Oh, advancements in science, the latest airship designs of Europe—she was Italian, did I mention that?—and the social impact Babbage and his lot could have never forse—"

"You really know how to engage the ladies, don't you, Books?"

His skin blushed, and he took a sip of the stout that had appeared in front of him. "No, Miss Braun, I do not."

That confession caught her off guard as a bludger from the shadows.

"I am solely responsible for the choices I make in life."

Eliza was not certain if that was his conviction or if he was trying to assure himself of this. She held her tongue as he continued, "I chose a career in the Archives for reasons that, I still believe, were right and best. But this recent turn of events, including your presence across my desk, has me wondering where I went wrong."

"You took a chance," she offered.

He nodded, defeated. "That I did."

Eliza's bark caused him to start. "So because some gammy tart pulled a flam on you, you're thinking yourself the Ministry's glock?"

He rapped a single knuckle against the table in reply. "No need to speak so common, Miss Braun."

"From what it sounds like, Books, you have been working too hard for Queen and Empire. You're forgetting that there's a world out here to experience."

"I experience plenty, Miss Braun."

"Really then?" Eliza took a long draught, and then deliberately licked the white foam clear of her lips. "So tell me, Wellington Thornhill Books, Esquire, what *do* you do for fun?"

Wellington blinked at her. Whether he was knocked back by the unexpected nature of her forwardness or the stout's bitterness, it was hard to tell. "I don't think that is an appropriate question."

Eliza let out a little sigh. Perhaps the cracks in his façade were only wishful thinking. "Look, Welly, I'm serving a yeoman's office. We could be stuck with each other for a long time, or we could get killed tomorrow—but either way, we should get to know one another as partners do. We have to work together for the moment."

"Which we would be doing, back in the Archives, if you had been a bit more honest with me. I'm sure your previous partners regarded trust as an understood assurance in the relationship, yes?" He took a slight sip of his beer, and set down the pint with something verging on satisfaction.

So, Wellington Thornhill Books, Esquire, had teeth.

"Touché, Welly. But the point still stands: we hardly know each other. Let's at least make an effort to understand how one another ticks." She leaned back in her chair, fully aware that the firelight and shadows played across her corseted breasts, making them unavoidable to him. "In my spare time I like to read the Romantic poets. By candlelight with a glass of wine.

"Now, your turn." Deliberately Eliza raised her pint, and didn't put it down until it was completely empty. *Beat that*, she thought with deep colonial satisfaction.

"I . . ." Wellington paused, fidgeted with his pint a moment, took a measured sip of his drink, and then replied. "I collect and collate tropical beetle species."

Not his first choice of revelations.

"When I find the need to relax," Eliza began, "I enjoy weekends in the country alone. Just me and the Great Outdoors." Her smile widened. "And nothing else."

Strangely, he didn't comment on that.

Again, he searched and blurted, "I take great pride in my work."

Eliza groaned, "Oh for God's sake, Welly, I know that! Whatever is the matter? Are you not having fun?"

"Oh, I suppose in some cultures this might be considered fun. Unfortunately I do not reside in those cultures." Through his glasses, his hazel eyes were stern.

He had already confided in her earlier that for the choices he made he took full responsibility, and now this was his choice. *Very well then, keep your secrets.* She had come here with more than chipping away at Wellington Books, Esquire, as her goal. Her gaze fixed on the publican. With a foot, she kicked a spare chair out and gestured him over.

While Books watched, the man blew out through his moustache, glanced around, and then came over, a fresh pint in his grasp. After presenting it to her, he took a seat with some reluctance, looking between the two of them.

Eliza leaned forward, her eyes locked on him. "Tell me barkeep, why did you direct us to this particular table?"

He shrugged, and as she expected pointed to the locket. "You're one of them."

"Them?" Books looked curious now, despite himself. "To whom are you referring?"

The publican looked around him for a moment and taking the hint, Eliza slid a few coins across the table to him. He smiled warmly, while the money disappeared into his pocket. "They paid upfront for a whole year just to make sure I kept this table free, with a set of cards always available."

Eliza gestured him on, knowing the amount she'd just paid deserved the whole story. Books shifted in his seat and leaned forward.

"They'd come in most weeks, different people, men and women. All of them would have that there thing worn as a locket or a pin, so I knew who to bring to the table. But no one has been in for months."

The fluttering feeling in her stomach told Eliza she was close to finding what Harry wanted her to find. She tried to sound casual. "How many months ago—as near as you can reckon?"

The man pursed his lips, and stared up at the ceiling. "Oh I would say maybe eight months. It was winter I think."

Books watched her like a hawk, but Eliza couldn't afford to worry about that now. Harry had gone missing at the end of last winter. In small increments she felt the reins of Harry's obsession slowly drawing her in. "Do you remember anything strange about the last time they played?"

"Not really. All as I recall is one of the younger men turned up, thought there was a game on, but none of the others did. I do remember that, 'cos he pulls out of his pocket a trinket like yours, miss, and gave it to me."

"Gave it to you?" Eliza could almost see Harry standing there by the fire. But a living person couldn't have a ghost, could they?

"Well, gave it to me to send to some shop down by the river."

The agents shared a look like lightning. Even the Archivist was getting intrigued.

"Do you," Books cleared his throat, "do you recall the name of the business, my good man?"

The publican shrugged, "Some woman running some warehouse down there I think."

Eliza swallowed. "Thank you. That's all we needed to know."

Once the barkeep was well out of earshot, Wellington slumped back in his chair, taking a long, lingering drink as he mulled over the story. "Well, at least we know how the locket ended up in the Ministry. Harry himself sent the locket."

"It proves he was onto something." She knocked back the last of her pint.

"Hardly," Books swirled the remains of his own drink. "One strange locket and the testimony of a publican barely prove anything."

Had he no imagination? The man was infuriating. He couldn't for a moment think it was coincidence that shortly after Harry, who had shown no signs of mental illness until that point, had been found a gibbering wreck?

"I need whiskey," she growled. This time, Books was not so dense as to miss his cue.

Alone for the moment, Eliza snapped out of her casual demeanor and swiftly took her chance to examine the table. Harry had been a world-class trickster. Always hiding little notes in her desk or even while they were on assignment.

The remembrance of one saucy epistle she had found hidden in the office of Thaddeus Morne, while they had been ransacking it no less, made her smile even now.

She traced the corners of the table, and then slid her fingers around the underneath, searching every crevice. And there she was: the Queen of Hearts, jammed between the leg and the top of the table. Eliza only had a moment before Wellington came back, only an instant to glance at it. She recognised Harry's precise writing, and her pulse began to race. Quickly she tucked the playing card inside her corset, against her own heart. Very appropriate.

Now she had her answer.

With the memory of Harrison Thorne biting deep, she took the glass Wellington handed her and quickly downed it.

When his eyes went wide, she laughed. "Now let me show you how we colonials drink."

CHAPTER NINE

Wherein Wellington Books Acts a Perfect Gentleman, but Is Not Above a Little Skullduggery Too

"*Aaaaaaaaaaaaand it's NO—NAY—Nev'rrrrrrrr . . . no nay never NO MOOOOOOOORRRRE . . . will I plaaaaay the Wild Rover. No nev'rrrrr no moooooooooorrrrre . . .*"

The woman's caterwauling was potent enough to wake the dead. In the Americas.

He stopped at the landing, hefting the woman slumped over his shoulder a touch higher before she ended up slipping off him entirely. This action made her giggle in a most unladylike fashion. Wellington took a long breath and cast his gaze upward. One more flight. His feet scuffed hard against the steps of Eliza Braun's building. Yes, there had been some effort on her part to climb them, but it had been more hindrance than help. There was no denying that the woman could drink. It was truly a miracle of God in Heaven Above that she had possessed the wherewithal to stand, gather her shawl, and tip her hat to the few remaining opponents of their long, surreal evening at Ye Olde Cheshire Cheese.

"You held your own, mate," Braun slurred.

The combination of scotch and beer wafting from her mouth was very off-putting. With any luck, her stomach was as strong as her constitution. "Well," he replied as evenly as possible, "I was most fortunate to place myself in your capable care once again, Miss Braun." He had thought there were fewer steps to climb when looking from the bottom, but they seemed to go on without an end in sight.

"Eliza! Me bleedin' name's Eliza!" she insisted. "Come off it, Welly. We're getting to know each other a bit better, 'ey mate?" She gave a quick snort. "Fancy a ding-dong?"

"It is a bit late, Miss—"

"*AAAAAAAAAAAAAAAND it's all for me grog, me jolly jolly grog . . .*" Her voice echoed in the stairwell as they reached the top floor, the only apartment there. "*IT'S ALL FOR ME BEER AND TOBACCOOOOOOO!!!*"

He fumbled in his vest pocket for the key and managed to get the door to Braun's apartments opened just before the chorus had finished.

"*. . . And across the Western Ocean I must WAAAAAAA AAAAANNNNDEEEEEERRRRRRRRR!*"

"Yes, yes, yes, Miss Braun, I do believe your building would prefer you were across the Western Ocean as we speak. Now there's a good lass, come on," he said, hefting her once more across his shoulders.

Her laughter disappeared, and the silence felt wrong.

"Miss Braun?" Wellington asked.

Her sobs were hard to hear at first, but on catching her breath, Eliza let out a soft, pathetic wail. "The Western Ocean," she blubbered.

"Miss Braun," Wellington stammered, "are you ill?!"

"The Western Ocean . . . the Western Ocean . . ." She then sniffled and said, "I want to go home."

"But you are home."

"I want to go home," she sobbed, "to New Zealand."

"Miss Braun, do remember, wherever you go, New Zealand is there. Besides," he grunted, guiding her through the near darkness, "I don't believe an airship will be leaving for your home shores at this ungodly hour."

In the back of his mind, Wellington's Basic Training stirred. It was not wise for an agent to enter any darkened room, even if it was one as intimate as their own dwellings. The possibility remained that someone nefarious could take refuge in the shadows, merely waiting for an opportune moment to strike.

Eliza's crooning, he mused, could serve as a deterrent—if not a repellant—for a small army of ne'er-do-wells:

"God of nations at Thy feet
In the bonds of love we meet,
Hear our voices, we entreat."

With a quick prayer that the lights would not reveal any surprises waiting in the parlor or the corridor leading to the bedroom, he reached for the closest lamp and turned the nozzle to illuminate where they stood.

"My Lord!" Wellington whispered.

His colleague fell to the floor with a loud thump.

The apartments of Eliza D. Braun, field agent of the Ministry of Peculiar Occurrences, were stunning to say the least. The decor showed a refinement, an eye for detail and a care for what it said about its occupant. There were small statuettes and woodworkings from all over the world, and two chaise longues of the richest colours and comforts sat on either side of the window. This could have easily been the apartments of minor nobility or someone of his family's wealth and history. It was stepping back to his origins, to when he had been to the manor born.

She groaned as her face turned to press against the rosewood floor. "Welly, remind me to order a better mattress for my bed. This one is far too firm."

"Oh, Eliza," Wellington gasped, now remembering why he was in these lush surroundings. "No broken nose, I hope."

"S'all right," Braun slurred. Her voice dropped to a whisper, "My ample bosom broke my fall." She broke out into a cackle as she threw her arm around Books' neck. "And this—" she chortled, rapping her knuckles against her corset. "Standard issue for female agents. It's bulletproof."

No wonder she is so heavy! "Ah, good show." Wellington heaved, lifting the agent back on her feet. "I'll know what to hide behind if we are attacked by a gun-welding chamber choir."

Braun found his comment hilarious. "Good one, Welly! Now . . . where was I? Oh yes . . ."

And her song started once again.

"From dishonour and from shame
Guard our country's spotless name
Crown her with immortal fame
God defend New Zealand . . ."

"See? Your patriotism, Miss Braun, assures you that whilst you're away, New Zealand remains safe and secure," he gasped, her feet now dragging across the floor, "within your most ample bosom."

Her nation's anthem paused yet again for her hysterical laughter. "You're a good bloke, Welly, you are! I knew that on first sight of you, back in Anttara . . . Antana . . . Arcani . . ."

"Antarctica."

"There. You were in that rather unpleasant-looking contraption, and your eyes—aww, Welly, I've never had anyone look at me quite that way." Her voice went up in pitch, as if she were talking to a newborn in a bassinet. "It was so bloody *adorable*! Like a puppy!"

"Provided the puppy is chained up and prepped for interrogation," he added, manoeuvring them both to where he was guessing would be the master bedroom. "But very kind of you to say."

"I like puppies."

His foot kicked open the double doors, revealing a very charming, very cozy boudoir, a vanity neatly arranged for a morning's routine and a large canopy bed taking up the center of the room. Wellington swallowed hard, hoping that the hangover cure he intended to quaff would erase the memory of these most intimate surroundings of his brash partner from the colonies. The contradictions were making him curiously nervous. It was easier to regard her as abrasive, not refined.

What other secrets did she harbour?

Braun flopped across the bed, the air rushing out of her body. All was still for a moment, and Wellington felt a small panic swell within him. Then she gave a tiny snore.

"Right then, Miss Braun," he said, allowing himself pride in a job well done. He had gotten one of the Ministry's own home from a night of revels. "I bid you goodnight. Remember—at the hour of eight—at your desk. Good—er, good morning, Miss Braun."

He had not made it three steps before "Welly . . ." the voice implored, "Welly, I . . . I have . . . a problem."

The Archivist turned to see her hands fumbling around her waist, scrambling across the outer bodice and bulletproof corset. Oh, for the love of God, she was not serious!

"I need a liiiiiiiiiiiittle bit of help here, mate."

Clearing his throat, Wellington returned to her side. "Um, Miss—"

"Seeing as you're about to get *very familiar* with me, I'd appreciate it if you started calling me Eliza."

Her apartments were feeling remarkably warm. "Eliza, I'm not quite sure if I can—"

"Lissen, mate, you can do this and I promise you that it's not going to go any further than a gentleman assisting a lady in a time of need." She chuckled again. "Besides, if your hands did wind up anywhere I didn't want them—"

"Let me guess," Wellington interjected. "I would lose the loss of that particular hand for a time, wouldn't I?"

"Eeeeeeeezzzactly!" she said, sprawling back across the bed.

"Right then." He pulled his collar loose and placed his

hands on either side of her waist, leaning in to inspect her bodice.

Braun giggled, and took a deep breath.

"Eliza," Wellington warned, his head motioning to her breasts now falling slightly, "you're not helping."

The laugh that came from her practically held a candle to the devil. "Who says I wanna be helpful?"

Undeterred, Wellington centred her as best as he could on the bed and started to cautiously feel up her bodice. He knew it had to be there.

Another giggle, and then, "Remember what I said about your haaaaands," she sang.

"I've not forgoooteeeeennnnn," Wellington chimed back.

He then gave a nod. It would have been foolish to think that Braun would have gone into that pub completely unarmed. From its concealed scabbard, the fine, smooth handle slid free and with a flip of a switch the knife's point snapped out.

The blade still managed to catch the light filtering in from outside. He looked down at the woman humming lightly, the smile on her face blissful and carefree. "Eliza, please, for once listen to me—remain very still." He gripped the blade, breathing slow and deep as he counted, "And one . . . two . . . three."

It was alarming how easily the stiletto sliced through the bodice. The fabric was apart in one graceful move, and Braun laughed so hard her breasts trembled lightly in the embrace of the bulletproof corset.

"Oh, Welly!" she sniggered. "I didn't know you had been on assignment in Singapore!"

Wellington sighed, retracting the blade back into its handle. He then began to undo the corset, one hook at a time. The body armor was impressive, and solid enough that he was convinced it would stop a bullet. As it was a corset, however, it would probably knock the wind out of her and leave a good bruise as a reminder of that brush with death.

When he reached the last hook, dangerously close to her bosom, he felt his heart quicken. "Eliza, about where my hands go . . ."

"It's the last button, Welly, and I know if you wanted to try anything you would have by now. So get me out of this bloody thing, there's a good lad."

He undid the last hook with little effort and her body, including the impressive breasts he had been stealing glances at all night, were now free.

She smiled wide and sighed, "Thank you, Wellington. A gentleman, you are." Another giggle, and then, "Give a kiss goodnight then. Go on. You've earned it."

Wellington knew his imagination must have conjured that up. He had also been in his cups tonight.

"It's okay. A little peck on the lips won't hurt a soul. It's how we do it back home." Eliza puckered her lips and made quick, kissing noises.

This situation had just gone from *entirely* inappropriate to a descent into madness. Just being in this situation with another agent of the Ministry was bad enough, but he would have been naïve to believe field agents didn't enjoy the more exotic fruits when on assignment. So, one agent helping another back to bed was, perhaps, standard operations. Seeing as the "mate he was helping out" was *female* did alter the parameters, just a bit.

Eliza pouted. "Now you're being a cad. I just wanna little kiss." She scrunched up her face, making a gesture of something tiny between her fingers. "Jus'sa li'l one."

Even in her current state his colleague was still a woman, and (the last time he checked) he was a man. He found her a beautiful sight back in Antarctica, although he tried to dismiss that later as just being relieved on being rescued. In that combative setting, she was strong, forthright, and brave, but still she maintained a strange elegance. Tonight there were no enemy operatives, no explosions, and no secret lairs. Tonight was just them.

And now she wanted a "quick kiss" to end what was a

night out with a colleague. She had certainly taken joy complicating his life both in the Archives and now in her bedroom.

Then again . . . maybe she had been right about him. Maybe he was overdue for a little complication. He glanced around the bedroom, and then back to her.

Wellington's gaze locked with Eliza's blue one and he had the distinct impression she was sizing him up just as she did in Antarctica but with different intentions. His throat felt incredibly dry. Was it possible that she wasn't as drunk as she was letting on?

Then the moment passed and Eliza stretched like a cat would in the noonday sun streaming in through a window. Wellington felt her leg brush his thigh as it rose slightly during this stretch, this relishing of newfound freedom, and then both leg and arms slumped down. It seemed that she had stretched herself into a deep slumber.

It didn't last long. "I need to sleep on my stomach."

"What?!" If she had been asleep, his question would have roused her easily.

"I can never get comfortable on my back so the options are either you spend the night so we can cuddle a bit, or . . ."

"All righty then, upsie-daisy," Wellington said, lifting her on her feet.

She swayed a bit, the clatter of her bodice and corset falling to the ground causing her to blink. Eliza looked around the room, then back to Wellington. She gently patted him on the cheek. "You're a blasted good bloke there, Welly."

Then she wobbled about to face the bed, and then fell as would a great oak cut down in a forest.

Thank you, God! Wellington praised to himself. He bent down to pick up the discarded garments, turning the ruined bodice in his hand back and forth. Wellington wondered if there was any way his tailor could repair it. *Wishful thinking*, he lamented.

Popping out from the dark wood of the floor was the outline of a single playing card. He held it up to the dim light.

The Queen of Hearts. Before he could look for where this could have come from, he instinctively turned the card over to discover an address scrawled in an all-too-familiar hand.

Dash it all, he swore inwardly. *She hid this from me!*

Wellington's mouth was open, the protestation on the tip of his tongue. Then he paused on hearing the rumble from her. She was finally asleep.

The card was still in his hand, and he considered for a moment where it had stayed concealed. It surprised him with all the flesh Braun had put on display that it had stayed put. With a final sigh, he tucked the card inside his coat pocket and then smoothed out his lapel. Wellington had served the Ministry by getting the inebriated colonial back to her apartments. Now, his own head spinning lightly, it was his turn. Hopefully, Wellington could whip up a batch of that cure for hangovers, and tomorrow morning he would be right as rain.

Albeit, the anger in him currently rising to a boil was quite sobering.

He waited for a moment, staring at Braun's sprawled form now facedown in the large, luxurious bed. There was no movement, but he could hear breathing. Steady. Perceptible. She would be fine.

One step. Two steps. Three steps . . .

"Welly?"

Dammit. he hissed in his mind. *If I hold my breath and remain perfectly still . . .*

"Don't let the bitch bother you, mate."

He straightened up, turning back towards the bed. She hadn't moved, but she was definitely talking to him.

"What did you say, Miss Braun?"

"I said, don't let the bitch bother you."

His brow furrowed slightly. "I'm sorry?"

"You know, that tart . . . in the tavern . . . with the green eyes. That was all about . . . the mission." She was on the verge of passing out again. Her voice was muffled by the bed linens and her own inebriation, but it was the effort that held him fast. She had something to say and the woman was determined to get it out before surrendering to the libations. "That was about the job. It weren't nothin' personal. You're good value, Welly. Good value. I did the right thing. I did . . . the right thing."

Whatever did she mean by that?

"Very well, in a few more hours at the Archives. At the hour of eight. I'll have coffee at the ready."

"See?" she said, her voice now fading off as she repeated again and again, "You're good value. Gooood . . . valuuuuue . . ."

"Sleep well, Eliza." Wellington knew she wouldn't remember him saying this, but he would. "This was fun."

Manoeuvring out the luxurious apartments and descending the steps of her building, Wellington stood for a moment on the front step, taking in every open alleyway within sight, looking up and down the main street repeatedly. It was late. In a few hours, the sun would rise and he would be in that familiar darkness of the Archives. He took solace in the fact that it would be dark in his workplace. Sunlight and hangovers never made good companions, not even civil acquaintances. So in the quiet of all that needed sorting and cataloguing, both he and Eliza could suffer together.

The playing card's corner brushed his breast, and he felt a slight pang of bitterness swell in his mouth. Tonight's little exercise, Wellington surmised, was some sort of game in trust. Perhaps it was an exercise within her parameters, seeing as this clue was being kept from him. Eliza had convinced herself that he would go off to Doctor Sound and reveal this new find. And while he kept her visit to Bedlam between them, this clue warranted proper protocol. Protocols were in place for a specific reason. Perhaps it would appear to Eliza as if he were running to the headmaster to tattle; but as juvenile as it seemed, no one was above procedure and process. Both kept order at the Ministry.

Still, it hurt. He actually had been enjoying himself. A bit. He'd thought he was taking the right steps in getting to understand his unexpected ward, and he'd thought he was building a sense of trust there.

How will she react when she finds the playing card missing?

"They'd come in most weeks, different people, men and women. All of them would have that there thing worn as a locket or a pendant, so I knew who to let at the table. But no one has been in for months . . . maybe eight months . . ."

Eight months ago, when Agent Thorne disappeared.

He remembered back then how activity at the Archives seemed to come to a halt. Wellington had considered going up to the second floor, to see what was the matter. Had there been a death? A case that spiralled out of control? Was the Ministry being shut down? Considering their eccentric nature and the mysteries they faced, it would not have surprised him in the least if the Crown closed their operations for good.

He'd thought better of venturing up to the office floor, reminding himself how the agents regarded him merely as a handy resource, an appliance that helped them get the job done. He vaguely remembered Thorne's ambivalence towards him when he had come to the Archives for research. Had Eliza been working with Thorne, Wellington wondered, the last time he loomed over his desk, considering the Archivist with an air of entitlement? He recalled Thorne describing his analytical engine as "amusing" and how it livened up the Archives. It was just another toy, just as he would be issued by the clankertons at Research and Design. Thorne, Campbell, and the others made it abundantly clear that agents came to the Archives only out of need, never for pleasantries or for small talk. The more efficiently Wellington performed his job, the sooner they could get out into the field.

Well, all of them except for Agent Brandon Hill. The tales of monkey knife fighting Hill would regale him with made the Archivist wonder if that particular agent was entirely sane.

And yet, Agent Thorne was part of the Ministry. They were compatriots, or so the shared coat of arms and Ministry rings implied, all part of the same machine that served at the pleasure of Her Majesty. Even with his distance from the offices, Wellington knew that something had happened. The confirmation came when Campbell delivered for cataloguing case files and notes that seemed to have no end in sight. In the eyes of the Ministry, closure for this particular case occurred with the demise of Agent Harrison Thorne. Wellington never did find out the details but he had read the loss in Campbell's face.

Wellington might not have liked Thorne, but he also felt the loss. Perhaps not as deeply as Eliza had, but still felt. Thorne must have been quite an individual to win her loyalties.

Now, in his pocket, was an address, an address that Wellington knew was not in the case files back in the Ministry. A new wrinkle in the mystery that no one knew about, at present.

"As I recall, one of the younger men turned up, thought there was a game on, but none of the others did."

And then Agent Thorne disappeared.

"Campbell found him, stark raving mad in one of the side gutters of the West End . . ."

This address had been the next move for Thorne eight months ago. He knew something was wrong, and that he was in danger. Agent Thorne had taken those few steps he could to see that Eliza continued the chase if something were to happen to him.

"The Archives is where the mystery continues."

Those were his own words to Eliza. Did he ever really believe that rhetoric until this very moment? The mystery did, indeed, continue in the Archives, in the cases that had been forgotten by the very agents sworn by duty to solve them for Queen and Country.

He felt the earth underneath him shift. Wellington's head was reeling. Yes, he had been in his cups. The alcohol would overcome him if he did not get back home for that Mayan hangover cure.

Wellington then caught a scent in the air, something he did not associate with his own basement apartments. Something he recognised, but wherever he was it wasn't home.

Above him loomed the entrance to the Ministry of Peculiar Occurrences.

He knew where to find the cure in the Archives. He was also well aware of the cure's side effect if taken without the safeguards he had introduced to the mix. Ascending the steps, carefully, Wellington took a glance to either side of him, and produced his clockwork key that turned the main lock while disengaging the added security measures of the doorframe.

There was no one else in, as far as he knew. When the security locks re-engaged after he cleared the foyer, Wellington was assured privacy. The lift's gate rattled throughout the building as the trident-shaped key once more clicked thrice in its panel before returning to his waistcoat. The shadows and featureless furnishings of the main floor disappeared on his descent. A few moments he would find himself awash in gaslight and standing before the hatch that led down to his corner of the Ministry.

Wellington was going to need privacy. After downing his trusted remedy, he had a good amount of uninterrupted reading to do.

CHAPTER TEN

Where Miss Braun Pays for Her Overindulgence and the Archivist Ventures Outside His Domain

Eliza wasn't exactly sure how she found enough strength to get into the Ministry the next day; yet by some residual instinct, she was up and moving, every inch of her being protesting violently, particularly at the smell of breakfast. With half-lidded eyes, she managed to get dressed and out the door, declining the breakfast her housemaid had prepared. She had no doubt it would have been lovely, but her stomach would not hear of it. The sound of carriage wheels rolling over the surface of the street outside was like thousands of gleaming knives fired into her head. The summer sun shone directly in her face, even in her vain attempt to shield aching eyeballs. She felt cursed this morning—like everything in London was out to get her.

Eliza recalled a previous mission where she had been dragged by a carriage through the streets of Prague. She could still remember how she felt the morning after. This morning was far worse. Everything ached, every movement hurt, and she was not looking forward to Wellington's dressing-down—because yes, she was several *hours* late. Now she was about to find out how much pity existed inside the Archivist.

Eliza crossed over the street and entered Miggins Antiquities. No agents met on the way, in the lobby, or even at the lift. It was a blessing for everyone. It would not have ended well for Campbell if he had tried his usual antics with her this morning.

Eliza made it to the Archives without interruption, and she found herself elated with her reassignment. There it would be dark and quiet. Wellington's refuge was now hers. She let out a long sigh and pulled open the iron hatch.

The high-pitched whine made her knees buckle.

She had made it to the second landing when Wellington greeted her with a cheerful, piercing, "Good morning, Miss Braun!"

Eliza winced. Her head felt like Quasimodo should be swinging off it. It took a moment for her to focus on Wellington, sitting at his desk as bright eyed and bushy tailed as no man had a right to be, especially not when she was feeling so miserable. She stumbled to her chair, not daring to reply until she was seated.

"A little worse for wear there, I see." If that was an "I told you so," it was delivered with unabashed cheerfulness. "Still wonderful to see your commitment to your job got you here only a scant few hours late."

It was hard to concentrate on his words when the room swayed as it did from where she sat. The worst of it was, she was embarrassed. No one had ever outdrunk her—*no one.* If she were back home in New Zealand there would be more than a bit of ribbing coming her way; but since she wasn't back home, it would be Wellington to loose upon her the jibes and playful insults.

When Eliza finally focused her eyes on him she realised he wasn't taking the ample chance to do so. Instead he was looking at her with something that might have almost been . . . anticipation? Sitting bolt upright in his chair, Wellington Books was waiting for her to say something.

Marshaling her fading resources, Eliza scrutinized him for some clue why. A large box was on one side of his desk, while the rest of it was covered in paper and folders. Then, as she looked closer she noticed something strange.

"Welly—those are the same clothes you had on yesterday." If it had been anyone else she would have made a joke about carousing the dark hours away with some "lady friend."

He smiled. "Yes, well I had some things to work on so I came here straightaway after escorting you home."

"Oh," she said with a light nod, and then her eyes went wide. "Oh, so *you* got me home and . . . in . . ."

Even in the dimness of the Archives, Eliza could see Wellington blush. "Yes, Agent Braun, I . . ." he began, his mouth open to form just the right word, ". . . aided you in your sleeping arrangements."

"Ah," and now it was Eliza who felt her cheeks burn, "well then . . . fancy that. I did say I wanted to get to know you better." She furrowed her brow as her eyes had now adequately adjusted well enough to read the label on the side of the box. "And you've been here all night? Investigating Harry's case?"

Gods, her own loud voice was making her head ring. She placed both hands up to hold it together, just on the off chance it flew apart and made a mess in the Archives.

Wellington got up, his chair making a terrible racket grating against the stone floor, and bought over the cup of tea by his elbow. "After last night, I felt I owed it to Agent Thorne to look into the matter. It seems he unearthed some intriguing leads that deserve attention, and since the Ministry is rather stretched right now—"

Eliza waved at him like he was a flying insect that she wished would buzz away. "Get to the point!" She tried not to shout, as it caused her pain, but Wellington was irritating her so much right at the moment she just wanted to lie down.

"There is a cab coming for us in fifteen minutes."

"Beg pardon?" And Eliza screwed her eyes shut as she weathered the ripple of pain tearing through her skull. "By the gods, Welly, can't you see I'm ready to swallow a stick of my own dynamite to make this hangover disappear?"

"Then drink this Miss Braun." He slid the mug of warm liquid closer to her. The smell that rolled off it was the last straw. It was a lucky thing she had done all her vomiting earlier that morning; yet as it was, Eliza gagged for a good minute. It was obviously *not* tea.

"For pity's sake man, are you enjoying making me suffer?"

"Perhaps a little." Wellington smiled. "Drink this, because I think you will find it will make everything better."

"Only a bullet would do that," she grumbled. "What is it?"

"An Ancient Mayan cure for the common hangover made with the native cocoa bean." His words were tumbling over each other a little, and Eliza had difficulty understanding him through the fog of misery.

She levered herself upright. "Hold on—you drank some of that last night?"

"Ah, yes." His smile was now definitely sheepish. "Just after our night of intoxication. Immediate consumption of the cure can mitigate the side effects." He looked at the cup, and then back to Eliza, his grin hardly convincing. "Sometimes."

"And what exactly *are* the side effects of this ancient remedy?"

Wellington returned to his side of the partners' desk. "Well, it does in fact act as a stimulant which means you do tend to stay awake for quite a while," he admitted, gesturing to the files covering his half. "I'm not positive, but I believe the aftereffects will probably involve a lot of sleeping. But for our purposes today it will do the trick."

The mixture still smelt vile. Eliza picked up the cup with suspicion. Would she talk as fast as Wellington afterwards? "And what exactly are our purposes?"

"We need to follow the footsteps of Agent Thorne," he said, pointing to her side of the desk, "as you were doing last night."

Eliza looked at where Wellington directed, and she felt

her fingers wrap more firmly around the cup. There was the Queen of Hearts she had concealed from him last night.

"Wellington . . ."

"Tosh, Miss Braun," he replied dismissively. "I am not expecting us to have full trust in one another until a time when you are more comfortable around me. At present, I just need you to be alert, so drink up."

And with a sigh she obeyed. What could possibly be worse than this hangover?

"Gahhh!" Eliza stuck out her tongue and shook her head. The protest made no difference: the taste lingered.

"Finish it," Wellington insisted.

With a final exhale, she downed the whole lot. Considering everything, she owed him as much. Her face remained fixed in a twisted expression of disgust, and not from the burn of the liquid. Scalding her throat would have been a lovely alternative to the bitterness. When she finally found her voice, Eliza already sounded far less groggy. "You know Wellington, I believe you cheated. Stacking the deck and all in not telling me about this cure of yours—but since you managed to not tip your hand—I have to admit you are a better man than I."

Wellington choked back a laugh on that one. "Thank you Miss Braun. From you that is a real compliment. Now the effects should kick in before the cab arrives."

"Where is it we are going?"

It was the first wicked grin she had ever seen on Wellington's face. It actually suited him. "Eliza, you wanted to know when I was having fun . . . well I believe I have found something that might be worthy of that title.

"In my research, I found where this address leads. It is the address of a certain doctor in Charing Cross." Wellington turned away from her and began flipping through the files on his desk. "It appears Agent Thorne had infiltrated some sort of underground society—an underground society that is *not* the House of Usher. After last night's conversation with the publican we can deduce that his identity had been compromised."

Eliza was starting to feel the headache recede, and her faculties return. She also felt that slight rush when a piece fell into place during an investigation. She hadn't felt that in nearly a month and it felt damn good. "So what does this doctor have to do with it?"

"An intriguing question. However there is nothing in Thorne's files on this fellow, so I presume it was a new lead." Wellington put on his bowler and coat. "Let's go and find out."

Certainly she was not going to challenge Wellington Books and his unexpected interest in this forgotten case. Eliza felt herself teeter for a moment, nearly swooning from the optimism that filled her. Could this be a side effect of Wellington's apothecary, or the fact that he had chosen to jump in with both boots that made her feel that way?

She didn't care, and they had a carriage to catch.

By the time they exited Miggins Antiquities, the cab was waiting, as Wellington had assured her. They both hopped in with the enthusiasm of children. London was busy around them, worked up to a noonday pitch. *So much better than being locked away in the Archives*, she thought selfishly. She dared not open her mouth and risk sharing this only to have Wellington turn the cab around. On the ride, Wellington droned on and on about the case, about the murder that she already knew of. His words continued to tumble, so fast that even the cab driver looked back in wonderment. Wellington probably sounded like he was speaking in tongues, and Eliza would have shushed him had he taken a breath and given her a moment to interrupt. She already knew most of what he was rambling on about, but Wellington felt the need to take her through the files once more, this time from his perspective. Her attention on him was polite, at best. Eliza was surrendering to the elation of being back in the field, even if that field was merely London.

Reaching Charing Cross, they came to a halt across from the doctor's practice. It was a two-storey building, white-painted stone like every other one in the row. This address did hold a distinction for her, though, as this particular address was a *lead.* She could feel her skin tingle. How many weeks had she been in the Archives? *Or is this the remedy? Of course not*, her mind retorted immediately after. *You're back in the field. You are where you should be. Harry would be so proud. Make sure you set aside some time later today to visit him in Bedlam. You did promise yourself to do so. Jolly good. Now, what was Books on about? A doctor. Yes. The Lead.*

All that came to her in a blink. *The Mayans must have been a fun lot*, she thought absently.

"Oi gent," a gruff voice from above her snapped, "payment is appreciated!"

Books scrambled through his pockets, producing his own wallet and fumbling for fare. As he rectified his oversight, Eliza took the chance to examine the building, tucked as it was behind a narrow strip of garden. The brass plate on its gate proudly displayed the name Doctor Christopher Smith, and it conveyed discretion and elegance—no doubt a reflection of Doctor Smith's success. The garden was well looked after, as were the brass fixtures in the door and the iron of the gate. A lovely business establishment. She could see nothing troubling about it.

And yet she was. Deeply.

Eliza hadn't truly realised how much she missed the thrill of the chase until this moment—the most fun to be had with clothes on as far as she was concerned.

The cab rumbled away as passersby continued along past Wellington and Eliza. Both of them took in the pedestrians, all very neat, proper, and a slight step higher than Wellington who was still wearing an outfit in need of a good launder. "I suppose," Eliza said, straightening his lapels and giving them a light press with her palms, "we will have to make do with your current state."

"I should have considered we were going to Charing Cross."

"No need to fret," she said, attempting to dust off his shoulders with her fingers. "We will just tell the good doctor your problem is you cannot sleep. Quite close to the truth, so the lie will not be hard to sell."

She turned back to the doctor's office. Something felt off.

"Right then, Welly," she resigned before taking him by the arm. "Keep a sharp eye."

"One moment, Miss Braun." He tugged back, halting her on the first step. "Now, remember we are here on a very tenuous clue. It is a stretch to imagine that any of this will lead anywhere at all."

She glared at him, feeling her blood beginning to rise. "Well, I can see you are going to be difficult."

"I am just cautioning restraint. You are probably feeling a little more . . ." Wellington stopped, taking a moment to consider his words carefully. ". . . aggressive than usual. A rather frightening thought, I must admit, but please bear in mind that is also one of the side effects of the Mayan cure."

Eliza tilted her head, pausing for a moment of self-reflection. "I don't feel any different, but if you say so. I will try it your way." She took another moment, and then added, "For a bit."

They had just stepped off the curb when a giant invisible hand picked them up and threw them to the ground. Glass from the top floor windows showered the street as Eliza and Wellington were tossed backwards like flowers in a storm, back to the curb where they started. Being slightly ahead, she took the full force of the concussion and actually landed atop him.

It took a moment for Eliza's mind to recognise the sensation. An explosion. A *big* one.

The concussion was enough to rattle panes on the opposite side of the street but not shutter them. Screams and wails of pedestrians were now joining the clatter of wood and stone, the fire coming from the house providing a low drone like that in the Archives. Eliza rolled over and covered Wellington as a second wave of flame and debris shot out of the house.

She held down the stunned Wellington until she was sure the munitions and gas had done their initial work. From a professional position—which, at present, was covering the Archivist with her body—it had been a very well-placed charge: enough to wipe out the doctor's surgery and trigger the gas mains within the accompanying apartments, but not enough to destroy anything else. That kind of precision and detail spoke of someone who had experience—someone like her.

When Eliza finally rolled off him, Wellington was pale but remarkably calm. Luckily it was not his first explosion, so she did not have to deal with any screaming from him. She hated the screaming, and there was now plenty of that from the injured and dying on the street. Since Charing Cross was not known for such things, general panic seemed to be ensuing. Traffic stopped. People gaped in horror. Soon enough the fire brigade would arrive. Police, as well. This kind of distraction meant Eliza could check herself and Books for any injuries which, thankfully, appeared to be none, although she knew they would feel the bruising on the following morning.

"So, Welly," Eliza asked, "still think this lead is a bit of a stretch?"

CHAPTER ELEVEN

In Which Our Daring Duo Indulge in a Dashing Chase Through London, and Mr. Books Finds a New Guardian Angel with a Most Jealous Disposition

Another billowing cloud of flame and smoke erupted from the remains of the Charing Cross practice. Wellington took stock of the gathering onlookers, some of the ladies swooning at the sight of destruction while gentlemen called out and cried in alarm. No journalists had appeared yet, a blessing as they were prone to do at moments of calamity. In the distance, mingling with the shrill whistles of the police, came the rapid ringing of the fire brigade.

He was about to turn back to Eliza and recommend they slip away when he felt her hand grip his arm tightly, just as the sound of a horse's cry reached his ears.

"I think we found the good doctor's previous appointment," Eliza said, pulling him back to his feet.

The onyx Concord coach was shaking—not from a nervous steed protesting at small explosions, but from its lone occupant dressed in what appeared to be black skirts that vanished as the cab's door slammed shut. Even over the fire, Wellington heard the snap of the driver's whip and the horses' shoes rattling against the cobblestone streets.

"Come on, Wellington!"

It was not that he had any choice in the matter as Eliza was pulling him towards one of the hansoms that had stopped to gawk at the fire.

Wellington pulled himself into the cab, shouting through the hatch above his head. "Driver—"

The cab lurched, throwing him to the other side of the seat. From the driver's perch, he heard Eliza. "We need to borrow your cab. Do you mind? That's a good chap!" And with a cry and snap of the whip, the hansom launched into the streets of London.

Wellington popped open the small hatch to see holding the reins, "Miss Braun?!" The effects of his hangover remedy were doing very little to calm his nerves.

"Have a care, Welly!" The Mayan cure, it appeared, was also having quite an influence on Eliza. "We got some ground to make up!"

Buildings and pedestrians were shuddering, blurry things as their ride shot through the streets of Charing Cross. Wellington wondered just how low key they were being, between the clatter of the hansom, Eliza calling out to the horse, and the crack of the whip. He pressed harder against the walls of the cab, its vibrations rattling him hard. He could feel their speed, and with each city block their horse continued to pick up its pace.

"Lean!" he heard Eliza shout over the cacophony of wheels and hoofbeats against stone.

The cab took a sharp turn, and Books felt his world begin to teeter.

"Dammit, Books," Eliza bellowed, "get on the *other* side!"

He pushed hard against the grounded portion of the cab, shifting his weight and pressing as hard as he could. He could hear the wood creak, but the cab was returning to a more level perspective. The bounce kicked him off the seat for an instant, knocking his spectacles clear of his face. Wellington wanted to scream, but it would accomplish absolutely nothing.

He did so anyway. It felt quite good.

"That will do, Welly!" came the voice from the driver's seat.

Wellington opened his eyes to a world lacking focus, and for a moment he was horrified. *My God*, he exclaimed in his head, *I'm blind!*

Then he recalled that his glasses were somewhere on the floor of the hansom.

Leaning forward he tried to keep his balance while the cab lurched this way and that. His fingertips bounced lightly against the floorboards until finally brushing against the delicate rims of spectacles. Another shock to the hansom sent the top of his head forward into the cab's frame. Wellington would have been surprised if Eliza had not heard that impact.

The crack of the whip. Their horse cried out. They were going faster.

He pushed his spectacles back to the top of his nose and looked up to see the distance between the ebony carriage and their own disappearing.

"Hold on!" was the only warning he got before the hansom popped up in the air, lifting him out of his seat and sending him back into the tiny floor of the cab.

Wellington pulled himself up to see the black carriage in detail, their own pace now matching it. Standing out in the door was a fist-sized crest centered just underneath the cab's window. He held his glasses steady in order to get a better look at the design of inlaid gold; but as he deciphered the Latin banner running underneath it, the carriage's tinted window slid down.

From its shadowed interior extended a rifle barrel.

Wellington ducked back into his cab's floor just as the bullet shattered one of his windows.

"Would you like a gun now, Welly?" he heard Eliza shout.

"Just drive the bloody cab!" he screamed as a second gunshot ripped through the air.

Their cab swerved away from the carriage, giving it a momentary lead. He heard two whip cracks and, once more, the gap between them closed. Wellington could see the rifle barrel—once again—sliding from the shadows and drawing aim on him.

"*Wellington!*" he heard Eliza cry out as his world went dark.

The gunshot caused his heart to seize up, but when he opened his eyes he saw no telltale mortal wound upon his person. He looked out of his window to see the rifle faltering for a moment, and then attempting to come around again. Sparks flew off the weapon as the second bullet struck, this time knocking it free of the unseen assailant. He watched the rifle topple from the window, and both hansom and carriage bounced as their respective wheels ran over it.

Wellington rapped against the roof of his hansom and shouted, "Lovely shooting, Eliza!"

"I agree," she replied. "Pity it wasn't me!"

With the black carriage pulling ahead, Wellington dared to peer behind them. His saviour had been a lone rider, also dressed in black, and brandishing a single pistol that he now holstered. This new ally spurred his ride, quickly drawing closer and closer to their own hansom.

The closer this friendly masked rider drew, the less comforted Wellington felt.

He never got a chance to note anything unique about the unknown rider's saddle, attire, or even his horse. The steed, unhindered by an attached coach or multiple fares, slipped through the space between it and the hansom, and then matched pace with Wellington. The fist suddenly shot out of the rider's cloak, striking Wellington's nose hard enough to disorient him and send his glasses once again to the floor. This jab had also shaken him enough that he couldn't slap free of the sudden grip this rider got on his coat.

"Bugger me!" Wellington heard through a haze, and the hansom lurched violently again.

His feet shot out in opposite directions while his hand grabbed hold of a strap meant for fares that preferred assurance when taking corners at a jaunty pace. This left Wellington one hand free to grab the rider's wrist. His body jerked forward and now he felt the air on his face and could see the stones and dirt of the road below passing underneath him in a blur.

The first tug he made against the cab's strap did nothing, but the second one pulled the rider in his saddle enough to loosen his grip. Wellington, his senses now lost in confusion save for one overwhelming desire for preservation, pulled and pushed with all his effort. The rush of air ceased, and the chaos around him abated slightly. He was now lying flat on his back across the hansom's seat.

Something shifted above his head once more, the cab shook, and Wellington looked up to see the black rider by his window, his face completely concealed by a black kerchief save for his eyes. Those eyes studied him as would an owl on catching sight of a lone field mouse.

The hand reached out once again, this time grabbing the side of their hansom.

His grip was fleeting as the hand wrenched back to where the coach whip wrapped around his neck and then went taut. The black rider's arms flail wildly as he plummeted from his saddle.

Wellington didn't hear the rider's neck snap, but the angle of his head on striking the street served as assurance. This saviour-turned-enemy was no longer a concern.

Wellington had just caught his breath when he was opposite of their original prize: the black Concord coach. This time, it was not a rifle barrel he saw, but a small, pearlescent puff of steam. A shrill whine immediately followed, and abruptly stopped when projectiles, small discs, just larger than his fist, their cogs filed to a razor's edge, bit into the wood just beside his head.

"Eliza!" he called through the roof hatch, his eyes not leaving these peculiar weapons.

"You know what would be just ducky right now?" she replied, snapping the reins and pulling *ahead* of the Concord. "A crack shot. You know, someone who would shoot while I drove the bloody hansom? That would just be lovely! I know you expect me to do everything, me being a woman and all . . ."

Then came a sound like Eliza's stiletto knife, only much louder. Wellington looked back at their closing quarry, noticed its new adornment, and swallowed hard. From its wheels' hub extended serrated blades that spun with the carriage's speed. From the glint off the blades, they could easily shred through their hansom.

"Bloody hell!" he spat.

"Welly," Eliza shouted, "now would be an excellent time to hold on."

They swerved suddenly towards the curb. Wellington braced himself, his teeth striking one another painfully as one side of their ride popped onto the sidewalk, sending pedestrians into the street. The death carriage continued pursuit, undaunted, much to the dismay of pedestrians caught by its lethal blades. At least two screams cut through the hansom's rumbling. Wellington attempted to turn, to see what damage that black coach reaped, when he was lifted from his seat once again. They had returned to the street, the Concord still behind them but seeming to position itself for one final attack.

Hooves pounded against stone. Wooden frames shuddered and clamored. The air filled with equestrian shrieks of fear, chaos, and anger, and then Wellington felt a surge forward. His grip tightened as their hansom swerved again, but this time skidded to a complete stop, their horse rearing back in protest, flailing its hooves in the air before returning to the ground.

The ebony Concord went rushing by them, its speed and greater weight preventing it from stopping as aptly as they did. Horses and carriage careened into a cart of produce, the Concord's driver launched from his seat with a scream that joined his fallen steeds'.

Wellington lowered himself out of the hansom and walked around to the sprung seat where Eliza remained perched. Behind her was the hansom's driver, looking very pale in contrast to the uniform of his office.

"Welly, pay the driver." And without a glance behind her, Eliza dismounted. "Pay him well."

Both their heads snapped to the Concord's wreckage as screams ripped through the street. Its sole fare, the woman they had only managed a glance of back at Doctor Smith's, had been freed from the cab. The gentleman who had apparently assisted her was now dead on the street, two fist-sized discs protruding from his chest. At point-blank range, the lethal gears that had missed Wellington had found their mark in this Samaritan without fail. Onlookers scattered in every direction providing enough cover and chaos for the mistress in black to slip away. Eliza, with Wellington close on her heels, ran into the fray, but her offensive was a futile one.

"Damn it all!" she spat, her eyes searching the alleyways.

"She's gone, Eliza," Wellington said, his own eyes looking around them, "and we should follow suit."

Giving a soft huff, Eliza turned to say something in reply, but instead rapped his arm and motioned to the wreckage. "Apparently, someone wasn't as deft."

Three men stood motionless on the other side of the Concord's scarred, damaged husk. Wellington and Eliza manoeuvred through remaining onlookers to look down on the driver's twisted body, his neck visibly snapped. His arms showed a final effort to save himself, perhaps trying to catch something—anything—in order to avoid the gruesome death that had found him anyway.

Eliza bent down and started feeling inside the man's coat and vest, much to the disgust and disapproval of those watching.

"Gentlemen, ladies," she began, her tone civil but still with warning, "I doubt if he will mind my searching his pockets. It's not as if he will complain about anything gone missing."

Wellington heard her hand strike something in the driver's left inside pocket. She pulled from the dead man's coat a small journal, worn and well used. A quick peek inside revealed grids of times and places.

"Eliza," Wellington whispered into her ear. "People are gathering. We *have* to go!"

With a final glance around them both Wellington and Eliza disappeared down a similar alleyway as the Concord's fatal fare. Behind them, policemen's whistles drowned out the curious queries and concerns of passersby.

INTERLUDE

Wherein Agent Campbell Is Scared Straight Out of His Socks

Bruce hated—*hated*—coming down to the Archives. It wasn't anything personal against Books. It was more of a feeling being surrounded by previous cases. When he arrived to the Ministry, he was a no-nonsense sort of fellow, fresh from the colonies and hardly one to believe in anything that resembled flights of fancy.

That was, of course, before his first year here.

When Doctor Sound offered him the position with this branch of Her Majesty's government, he was entreated by his own Prime Minister to accept and represent Australia. This was a grand opportunity to show Her Majesty exactly what stock Australia could produce. Bruce was eager to do his country, his real home, proud. There was also the opportunity to travel. That also appealed to him as this meant meeting ladies of all backgrounds, a little fringe benefit to catching airships bound for destinations far and wide.

The ladies were a cold comfort in light of the things he'd seen and what he dared to bring back to England. As the Archives were underneath him (in many ways) and kept out-of-sight, it was easy to keep them out of mind. Then there would be the cases that gave him no other choice but to descend into the Ministry's darkest corners. There were trinkets in here that altered time, statues and talismans that could affect a man's manners, and things on these shelves that were just not . . . normal. He heard a whisper of a portrait down here that, on glancing at it just once, could trap your soul and kill you in a moment . . . or, with the right handling, grant you immortality.

That just wasn't right. Not at all.

The whine of the Archives' door as he closed it behind him echoed dreadfully. If there was anything that could turn the Crown against the Ministry once and for all, his instincts told him that it would be in here, somewhere amongst these numerous shelves.

Bruce walked over to the partners' desk and set on Eliza's side his morning's newspaper. His Kiwi Cousin was now here, amongst the other unwanted antiquities of the world. All jibing aside, she was the closest link to home and had been handpicked to represent her country. It was sad to see her fall so far. For her career to end here was a travesty.

His eyes jumped to the other side of the desk. There was something about Books that left Bruce unsettled. He felt like the diminutive gentleman was more than he appeared, like many things in this place. Just as dangerous, too. He didn't know why the pom made him feel that way, but he did.

Neither Books nor Braun saw Bruce this morning when they left the Ministry shortly before lunch. He wondered if Braun was cozying up to her new partner. It wouldn't be surprising—whispers amongst the other agents were she'd been quite smitten with Thorne.

Bruce moved to Books' side of the desk and attempted to open the main drawer. Locked. He tried the other two drawers along the side. Also locked.

"Not a problem," he whispered aloud, reaching into his coat.

He lightly bit the inside of his cheek and groaned. His lock picks were back upstairs in his own desk drawer. Too risky to head back up there now—Books and Braun could return at any moment.

He pulled at the desk blotter, revealing a series of codes. "Blimey!" he swore, looking at all the various combinations and sequences available for the Archives' confounded difference contraption. A code for making tea. Various codes to play music. "Does this bloody contraption actually do something for the Archives?

"No worries, then," he conceded, sliding the blotter shut. "I'll do this the old-fashioned way."

Bruce gave his coat a tug and descended into the depths of the Archives.

He stopped and rubbed his massive square jaw for a moment. "1890," Bruce muttered, "where it all began for me."

It wasn't just his cases, but the cases of his fellow agents. Bruce wasn't the only one who was dealing with the strange, the confounding, and the downright unnatural. He was sure if he couldn't come up with incriminating evidence against the Ministry from his own history, he could find something from another agent.

Bruce grumbled a bit as he got on his hands and knees, checking each case box as he started at the beginning of the bottom shelf.

"Agent Hill . . . Agent Donaldson . . . Agent Thorne . . . Agent Thorne . . ." He wasn't even sure what he was looking for. This was over six years ago, his first year in the Ministry. And he honestly didn't know how this filing system worked. "Bugger it," he snapped and grabbed the next case crate. He strained to read by the gaslight the small card fixed on its side:

AGENT DOMINICK LOCHLEAR
ASSIGNMENT: CAPE COLONY
CASE #18901022CCAS

"As good of a starting place as any," he said, opening the box.

The case book in this box was thin. This usually meant the case was of the open-and-shut variety, Bruce's favourite kind. Two days of case work, the remainder of the week (or two, depending on how the circumstances had depicted the matter) enjoying the local ladies. At least, that was how he handled things in the South Pacific and Asian sectors. He had only visited Cape Colony once; and while parts of it reminded him of home, he had little desire to return there. While Australia and Africa both faced challenges in managing indigenous populations, Cape Colony's savages were a tenacious lot.

In the Archives' dim light, Lochlear's handwriting told Bruce the story of Case #18901022CCAS, and thankfully Lochlear's penmanship was polished and refined. Less eyestrain.

"Unrest in Zululand has always been of a concern to Queen and Empire. This is a known fact. Recent events, however, have called the Ministry of Peculiar Occurrences to action. In the past week, several heroes of the Zululand Campaign of 1881 had been found dead, the circumstances behind the deaths unable to be explained by conventional science. Autopsies of Lord Richard Castlebury, Sir Frederick Roberts, and 1st Lieutenant Randall Morrison revealed no signs of chemicals, mortal wounds, or even scorch marks from hyper-oscillating aether-armaments. Their bodies, both inside and out, had been naturally petrified. Doctors concluded from the rate of petrifaction that had the bodies remained unchecked for another two days, Lord Castlebury, Sir Roberts, and Lieutenant Morrison would have fossilized, making any further investigation a challenge."

Bruce looked around him, suddenly noticing how quiet the Archives were. There was the constant droning of the

Ministry's generators; but after a few minutes it seemed to become synonymous with the silence, as if they were working in concert with one another to create this atmosphere that sent goose flesh racing along his arms.

"Eliza," he muttered, flipping a few pages ahead, "How the bleeding hell can you manage working down here?"

"The Amulet of Shaka, on careful research by myself and Agent Atkins (on temporary assignment from the London office), while hardly the most powerful of amulets I have encountered, does possess startling abilities that anyone within reach of said amulet should take caution."

"Here we are," Bruce chuckled softly, continuing deeper into the notes of Agent Lochlear.

"The amulet is nothing remarkable in itself—a carved chunk of petrified tree-bark that has been hollowed out, making it able to hold small amounts of fluid. The design of the amulet is a common image for the people of Zululand, a shield with two spears cros—"

"Get to the point, mate," Bruce swore, running his finger quickly through the notes. "Just tell me what makes the bloody thing so dangerous!" If he could confirm the Ministry was holding on to truly dangerous artefacts, that might satisfy Sussex.

". . . unable to explain, perhaps it is a quality of the wood or its own petrifaction process, but the fluid—in this particular case, the blood of Shaka Zulu himself—has remained preserved, down to its temperature as if it has been drawn from the savage chief just today."

Bruce swallowed, and he winced lightly. His throat hurt. He desperately needed a drink. Preferably a whiskey.

> "The legends, from what we are able to surmise as locals seem to be reinterpreting the core story and embellishing it to suit their own needs and status amongst their respective communities, tell that Shaka was revealed in a vision the fact that his half-brother Dingane and his brother Mhlangana were plotting his assassination. Shaka traveled in secret to a tree, believed sacred and possessing the power of the gods in that the tree had been struck several times by lightning but continued to grow and flourish as if it lived in the tropics. There, Shaka and a trusted witch doctor engaged in a bloodletting ritual that, by our calculations based on folklore, should have killed King Shaka outright, or severely weakened him."

Bruce shook his head. Life before the Ministry might not have been as exciting, but it was certainly more simple. Marking his place with his thumb, Bruce looked into the box and felt a chill crawl through him.

The gaslight barely reached inside the box, but shadows danced across the carvings and tiny crevices of the Amulet of Shaka. It was one thing to read about it, but a far different matter to actually see it. He had been on an assignment in Batavia where he found himself facing a cobra. Calling on that same control he'd used against the serpent, his hand reached into the box, his movements slow and even. The only difference between then and now was that Bruce truly felt fear.

Smooth. With all its detail and cracks, the wood amulet was smooth, like a silk cloth. And warm. In his head, he could hear his heart pounding. Or was that his heart he heard? The rhythm resonating in his head was faint, but still reminiscent of the drumming he heard while on assignment in Cape Colony.

Bruce flipped the case report open and resumed reading.

"It is believed the wearer of the amulet, on placing the blood of Shaka across the brow and in the centre of your chest, gains the power of the tree gods. The amulet required one more blood ritual before it could become active, but Shaka was assassinated before the ceremony could be carried out. The amulet disappeared shortly after the capture of King Cetshwayo in 1882, and our local sources lead us to believe that the Amulet of Shaka was bestowed on leaders of various underground factions. With the recent deaths of these war heroes, we can only surmise that the final blood ritual had taken place, and that those who carried it to fruition must have some sort of blood-tie to either Dingane, Mhlangana, or—considering the immense power of the amulet—King Shaka himself."

The amulet now shook in his hand. Was that really all it took to be a god? A drop of a dead savage's blood on his head, and his heart, and then he would be able to call upon the powers of nature—and he would be unstoppable.

In his ears, the drumming grew louder.

It was his imagination running rampant. Had to be.

"As we observed, the wearer, preferably with the amulet itself under unfettered light from a waxing or full moon, would be able to bring forth revenge against their foes. The ritual must begin with the intended target's name spoken aloud—"

"Agent Campbell?"

The scream that came out of him was hardly fitting with his reputation in the field for being a bare knuckles brawler. Bruce stumbled and fell hard on his ass, the report tumbling back into the box and the amulet held tight against his heart.

"Agent Campbell," Doctor Sound said again, his head cocked to one side, "Would you be so kind as to explain to me why you are down here in the Archives, unattended, rummaging through a case file?" He adjusted his spectacles and looked harder at the amulet Bruce was absently clutching. "A case that wasn't even yours."

Bruce looked at the trinket and quickly tossed it back into the case box. "Ah, yes, Doctor Sound, "I was just—" And his words caught in his throat. His eyes immediately darted to the front of his shirt.

"Seeing as the unfettered light here is gaslight and not moonlight," Doctor Sound jested, "you—and anyone else you might have a disagreement with, at present—are perfectly safe."

"Ah, right then," Bruce muttered in reply, replacing the lid of the case file.

"Better make certain that case file goes back to its proper place." Sound chortled as he added, "Lest you invoke the wrath of our fine Archivist and his assistant."

Bruce cast the Fat Man a glance and replaced the case back onto its shelf.

He towered over Doctor Sound, but somehow Sound still managed to intimidate the hell out of him.

"You were about to keep my rapt attention with the reasons why you are down here in the Archives, unattended?"

He had to get into that frame of mind when an adversary would stumble upon him during a surveillance. Granted, his usual instinct was to start throwing punches; but as this was the Director of the Ministry, that option was unavailable.

"Well, Doctor Sound, I was considering a change of pace from my South Pacific duties."

"Really?" scoffed Sound. "And you were considering Cape Colony?"

If Bruce didn't tread gently, this lie could easily get him transferred, and then he would be truly sunk. "More like I wanted to come down here and ask that bloke Books to pull a few random cases from my first year here. You know, just get a look back on where I walked about then. I wanted to see where I was the most wide-eyed."

Doctor Sound's expression remained stoic. "Why, Agent Campbell, I had no idea how poetic of a man you were. I suppose it is not out of the ordinary to have agents keeping a few secrets for themselves, now is it?"

A sweat started to form at the small of his back, but he shrugged and replied, "I suppose not, Director."

Bruce went to return to Books' and Braun's shared desk when he noticed a suitcase tucked in the aisle behind Doctor Sound. "Is that yours, Director?"

"Oh?" Now it was Doctor Sound's turn to fidget. "Oh, that—yes, I, uh, have an unexpected call to attend to tonight so I brought my suitcase with me. I will be taking the first airship leaving at the end of our day."

Bruce gave a nod, and then returned to the desk, picking up his paper. "Well a safe travel and bon voyage to you, Doctor Sound. I'll be getting back to it."

"Just a moment, Campbell," Doctor Sound called, his suitcase rattling lightly as he approached.

If this were it for Bruce and his deception, maybe Sussex would understand him having to punch the Fat Man in order to get away clean, without revealing Sussex's intentions.

"Is that this morning's paper?"

Bruce blinked, and then looked down at the newspaper in his hand. "Yes, Doctor. Do you have a need for it?"

"I do," he said, his smile pleasant and affable.

The newspaper unfolded with a snap, but never opened. Apparently what Doctor Sound was looking for was the headline; and as he read the accompanying story, Bruce heard a soft grumble come from the Fat Man.

Sound shook his head slowly. "So, here's where it starts. Interesting. Not quite what I anticipated, but very well." He then turned his attention back to Bruce, as if he was just bumping into him in the office upstairs. "Do you mind if I hold on to this?"

"No," Bruce answered, the hammering in his head finally subsiding. "Not at all, Doctor."

"Capital," he said with a nod.

They both headed for the staircase leading back up to the main offices, but Bruce stopped just short of the first step and called out to the Director. "Pardon me for asking, Doctor Sound, but . . ." His eyes jumped to the massive, heavy, and—its most notable characteristic—*noisy* iron hatch and then back to Doctor Sound. ". . . I didn't hear you come in here."

"No, you didn't." Doctor Sound stood there for a moment, saying nothing but keeping his gaze locked with Campbell. As he was a few steps ahead, he was now looking down at him. "But *I* heard *you* arrive."

Sound was down here the whole time? And it took the Director that long to confront him about digging through the Archives?

"I should have that hatch tended to," Doctor Sound said, casting a glance to it.

"So, Doctor Sound," Bruce said, leaning against the staircase railing, "mind if I ask what *you* were doing here in the Archives, unattended, before I got down here?"

"The same as you, Agent Campbell," Sound answered, his voice never faltering. "Research."

The Ministry Director resumed his walk up to the hatch, leaving Bruce at the bottom of the staircase.

"Guess you are right, Fat Man," Bruce muttered to himself. "A few secrets kept to yourself isn't out of the ordinary, now is it?"

CHAPTER TWELVE

Wherein the Agent and the Archivist Uncover Nefarious Goings-on in a Somewhat Less Than Salubrious Factory

Eliza adjusted her Ministry-issue bullet-resistant corset, and her hands absently came to rest on where her weapons were concealed. Glancing out the window, she ascertained that they were nearly at the site of the foundry—the place she had never wanted to return to. In addition to her usual array of throwing knives, she had made sure to strap the *pounamu* pistols into back holsters, concealing them further with a loose men's jacket specifically tailored for her. (After all, pistols holstered in the small of the back were nothing more than absurd fashion statements unless you could reach said pistols.) Usually she hated to combine male and female attire, but today, this investigation warranted the benefits of a corset and the freedom of male pants.

A smile crossed her lips.

"Miss Braun," Wellington spoke, "I fail to see amusement in this situation."

Eliza concentrated on cladding her hands in black silk

opera gloves. "Perhaps it is your abrupt change in attitude I find so funny."

Wellington opened his mouth a couple of times, then closed it with a snap and turned his attention to the journal on his lap, but not for long as their transport lurched for a few more feet on the cracked pavement before coming to a sudden stop.

The carriage window framed where, in her first case with the Ministry, she and Harry had stood over the exsanguinated body of a young woman. This place had looked very much different then. The chunky brick building of the Ashton Foundry with its great chimneys bellowing out thick smoke was now reduced to abandoned ruins, consumed by the elements it lived on.

"It appears," Books flicked open his own notebook, "That the foundry caught fire just over seven months ago. By the time the fire brigade reached it, the conflagration had taken hold."

"Very convenient," Eliza muttered as she opened the door and stepped down. "Thank you," she said to the driver, "We would be grateful if you would wait." She passed up enough firm currency to hold him to it. They had no chance of finding a hansom or any other kind of carriage in this industrial wasteland. As far as they were from the bustle of London, they might as well have set foot on the surface of the moon. The silence of abandon embraced them, consumed them, the screams of distant crows shattering the unnerving quiet. New Zealand had none of those evil creatures, and for that she remained eternally grateful.

"Miss Braun?" Wellington asked, his voice seeming out of place.

Eliza looked down and realised she was holding his hand, her grip tightening when one of the crows cawed.

She yanked her hand up away from his as if his touch burned hotter than the tingling in her cheeks.

"Sorry, Welly, it's—" She had to get ahold of herself. They were just birds. Nothing but scavengers with feathers.

"Not much to look at, is it?" she suddenly quipped to the Archivist. "This paragon of the era?"

One raised eyebrow was the only reply she received, as he continued to scan the journal. Eliza wasn't sure how comfortable she was with him being so calm. She much preferred him prickly—at least she knew what he was thinking then.

Well, at least today she had made one good choice—this was not the time to be weighed down by skirts.

Not that skirts weighed down that other woman yesterday, she thought bitterly to herself.

Annoyance gnawed at Eliza's exterior, the assassin continuing down the alleyway and disappearing from view clear and vivid in her mind's eye. Over a hearty breakfast that morning she had contemplated the facts. Skirts. Those had definitely been skirts disappearing into the death coach. That had to mean a woman—or perhaps a man dressed as a woman? It wouldn't be the first time she'd run across that in the field, but it was not the greatest possibility. A blind man would have seen that the figure was hourglass in nature, hardly the stock and build of a man, and one harder to mimic when cross-dressing. So, a woman then. Like her. One with a fondness and skill for the art of the black powder, now pitted against her.

Eliza didn't dare tell Books this new adversary made her blood race.

The Archivist let out a great huff, a sound she was used to hearing in the Archives when his work was disturbed by her presence. Closing the little black book with a snap, he peered over the rims of his glasses, this time his ire directed at the scene of Harry's unsolved case. Eliza swore that the Archivist was disappointed the coachman's notations were not in code. Closer inspection of the book revealed it was merely a list of dates and locations, along with a series of initials—presumably people that the coach had been scheduled to pick up.

This one address had immediately caught Eliza's eye—

leaping forth as both familiar and out of the ordinary in amongst the very high-class residences and usual destinations such as tearooms, theatres, and arboretums. Ashton Foundry was not a place she was ever likely to forget.

"Over there," Eliza gestured towards the distant river, "that was where we found the last victim—drained of every drop of her blood. The killer was just unlucky. One more tide and the body would have been carried away by the Thames, but fortunately some mudlarks found her."

"Mudlarks? Reporting a dead body in the Thames?" Books' eyebrows shot up at that. Scavengers on the river regularly found corpses, usually stripping them and letting the river carry them away.

"One poor old widow. Told us the corpse reminded her of her own dead daughter. So she pulled her up above the high-tide mark."

"Strange."

"Even the poor, destitute, and forgotten can have feelings, you know," Eliza snipped.

Wellington frowned and, like a good gentleman, disregarded her with a quick sniff and walked ahead of her to get a closer look at the remains of the foundry's massive chimneys, which continued to tower over the scene. "I read in the report that you questioned workers at the foundry. How thorough were you, would you say?"

Eliza chose not to bristle. What kind of agent did he take her for? "As thorough as could be expected," she said, proceeding even deeper into the rubble. "They didn't have very much to say—only one step away from slaves. Poor things."

"And the owners?" Books followed gamely in her footsteps.

Eliza snorted. "As if Harry and I could ever get that high up. It didn't seem worth the bother since the owners left the place in the hands of some truly cruel managers. Naturally, they claimed to never have heard a thing."

"Which was probably true. I imagine when it was working, this place made quite a din."

Eliza paused. The faces of the workers, reflected red in the light of the furnaces, grimy and flat with hopelessness, had made more of an impression on her than the dead girl's pale one. "It certainly did."

Glancing over her shoulder, she noticed Books seemed a little unsteady on his feet. "You should have joined me for breakfast, Welly. Alice makes the best scrambled eggs in London, would have fortified you for this sort of hike."

"Alice?" He stopped and stared at her. Did he imagine she had some female companion—what was going on in his mind?

"My housekeeper."

"You have—" And then Books' brow furrowed. "Ah, well . . . I see."

Eliza twisted her mouth into a smirk and picked up her own pace over the broken brickwork, suddenly desiring more space between herself and Books. Charming as he could be, and there were moments she wouldn't deny, Wellington Books was severely lacking in diplomatic skills. Naturally Books didn't expect her to have a servant. "Pauper colonial" had obviously been what Books had cataloged her as, and yet he had no clue of her childhood, her upbringing. Perhaps her own polish suffered a few tarnished spots, but the assumptions he made truly rankled her.

Then again, she was finding great satisfaction in surprising him. How she wished she could have been conscious when he first laid eyes on her apartments.

They made their way to the heart of the factory ruins. Here the bottom storey of the once towering foundry works hugged the earth like an upturned and broken red hand. Remains of machines and equipment lay scattered about, while great furnaces to the rear of the building could be seen lurking in the shadows, their doors hanging off or missing entirely.

"Must have been quite the impressive burn," Eliza said in a flat tone, thinking of the hundreds of workers who had laboured here. "Some of these ironworks melted. You wouldn't imagine one fire could do so much damage."

Wellington asked, "Could it?"

"Depends on the chemicals involved, what was the incendiary, and the skill of the arsonist."

"You suspect arson?"

"When I heard about this place going up in flames so close to Harry's disappearance, I found it suspicious. On attempting to follow in his footsteps and investigate on my own time, crushers were everywhere and guarding the scene around the clock."

"Guarding a burned-out husk of a foundry? Around the clock?"

"That's when I started to think that maybe Harry's assumption of 'something bigger' could have credence. Doctor Sound, on my return to the Ministry, then started sending me on more remote assignments. Good bit of sidetracking, that was." Eliza looked to either side of her and motioned ahead. "Let's poke about a bit."

"Quite a lot of ground to cover," he observed. "I'll look around the back, you check the front."

She would give Books this: as immaculately dressed as he was, he didn't even give one complaint at the idea of mucking about in soot-covered remains. A gentleman who didn't mind getting dirty? Eliza chuckled at how attractive she found that in him.

Setting her mind to the task at hand, Eliza focused on the remains of the foundry's interior surrounding her. Wellington was right: a lot of ground to cover. Overwhelming as it appeared, goose pimples prickled along her arms and chest. Something was here. Instincts insisted she had to be looking right at it. She continued to a small clearing on the factory floor, and that tingle was now a burning. It was right in front of her. Eliza paused here, and closed her eyes. This was no accidental fire. Her experience with dynamite and flame told her that almost immediately. She told Wellington as much just now, but Eliza couldn't see what she needed to see. What was throwing up a stone wall between her and the next step forward?

I'm too close, she thought, her eyes flicking open.

Those words made her stomach tighten, but the truth was evident. She was too close. Both in the crime scene, and in the reasons behind her investigation. With a deep breath and her epiphany coming to roost, she turned back towards Wellington to suggest returning to the Archives.

Eliza now saw what he could not: a panorama of where the foundry's furnaces had been, this area scorched more severely than where she stood. That was the foundry's incendiary: the furnace. That was where the fire had started. The plant's power source had not reacted to the fire, but had been its origin. Someone had wanted to make very sure that the place went up. Her hand traced in the air the scorch patterns in the brickwork, their long ribbons serving as the accelerant's signature in where it all began.

The weather had long washed away any smell that could have helped her identify exactly what that accelerant might have been, but Eliza wanted the other clue that could unlock details of a fire: its flashpoint.

Industrial accidents were rarely investigated—not when the right families knew the right words to put in the right ears. It was how the world worked. Apart from this evidence of foul play, there was nothing but destroyed and charred equipment, most of which she wouldn't have been able to identify even when it was whole.

Eliza was just craning her neck to find Books, when she heard him call out. The note in his voice caused her to start running. With a racing heart she heard him again. *"Miss Braun!"*

He must be in one of the large storage rooms. The door was charred and hanging at an odd angle. With a deep breath, Eliza reached through the slits cut in her coat and produced her pistols, cocked them, and kicked the door open.

Books blinked at her and the weapons in the half-light. He was alone, and crouched at the far wall with an excited grin on his face.

"Do me a favour, Welly." She released the hammers on

the pistols and holstered them once again. "Only use that tone if you are in imminent danger."

"But look what I have found." He gestured her over to the wall, scorched like everything else in the building.

"Another burnt surface of brick?"

"Perhaps, perhaps not—do you have a mirror?"

Eliza knelt next to him while fishing out her compact. "What sort of woman would I be without one?"

Wellington's excitement diminished for a moment as he pondered the square accessory of Eliza Braun's: gold and pearl with the initial "E" encrusted in diamonds.

"A gift from a handsome Texas rancher turned oil baron," she said with a sigh. "That was a very special assignment, so do have a care."

The Archivist shook his head and motioned to the wall. "See—there was some sort of mark here." With one hand he brushed away as much of the scorching as he could, then placed her mirror against it and tilted it. "And now can you see what it is?"

And she could indeed. It looked very similar to the pattern on the playing cards. "A Phoenix," she whispered, tracing the shape.

"And look," he went on, "there is some sort of banner at the bottom. I hazard perhaps with a Latin inscription on it—but I cannot possibly work it out from this fragment." Wellington sat back on his heels. "I will need to get back to the Ministry and do some more research into who would lay claim to such a heraldic symbol. I know the phoenix is a popular moniker, but this particular design is fairly intricate."

Eliza could feel dread building inside her. What sort of people could be responsible for fire, explosions, and madness? She was beginning to wonder what Harry and his odd little locket were leading them both into.

Apparently, so was Wellington. "We have made at least one connection between yesterday's events and the Rag and Bone Murders: this coat-of-arms. But we are now faced with a new intrigue."

"We are?"

Wellington produced the coachman's ledger and flipped to their current address. "This foundry was burned down shortly after Harry's disappearance and eventual admission into Bedlam."

"Yes."

"The fare recorded here is from this week."

She stepped out of the storage room and back into the ruins, her eyes scanning across them quickly. "They came looking for something."

Whatever could be here that would bring the perpetrators of this crime back, after such a long period of time? Rocks. Rubble. Scrap iron. There was nothing in sight, but something had to have brought them back. Something vital, something important. Something right in front—

Eliza's sapphire gaze jumped back to Wellington Books, his complexion pale and sickly as he joined her, his eyes still in the coachmen's ledger.

"What is it, Books?"

He swallowed, and flinched. "I know what they were looking for."

By the gods, he really did need to learn better skills in sharing with his partner. "Out with it!"

"Eliza, this fare occurred following your visit to see Agent Thorne." He looked around. There were no other souls to be seen by him, apart from herself and the driver watching them from a distance. "These people were looking for *us*."

Harry, you were right.

Swallowing hard on her own concerns, she took Wellington by the arm and led him back to their carriage. "The time has come to divide and conquer, Welly. Get back to the Archives. You do what you are good at. I will do what I am good at."

He glanced at her, "Blowing things up?"

Eliza gave a nod, shrugging lightly. "I stepped into that one. No, I have *other* skills, you know," she returned. It was fun to see him blush. "Interrogation."

"You mean investigation."

She was barely able to contain a little snort. Life had sheltered dear Mr. Wellington Books down in the Archives. Unfortunately life had not been so kind to her. "Investigation. Interrogation. What you will. As you'll be in your element, I'll go back to Charing Cross and see if I can find out a bit more about the good Doctor Smith. Is that all right with you?"

"Of course, Miss Braun."

Eliza returned a nod, and then cast her eyes to the Thames slowly progressing by them. If she were exceptionally fortunate, her "investigation" wouldn't involve employing her other skills—the skills she was terrified of losing while serving in the company of Wellington Books.

CHAPTER THIRTEEN

Wherein Agent Braun Causes a Bit of a Ruckus While Making Friends

It felt so good to be out pounding the pavements again, Eliza thought as she stood in the alleyway opposite Royal Hospital. She was actually smiling. Not a put-upon, cordial smile one wears about the office, but an honest-to-goodness smile of joy and delight. Usually this kind of legwork, with its long periods of doing nothing, was her least favourite, but after weeks away from it she was enjoying the moment. A thicker than usual London Particular had swept in off the Thames and that made the whole setup just about perfect in her eyes.

Whitechapel was certainly not the kind of place people like Wellington Books would be comfortable with, especially at night, but to her it was very familiar. She and Harry had spent a great deal of time down here as many Peculiar Occurrences happened in the cramped houses and narrow alleyways of this part of London. This was the corner of the City, forgotten and ignored by the upper classes, full of rabble-rousers, Fabians, cut-throats, and Dollymops. It was dirty, dangerous, and dank.

It also felt like a warm and welcoming home following her time in the Archives.

She fished out a warm chestnut from the little bag she'd bought off a street seller, popped it into her mouth, and bit down on it with relish. Across the road, even with the fog diffusing its warm lights, she could still make out the imposing brick and stone façade of the hospital and catch sight of people coming and going.

When trying to get information about a recently deceased person, there was always a critical moment when the cracks would be easier to find. It was usually within the first two days. Lovers, enemies, and co-workers were at their most vulnerable when in shock, before they could apply a varnish of respectability over the dearly departed. Eliza had considered this when planning her attack on those touched by the oh-so-recently exploded Doctor Christopher Smith.

It would have been effortless to access the Thames Pneumatic Dispatch from her old office to find out the basics; but if she were by the receiving centre, awaiting the cylinder addressed to her, that would have got people wondering and—more importantly, less helpful—asking what she was up to. She had spent the afternoon assuming the role of a journalist investigating the tragedy of Charing Cross. Her efforts granted her access to public records that revealed Smith was a single man whose parents had died when he was young, and had left him with no siblings. Nothing beyond that.

Then she discovered his residency was at the Royal Hospital. It was not a surprise but more of a confirmation that this doctor's demise would be connected to Whitechapel. Whatever answers waited for her had to lie within these walls.

Finishing the bag, she crumpled it up and stuffed it in her pocket. Under her cloak, the brass of the *plures ornamentum* arm had finally warmed. Taking out her favourite weapon once more onto the London streets was the icing on this evening's cake. The contraption had cost her an evening on the town with Axelrod, the least-annoying of the two clankertons in Research and Design. That sacrifice was ample compensation for getting her hands on it. Or rather her arm in it. The *plures ornamentum* had been the last privilege she'd weaseled out of the gadgetheads before heading off to Antarctica—but she had decided at the last moment not to pack it. It stood to reason that encasing her arm within brass in the freezing cold was a truly bad idea.

Luckily, clankertons were not the best keepers of paperwork.

The gauntlet moved seamlessly when she wriggled her fingers and a deadly part of her hoped that their elusive assassin would make another appearance. *Things would be very different then*, she thought smugly. The cogs ticked and whirred as she rotated her wrist and went from splayed fingers to a tight fist. Her heart thrummed in her ears lightly, as it did when she chased an enemy of the Empire through the city streets, or made love to an overseas operative when the assignment drew to a close. Tonight, Eliza D. Braun was finally back where she belonged.

Let Books have his Archives. *This* was living.

So engrossed by her elation was she that Eliza almost missed the group of men she'd been waiting for, coming around the corner of the Hospital. They had not come through the main public entrance, for that was the domain of visitors and nurses. These men were either the porters or orderlies of Royal Hospital, the medical equivalent of mill workers.

As they made off up the street, roaring with laughter, glad to be free of their work, Eliza followed a short distance behind. She could have forgone the gauntlet and, continuing her guise as a journalist, interviewed Smith's fellow doctors, could have heard what a fabulous man he was, how they would miss him, and how they could not understand why such a terrible thing befell such a kind soul.

It was what those well off would do—hide true feelings behind good manners.

If you wanted the truth about a person, you asked those

subordinate to him—especially if they were working class. They'd tell you what they really thought of him, no matter if he'd been blown all over Charing Cross that very day or not.

Three streets later, the men disappeared into a little corner pub. Eliza paused outside, taking note of its name—the Liar's Oath. She gave the working men a few moments to their beers and to settle in for a time between mates. Her dress this evening was more subdued, so she did not expect to be mistaken for a Judy. Even so, feeling her brass-encased hand pressed against the Ministry-issued corset reminded her how perilous walking the streets of Whitechapel could be for an unarmed woman.

For a woman as armed as she, an evening here was an invitation to trouble.

Pushing open the oak door, Eliza entered the Liar's Oath. As it was with the multitude of small working-class pubs in this part of London, it was packed. The smell of smoke and alcohol easily catapulted Eliza straight back to childhood, and for the briefest second she thought if she turned her head she would see her mother pulling pints behind the bar. Yet when she did catch a glimpse of the bar through the crush of people, there was no one there. What she did see made here eyes wide. How she loved the technological marvels.

Lord McTighe, an aristocratic inventor from the Highlands, had created the Combobula bar; and in a gesture of eccentric philanthropy, had given it to working-class public houses all over the nation. His reason for the invention apparently could be traced back to the fact he was, aside from being as mad as a March hare, madly gallant. "*Women shouldna be pawed by drunk patrons!*" he had been overheard to slur at his favourite Edinburgh pub.

The shiny brass-and-wooden bar was probably responsible for the overcrowding in the small space, but even Eliza could not deny its grace, beauty, and sheer novelty. Using her elbows she managed to get closer to the contraption.

On closer inspection, the bar was divided into sections with a menu set into its gleaming brass surface. Eliza nodded appreciatively at the wide array of drinks the Liar's Oath offered. It was evident to her now why this place was so crowded: variety from the clockwork barkeep.

She dropped her coin into the slot closest to her and ordered a pint of bitter by pressing the appropriate button, and heard, even over the din of people, the cogs begin to spin. The rather odd tune it selected to play while she waited for her drink was "Onward, Christian Soldiers," another fine example of McTighe's madness. However, no one seemed to take much notice or even bothered to sing along. The laughter, mirth, and friendly chatter was the house's true music. This was where the working class of the City came to revel and repast.

One pair of the half dozen arms sprung out from under the back of the bar, giving Eliza a start. Articulated fingers of brass wrapped themselves around the tap handle and slowly pulled in a precise fashion that only an experienced bartender would manage, while a second arm tipped her tankard at an angle, slowly righting it the fuller it became.

Eliza took stock of the bar and how it segregated itself. At the Combobula, it was men, as it was throughout the Oath. Against a far wall women put up their feet and chattered amongst themselves.

She smiled as the pint was level, and the arm once pulling the brew now produced from its metal skeleton a long file that dragged itself over the tankard's rim, removing any excess foam from the bitter's head. An experienced barkeep would have done this smoothly, gently. As this was one of McTighe's creations, the file whipped across at the end of the rim, flecking the drink's foam onto patrons who didn't flinch when the bubbles struck. One worker merely wiped his cheek clean and continued talking to his mates while another sampled the bitter, nodded, and proceeded to order one for himself.

With libation now properly prepared, the serving arm

swung over to where Eliza stood while the other returned to a neutral position under the bar. She picked up the bitter carefully with her left hand, keeping her gauntleted right under her cloak. As Eliza took her first sip and glanced down the length of the Combobula bar, she decided perhaps Mad McTighe hadn't been totally mad. The arms did serve a lot more people than three barmaids ever could.

Though there had been that *incident* in Colchester last year. Eliza counted off in her mind how many had been rushed to the local hospital . . .

She took a careful step back from the bar just on the recollection, and stepped right on a man's toe.

"Careful, love," his hand actually slipped around her waist and she controlled herself enough not to elbow him in the gut to get free. The grateful man could hardly be held at fault—the Oath was heaving with women on the make.

Wriggling free she worked her way back towards her targets. Their burly forms were clustered at the far end of the bar and as she managed to move closer, she caught some very interesting conversation . . .

"Best bloody news I've heard all day," barked one of the men just before wiping foam free of his impressive moustache.

"Only sorry I weren't there to see it." Another chuckled. "Bet he made a fine ol' mess all over Charing Cross."

Yes, these were indeed the right people, so she planted her toe in the floor and tripped. It was better than any music-hall actress could possibly have managed—though she lost half her pint down her front and knocked into the largest of the three so hard he lost most of his on the floor. A noble sacrifice.

The giant of a man spun about ready to pound the drunk who had soaked him, but then he stopped. Eliza smiled her most winning smile. "Sorry, mate, some bugger tripped me up. Let me buy you another?" Her accent was carefully chosen East End, and—if she said so herself—damn well done.

"That's all right love," he muttered, still hot from being doused with bitter. "Needed a bath anyway."

She pursed her lips and gave them all a saucy look over. "You boys look like you've had a hard day, and I can't take a man's hard-earned drink away from him. Wouldn't be right." The men made way for her so she could slip more coins in the bar. The mechanical wonder whirred and the beer was poured. "Name's Emma. Emma Kincaid. You boys don't mind a lady buying you all a round, do ya?"

"Well now," the big man said, his demeanor softening a bit, "if a woman wants the right to vote an' have a voice an' all, I sees no fuss in a woman buyin' th' rounds."

The guffaws and raised tankards were Eliza's invitation. Never failed. The way to a man's heart was best fueled by beer.

They were quick enough to introduce themselves: Buford, Seth, and Josiah, all orderlies at the Royal Hospital and all possessing the most magnificent moustaches. After some prodding—and two more rounds for the lads while Eliza continued to nurse her original tankard—Seth admitted their facial hair was a competition the orderlies in the hospital were hosting. On the following round, they were calling on her to judge, at least the three of them.

"Oh now, come along, sweet Emma," Josiah urged, his gravelly voice attempting to smooth itself into something seductive. "Fine blue eyes as yours should declare a lucky lad a winner, eh?"

"Please," she held up her hands, genuinely laughing, "I cannot possibly chose between you fine gents." She paused, taking a sip of her dwindling cup. With a silent prayer that the men wouldn't notice how little remained in her own pint, she looked at each of them before asking, "Fine 'staches you gents have. Why I would not reckon any of the high-class types could hold a candle to you three." She waited for their chuckles to subside. "So exactly what are you handsome, strapping lads celebrating tonight?"

Seth, the tallest of the three, twirled the end of his ginger handlebar moustache, and raised his glass. "The death of the biggest bastard in London!" The other two whooped and hollered in agreement.

"That's quite a title," Eliza laughed with them, her ears ready for what had to come. "Who's the winner?"

"Doctor bloody Christopher Smith," Buford slapped her on the shoulder, his careless gesture nearly knocking her down. "Always looking down his nose at us, at the nurses. Even the bloomin' patients!"

"Like we were something ripe on the bottom of his shoe," Seth added, swaying a bit against the bar. "But worse than that . . ." He looked around and then leaned forward into the group. "That clinic of his down on Ashfield Street—"

"You'd never catch me going down there." Buford knocked back another swig of his beer. "Bloody deathtrap, it is."

Eliza's stomach clenched. So there was another side to this respectable doctor. She should hardly be surprised. Still she kept her voice light, "Oh come off it, lads . . ."

Buford suddenly grabbed her arm and stared at her hard. "No, really, Miss Emma—don't go there. *Ever.* Even with that butcher in the ground, just don't go there."

Death was everyday in Whitechapel, and so anything that caught the eye of the locals must have been gruesome indeed. She gave a little nod, a nod that anyone who had ever lived in reduced circumstances understood.

"Anyway, he's dead now," Josiah muttered. "And it won't be us grateful for it—them nurses copped it good. Especially her." He jerked his head to a dark-haired, sturdy-looking woman in the corner of the pub. Whether by chance or by personality, she had cleared a space even in this crowd.

"Who's she?" Eliza downed the last of her pint.

"Mary Grissom. Finest lady to ever grace the halls of the Royal Hospital, if'n you ask me, which you did, miss." Josiah's wide face wrinkled in something bordering on sympathy—another emotion rarely found in Whitechapel. "Even that tosser Smith agreed as much and that is why she went on an' worked for Smith at that clinic. But she saw something at Ashfield. Something bad. Tried to blow the whistle on what he was doing down there, and Smithy caught wind of it. Now she can't get no work at all—not even in Bedlam."

Buford let out a long burp, before pronouncing solemnly, "Poor cow—still hangs around the hospital though. Like a beat puppy coming back for another hiding." He slammed his fist against the bar, making the other tankards jump. "It's not right. Not bloody right. Smith said horrible things what made her a leper. She deserves better!"

So that was the person she needed to talk to. "Gents, you all have earned another round. God bless you," she said, plopping some coins in front of them. "But if you will excuse me, lads. Looks like Mary could use the ear of a lady."

She worked her way to the other end of the Combobula and ordered a pair of sherries. Cradling the two glasses between fingers of her left hand, she slinked her way through the crowd until she came to stand before the solitary table where Mary Grissom sat. When Mary looked up into Eliza's own gaze, the disgraced nurse did indeed look rather like a lost, confused puppy.

"Here you go, love," Eliza spoke gently, placing the sherry in front of her. She motioned her head back to the orderlies. "Them lot were telling me you could do with one of these."

Grubby hands hesitantly took the drink. "Thank you," she whispered, raising it to her lips.

"Don't think nothing of it—got a bit of a soft spot for my fellow woman who's been kicked about by the toffs."

Mary gave her a hunted look. "What you on about?" She was trying very hard with an East End accent, but underneath was running a strain of education. Whatever Mary Grissom was now, once she'd been something else. Doctor Smith had beaten that Mary Grissom into submission, and now this ghost of a woman that once helped people on the mend was all that remained.

Eliza needed to take a different tactic with this one. Mary was not the normal sort to the East End. The absence of a drink in front of her told Eliza that the fallen nurse wasn't coming here to forget. She was hiding.

Leaning across the small wobbly table, she fixed Mary with the look of a hawk. "I know about that bastard Smith blacklisting you from the only honest work you could get—from the work you *should* be doing. In light of his untimely death, as well as the reasons behind him sullying your reputation, I am assuming you know something, something that could well get you killed."

"Who . . ." Mary's bottom lip quivered. She blinked her eyes, a tear managing to escape as she finally asked, "Who are you?"

Eliza went to answer, but the sound of the pub's door opening grabbed her attention. If she hadn't seen through their guise, she would have laughed at these two "blokes of the working class." When one of them pointed at Mary, Eliza caught the glint off a ring that clashed with the rest of his simple ensemble.

Her heart began to race, and she clamped her hand down on Mary's arm. "Right now, I am your best mate and the one chance you have in leaving here alive." Eliza leaned towards Mary, her blue gaze hard and insistent. "Do you trust me?"

It was a crazy thing to ask, but on such moments many things could hinge.

Mary gaped, but she had not become a nurse by being a shrinking violet. Her jaw tightened and she nodded, "Yes—yes, I think I do."

"Then just stay behind me, and whatever you do, no matter what happens, don't run."

"Unless you tell me to?"

"Exactly," Eliza spoke evenly, turning in her chair to welcome the newcomers. "If you leg it, their man outside will have you for certain. Understand?"

"Yes, miss."

"I mean it," she insisted. "No. Matter. What."

She caught Mary knocking back the sherry quickly. It was a pity Eliza didn't have the time to return to the bar for another.

The men looked over the table, their eyes not leaving Mary Grissom, even when Eliza greeted them with a cheery, "Hello, chaps."

"Piss off, whore," one of them hissed. "We need a word with Miss Mary here."

Eliza shifted in her chair. Her feet needed just the right leverage. "Got a sick friend?"

"You could be saying that, yeah," the other one grunted. "Needs some attention."

"Sorry about this, lads," Eliza said, broadening her East End accent, "but the good nurse here is off duty. Ya follow?"

The lead one frowned, leaning forward to stop only a few inches from her. "If you want to have that pretty face of yours carved like a Christmas goose, then please, stay."

Eliza looked over her shoulder.

Mary nodded, mouthing the words, "No. Matter. What."

"If you would rather wish to walk out of here," the thug spoke again. Eliza turned back to him, and his fetid breath caused her to blink as he said, "then I'll repeat myself, you dozy bint—piss off."

She just grinned at him in reply, and that was when her gauntleted arm shot out, the brass fingers grabbing hold of the man's balls. With the sound of gears spinning and a tiny hiss of hydraulics, Eliza's armoured fingers squeezed.

The man could barely scream, let alone breathe.

"Mate," Eliza said, keeping the first thug firm in her grasp, but addressing the second one as if sharing a high tea, "if you want to make sure your pal here doesn't become a soprano in the church choir, I'd suggest you both lea—"

The partner blew hard on a whistle, its shrill tone higher than that of a Blue Bottle's. Two more lummoxes, dressed head to toe in black, burst through the door, looked in their direction, and started pushing patrons aside, not a care where those in their way landed.

Eliza's gauntlet released the thug, his breath coming back in a hard, sharp gasp. As he took a second gulp of air, the brass fist clocked his chin. He remained suspended there for a moment, his arms reaching for her in a feeble, futile way. Before he fell back, though, Eliza grabbed his wrist and removed the ring from his finger.

"Thanks, mate," she quipped. "My partner's been on me to get a clue. Mayhaps this will appease him."

The first thug toppled on top of his partner, but reinforcements—considerably larger than the two on the floor—had already made work of the crowd and now closed on her. *Two,* she thought. *Whoever these people are, they really want this woman dead.*

The newcomers apparently hadn't seen Eliza's gauntlet, and the lead thug might have wished he had after feeling it backfist him in the nose. The last man in, however, evaded her hook punch and slapped Eliza hard. His follow-through sent her into the crush of pub patrons.

Eliza's head spun, her senses swimming in a fog of confusion. *Don't you* dare *swoon, Braun,* she chided herself. *You haven't been out of the field that long that you've forgotten how to take a punch. Pull yourself together!* Her vision cleared first, and that was when she heard the scream. She saw Mary recoiling on account of the killer reaching for her. *Bugger!*

The thug's wrist suddenly disappeared under a mass of flesh and muscle. Eliza would have thought only someone from her home's national rugby team could possess such speed and still carry that much girth. *What a shame he's English.*

"That's Miss Emma you're shoving about there!" Buford bellowed, bending the thug's wrist back. If it snapped (and judging by its angle, it should have), no one heard it over the raucous crowd. "She's going to be judging our moustache competition!"

The thug flew into another unsuspecting group of patrons, who did not appreciate losing their drinks to some bloke dressed like an undertaker. Both reinforcements were now lost in a sea of uppercuts and kidney punches. Eliza was free to return her focus to the original pair, the first one still unconscious but the second regaining his feet. She didn't bother to look for a blade or a pistol. Eliza flicked the switch on her brass-encased arm, felt the mechanisms within whir and spin against her bicep, and fired the *plures ornamentum* in one smooth motion.

The weighted bolas shot from the arm, the long outer cord sending its attached brethren wide, wrapping the man's legs against each other. He went down cursing, tipping into the arms of Josiah and Seth. Both men returned him upright, and then lifted him off the floor with a double-dealt uppercut.

The Oath's crowd, now enjoying the theatre of the brawl, roared with a delight as the last man fell backwards, his eyes rolling in his head. Eliza could feel her blood pounding in her ears, her warrior's urges encouraging her to leap into the fray. Ministry training, however, took hold: *Grab Mary and make for the most convenient exit.*

A pair of arms wrapped around her in what could have been a very intimate bear hug, just as she turned towards her table. The air was being squeezed out of her, and her ribs felt hot and in danger of cracking. The brass of the gauntlet pressed painfully into her corset, and stars exploded in her vision.

"Don't know who you are, bitch," the gruff voice wheezed into her ear. She must have really squeezed the life out of his manhood. "But you are making my job most difficult tonight!"

The impact of the back of her head into the bridge of his nose made a snap that could just be heard over the general chaos of the brawl. When he howled, his grip relaxed slightly, and Eliza followed it up by scraping her boot hard down his leg. That and a brass-covered elbow in his gut got her free enough to spin about and deliver a snap to his jaw. His crash to the floor was most satisfactory.

Eliza turned back to Mary who gave her a polite wave. She had done exactly as she was told.

"Now we run?" Mary asked anxiously.

"Now, dearie, we run," she said, pulling the nurse out of the chair and into the crowd.

The Combobula whirred and buzzed as it closed down to protect itself. Just how it sensed a brawl was in progress Eliza had no idea—but she got a new appreciation for Mad McTighe's invention. The two women had made it to the door just as pints and chairs began flying.

"Wait!" Eliza poked her head out of the pub and looked around. No one about. She then shouted over the brawl, "Buford!"

The orderly had just taken down one of the men in black when he heard Eliza. He cheerfully waved back and pointed to the unconscious assailant. He seemed quite proud of his brawling proficiency.

"I vote for Seth!"

He blinked, pointed at Seth, and then cocked his head to one side.

"On account of the colour!" Eliza shrugged and added, "I have a fondness for redheads!"

She chuckled as the thug Buford had taken down was apparently struggling to get back on his feet. This time, Buford helped him up, and then decked him again. Then, he helped the thug back on his feet. And proceeded to send him back to the floor again.

"Oh dear," Eliza said to Mary just before opening the door, "Buford isn't taking my judgement well."

Once outside in the relative calm of the street, Eliza pulled Mary along, ducking into the first dark doorway she could find. She pressed a finger to Mary's lips and kept the nurse concealed in the shadows as she looked down the alleyway and then out into the open street. They were safe, but only for the moment. The refuge of her apartments felt leagues away.

Removing her finger, Eliza smiled and patted the nurse's

hand. "I would love to hear everything you can tell me about Doctor Smith and what nefarious antics he was up to at the Ashfield Clinic."

Under her grip, Mary was trembling, but her gaze was steady and strong. Not bad for a destitute woman who had just brushed her own imminent death. "Whatever you need."

Eliza's heart went out to her. Pushed around by powerful men, denied her trade, hunted, and still she would tell her story. The courage in her eyes was admirable, but whoever had sent those men now lying comatose on the public house floor (save for the one that Buford was taking his aggressions upon) would be unlikely to stop at the Liar's Oath. London, and perhaps all of England, had just become even more dangerous for Nurse Mary Grissom.

A plan began to form in Eliza's mind. "Mary," she said brightly. "How familiar are you with tropical diseases?"

CHAPTER FOURTEEN

In Which Our Heroes End Up in the Papers and in Rather a Pickle with Doctor Sound

The woman's feet scuffing against stone took his attention from the massive volumes and smaller books arranged before him. Wellington looked at the clock with a start. Close to the end of the morning. Simply amazing.

"I was wondering if you had in fact slipped through a looking glass and were lost in Wonderland, Miss Braun."

"I was busy," Eliza's voice echoed through the Archives, "you know . . . investigating?"

"Interrogating," Wellington reminded her.

"Same thing, different perspective," she said, reaching the bottom of the staircase. "I was looking into what seems to be quite the colourful lifestyle led by Doctor Christopher Smith."

He waited until she flopped in the seat opposite him. Eliza rubbed her eyes slowly, the gesture accompanied by a faint groan. Apparently, the previous evening had stretched into the waning minutes of this morning.

"You're late," he reminded her, punching into the engine his tea sequence.

Eliza's hand dropped to her lap as she let her head fall

back. "Yes, Books, I know. I'm such a bad, bad agent. I should be put across your knee and spanked."

"Your fantasies are not my concern," he observed dryly, "but if you are going to run this investigation without Doctor Sound's knowledge or permission, you may wish to have a care concerning the schedules you keep. You're in the Archives for a reason. If you continue holding the hours of an active field agent, you will be noticed."

"Don't you mean 'we'?" Eliza's head tipped to one side. "You are in this investigation with me, aren't you?"

His reply cracked a bit as he answered, "I suppose I am."

"You *suppose*?" She sat up, something working at her already stretched-thin nerves. "You mean if things get tight, you are going to leave me out to fend for myself?"

"I didn't say tha—"

"You insinuated it!" Miss Braun snapped. Her words were already filling the grand space underneath the Ministry, and still she grew louder with each word. "I have endured one hell of an evening, and I would like to know if I am in this alone or not. I need to know if I can count on you, and if I can't, we'd better be clear on that *right now*!"

Wellington raised an eyebrow, waiting for her echo to subside. When it did, his own tone was as calm as a millpond in morning. "Are you done, Miss Braun, or would you care to have another row again? I don't think the Dalai Lama in Lhasa heard your earlier train of thought, so please, oblige His Holiness."

Eliza leaned back in her chair again, her gaze never leaving his own.

"Perhaps you would rather hear what I have discovered in your absence?" he asked, and, on the sound of the chime, began putting together for Eliza a fresh cup of tea.

"Please, go on, Welly."

After gingerly placing a steaming Earl Grey in front of her, Wellington licked his fingertips and began turning pages, finally stopping on one and then offering the open book to Eliza. "That is the symbol from the playing card, the Death Coach, and as far as I can tell, the scorched sigil at the foundry."

"And the signet ring."

Wellington tipped his head to one side. "What signet ring?"

The bauble landed square in between the open book Wellington cradled in his arms.

"That signet ring," Eliza said, dropping three cubes of sugar in her tea. "Took it off a bloke the other night hired to kill Nurse Mary Grissom."

His brow furrowed. "Who?"

"You first." She took a sip, and then motioned to him with her teacup. "Tell me about this crest."

"This is the coat of arms for the Phoenix Society," he stated, placing the open book between them.

Eliza leaned forward, setting her tea aside. "The Phoenix Society? I thought that was some myth. One of those society clubs formed to give proper poms a reason to go cheat on the wives?"

"Actually, this group is hardly a myth. They possess some fascinating history," he said, motioning across his cluttered desk, "possibly predating the Freemasons."

That made her look up. "Really?"

"The first recording of their crest was in the South Pacific, the Philippines as a matter of fact. There was a grave site that had, emblazoned in gold, the emblem of the Phoenix Society. In fact," he began, lifting book after book until finally finding the desired volume and covering the detailed rendering with a new image: a woodcut of a Spanish seaman from a far-off age standing by what appeared to be an ornate gravemarker. Wellington tapped the emblem clearly visible, and added, "It was believed that Ferdinand Magellan was one of its members."

Eliza blinked. "Hold on. Magellan? How does a Spaniard—"

"Become a member of an English Gentlemen's Society? Because this English Gentlemen's Society has deep roots that extend to cultures other than Britannia. This group could very well stretch back to Roman times, when the world was part of the Great Republic and comprised of people from various conquered lands. One thing I have noticed in my research of the Phoenix Society: no instances of this emblem appear in *Roman* artifacts, both documented publically and in our own Archives."

"So . . . a gentlemen's club that apparently excluded the Ancient Romans. Not very gentlemanly."

"Unless," he said, flipping through pages of a volume still on his side of the desk, "that was intentional. Perhaps the Phoenix Society started as a dissident group. An underground movement dedicated to one goal."

"The fall of the Roman Empire?"

"A common goal for a group of people from all parts of the world, all of them conquered."

Eliza nodded her head, a wry grin forming on her face. "And from the ashes rises the great phoenix. An interesting theory you have there, Welly."

"Yes, a pity I have no definitive proof to back it with, but definitely a theory. This is, however, the mantra of the Phoenix Society as seen by this inscription in the crest." He pulled the more detailed rendering back to the top of the pile. "There you are, Miss Braun," he said. "The Latin translates roughly to . . ."

"From Ashes and Chaos Arises Order and Balance." Her own fingertips traced the coat of arms as she studied its detail. "I can read Latin, not that I enjoyed my classes." Her expression softened as she took in a deep breath. "My Latin *teacher*, however, was a different matter entirely. Quite dashing enough to turn a schoolgirl's head."

A prickling rose along the nape of his neck, and Wellington tugged slightly at his shirt collar. "Yes, well . . ." he stammered. With a quick clearing of his throat, he continued, trying to ignore the warmly wicked grin now on her face. "The Phoenix Society's history—at least, their *public* history—is sketchy if not outright fantastic. Queen Elizabeth, the court historian noted, had made the Society quite the subject of interest." He adjusted his spectacles, glancing over an open volume on his desk. "One could argue it was an obsession of hers, really. She was convinced they were determined to undermine her rule, and therefore passed a law condemning anyone found in association with them punishable by death."

"So underground they remained and Good Queen Bess ruled happily ever after?"

"Apparently."

"So when do we hear from the Phoenix Society again?"

Wellington nodded, giving a little chuckle as he opened yet another book.

"Good Lord, man, how many books did you go through while I was out . . ." Eliza sounded as if she were about to say "interrogating" but she swallowed back the word and said, ". . . investigating?"

"We all have our methods of madness, Miss Braun," he said, producing a parchment, "and the Archives are mine. Here," he said, passing her the document, "is the next instance of the Phoenix Society turning up in England. Perhaps the only real hard proof apart from the instances of the sigil."

At the very bottom, almost resembling a Royal Seal, was a gold-leaf printing of the now familiar moniker. Age had tarnished the gold and some of the detail had worn away, but it was the emblem they had seen again and again, only this time accompanied by seven signatures.

Her eyes considered the parchment from top to bottom. "What exactly am I looking at?"

"A declaration," Wellington stated, his smile widening, "bonding those who signed it to reach out to Mary, the daughter of King James II, and William of Orange, in order to usher in an age of change."

Eliza's head popped up. "The Immortal Seven were members of the Phoenix Society?"

Wellington shrugged. "From the ashes . . ." He gingerly took the parchment from her hands and said, "I need to make sure that this is returned to its proper place here." Slipping the declaration into a protective leather binder, Wellington continued. "With a throne grateful to them for restoring order to the country, the Phoenix Society could now enjoy a less covert existence. And much like the Freemasons, the Phoenix Society became a secret society that revitalised themselves. First, they became exclusive to Britons. Next, they felt the need to flaunt their influence by emblazoning their crest everywhere. At least they did so until the turn of the century, when their 'influence' just up and disappeared."

"Just like that?"

"Just like that," echoed Wellington. "The last sighting of their mark was in 1810. A group of doctors tending to His Majesty King George III, on the orders of his son. It was their diagnosis that served as the prince's permission slip to usurp the throne via the Regency Act of 1811."

"Wait a moment," Eliza interjected. "Are you making the claim that this Phoenix Society led a coup against Mad King George?"

"I'm saying that these doctors brandishing the bird were the same doctors charged with the health of Princess Amelia, when she was on the mend in 1809. A year later, she was dead."

Eliza went to say something, possibly to tell him he was wrong. She opened her mouth again, but only a dry, hard laugh came out of her.

"And these books, these documents," she said, motioning to the trail of pages and papers strewn before her, "all this was here, lurking behind the details of *other* cases?"

"Welcome to the Archives, Miss Braun," Wellington answered wryly. "That one particular document was discovered in a raid of the Immortal Seven." He shrugged and added, "Seems that in a case back in 1857, Ministry agents discovered their moniker was not too far from the truth."

She crooked an eyebrow at that, then dismissed her impulse and asked instead, "So with this much influence, why did the Phoenix Society go underground again?"

"That's open to conjecture. No records, no dedications, no formal events, or correspondences ever carried this particular seal of the Phoenix. This time, the Society wholly and truly vanished."

"Until now, when we find three instances of their crest within a week? That sounds a bit off for their modus operandi, particularly the crest appearing at the factory. Why, if you're a secret society believing that from chaos comes order, would you invest in that which is giving the Empire a solid foothold?"

"Good question," Wellington conceded.

"Could this be what Harry had discovered?" asked Eliza, her eyes returning to the emblem open before her. "The return of the Phoenix Society?"

"I think *Agent Thorne* discovered them without knowing what they were capable of." Wellington continued, dismissing her reaction to his correction. "I think the Phoenix Society took measures to mend any possible leaks of their rebirth, and they appear to be growing bolder in keeping their secrets safe. We are most lucky."

"Lucky? How do you come to that conclusion?"

"We are entangling ourselves with a secret society that dates back to the fall of the Roman Empire, and has steered the course of the British Monarchy for centuries. Look at the fates of anyone who discovered one random fact too many. The Rag and Bone Murders, and Agent Thorne residing in Bedlam."

"And Nurse Grissom last night at the Liar's Oath." The colour suddenly drained from her face. "Oh dear God," and her hands went up to her mouth as she tried to catch her breath.

"Eliza!" Wellington rushed over to her and bent to one knee. He looked up at her, resting a hand on her cheek, "What is it?"

Her eyes sparkled for a moment and then shut tight. Wellington gently took her hands away from her mouth and held them fast as she shook her head. With her eyes still closed, she whispered, "Harry. In Bedlam, he had a tiny scar just behind his ear. A surgeon's signature, if you will. Smith . . . the Society . . ." she hissed through clenched teeth as she said, "They *did* something to him."

A valid conclusion. One he wished had not been so solid in reasoning. "And that is probably what is keeping him safe at present. As for us, we're still shrouded in secrecy, for the moment."

That's when Eliza's eyes flicked open, any sign of tears effectively held back. "You know that won't last."

"Perhaps not, Miss Braun, but right now there is only one thing that protects us—our anonymity."

With a nod and a deep breath, Eliza went for her coat pocket and then smiled. "Welly." She chuckled. "My hands?"

He tightened his grip on them. "Yes, Eliza, what about your hands?"

"I'd like them back, if you please."

Wellington looked down and felt his skin heat up slightly. "Oh dear," and he tore them free of her as he returned to his feet. "I . . . I thought there was something wro—yes, right then."

She watched him return to his side of their desk, and her grin made his skin prickle with sudden heat. From her own pocket, she produced a small, worn journal of her own. "Along with being ghosts to the Society, we also have an insight into their company. I was doing some digging of my own, Welly, remember?"

"Ah, very good." He cleared his throat and asked, "What do you have to add to the pot?"

"Well, the good Doctor Christopher Smith was just that, an outstanding man of his profession. The man was very talented, very gifted." Eliza then flipped to the marked page of her journal. "I also found out that the impressive Doctor Smith was something other than what he appeared. I spent a good portion of the early morning talking with a nurse formerly of his practice, a Miss Mary Grissom, the name I dropped earlier? She had worked alongside the doctor at both his general practice and a clinic located on Ashfield Street until a few months ago, when she was dismissed."

"Perhaps Nurse Grissom wants to blacken Doctor Smith's name?"

"Now, Welly, is it polite to interrupt someone when they are talking? It is behaviour such as that which breeds ignorance." With a very satisfied smirk, she took a sip of her tea and then returned to her own notes. "Had you let me continue, you would have heard me tell you about experiments Nurse Grissom witnessed at the Ashfield clinic. She happened to note a patient's reaction to one of Doctor Smith's treatments and brought it to his attention. He *increased* the dosage. Grissom, from that point, then noted that this was Smith's process: Any sign of an adverse reaction, Smith would continue treatments with keen interest. The more dramatic the reaction, the more he would intensify treatments, as if testing subjects' tolerance levels.

"It seems that Smith was running the clinic for two reasons. The first was for his own standing in the eyes of the Society. The charitable work did win him many accolades. The second reason, though, was a bit more diabolical as Nurse Grissom discovered. She was, near the end, asked to assist in surgeries that were not only unnecessary but unethical. All these trials, and the deaths that occurred, all centred around the human muscular system. When she insisted on understanding what she was party to, he apparently answered with, 'The betterment of the Empire.' " Eliza closed her notebook and looked up at him. "It fits. Considering the condition of the corpses Harry and I found, it would have taken a curious surgeon with a great amount of skill."

"Indeed." Wellington then went pale. "Wait a moment. Nurse Grissom—"

She raised a hand, silencing him. "Already taken care of, Welly. I saw her off on the first airship leaving the country this morning. I called in a favour and now our Singapore office has a new head nurse."

He pushed his spectacles higher up his nose. "A lovely

notion, Miss Braun, but what will Doctor Sound say when he receives a communication from—"

The hatch unlocking boomed throughout the Archives, making them both start. Even in the sparse lighting that reached the top of the staircase, the portly man descending was most distinguishable.

"Ah!" His voice was cheery and bright, providing an odd contrast to the darkness of the Archives. "There you are! How fortunate to find both of you present!"

Wellington felt a sudden urge to flee, or perhaps excuse himself to use the lavatory; but that would have been far too conspicuous. Eliza, her movements in his peripheral seeming graceful and fluid, merely straightened up to her full height while closing the books on her desk. Wellington's eyes quickly glanced down to the open volumes under him. No etchings, photographs, or sketches. Merely dates and notes that might go unnoticed.

Yet this was Doctor Basil Sound, Director of the Ministry. His fingertips locked under the book's edge in order to close it before Sound reached their desk.

Too late. "So here are the unsung heroes of the Ministry, eh what?" Doctor Sound chuckled. Under his arm, a collection of papers crinkled as he clasped his hands together, considering them both. "From the looks of the shared desk, you two are keeping yourselves quite busy."

"Yes, sir," Eliza answered back, her voice that of a respectful soldier to her commanding officer. "Tea, Director?"

"No," he replied warmly, "thank you."

Eliza finished her cup and motioned to Wellington. "What Books does here is par excellence. I do have a great deal to learn."

"Well, I assure you, Agent Braun," Doctor Sound beamed, "when it comes to the facts and the figures, no one does it better than Books. A walking, talking analytical engine, you are, aren't you Books?"

"I suppose so, sir," answered Wellington, his voice wavering slightly.

Doctor Sound gave a hearty laugh, but then focused his attention on the six jars lined up between the two piles of books.

"Forgive me, Agent Books," Sound began, his eyes recounting the jars, "but didn't Agent Hill bring back *seven* jars from South America?"

"That was before Agent Braun's assignment here, Director. I'm sorry, sir."

Wellington went to glance at Eliza a silent apology but found himself caught in her astonished gaze.

"Yes, I was a bit of the butterfingers when I first got down here," she stated, her eyes never leaving Wellington's.

The Director sighed, and then seemed to cast off the disappointment. "Well now, that is the price for change, I suppose." He leaned in. "I should have warned you that when you were to break in a new partner, it would be in the literal sense with this pepperpot."

Was the Director *winking* at him?

Wellington took his seat and drew in a slow, deep breath. This couldn't be good.

"There is that old saying, Books, that you cannot make omelets without breaking a few eggs . . ." Doctor Sound counted the vases again, and shrugged. "Or in this case, irreplaceable vases leading to El Dorado."

"It won't happen again," assured Eliza. "I am still adjusting to the change, and I am learning, sir. I am learning quite a bit."

"Excellent," Doctor Sound replied. "I would be disappointed if you were not, or if I had made an error in my reassigning you. You are a superlative field agent, Braun, but I believe to round you out, to temper your need for mayhem, you must find a place here. It is also my intention that you would find a mentor in Books here, because he is—in my humble opinion—one of the most disciplined agents we have at the Ministry."

Wellington blinked. "I am, sir?"

"Of course you are, Books." Sound chuckled. "You work

down here diligently . . . undisturbed. You keep your own hours within the stacks . . . unsupervised." The mirth was receding from his tone. There was no malice or warning in his voice, but he was speaking with a slight air of curiosity. "What I mean is that you have been down here for years working without immediate supervision, and still you have worked wonders in restoring the Archives and remaining reliable as clockwork. That is a true mark of discipline and dedication to work."

"Yes, sir," Eliza answered.

"With the Archives seeming to be a world unto itself, practically detached from the Ministry's offices," Doctor Sound continued, "it is a wonder you two are, in fact, doing your assignments at all and not gallivanting on your own through the streets of London . . ."

Then, Doctor Sound unfurled one of the papers from underneath his arm and placed it on Eliza's side of the desk.

". . . Like *this* couple that I've been reading about in the papers."

Wellington slowly rose from his seat, the creak of his chair conjuring in his mind the sound of the gibbet. The headline screamed back at both of them:

CHARING CROSS SLAUGHTER!
Unknown Samaritans Attempt to
Apprehend Dealer of Death

"A most fascinating story from the *Times*," Sound said, nodding his head while unfurling another newspaper. "But no need to worry if you missed it there, because the *Daily Telegraph* also covered the story."

THE BLACK DEATH!
Mysterious Coach Kills Innocents
While Brave Husband-Wife Attempt
To Save the Queen's Subjects!

This story landed in front of Wellington, and his earlier desire to run to the lavatory increased tenfold.

"Oh, but I must give credit to the *Daily Mail* for their coverage of this calamity," Doctor Sound said, unfurling the last remaining newspaper. He held it before them, displaying the chronicle's impressive, imposing headline that Wellington did not doubt sold papers. "They captured, perhaps, the excitement, the madness, and more importantly, the *detailed eyewitness accounts* of what happened."

CARNAGE AT CHARING CROSS!
Woman in Black Ministers Death
But Flees in Sight of Daring Duo!

For a few moments, only the low rumbling of the Ministry's generators filled the space. Wellington read the *Daily Mail* headline several times and tried to remember to breathe. He felt the confession on the tip of his tongue, but he was too far invested into this forgotten case now. He would probably meet the same fate as Agent Braun, even if he withheld nothing from the Director about what he and Eliza had really been up to in their brief time together.

As if in answer to Wellington's prayer, Eliza asked, "Could it be the House of Usher, sir?"

"Well, Agent Braun, the black carriage with—" Doctor Sound turned the newspaper back around and, after a moment, began reading. "—'wheels of nefarious construction smiting down innocents as would the scythe of the Reaper' does sound very House of Usher, but then I have to stop and consider the other particulars in this story.

"Note, if you will: 'Eyewitnesses report that Mistress Death was locked in mortal combat with a hansom that kept chase, its drivers a man and a woman lacking modesty most proper.' Now, here is a detail I find most curious: 'The heroic hansom did carry a lone passenger, the man's purpose unclear as all he seemed to be doing was screaming as would a banshee of the rolling moors of West Yorkshire.' What do you make of that, Books?"

Wellington felt his tongue swell. He found himself totally paralyzed by the cool steely gaze of the Director. His mouth went to open, his throat dry as if he had been walking though an Egyptian expanse.

"As I read about such outrageous behaviour from the subjects of Her Majesty," Doctor Sound said, folding the newspaper and placing it where the seventh vase should have been, "I thank God in heaven above that I am the director of a *clandestine* organisation where our specialty is our subtlety." He slowly turned to Eliza, his eyes narrowing on her. "Isn't that correct, Agent Braun?"

Eliza nodded. "Most of the time, sir."

"Yes," he agreed. "Most of the time." Sound's eyes went back and forth between them both, and Wellington could feel a tightness in his chest. "Well then, I shan't keep you. I just thought I would pay my Archives a visit, and I am quite glad I did so." He took in the shelves, the massive analytical engine and its vast network of pulleys, and finally their shared desk, and he nodded approvingly. "I should do this more often. So please, if I ever do pop down here when the mood strikes me, just go about your business. Pretend as if I am not here." He lifted a finger up to his moustache and tugged at it a bit. "You can do that, can't you?"

With a final look at the two of them, Doctor Sound headed for the stairwell. "Agent Braun, Agent Books, good afternoon."

They both watched in silence as he made his way up the stairwell, opened the hatch, and disappeared.

"Books," Eliza said, shattering the silence. "How many times has the old man paid you a visit like that?"

"Including your arrival down here?"

"Yes."

"Twice." Wellington finally tore his eyes away from the metal hatch and glared at Eliza. "What in God's name have you talked me into, woman?!"

"Oh, this is my fault, is it?" She stopped for a moment and then nodded. "Yes, I suppose it is, but you were hardly coerced. You could have left me out on my own . . ." Then she leaned forward, her gaze seeming to chill in the glow of the warm gaslight. ". . . Or did you want the pleasure of turning me over to Doctor Sound yourself?"

He jerked upright in his chair. "I beg your pardon?"

"Didn't hesitate to mention the broken vase to him, did you?"

This woman was intelligent, resourceful, and sometimes thicker than clotted cream. "Eliza, do you really think he gives a toss about that bloody vase? He is onto us!"

Wellington could see it in her face, and this was one of those rare moments where he hated being right. "Then we will have to be more careful, won't we?"

The woman's tenacity could not be denied.

This colonial is hardly worth a thought, he heard his father speak in his head. *Do as I raised you, and send the strumpet packing! 'Twill do England and the Empire a spot of good.*

"I suppose we will have to be, yes."

In the abrupt silence, Eliza looked to be having some difficulty choosing her next words. "So in the interests of being careful, we need to discuss the wild card in all this—the gentleman that tried to cut in on our carriage dance. Did you get a good look at him?"

The Archivist let out a long slow breath. "Unfortunately, no. All I saw was he was dressed in black, his face concealed by a black mask, and he rode a black horse. Oh, and he was quite the marksman."

His colleague nodded, while her gaze remained fixed on the desk between them. "Do I have to say it or will you?"

The conclusion Wellington drew was the same one he had arrived to when he had come home. It had been thoroughly unpleasant then. It was even more so under Eliza's stare.

Her voice was so low it was nearly drowned out by the

analytical engine. "The House of Usher are still after you, Wellington."

He pinched the bridge of his nose and pushed back what threatened to be a splitting headache. "I pray to God you are wrong, Miss Braun."

Her hand slid across and just for an instant clasped his. "I am afraid I very seldom am."

"Regardless, we cannot tell where they will next strike, so I suggest we concentrate on the task at hand." With another deep breath he opened the top drawer of his desk and flipped through the ledger they had retrieved from the death coach's driver. "So as we are now destined for destinations of onward and upward, what are your plans tomorrow evening?"

Now it was Eliza's turn to blink. "Excuse me?"

He held up the book, looking at Eliza over his spectacles. "The driver's next appointment. There's a fare scheduled tonight for the London Opera. I believe the current production there is Verdi's *Macbeth*."

"Opera? As in the bustiers, the Viking helmets, and suicide scenes that last about fifteen minutes too long on account of the caterwauling?"

Wellington pursed his lips together as he considered her. "So," he said, returning the book to his desk, "I have discovered where your refinement ends."

"An abrupt one at that," she grumbled, as she tugged at her bodice. "Are you sure that is our next lead?"

"Oh, this ought to be delightful," Wellington said, leaning forward over the book-cluttered desk. "I get to watch the astounding field agent Eliza D. Braun *squirm*." He sighed. "I do so enjoy the Arts."

"A night at the opera, is it?" groaned Eliza. "Gods . . . the sacrifices I make for Queen, Country, and the pommy bastards that live in it."

CHAPTER FIFTEEN

Wherein Agent Books Almost Keeps Agent Braun Waiting

For the fifth time that evening, Wellington peered into the mirror and attempted to affix his tie properly around his neck. Maybe this time would be the last.

He had always preferred the ascot to the necktie as it was a far simpler fashion statement. The necktie meanwhile stood for elegance and refinement. Hardly surprising then Books was out of practice.

It wasn't as if he didn't put forth some effort to keep the manners his upbringing had taught him, as he believed in them and the civilisation they were the hallmark of. He might not have been what his father wanted, but he was still a gentleman.

Tempting as it was to break out a simple ascot, Wellington struggled on with the necktie. Tonight he needed to dress to fit into the world he had left behind shortly after serving in Her Majesty's cavalry. His eyes drifted into his reflection and to the open wardrobe behind him.

No, it was out of the question. He needed to blend in, and wearing his military dress, even free of the medals and commendations, would attract attention. Tonight, he needed to hide in plain sight.

"*You do not have to enjoy the Arts, Wellington,*" he recalled his father telling him, "*but simply put in your time at the theatre. There, you meet those that matter, and you must—above all—be better dressed than everyone else. Your breeding should be on display at all times.*"

Perhaps his father's first disappointment was when Wellington expressed an actual appreciation of the opera and theatre. He should have known better than to reveal such a thing.

Wellington pulled at the wings of his collar gently. He almost had it. His nerves were rattled enough. What he did not need now were memories of his father sneaking up on him. That's all they were: Memories. Bad memories. Nothing more.

"*It's that colonial. You've let her get ahold of you.*" His father's voice was so clear that for a moment the Archivist dare not turn around—just in case he was standing behind him. Impossible as that notion was. Wellington swallowed as he tightened the knot centred on his neck. "*She will drag you down with her into the mud.*"

When he took his hands away, Wellington finally let go of the breath he had been unconsciously holding. The tie was perfect. Immaculate. He gave the lapels of his black jacket a light tug, inspecting his reflection one final time. He gave a smile at how he looked, but still picked up the clothes brush and gave a few strokes along his arms for good measure. It had been too long since he had indulged in an operatic performance.

He felt the finger where his Ministry ring usually resided. That was another recommendation of Agent Braun's. While the tracking system was reserved for emergencies, Doctor Sound could very well consider them a threat to the Ministry's overall security and activate the ETS.

I'm sure Thorne considered the same thing, he thought to himself, a slight tremor creeping into his hands.

He afforded himself a compliment: *Wellington, old boy, you look quite dashing tonight.* Granted, this occasion was not about a night of elegance and gentility in the City. He could not afford to lose himself in the embrace of music, voice, and tragedy.

Perhaps the real tragedy resided in the fact that Wellington finally had an engagement with a beautiful woman, and it was all in the name of Ministry business. Ministry business that he had to keep secret from the Ministry itself.

Wellington was certain that somewhere in Heaven, William Shakespeare was smiling.

"Right then," he said, donning the top hat. Wellington was not fond of that particular accessory, but there it was: The final touch on his disguise for the night. "In for a penny . . ."

A soft rattling came from outside. The tenants of this convenient apartment were apparently coming home.

He slipped into his long coat, took up the cane, and finally hoisted the bulky case up to have it rest by his hip. It didn't feel heavy; yet its size and weight would eventually catch up with him, perhaps as he made his way to the appointed address where the hired coach would be meeting him.

On Eliza's suggestion, she would meet Wellington someplace other than his home. "*A precaution,*" she had assured him, "*in case Doctor Sound is really keeping an eye on us.*" She also recommended finding another apartment, preferably with a back entrance, to change into his evening wear, again in case Ministry personnel were watching.

The tenants were lingering in the main foyer, and now moving to the parlour. He smiled as he calmly, quietly moved for the apartment's back door. Slipping out, Wellington crossed the walled garden, unlatched the gate, and continued into the night. Fortune was, at least for tonight, favouring the bold.

"Spare a coin, sir?" the voice spoke from a darkened alcove.

Wellington shouldered his case and forged ahead, past the voice.

"Why so cruel, Mr. Books?" the beggar asked.

He froze and turned to look behind him.

Two shadows had come to life, and were blocking his way back. He took another glance to the street ahead. There was a third, standing deliberately in his path.

"Gentlemen," Wellington said, slowly lowering his case by his feet and placing his hat on top of it, "I have an engagement tonight, and the lady I am meeting will not take it kindly if I keep her waiting."

The two men closest to him remained still while the third began walking towards him.

"Very well then." He sighed.

Wellington took one more look at the man coming from the main street. *At least thirty paces away. When I engage, he will most likely run.* He turned back to the two shadows. *I will have to make this quick.*

The two thugs shared a glance as Wellington moved for them. His cane came up for the man to his right, but the feint was enough to make the large man step back. The cane shot for the other man, its handle striking his thick neck. As the thug stepped back, his hands at his throat, Wellington swung his weapon around. The cane slammed into his partner's knee, and the crack assured the Archivist that his opponent was not getting up.

Wellington turned towards the sound of running footsteps. The third man would be close. This is why Wellington brought his left arm up as he pivoted, and his attacker's arm was brushed out of the way.

At first.

The brushing arm slipped around the lumbering man's forearm, and then bent it upwards in a manner it was never meant to. Wellington brought his cane up, its top slamming into the thug's chin. The man's head snapped skywards, causing him to stumble backward. This misstep made it easy for Wellington to send him to the ground.

And back to the beginning, once more, Wellington thought as he turned towards the coughing. The attacker struck in the throat had now pulled himself up on all fours, and was still straining to catch a breath.

His foot caught what the third attacker had dropped. Even in the shadows he easily identified the sidearm as an 1881 Remington Elliot three-barrel Derringer. Its compressor glowed softly, the indicator lights reading green for each barrel.

"*Go on, my son*," his father told him. "*A smart boy would have the good sense to do right now what you refuse to. Three men, three high-velocity hyper-projectiles. Finish this.*"

Wellington kicked the weapon away from all four of them.

"*Bloody coward*," his father spat.

The thug had managed to bring himself up to one knee, but he never made it to his feet. Wellington's cane struck across his attacker's nose, planting him on his backsides with an audible thump.

"The level of crime in London is just disgraceful," he said, brushing himself off and once more placing his top hat where it should be.

He picked up his case and took one step when his cane snapped under his grip.

"Damnation!" The Archivist allowed himself one crass word, considering the only ones to hear it were the groaning ruffians. "They certainly don't make these like they used to."

Wellington tossed the ruined accessory aside and made a mental note to visit Savile Row as soon as possible for a replacement: something in ebony, this time with a silver handle.

He paused on hearing the groan behind him. They were still on the ground.

Perhaps a concealed sword in the replacement would be worth considering.

He made his way again to the street to pick up his coach, checking his watch as he did. He was running late.

Eliza would make quite a joke of it to be sure.

CHAPTER SIXTEEN

In Which Beautiful Attire Still Fails To Make Miss Eliza D. Braun Happy with Opera

The cost of hiring a truly grand carriage was worth it, Eliza decided, as she waited outside the gentlemen's club. The coach was warm, comfortable, and even she—occasionally—enjoyed feeling like a lady. It was definitely against the social norms, however, for the lady to be picking up a gentleman for a night at the opera; however, she was well used to working outside the lines of society.

Eliza adjusted the line of diamonds and emeralds at her neck. Her right wrist was weighed down with a thick bracelet of matching jewels, while her long dark hair was held off her shoulders with a fine hairpin decorated with another spray of gems that formed a peacock, a pretty bauble she had picked up in Persia that doubled as a very serviceable stiletto. Eliza was looking forward to seeing the effect the whole outfit would have on proper Mr. Wellington Books when she removed her cloak.

As if summoned, he emerged from around the corner and strode towards the carriage—but it was not an easy perambulation, because he was carrying a large odd-shaped box before him.

Eliza threw open the carriage door before the driver could get to it. "Perhaps you have mistaken the point of the excursion. This is an evening of opera. I am not helping you move your residences."

He slid the object, which she could now see was the breadth of his chest and as wide as her skirts, into the carriage. "I am perfectly aware of our destination Miss Braun. But this," he said, patting on the wooden crate, "will make all the difference in our little mission tonight."

"Good gracious, Books!" In the flickering gaslight, she could make out smears of dirt on his face, and his coat and necktie—while the definition of a proper knot and fashion—were in need of adjustment. "A moment, driver, and we will be on our way." She exited the cab and was immediately on Wellington, preening and fussing over his attire. "You look lovely, just a touch disheveled. You didn't nap in your evening wear, did you?"

The joke fell flatter than her usual jibes did with him. Once they were both in the close confines of the carriage and underway, Eliza tilted her head as she considered his fidgeting. "Welly?"

"It's nothing," came his sharp reply. "London is full of ruffians, and a gentleman must be on his guard."

She slapped him on the knee. "I'm afraid you will have to do better than that!"

He pressed his lips together, but finally blurted out, "Let's just say God didn't hear my prayer this afternoon."

The carriage lurched while Eliza digested that particular hard nugget of information. She usually liked being right.

"They attacked me in the street," Wellington stared out of the carriage window, sounding more outraged when he added, "They even called me by name."

Eliza's jaw twitched. "And the Mad Hatter's tea party rolls on. You know they're not going to stop, Wellington."

He adjusted his necktie; and now his gaze, surprisingly hard, fixed on her. "I am fully aware of that, Miss Braun—however, it is not as though we can take the matter to the

Director. He would only have his suspicions about us both confirmed."

That one stung, Eliza leaned back in her seat, unable for once to find a truly pithy reply. Silence would be the most appropriate response.

It did not last long as Wellington's eyes flashed to her neckline. "Where in the blue blazes did you get those?"

Eliza reclined a little, giving the gems following the curves of her breasts a chance to catch the waning light coming in the carriage window, "Wonderful, aren't they?"

"I beg your pardon?"

The poor man really needed to get out more. "I was referring to the necklace, Welly."

Just by his shocked expression she discerned he was imagining all sorts of nefarious ways she had gotten her hands on them. Best to put his mind to rest. She laid a silk-gloved hand on his arm. "There was a very grateful sheik that was happy enough to give them to me."

The resulting confusion and embarrassment was quite satisfactory. Wellington sniffed, and then returned his eyes back to the street passing by. "I don't think I need to hear the rest of the story."

"Good," she replied mildly. With a tilt of her head she examined his worthiness to enter the hallowed halls of the London Opera. Music Hall was more Eliza's cup of tea but she had to admit that she liked dressing up—something she obviously shared with the Archivist. Immaculately attired in a very smart evening suit, Wellington Books outdid her impressions of him. In fact, he looked quite dashing in it. "You'll do," was her final assessment.

"Why thank you." And those words were the last they exchanged for a long time. They sat in silence most of the way to Drury Lane. Eliza stared at the odd suitcase shape his fingertips rapped lightly against, and Wellington stared out the window, studiously ignoring her curiousity. The closer they got to their destination, the more a self-satisfied smile began to form on Wellington's lips.

It appeared that most of London's high society was attending Verdi's *Macbeth* this evening. Wellington stepped down from the cab and assisted Eliza in her descent—which was most helpful because it had been a while since she had worn so much fabric. Her expression reflected many of the patrons' excitement for the entertainment, but inwardly Eliza dreaded what lay in store for her tonight. Ye gods, how she *hated* opera. However, the game was, once again, afoot; and she needed to perpetuate the façade and so came the smile and outward appearance of anticipation.

When she inclined her head in Wellington's direction, she wanted her smile of gratitude to be sincere. Her evening's deception faltered for only a moment when Wellington slung the strange suitcase in their carriage over his shoulder. If she'd been hoping that the Archivist would leave it behind she wasn't that lucky. It most definitely did not go with his evening wear, and it would attract attention. By the list in his posture it had to be heavy—but she was damned if she was going to ask him why.

Even with this awkwardness, Wellington still managed to win back her sincere smile on offering his arm to her. There was a charming chivalry in his determination to keep up appearances.

They climbed the stairs to the entrance, in the stream of other fine looking people. Books bumped a few of them with his ridiculous case, but he was so effusively polite and so was everyone else that they made it in with little trouble.

Once in the warmth of gaslight, Eliza took off her cloak and draped it over one arm while a ridiculously tiny evening purse and a vibrant fan hung over the other. The indrawn breath at her side was just what she'd been hoping for. Admittedly she had briefly considered wearing red, but much as she loved that colour it would draw the wrong kind of attention. Her deep green dress drew notice but the kind that she wanted. The sleeves were stylishly ballooning, but set low so that her shoulders were just as fashionably exposed. The dress turned her form into a long serpentine swathe, and exposed enough décolletage to set off her jewels perfectly. Wellington was not the only one that was looking—she could feel many admiring glances. Eliza might have been stripped of her power within the Ministry, but at least she still had this.

Turning to the Archivist, she inclined her head. "Is something wrong, Wellington, dear?"

"Not . . ." He cleared his throat. "Not at all, Miss Braun."

She raised her fan and pointed it at him, her voice just above a whisper. "I believe in this particular, *under-cover* situation, you should call me 'darling,' 'sweetheart,' or at least 'Eliza.' "

"I think I can manage the last." His expression hardened, but there was a bit of blush remaining. He then managed, "Eliza dear."

"Very well," she nestled in against his side and directed him over to the cloakroom attendant.

After the young man took her cloak he looked with befuddlement at Wellington's valise. He was trying to be very polite and not ask directly. Finally he had to. "Sir, are you planning to take this into the theatre?"

The Archivist made a stern face. "I am dreadfully sorry but I have to—doctor's orders."

"We have a box seat, especially for that reason," Eliza picked up the hint and ran with it. "My husband must be comfortable." A little flash of her smile and a switch of posture that displayed her bosom and the jewels resting there, and the young man melted.

"Well, I am sure we can make an exception for medical reasons." He gave Wellington a small yellow card. "Hand that to the usher." He leaned forward slightly and added in a hushed tone, "Some patrons insist on bringing their dogs in, so I am sure this is fine."

"Very sly, Wellington Books," Eliza muttered as they walked through the main foyer. She had been genuinely impressed at his acting skills. The glance he gave her was indeed most self-satisfied.

After handing in both their regular and irregular tickets, Eliza and Wellington entered the hallowed halls of the London Opera. The theatre, only opened a year before, attracted enthusiastic crowds for more than just a night's entertainment. This was a place where people wanted to be seen. No one rushed to their seats. Patrons milled about either to admire the fine surroundings or chat and gossip with those they knew. The opera house was a fine confection though: all scarlet and gold, and spiraling curves. The box seats, of which there were six on each side of the stage—grouped in three rows of two—were held aloft by half-naked goddesses. Some of these plainly displayed in a cartouche the crest of the family that paid some exorbitant fee for the privilege of a regular box.

"Do you see it?" Wellington hissed, slipping his arm around her waist and guiding her over.

"Yes, yes." She replied just as quietly.

On the left-hand side, middle row, middle column, the Phoenix painted in gold seemed to shimmer and gleam in the firelight of the theatre's grand chandelier. Currently this box was empty.

"You know," Eliza commented under her breath, "for a secret society they aren't being that secretive."

"Hubris is a wonderful thing, and it is only obvious to us as we know what to look for. But here's the sticky thing—we need to be in the box right above that one," Wellington tapped his case meaningfully.

"Do we?"

"Absolutely." His expression brooked no further discussion. Whatever he had in that mysterious case of his, he was certain.

"Very well," Eliza snapped open her fan and turned away ready to make the impossible happen . . . as usual.

"Darling," the Archivist pulled her close, "do hurry back," he said for the crowd milling around them. Into her hair however he murmured, "Please don't kill anyone."

With a charming laugh, Eliza moved off. *He really*

doesn't know me—Harry would realise exactly how far I would go. She sighed as she slipped her way through the crowd. It was an easy enough thing to do really: stand at the entrance to the box seats, tickets in one hand, her handkerchief in the other, and look pitiful. She only had to stop two groups of people before finding the right ones.

A tall old man wearing a smart evening's ensemble and his diminutive wife in a bright blue dress stopped when she asked politely, "Excuse me, but are you in Box Seat Five?"

"Why, yes," he replied.

Eliza held out her own tickets, her lip trembling a calculating amount. "I was wondering terribly if you would mind swapping with ours."

The gentleman looked down, "But these are—"

And that was when Eliza's acting chops kicked in. Turning, she pointed over to where Wellington stood in the crowd, looking lost amongst strangers. "I know, they are perfectly good box seats, but my husband . . ." She flinched. "Well, he has an awful temper and I was supposed to get Box Seat Five." Eliza fixed them with a pleading look. "He is very particular."

He looked between Eliza and Wellington, his eyes fogging a bit as he asked, "Particular? Dear lady, I fail to under—"

Eliza drew in a breath and shook her head, "No, no. It is quite all right. I should just . . ." And her voice trailed off. She felt her eyes tear up as she spoke with plenty of tremble and fear, "This is my fault and I should bear the responsibility. Thank you."

"Henry, dear," the wife chimed in, "I'm sure the view is more than adequate at this sweet girl's seats."

"Oh, that is so kind of you, madam," Eliza said, pursing her lips tight as if to keep from sobbing, "but no, I have failed as a wife and should stand for my shortcomings."

Both of them gave a start. The wife took Eliza gingerly by the arm. "My dear, these are just seats at the opera."

"Yes, but he is most . . ." Her voice faltered, and after the moment lingered to where things felt most awkward, Eliza lightly traced her cheek with the backs of her fingers and added, "insistent. But no, it's all right. I am sure I will enjoy tonight's performance. It will tide me over in the future."

They both gasped. Eliza brought the kerchief up to her face and gave a muffled sob, thankful the fine lace and embroidery hid her smile. It had been too long. Eliza so loved her work in the field.

"Give her the tickets, Henry," the wife insisted.

The man's shoulders fell, but surrender the tickets he did.

Eliza was about to leave when the woman caught her arm. "My dear, I want you to have this. Please. I insist that you make it a point of joining us for next week's meeting."

The card shook in Eliza's hand.

Clapham Committee for Women's Suffrage
Felicity Hartwell
7 Ashburn Grove

"I hope to see you there," Felicity said, giving her arm a tight squeeze.

The laugh was in her throat, but Eliza managed a tight, wavering, "Thank you."

There were other ways she could have played them, but that had been fun. Eliza strode back to Wellington with the swapped tickets in her hand, giving a long, heavy sigh of satisfaction.

"Everything all right, darling?" he asked, his eyes darting around the room.

A little tilt of her head was all she gave him before leaning forward, whispering in his ear as he had to hers. "They'll never find the bodies."

As he went to ask her whatever she had done, Felicity Hartwell of the Clapham Committee stepped free of her husband and struck Wellington hard against the arm with her fan. "Brute," she snapped, loud enough for attendants and opera patrons to hear.

Wellington looked at the older couple for a moment, then back to Eliza who oddly looked terrified of him.

Then, once they were gone, Eliza's fearful expression melted away to one of mischievousness.

The conclusion was obvious and he let out an annoyed huff, "Well then, shall we take our seats?"

Eliza smiled sweetly. "One moment, dear," and then she turned him about towards the box seat bearing the crest of the Phoenix Society. "Our friends are arriving, and I would quite like to have a look at them, quick and fleeting as it may be."

"Very well then," he nodded, casually looking away. "Please, do not dally."

Laughing and lightly touching Wellington's shoulder, she was able to get a reasonable glimpse out of the corner of her eye at the occupants just arriving. "Two men; one elderly, one in his late twenties to perhaps thirties. Two women. One elderly, smartly dressed, the other in her middle years." She tittered as she added, "The second woman is in dark blue and wearing enough diamonds to drown an elephant."

"I wonder if she will get to keep them," Wellington chortled back as he took Eliza's hand and led her towards the box-seating entrance, "knowing your love of fine gems."

"Oh, dear, dear Wellington, what do you take me for?" She sighed and gave a polite laugh as she continued, "I am merely an agent in service to Her Majesty."

"And the benefits are most evident, from the looks of your apartments."

"Are you critiquing my refined lifestyle?"

"Merely observant." He chuckled.

Her fan snapped open as she allowed herself to be led through the crowd. "You know, if I didn't know better, I would swear we were actually married."

"I can't think of anything more off-putting," Wellington placed his hand in the small of her back as he continued, "than being married to a walking armoury. You, my dear Miss Braun, are a living, breathing advocate for bachelorism."

Unfortunately they reached the usher and Eliza had to swallow a comeback on that particular jibe. When the attendant opened the door, she glided into their recently acquired seating with all the meekness of a proper English wife.

Once the door was closed, Wellington laid his valise on the floor behind his chair, flicked out his tails and sat. His eyes were on the stage. "I have heard this production is quite magnificent."

Eliza glared at him, but it was quite ineffective since he didn't even glance her way. "I hope you have a good explanation for having us be situated *above* our prey? The usual practice is to be in line of sight."

"I know that," he replied mildly.

"So you are going completely against Ministry protocol?" She didn't enjoy the realisation that her tone was a little bit like that of a fishwife.

"It seems that way, doesn't it?"

Eliza's corset wouldn't let her sit any other way but straight. If she'd been able she would have slumped in her chair and glared at him.

Dammit, now the orchestra were tuning up.

"So, what do we do now?" Even to her ears, her voice sounded petulant.

"Now," Books said with evident amusement, "we wait."

"Oh." And the houselights dimmed. "Lovely."

It wasn't going to be. She knew this. This was, after all, opera.

CHAPTER SEVENTEEN

Wherein Mr. Books Reveals His Device and Our Daring Duo Engage in a Spot of Proper Eavesdropping for Queen and Country

Opera is an acquired taste, and no two productions are the same. Beyond the core basics of the art, opera offers a wide variety of possibilities both for the visual and aural senses. An opera by Mozart will not have the same emotional range as one from Puccini; and as lovely and lush as Bizet's music is, there are few composers that can capture the epic grandeur in the same way as Wagner. So it is with Verdi and his operatic treatment of Shakespeare's cautionary tale of ambition. Through his sweeping arias, powerful chorus numbers, and staccato movements, Macbeth's rise and fall from power took on an even more ominous quality between the haunting melodies of the witches and the prophetic warnings of ghosts and evil spirits.

As Wellington's eyes drifted from the image of Macbeth and his wife plotting to kill Macduff's family to his sole companion in Box Five, his smile widened. Agent Eliza D. Braun looked ready to throw herself out of their exclusive seats.

"Do you know what would be a lovely addition to this production?" she asked, her frustration simmering underneath a marginally thin layer of concealment. "Dynamite. Lots and lots of it."

"Miss Braun," Wellington chided lightly, trying very hard to quell his amusement. "Remember that we are here for Queen and Country. Keep in mind the task at hand. And besides," he said, tipping his head back as he reclined slightly in his chair, "this is culture at its peak. Refined tastes for refined palates."

"It's *opera*, mate," Braun seethed. She watched the stage for a few moments, and then growled, "I know enough Scotsmen to know that if a group of men were wandering across the moors screeching like this lot, they'd be tossed like cabers back here to Pommyland."

With the scene drawing to a close, a light applause rose from the house. Wellington joined in. He looked over to Eliza who was considering her fingernails.

"Oh, do make an effort," he said over the applause.

"I don't like encouraging such behaviour," replied Eliza, her disinterested gaze returning to the stage as the scene changed to the hills of Scotland. She sighed heavily before whispering, "I'm still a bit confused as to what we are waiting for."

"We are waiting for one of the constants in our world, Miss Braun," Wellington assured her. "At the end of every opera, there is the grand finale, where the music continues its gradual crescendo, the tenor and tempo rising ever so gradually for that pinnacle of dramatic tension, that moment of anticipation—"

"Welly, are you talking about opera or about sex?"

His next words caught in his throat. For a woman of higher tastes and seeming refinement, this woman could be utterly crass.

The grinding noise ripped in both their ears, and Wellington's gaze narrowed on her.

"That," Eliza whispered harshly, "was *not* me!"

It came again, not as loud at last time but still as grating. Both Wellington and Eliza looked out over the audience, their collected attention rapt with the opening of Act Four. They did not hear the slight rattle. Wellington looked at Eliza, this time motioning with his head to the box beneath them; a few minutes more, and just at the end of the music's decrescendo came the light, relaxed rumbling.

Someone in the Phoenix box was snoring.

A voice from the box whispered harshly, "Ye gods."

"Yes, Father always did complain about the snoring," they heard in retort. "Help me move her to the back. Otherwise she will attract attention."

Wellington stood, smoothing out wrinkles in his coat that were not there. Eliza watched him carefully as he undid the ties of the curtains, casting more of their visible seats into shadow. Her eyebrow crooked as he offered him her hand. For a couple, such as they were posing to be, lowering the curtains after the show's opening usually insinuated one's boredom with what was happening onstage and therefore devising other entertainments, discreetly of course.

Doing my part to perpetuate the illusion, Eliza thought with a smirk as she slipped her own lace-decorated hand into his. *Apologies, good thespians, but this is for Queen and Country.* Together, they disappeared into the shadows of their exclusive seats.

"Are you ready?" he whispered, crouching low as he slid his suitcase between them.

"Ready for what exactly?"

The locks snapped open, and the top half of the case split and folded back, "A bit of modern technology in the field."

The music was now beginning to pick up in its pace, and this was Wellington's cue. From his inside coat pocket he produced a set of brass keys, one of which he turned over to Eliza.

"On my cue," he said, inserting the key in the opening closest to him. His head bobbed a bit as he kept time with the music. "Eliza, the—key—in—the hole—if—you please . . ."

She quickly slipped her key in place, and waited. More voices were joining in, the violins building in their tempo. Wellington kept time with the musicians, and then gave a sharp nod to Eliza. Their keys turned, and—as Wellington had timed it—the brass sounded in full, the voices and strings giving way to the call of trumpets, trombones and tubas. This "call to arms" from the orchestra effectively drowned out the hiss of steam jetting out through the two escape valves. Now Wellington could see her curious smile clearly in the glow of the two glass orbs that pulsated to life. Gears now spun and clicked, keeping time with Verdi's musical creation. The amber glow illuminated the device well enough for them both to see a small control panel collapsed against the clockwork apparatus, and two long coils with cylinders at their respective ends flanking the contraption. One of these coils Wellington handed to Eliza.

"Welly, what in the name of God is this thing?"

"In good time," he said, pulling the control panel down and away from the whirring device. "Right now, we must remain quiet. This will be hard enough to filter out the opera."

"This device can filter out opera?" Eliza grinned. "I love technology."

Wellington shushed her as he pulled from the machine a small cone attached to a coil that ran back into the heart of the machine. With the cone cupping his ear, he motioned for Eliza to place the extension in her hand down to the floor. He pressed one of the keys on the pad, and the amber glow darkened slightly. Then he reached inside the suitcase and worked an array of knobs connected to the chassis. The device's gears sped up slightly, but still the ticking kept perfect time with *Macbeth*. He waited a few beats and, on the call of Macduff's troops at Birnam Wood, adjusted the settings. Quick blasts of steam were once again smothered by the orchestra.

"And the other microphone," he whispered, his own cylinder reaching parallel to Eliza's, "here."

He then returned to the case and gave a second array of

knobs their own adjustments. "And now, this should . . ." The glow of the two orbs turned a rich honey, outshone only by his bright, radiant smile.

"Should what?" hissed Eliza.

Wellington removed the attachment from his ear and offered it to her. "Have a listen."

Eliza stared at the cup cradled between her fingers, its coil seeming to tug back when she lifted it up to the side of her head. She immediately pulled the earpiece away from her, as if it burned her skin. She caught her breath, and looked at Wellington, her mouth slightly agape.

"The *auralscope* is still a prototype, Miss Braun," he admitted, "but with the music being as intense as it is and their voices coming in that clear, I think it is performing admirably."

Her soft laugh was her reply for the moment. Wellington assumed that his invention was a rousing success, at least for her. He afforded himself a small accolade. The auralscope was a real accomplishment, he knew that; but to impress Eliza, considering all she had seen? It felt good but he kept his elation in check. He would know for sure exactly how successful its field test had been after they returned from the opera.

Extending from the auralscope its second phone, Wellington joined Eliza in her eavesdropping on the box underneath theirs.

"I assure you," the male voice insisted, his voice in the auralscope clear but still seasoned with pops and crackles like distant fireworks, "we could be at a performance of the *1812 Overture* with cannons and my dear mother would remain in a deep slumber. I'm just astounded at her stamina tonight. Normally, she's out by Act Two."

A second voice chimed in. "To discuss this matter in a public place, though?"

"That has always been a weakness of yours, Simon," a third male voice sneered. It seemed that the gathering in the Phoenix Society's private box had picked up a new guest.

Wellington produced from the pocket of his evening coat his journal, unlocked it, and jotted down the name "Simon" while the conversation continued.

"A lack of daring," mocked this voice. Not Simon. Not identified, yet. "When our time comes, people will look to this box not out of curiousity but out of reverence. At present, we are simply set dressing. There will come a day when they will look for approval from whomever occupies these seats."

"So, my dear associates," the first voice resumed, "concerning recent events—"

"Damn sloppy, if you ask me," the voice which had spoken of "reverence and approval" interjected.

"Stuff it, Barty!" Simon shot back. "I had the situation well—"

Wellington and Eliza both shot glances to each other as the voice grew faint. Setting his pencil aside, he adjusted the dials, earning him a quick hiss of steam . . .

Unfortunately during the opening of "Una Macchia Qui Tuttora." Christina Nilsson's tormented Lady Macbeth and a few strings. Nothing more.

Both of them froze. Eliza's eyes motioned to her earpiece, then she slowly shook her head. He found he was holding his breath. Wellington was convinced, irrational as it was, that those underneath them could hear the ripples of his muscles and the sweat running down his back as he slinked over to his own headphone. He placed it to his ear, his heart tightening in his chest, pleading for a breath. The silence coming from the box below them was chilling.

"Are you sure you want to reconsider that answer, Mr. Ross?" the still unidentified voice asked.

"Smith was no longer a threat," he insisted. "Besides that, he was one of our order."

"Then let this be a hard lesson learned, Mr. Ross. The Society had been breached, and we never did find out where that gentleman's loyalties resided. Once upon a time I would have agreed with you, that the matter had been handled. If only our former initiate had not received that visitor at

Bedlam, I think Doctor Smith would have enjoyed the performance right where you sat."

"Go on, Simon," a female voice implored. Timid as she sounded, there was a touch of entitlement in her tone. "Admit that my Bartholomew tidied up your mess. After all, it was you and Christopher who invited that man into our ranks."

They finally had a full name: Simon Ross. That left "Barty" and the dominating voice that seemed to be the leader.

"Olivia," Bartholomew cooed, "as sweet as your gesture may seem, I do not need you gallantly coming to my rescue." His voice dropped, but carried such intensity that both Eliza and Wellington could still hear him. "Do my family name proud by being silent and speaking when addressed, like a good and obedient pet."

Wellington's eyes immediately went to Eliza. She was not looking at him. Her gaze was boring through the floor. He glanced at her fingernails, digging into the carpet of the theatre's box. With a long, slow exhale, Wellington wrote down the names "Bartholomew" and "Olivia" as, after a moment's pause, the conversation continued.

"Mr. Ross, I am not holding you responsible for what happened. You all found him charming, educated, and a most suitable candidate. Had I not this God-given suspicious nature, he would have charmed me as well."

"And we are thankful, Doctor Havelock, for your insight into this matter," Simon admitted.

The small peep escaping Wellington earned him a sharp, cold look from Eliza. He immediately scrawled out on a blank page of the journal a name that warranted all capital letters, an underline and several exclamation points:

DOCTOR DEVEREUX HAVELOCK!!!

Eliza looked at the name, shrugged, and returned her attention to the conversation underneath them. Crestfallen, he did the same.

"But to assassinate your colleague in such a—"

"That man," Havelock snapped, "was hardly my colleague. He was a member of the Society, but he suffered delusions, and these delusions nearly exposed our plans to that rogue attempting to infiltrate our ranks."

There was the *click-click* of a door opening, followed by the rustle of fabric.

"Ah, and here is our late arrival." Havelock then spoke as if the language of the opera were second nature to him. "*Buona sera, Signora. Come sta?*"

"*Ci sentiamo bene*," a low female voice cooed through the crackle of the auralscope, "*E voi?*"

"*Ah, mi va bene, ma lei sa come stanno le cose.*" He chuckled, and then switched tongues. "But where are my manners? *Signora* Sophia del Morte, may I introduce you to Simon Ross, your companion for the night."

"*Signor* Ross," the voice, luscious and exotic, conjured romantic images for Wellington; and he longed for her to grow tired of the opera and simply read poetry out loud. To him. "I must apologise for my tardiness." A pause. "I was delayed at my previous appointment."

"Oh, that's quite all ri—*ouch!*"

Her gasp hissed through the auralscope. "*Oh, mi dispiace terribilmente*, forgive me. I think this family heirloom I wear needs tending to from a jeweler. It has been in my family for years."

"No matter," Simon replied. "Simply a pinprick. Sometimes, well-loved heirlooms can develop jagged edges if not worn often."

"Yes," she said, a soft laugh falling from her, and trilling into her words. "This ring was my grandmother's."

Wellington pressed the cup harder against his ear as he returned to the auralscope's control panel. He needed cleaner sound, particularly of the Italian. Something about this new arrival made him uncomfortable.

"So," Havelock interjected, "I assume things have been taken care of."

"Only a few loose ends to contend with, but well in my control."

"But I thought, for what we are paying, you would resolve loose ends, not keep them under control," Bartholomew hissed.

Wellington felt that dryness in his throat grow worse. He had just finished writing out the Italian woman's name, staring at it intently as her voice filled his headphone.

"They are, *Signo—*"

"Lord," he snapped.

"Of course," the *signora* replied—a reply that strangely felt like a warning. "Lord Devane, when you first hired me to . . . how you say . . . *resolve these issues*, you failed to inform me of the gentleman and lady who gave chase in the streets."

His shoulder suddenly stung. He looked up to see Eliza waving madly to the journal, and then a thought screamed at him: *Write down his last name!* Why was he so distracted by this newcomer?

"A most unfortunate turn of events, I agree," Doctor Havelock added, his voice accented by a strange knocking sound. "Do we know anything more about them?"

"Welly," Eliza whispered, breaking the thick silence of their own box, "What is that?"

"Some sort of interference," he muttered. While still holding the phone to his ear, Wellington reached inside the auralscope for a row of tiny levers. Steam hissed softly with each lever engaged, but still the knocking sound continued. "I'm trying to isolate—"

"I thought you were subtle!" Bartholomew snapped. "First, Smith's practice and now this?" He let out a disgusted snort. "Olivia, tend to this."

They heard a rustle of fabric and the knocking sound subsided. It was not completely silenced, however; and now something else filtered into the conversation. There was a gurgling, and what sounded like someone practising proper theatre etiquette in smothering a cough.

Over a tiny whimper which, considering the pitch, had to belong to Olivia Devane, the conversation resumed.

"There was a rider, as well, wasn't there?" Devane asked. "Killed on the scene by the woman driving the hansom?"

"That is not a loose end, Lord Devane, to concern yourself with," del Morte interjected, her tenor decorated with annoyance. "That was a disagreement between professionals, and it will *not* happen again.

"If you want me to take care of that somewhat adventurous couple, however," del Morte continued, her demeanor neither wavering or faltering as someone gasped for life beside her, "my compensation will have to reflect as such. I was not made aware of any other parties involved."

"We became aware of them at the same time you did," Havelock said. "We can only assume they are of the same organisation that our candidate was a part of."

"But why now?" Devane asked, "That was nearly a year ago?"

"It does not matter how much time has passed," countered Havelock. "What matters is this unknown couple are looking into his previous affairs, and at present we are giving them a trail to follow, aren't we?"

"I would not call it a trail," del Morte interjected. "Your servants will take care of *Signor* Ross here after the theatre has closed. I took care of that poor wretch in the asylum just tonight. Considering he did not receive any visits for months, I doubt if he will be discovered by his allies anytime soon."

Eliza's earpiece bounced against the thin carpet. Wellington grabbed her arm, only to have it wrenched free from his grasp.

"No, Eliza," he whispered sharply.

"That bitch killed Harry!" she hissed through clenched teeth.

A thought flashed through his mind that Eliza, for all her faults, remained a disciplined agent. In the midst of her turmoil, she still managed to keep her voice down. Her hands in her fine opera gloves clenched, and her eyes grew glassy, but there was still an undercurrent of control.

"I know, Eliza, I know, but we cannot just barge in on them. If we do that, it stops here and Harry's death—his desire to know the truth—will be meaningless." Wellington locked his gaze with hers on grabbing her wrist and whispering tersely, "Pull yourself together, Agent Braun, and see this mission through."

Wellington felt her tremble in his grasp, but she remained in place when he let her go. Eliza swayed slightly, and with some shock he saw that her eyes were filling with tears. A small muscle was flexing in her jaw, telling that she was repressing the normal female reaction to howl or scream. His colleague looked fragile in that moment—as if the wrong word or gesture could crack her. She swallowed, took a long, wavering breath, and brushed the nascent tears out of her eyes before they could fall.

Carefully Wellington raised the headpiece to his ear. Below, the rustling of skirts was only drowned out by a barely perceptible chiding.

"Olivia, compose yourself, eyes front. Do not shame my family any more than you normally do." Another snort of derision, and then, "For God's sake, wipe the spittle off your face."

"Eliza," Wellington whispered, "the assassin's leaving."

Her eyes were dry and hard. "What about the rest of that lot?"

"They are still in the box, watching the show. I don't know if they are done or not."

"Keep listening, Books," Eliza said, making for the door. "I'll meet you back here."

"And just what are you intending to do, Agent Braun?"

The knives seemed to appear in her hands from thin air. She cast a glance over their sheen and smiled. "Introduce myself, from one professional to another."

CHAPTER EIGHTEEN

In Which Miss Braun Treads the Boards and Brings the House Down

After the torture of opera it felt good to Eliza to be out of that damn seat and hot-footing it away from the screaming on the stage. How Wellington could be so entranced with that glorified caterwauling was beyond her.

However, all discomfort at the performance had melted away when she had heard the assassin's words. *Harry was dead.* It mattered little to this Italian bitch that he'd been nothing but a shattered wreck in the asylum. So long as Harry had been alive, recovery was always a possibility, no matter how small the chance he could have been rescued from madness. The edges of guilt pricked her as she wondered if she should have just broken him out of Bedlam and nursed him back to health on her own. Considering her own ghosts and the brother she left in New Zealand, tending to Harry would have been a delight. Perhaps the chase had become everything, and she'd lost sight of why she was here at all.

Yet she could not seek vengeance—not yet. They had to follow the clues, just as Harry had taught her. Then, and only then, would there be a reckoning.

In the civilized atmosphere of the opera, pretense had

to be maintained. This situation required a little stealth, so she didn't bolt out the door as her impulses demanded. Eliza shut the door firmly between herself and Wellington, leaving him to tidy up his contraption. Where in the blue blazes he had got that thing? The clankertons in the armourey were damn tight with their toys, and Books wasn't exactly their chum. Another creation of Welly's, like the Archives' analytical engine? So very strange.

That little mystery would have to wait however—there were villains to track down. Admittedly, tailing anyone in the height of evening fashion was not an ideal scenario, but like all good field agents Eliza knew opportunity was not a thing to be squandered. This was as close as they had got to those who had destroyed Harry. The only thing better would have been if he were here to share in the moment.

No, I must not think of Harry. Not yet.

Just outside their box, Eliza kicked off her satin high-heeled shoes and left them next to the door. Wellington could not fail to stumble over them and pick up after her. He better—those shoes had cost her a pretty penny in Paris.

She crept down the stairs, her ear tuned for the quarry from the box below. An usher passed her, heading up, and his eyes turned in shock to the length of calf she was showing, but he was too well paid to question the goings-on of the gentry. Still he did let his gaze linger there several good moments longer than propriety would have dictated. When he made eye contact with Eliza, she granted the boy a wicked wink before continuing down the stairs.

When the door to the box below popped open, she flattened against the curve of the stairwell, her heart picking up its pace. Forcing herself to breathe slowly, Eliza waited to see if she would have to beat a hasty retreat up the stairs, or if the occupants of the booth would exit along the corridor. However, the sound of footfalls did not approach. After giving them a moment, she darted down the stairs and glanced to her left where the corridor led to the front of the theatre. It was empty.

A quick glance to her right afforded her a glimpse of skirts dragging across the carpet. It would seem the conspirators, while flaunting their Society's influence, were not above employing stealth when desired. As this one had just eliminated one of their own, stealth would have been paramount.

Her hands dropped for a second to pat the outside of her skirt: the tiny, compact Derringer 1881 pistols were still there, strapped, one to each thigh. For a brief instant she considered bailing up the whole Phoenix group—but she knew without backup that was foolish.

Also there was thought of Doctor Sound's reaction of her unsupported accosting of the London's upper crust—this stayed her usual inclination to rashness. Wellington, unfortunately, was not here to appreciate her restraint.

No, she decided, the best thing was to identify them, maybe trail the lead suspect and find out where he was staying in London, watch who went in and out to meet him, pinpoint the rest of the conspirators that way. "*When in doubt,*" Harry's voice whispered in her mind, "*back to the basics.*"

If she truly went back to the basics, she wouldn't be merely tailing this bitch. Her stiletto would be in hand, and Eliza would be avenging her fallen partner and friend.

Damn theatres—this was just like at la Scala: always too many cursed entrances and exits. A glance up and down the corridor told her that everyone else in the boxes was too entranced by the opera—another indication of inbreeding amongst the aristocracy, as far as she was concerned.

A shadow moved in the corner of her eye. She froze, held her breath, and watched the Italian disappear behind the door labeled "Backstage." Five seconds—that was all she gave Harry's killer before sliding in after her, the two blades Wellington caught a glimpse of back in her grasp.

Verdi's score nearly knocked her down as it enveloped her. It was so damn hard to hear anything with the opera still wailing on, and the commotion within the wings was even more distracting. This close to the action of opera,

Eliza had no way of avoiding it, and the music seemed far more frantic as apparently they were reaching some sort of crescendo. Stagehands were watching the action with hawk-like intensity, at the ready to lower the curtain. Ahead, a crush of actors bearing weapons and foliage waited for their cues, seeming to trickle on to the main stage to join their cast in the wall of music and voice. Lowering her head, Eliza did her best impression of just another actress—hard work considering the dress and jewelry she was wearing.

Luckily there were few here who could spare a moment to complain.

Then a hand grabbed her hard by the hair and spun her around, the swiftness of the attack sending her blades out of her grip and into the darkness. This was no stage manager: the grip was too confident, too professional in its application. Spinning under it, Eliza managed to break the hold, and found herself face-to-face with a neat little woman, at least a head shorter than her. A beautiful olive-skinned face framed by waves of dark curls smiled at her, but not in greeting. Anticipation, along with a touch of challenge and outrage, blazed in the woman's eyes. Eliza had not actually seen the assassin from the doctor's office, but instinct, experience, and the grip on her hair confirmed this. She was the kind of lady who might grace any salon in Europe: comely, intelligent and whip-smart—that and the knowledge of dynamite she had applied upon Doctor Smith's practise made *Signora* Sophia del Morte a lethal combination.

The grip Sophia briefly had upon her also told Eliza something else—this was not a woman who relied merely on explosions. *Very well then*, Eliza thought with detachment. *Neither am I.*

"A little early to leave your seat, madam." The assassin's accent was even lovelier in person.

Around them, actors readied themselves and stagehands flitted back and forth between props and set machinery. The basics Eliza had pledged to follow just got very complicated.

"And a little early for deaths at the opera," she snipped

back over the building. Motioning back towards the box seats, so there could be no mistaking her point, Eliza crooked her eyebrow. "Macbeth doesn't drop dead for another five minutes at least, Sophia." *Take that, bitch, I know your name.*

The assassin's smile was thin and deadly as she heard her name on Eliza's lips. "Not so cultured to know the curse of the Scottish play?" She took a daring step forward, and Eliza just as quickly danced back to keep the distance between them. "It is very bad luck to speak the name back here. But from your manners at Charing Cross, perhaps you enjoy tempting the fates, yes?"

So nice to be recognised for a day's work. "Why not retire to the lobby, exorcise your bad luck?"

"And miss the grand finale?" Eliza chuckled. "Tosh."

She seemed to shimmer before her. The assassin was fast. *Damn* fast. Eliza felt hands grabbing her fashionable billowing sleeves in order to swing her about, slamming her into the mass of pulleys and ropes at the side of the stage.

It would leave bruises, but that would hardly be enough to keep Eliza down. She pushed herself off the wall, grabbing the assassin by the arm. This time it was Eliza who spun her opponent to face her, immediately backhanding the dark woman in a sweeping, graceful follow-through. While the backstage area was not well lit, Eliza could just make out crimson marks her rings had left across the assassin's skin. *First blood to me*, she thought with pride.

However, she felt a chill when the assassin grinned back as trickles of red ran down her sculpted cheek; and then she threw a slap with her open hand.

Her ring, Eliza realised in the moment. *Bloody hell, her ring.*

Eliza just caught the blow before it landed, snapping her fingers around Sophia's wrist and jerking her opponent forward and around, her hand still clamped tightly about it. Quickly she turned the assassin's hand back and upwards, causing Sophia's fingers to splay wide. Eliza removed the deadly ring from the olive finger, avoiding the curl of points on its underside, and then with a shove, she slammed Sophia into the backstage rigging, her impact sending ripples along the taut hemp holding Macbeth's stronghold together.

Both of them were encumbered by their dresses, though the Italian's was a far simpler affair, less bulky, without the frills and ruffles of Eliza's green evening gown. As they circled each other warily, Eliza sized up Sophia. Eliza pushed back a whisper of doubt. So far, she had been lucky. She knew in their grapples that she was the more muscular of the two of them, but this creature possessed the same skills as she did.

Out of her now slightly ragged hairstyle Eliza drew the stiletto with the peacock hilt, knowing the smile on her face was triumphant. However, when the assassin produced two similar long, thin blades out of her own elaborate coiffure, her smile was just as fierce.

A shadow moved in Eliza's peripheral, but it was moving away from them both—a stage manager running for help perhaps? They did not have long, not that Eliza needed time. The curtain would come down on Harry's killer before it came down on the Scottish king.

With a graceful lunge and the flutter of fabric, the assassin drove both blades in separate arching angles, one for Eliza's head, one for her gut. Eliza blocked the attacks, one with the thick bracelet of diamonds on her right wrist, while she caught Sophia's head assault in a bind. Sweeping the attack aside, Eliza's target opened before her and she jabbed forward just as Sophia slipped past the wrist block and thrust.

Both women froze, their eyes studying each other, looking for the sign of their blades' purchase. Then, on the sound of metal clattering at their feet, they looked down.

Their blades now vibrated gently on the floor, empty hilts merely resting against where their kidneys would have been skewered.

"Who *is* your seamstress?" They asked simultaneously.

When no answer came, they pushed against each other,

casting their useless weapons to one side. The similarities between them Eliza found distracting: a love of explosives, relishing the chase, and an appreciation of strengthened undergarments. If Sophia del Morte were anyone else, they would have been friends.

With Sophia's second blade catching the dim light that crept backstage. Eliza silently added "concealed weapons" under their mutual interests.

The knife flicked forward several times, back and forth, like a mongoose's head attempting to strike a cornered cobra. When Sophia lunged the third time, Eliza finally took advantage of her fashion sense; using her large, billowy sleeves to entangle Sophia's weapon within the layers of fabric. The assassin pulled back only to lose her balance and fall forward—

—right into Eliza's waiting fist.

The agent pulled on her sleeve a second time and again connected with Sophia's nose. The third punch she dealt was building on her euphoria, so much that she did not notice Sophia's head angling itself to connect with Eliza's bottom lip and chin. The assault freed the blade from the folds of fabric, but Eliza's other hand shot out and clamped hard around Sophia's wrist. In the shadows, they wrestled for the remaining weapon, tugging it between them, like two adolescent girls fighting over a bauble. Eliza's elbow connected with Sophia's chin, and the knife flew free and slid from the wings and out onto the stage, disappearing beneath the feet of Birnam Wood which now reached ear-splitting heights for Verdi's grand finale.

Both women scrambled after it, Eliza yanking Sophia's hair to pull her back, only to have her own balance thrown off by a knee striking her reinforced corset. Eliza pushed against the floorboards, wrapping her arms around the Italian, and cursed softly on the feel of warm amber light against her face.

The cries from both actors and audience confirmed it—their fisticuffs had stumbled into Birnam Wood.

Eliza shoved Sophia further downstage, and growled, not at her opponent but at the horrified chorus around them both who were *still* singing and dancing the grand finale of Macbeth's fall. *The show really does go on*, she thought to herself as her eyes narrowed on Sophia.

The assassin was on her feet, backlit by the footlights, and suddenly—the screams of opera patrons now joining the tenacious performers on stage—her skirts fell away. The Italian's undergarments were hardly proper as they were fashioned of leather and suede. Eliza could easily see the shadows of four small pistols, two strapped on each thigh. There was a strong possibility there were some blades secured there, too.

Eliza charged for her, but Sophia—with her newfound freedom of movement—spun around and delivered a well-placed kick that Eliza felt through her armoured corset. She fell hard against the floorboards and the knife was next to her. Her fingertips did not even brush its hilt before prancing feet kicked it away from her to the other side of the wings.

A scream of outrage from onstage whipped Eliza's head up, and immediately the agent rolled to one side as a pike, most likely liberated from an actor by Sophia, bore down on her. The whirling display was a little unnecessary, but something that Eliza probably would have done as well. She however would have possessed the wherewithal to know that prop weapons—while still dangerous—were not built for a full impact against a solid surface like, say, a performance stage.

On hearing the pike connect with the floorboards and then shatter, Eliza rolled back and kicked, sending Sophia once more into Birnam Wood. Pushing her skirts down and pulling herself back to her feet, Eliza liberated a Scotsman from his sword. It was more of a club than a true sword, but it would have to do.

She then heard Macduff's aria stammer. Not missing a beat, the orchestra continued as the actor moved to the centre of the stage, while Sophia lifted up Macduff's sword. Her smile said this one was nice and heavy—a genuine weapon used for stage combat. The movement may be choreographed, but the weapons were more than authentic, making for high drama on the stage and trouble for Eliza.

Why did it have to be Macbeth*? Why not* Figaro, The Barber of Seville, *or* 1001 Arabian Nights*—something with pillows*, Eliza thought as the sword cut for her head. She went to block, but her cheap replica shattered on impact. The momentum of the swing and the broadsword's less-than-balanced weight did manage to throw Sophia off kilter.

"Next time, mate," Eliza quipped to the actor she had taken the weapon from, "land a bigger part than third git from the left!"

The chorus of men scattered, parting like the Red Sea as the now snarling Sophia whirled the blade over her shoulder and charged. Ducking and dodging, Eliza tried her best to keep beyond the broadsword. How had the woman got so damned lucky to land by the blasted lead of the opera? This weapon could pierce the corset or take her head off, and then there would be far less stage blood required for the finale.

Many of the cast were fleeing to the wings in Sophia's wake, but others held out manfully, singing hard but shooting worried glances at the battling women in their midst. Eliza would have loved to take a moment to appreciate this dedication, had she not been so bothered in fighting to stay alive.

"Bloody hell!" Eliza snapped over the orchestra's crescendo. The pistols were still strapped on her thighs—merely a fabric fold away. Reach in, draw, and aim. She could have at least knocked the wind out of her. A headshot would have been asking for far too much. All she needed was a moment where Sophia stopped charging.

Sophia lunged, missing Eliza and tripping forward.

That was when Lady Macbeth screamed. Right in Eliza's ear.

No one could fault the singer's professionalism. *Good*

lungs, Eliza thought as the blast of sound knocked her to the lip of the stage. In the disorientation of prima donna, music, and mayhem, the train on Eliza's skirts caught her foot, turning her less-than-graceful stumble into an ungainly tumble. Behind her, three footlights smashed as Sophia swung with the sharp blade.

The sword was about to connect with Eliza's neck when another stopped it short. Eliza let loose a relieved sigh at the sight of Macbeth's sword.

She'd always loved the Scots.

Sophia was about to take the actor's head but Eliza knocked her back with another elbow to the nose.

"Thanks, mate," Eliza said, taking the *lead* actor's sword this time. "If I live through this production, first pint's on me!"

The broadsword felt a trifle light in her hand and not as balanced as she would prefer; but it was, at least, made of metal. Both women glared at each other along the edge of their blades, the smell of gas stinging their eyes and nostrils. Around them the gamest of the performers continued singing, though probably not at their proper marks. Eliza and her opponent had cleared a large circle of the stage, making for quite the show closer.

Sophia glanced up to the audience as if for the first time realising where they were. The corner of her mouth twitched.

"I do not like to conduct business so publicly," the assassin shouted over the music that still refused to end. "And frankly, darling, this would be so much easier if we were in breeches—what say we reconvene when we are both better attired?"

Eliza would have made a snappy comeback to that one, all the while easing her left hand to one of her pistols—when the other woman turned away as if it was already decided. A heartbeat, a split second, passed to see what her real game was: a lit torch from one of the terrified chorus was now in Sophia's grasp.

Damned authenticity was going to make a very big mess.

The flame fluttered as it flew through the air, towards the shattered footlights. *Hell's Bells!* The front of the stage, swimming in gas, didn't require dynamite to explode as the doctor's Charing Cross practice had; but lit so much closer to her, it propelled her a further distance than what had knocked her and Wellington to the ground. The heat was a slap against her body—throwing her into the orchestra pit. The concussion echoed through the opera house, helped by the most excellent acoustics.

Eliza, her once magnificent dress torn and blackened, found herself sprawled across a deeply surprised pair of cellists and their instruments. They eyed each other for a moment, both uncertain of the proper etiquette of the situation. The silence after the explosion was monumental—but for the first time in the evening, no one was caterwauling. The musicians were utter gentlemen, mutely helping her slap out the burnt patches in her once glorious evening gown.

Cautiously Eliza levered herself out of their awkward embrace and stood up gingerly. Readjusting her hair as best she could she glanced up to the box seat. Yes, there was Wellington, and his face was white as Italian marble. It was true—people's jaws did hang open if you shocked them enough.

Eliza gave him a little wave, just as scattered applause began to run through the theatre. Then she called up to him. "Sweetheart, please be a dear and call for the carriage, I think the show is done."

CHAPTER NINETEEN

Wherein Mr. Books Learns a Little of Colonial Hospitality

A melody tripped off the tongue of Wellington Books as he strode through the streets of London, the brisk walk doing his body and his brain a world of good. The tune, he knew, was an echo from the previous night's performance of *Macbeth*, and the quick spring in his step he also knew was on account of what he had heard last night with help from the auralscope.

His shoes scuffed up to the large, ornate door to Eliza D. Braun's building that looked far more impressive in the daylight than it did at night. In fact, the entire building appeared far more imposing than he remembered it. In the back of his brain, a flurry of curious queries percolated. As he made his way up the stairs where he had so recently carried his colleague, he felt the cylinder in the satchel bump against his hip. When he reached his fellow agent's apartments he rapped the pattern of Verdi's "S'allontanarono!" on the knocker.

The door opened, and Wellington took a step back. The face that greeted him was certainly not that of Eliza D. Braun: freckled, cherub cheeks that were naturally rosy, and a riot of red hair barely contained under a mop cap.

And the voice that spoke was definitely not of the colonies—more like the East End. "Mister Wellington Thornhill Books, Esquire, is it?"

He cleared his throat. "Um . . . yes?"

"Very good, sir. Do come in. The Missus is waiting on you in the parlour."

The Missus? In the parlour? It must have been one of the rooms he hadn't yet explored. Already the vastness of Eliza's abode was impressive. "Ah, yes, of course." Wellington then snapped his fingers and smiled. "Alice?"

She returned his recognition with a polite grin and a curtsey. "Thank you, sir, I am. Now if you will be following me please."

"Certainly." It was only when the maid turned away that Wellington observed the sheath of gleaming, articulated metal that made up both her legs and the slight limp to her gait. In the silence of the hallway he could make out the sound of tiny pistons pumping.

"Quite remarkable," he commented, while fighting back the urge to lift Alice's skirts and examine her prosthetics more closely.

With the light of morning filling the apartments, Wellington could now enjoy the details of Eliza Braun's private sanctuary. She was hardly a woman of the time, but apparently ahead of it as she collected what seemed to be fine antiques and figurines. How did a woman as abrasive as this field agent from the colonies nurture such fine . . . taste?

Alice called into the sunlit atrium, "Pardon me, mum?"

"Alice," Eliza's voice replied, gently, but still with a firm tone. "Try again, please."

The house servant paused, cleared her throat, and then said, "Pardon me, Miss Braun?"

"Excellent. What is it?"

"Mr. Books has arrived."

"Lovely." She sighed. "Show him in."

Alice curtseyed again and beckoned to Wellington to join her in the parlour.

"I must know—*oh my God!*"

He had wanted to hold an interrogation of his own on the subject of her remarkable maid and her luxurious dwellings, but what was waiting for him in the atrium scattered any notion of thought.

Eliza's voice echoed in the small sunlit room for a moment, along with the gentle lapping of water. "Books, if this is the first time you have seen a woman in a bath, then I believe we need to get you out in the field more."

Wellington turned towards the voice, his eyes covered. "Perhaps modesty is regarded differently in the colonies, but if you would—"

"Welly," she snapped, "when you're in my apartments, you are on New Zealand soil." She motioned to the table on the other side of her bath. "So pull up a chair and enjoy breakfast. Unless . . ." And on her pause Wellington peered through his fingers. She was pursing her lips in that way that made him uncomfortable and uncertain all at the same time. ". . . you care to join me?" she cooed, flicking the bathwater.

As he tried to formulate an appropriate answer, someone guided him to a chair. The almost imperceptible hiss of pistons told him it must be Alice. Slowly his hand came away from his eyes, and indeed there she was, hardly fazed by the notion of her mistress enjoying a bath on the other side of the breakfast table. "There you are, sir: toast and marmalade, two eggs, and bacon. Help yourself to kippers or kedgeree. I'll bring you a fresh spot of tea."

With another slightly awkward curtsey, Alice returned to the kitchen.

"A lovely girl," Eliza started. "Reminds me a bit of me when I was her age."

"Did you have brass legs as a wee hellion?" he asked while buttering his toast.

His fellow agent shot him a wicked smile. "Ah, you noticed that, did you? Another fine example of Axelrod and Blackwell's work." Eliza's gaze tightened on him. "A little off-the-clock job for me. One Sound knows nothing about, and I would prefer to keep it that way."

Wellington finished his mouthful of warm toast before replying. "I see, but where did you find her in the first place?"

"The workhouse." Eliza adjusted the towel across her eyes and stirred the water lightly. A delicate bergamot scent tickled Wellington's nostrils. "She was injured in a mill accident, but even so, she attempted to pick my pockets. I offered to help her, but only if she came to live with me here as my maid. And seeing as the Ministry's clankertons were wanting to try a new trinket Sound showed little interest in, it worked out well for all involved. I think it has been a few years since anyone has shown Alice this kind of generosity, and she's coming along well in her education."

"Education?"

"Oh yes." Eliza nodded, churning the water lightly as she listed, "kitchen duties, proper addresses, marksmanship, table manners. These are the things a lady should—"

"I'm sorry," Wellington interrupted, "but did you say *marksmanship*?"

Eliza sighed again. "Tosh, Welly, surely you don't expect a woman of my profession and my occupation not to have another line of defence at home?"

Wellington took a few bites of egg, and then helped himself to a kipper as well and only then did he note the additional setting next to him. Then another. Looking over the round table, there were quite a few place settings all waiting patiently for guests.

"Do you expect other callers during your morning bath time?"

Eliza chuckled. "No, but I do have a later appointment—some people I want you to meet."

Wellington finished a mouthful of fish before asking, "Will you be joining me, Miss Braun?"

Her fingers idly flicked at the water. "I've already enjoyed my morning's repast, so don't mind me," she said, giving a slight sigh as she felt sunlight creep into the atrium. "The Phoenix Society can wait until after breakfast."

Wellington, even with the extraordinary setting of his meal, started feeling hints of comfort wrap around him. Languidly soaking in the exquisite tub, Eliza seemed as if she was about drift off to sleep.

"Do you often bathe in your atrium?" he finally asked.

"Only when I have been in knife fights and tossed into orchestral pits," she quipped, her eyebrows wiggling playfully above the cloth draped over her eyes. "I'm a young, healthy woman, Welly, but I hurt right at the moment and a hot bath is what is needed. I hope you will allow me to inconvenience you for a few moments in my own home."

She had him on that point. Her home. New Zealand soil. "Considering the previous night, you have earned this, Miss Braun. As you say," he replied, turning his attention to the morning's newspaper next to his plate, "you are a young, beautiful woman."

"Healthy," she corrected him. "I'm a young, healthy woman."

Wellington paused. "Yes, that's what I said."

He noticed the lull in conversation, and looked up from the paper to see Eliza in her bath, her smile something akin to the Cheshire Cat. "Now, while I was getting to know our favourite bitch," she began, "what did you, my clever Archivist, find out?"

Wellington set down his silverware for a moment and dabbed his mouth clean as he reached for his satchel. "Eliza, perchance would you have a gramophone?"

"Certainly. Just ask Alice to bring it in here." She snickered. "Do you need an orchestral background to give me the news of what you heard?"

He opened his mouth to reply, but Alice appeared around the corner with the promised fresh pot of tea.

"Actually, Alice," Wellington said, returning her bright smile. "Would you be a dear, and bring Miss Braun's gramophone in here."

"Certainly, sir." She settled the teapot on the table and trotted out on her mission. Soon there came a soft clatter from the main room and Alice reappeared pushing a handsome gramophone, its clockwork gears, tiny engine, and giant twin bells opening like lilies in springtime.

Eliza spoke. "Thank you, Alice. My clothes, if you please?" The maid then gave a quick hiss-accented curtsy and retreated to the master bedroom.

"You must know how much I enjoy bathing to music," Eliza slipped lower in the bath.

Wellington clicked his tongue as he flipped a switch on the polished brass panel, extending from the casing a tray of gears surrounding a cradle big enough for the cylinder he produced from his satchel. The object snapped easily into the device, and retracted with a soft hiss.

"And what is the musical selection for this morning's bath and breakfast?" Eliza asked.

"Verdi's *Macbeth*," he replied.

Eliza was silent for a moment, and with a deep breath, she sighed. "I think I know how that ends. The Witches put him up to the deed, they leave him out to dry, and the Scottish king loses his head to Macduff."

"This," Wellington spoke over his winding up of the gramophone, "is a new adaptation. In this performance, Macbeth gallantly saves the life of a Maori warrior who blundered onto the stage during the finale."

The water sloshed, and this time Eliza was correcting him in earnest. "I was born in New Zealand, Books," she began, her tone definitive, "but I am not Maori—at least, not by blood."

Extending the player's arm earned him a quick high-pitched burst of steam, its mechanisms *clickity-clacking* softly. He slowly moved the main control lever towards him, and flinched at the rapid notes blaring out of the twin bells.

"Audio controls are to the left, Books!" shouted Eliza over the clamor.

Much like he did with the auralscope, his fingertips adjusted the controls, slowing the gramophone's gears. Between hisses and rapid clicking, the garbled noise shifted and changed, taking on the semblance of voices deep in conversation while Verdi's *Macbeth* continued in the background.

A swell of water, and then Eliza asked, "That contraption of yours *recorded* last night?"

Wellington turned towards her. "The auralscope did just—" His voice stopped as he caught sight of Eliza's posterior just before disappearing behind the towel.

"Did just what, Welly?" she asked, pulling it tight around herself as she slipped behind a blind. "Are you all right?"

"Sorry, was fine-tuning the—volume—on your gramophone. I'm not used to your"—he cleared his throat—"fixtures." He quickly turned back to the gramophone, trying to force away the startling—and yet delightful—sight he had just caught. Trying, and failing. "The *auralscope* cannot only home in on certain sounds, it also records them for posterior—I mean, *posterity*—on standard-sized phonograph cylinders."

"Truly?" Eliza asked. "That is—" And then she grunted, "*Fascinating!*"

"You all right back there, Eliza?" he asked.

"Just—fine." Then Wellington heard the slip of fabric being pulled tight. Alice, it appeared, had returned. "Just—suiting up—in my battle dress. Do—continue!"

"With the quality of earphones you have here, the conversation should ring as true as we heard—"

"*Olivia*," Lord Devane's voice crackled through the bells, "compose yourself, eyes front. Do not shame my family any more than you normally do. For God's sake, wipe the spittle off your face."

"This was the point where you had left," Wellington said, "before you ended the evening in your usual, subtle manner."

"Don't start, Welly," Eliza warned from the other side of her dressing screen.

There was the click of a door closing, and Devane's voice spoke again. "Is the enlistment of that . . . *foreigner* . . . truly necessary, Doctor Havelock?"

"She is merely a tool," he replied coolly, "and like many tools in a work shed, some are very dangerous if not handled properly. You may wish to keep that in mind when addressing her, Bartholomew." Havelock's voice paused, and then, "So, Olivia, you were about to run down the suitable initiates for this weekend?"

"Yes," she began, her voice still trembling a bit. There was the sound of a breath, and Olivia seemed to have her composure again. "There are four couples we are looking at this weekend. There are the Collinses, Barnabus and Angelique. No children. Barnabus has been referred to by some in the Brethren as a man to watch."

"His specialty?" Havelock asked.

"Finances. Straight from University, he was snatched up by the firm of Harcourt and Sturgis." She paused, and then added, "No formal introduction had been made."

"Harcourt and Sturgis, without an introduction?" It was the slightest of inflections, but Havelock sounded genuinely impressed.

"Then there are the Fairbankses, Harold and Dahlia. Delilah's family owned a distillery."

"So Harold earned his fortunes from the wife? How then did he catch our attention?"

"Harold expanded the distillery to other locations. Acquired two more that were his fiercest competitors. One sold his family's label outright. The other . . . fell to ruin. A scandal involving the competitor and his secretary. His *male* secretary."

"A man of ambition," he conceded.

"A man of substance, as well," Devane added.

"The St. Johns. Seems they are doing quite well for themselves in textiles. Lovely people, what we know of them."

"Lovely people, are they now, Olivia?" Bartholomew hadn't snapped at his wife; but even with the crackle and tinny quality of his recorded voice, Devane's syrupy contempt was evident. "Tell us more of your assessment then. You think they will make a delightful addition to the Society?"

Wellington noticed there was something truly deafening about the soft pops and hisses coming from the cylinder rotating in time with the cogs of the gramophone. For an instant, he imagined how thick the silence—even with the power of Verdi's opera in the background—must have been in the Phoenix Society's box seat.

"Finally," Olivia continued, her voice lacking its earlier confidence, "there is Major Nathaniel Pembroke and his wife, Clementine. Two children. A decorated soldier from a long lineage of military men, dating back to Queen Elizabeth."

"Really," sneered Devane. "Was his ancestry a powder monkey at the battle with the Spanish Armada?"

Olivia cleared her throat and said, "He says his line reaches back to a commander four ranks under Drake. Records do show one of the vessels captained by a Lord Pembroke. The Major has been upholding his family's reputation quite well. May become the youngest soldier to reach the rank of General."

The laughter was coming from where Havelock sat. "A fine collection of initiates, which will make for a good weekend."

"A good weekend," agreed Devane, "provided the wives are not as priggish as the last lot were."

There was a sudden stutter from Olivia, and then a scream bled in from the background. The music seemed to accompany the improvisational drama occurring on the stage.

"Well now," Doctor Havelock began, any interest in the opera notably absent from his voice, "it seems that Jossepe has incorporated a few rewrites since the last performance."

Bartholomew's tone betrayed that he was teetering on the edge of panic. "Shall we call it a night? Brandy and cigars at our apartments?"

"Yes," Havelock said, "that would be lovely."

With a clatter of cogs and a soft hiss, the needle lifted free of the cylinder, and the cradle slid outward, as if it were a kitten imploring for another aural snack. Wellington's eyes glanced over his notes and then looked up to Eliza, now dressed in her regular fashion choices: a blouse and trousers.

He wondered if he was becoming used to her strange taste in attire. "As you can hear, it seems that the Phoenix Society is going to be enjoying quite the weekend."

Eliza rolled her neck from side to side, and then twisted at the hips. She then spoke over her shoulder to Alice, now carrying wet towels. "Capital work, Alice. Now, please keep an eye on the door, and show my other morning appointments in when they arrive, if you please."

"Very good, Miss Braun." She curtseyed, and repeated the gesture to Wellington. "Mr. Books."

He watched Eliza consider the girl with what appeared to be pride; a rather unusual sentiment to bestow on the hired help, but there it was, clearly in her face.

"Welly," Eliza began, pouring herself a tea as she did, "you seemed quite excited concerning this bloke Havelock. I wondered if your zeal wouldn't have tipped our hand early."

"Naturally, I couldn't expect you to know, considering the different circles we move in."

Eliza scoffed. "Oh this had better be good."

"It depends on your interests." And he produced his journal from his coat pocket. Setting it by his breakfast plate, he took a sip of tea before continuing. "Doctor Devereux Havelock is a pioneer of modern technology. It would not surprise me if Axelrod and Blackwell have not attended one of his symposiums for inspiration."

"I take it you have?"

"Several of them, as a matter of fact. The man is a genius, his work in engineering unmatched. He was the principal scientist in charge of the 1887 restoration of Big Ben's internal workings. In 1889 he designed the HMS *Pegasus*, a new class of airship that reset all records for commercial air travel. In that *same* year," Wellington said, feeling elated at this particular memory, "Doctor Havelock developed, designed, and successfully launched the HMS *Mercury*. I remember watching in my telescope its impact in Mare Serenitatis. I have seen some of his work up close and his articles concerning theoretical studies in automation mechanics is fascinating. Some of his ideas are a bit incred—"

"Welly," Eliza, interjected, "you lost me at Big Ben. So for those of us less stimulated by the sciences, give me a more simplistic picture. How does a man of letters and prestige as Havelock find himself as the grand master of a secret society?"

He paused, staring into his teacup for a moment. "Well, yes, Doctor Havelock is quite the genius, but the reason you may not know his name alongside other scientists like Tesla and Mad McTighe is that only a few years ago he started writing columns that had nothing to do with the sciences. The tenor of these commentaries was more . . ." He shook his head and drained his tea. "Political."

"Ah, the more critical looks at Queen Vic and her empire?"

"Yes, but they didn't just stop at the House of Parliament and House of Lords. He was calling for outlandish changes in our society."

"Such as?"

Wellington shuddered. "Imagine a governing body that judged your standing by your family history, to which families you married into, and your upbringing? Havelock was commenting on such matters as the purity of minor nobility bloodlines. He called for a total restructure of the English class system, and the complete and total expulsion of colonials from Mother England."

Eliza nodded, taking a sip of her now sweetened tea. "And you hold in high regard this stall whimper?"

He looked up from where he was helping himself to another cup of tea and his eyes narrowed.

"*She would object*," jeered the voice of his father. "*She's a colonial. First against the wall when the Empire opens its eyes and pays attention to its own people.*"

"I respect and admire the man's works in the sciences. I find it tragic that a mind so brilliant is marred by such"—he noticed the teacup in his grasp was rattling lightly—"idealistic politics. His railings of anarchy, sadly, pushed him out of favour with the Queen; and while rarely invited, he is still welcome to speak on the sciences. His name just is not as widely publicised as once was." Wellington took a sip and added, "And the invitations have been fewer and fewer in the past years as his talks tend to stray off-topic."

"And somewhere in all this, Havelock has taken up the mantle of the Phoenix Society."

"Yes," Wellington then motioned to the gramophone and said, "and it is Initiation Weekend for them."

"And it would seem that with the untimely death of Simon," observed Eliza, "there is an opening in the ranks."

"Two, I would think," Wellington said, flipping between pages of his journal. "I doubt they would be screening couples and families like this to replace what had become a loose end for them."

"So you don't think Simon's death was a setup?"

"Oh, it was most definitely arranged, but not an arrangement of a rash nature." Wellington unlocked his journal and flipped back a few pages to notes he had made during the night's eavesdropping. "I think the assassin's services were called upon more out of convenience and less out of impulsiveness. After all, she was in town. Why not add to her fee for additional services?"

Eliza's lips curled in distaste. "You make it all sound so proper, Books."

His eyes flicked up from the journal to her own gaze. "Don't mistake my clinical review of facts and theories for approval, or even the slightest admiration for that matter. I find this Society's actions and demeanour, in particular of that cad Bartholomew Devane, reprehensible. I am merely making a conclusion based on what I see. The Italian . . ."

"That bitch," Eliza seethed.

Wellington felt his jaw twitch before continuing. "The *assassin* had been hired to eliminate the good doctor and—"

He swallowed. How could he chastise her for feeling? It made perfect sense.

No, he reprimanded himself sharply. *You have to detach yourself from this case and the people therein if you wish to solve it properly. Otherwise, your work will be for naught.*

"The assassin had been hired to eliminate Doctor Smith and Agent Thorne. The assassin might as well have taken care of all loose ends, so why not Simon as well?"

"Yes," Eliza repeated. "Why not?"

He furrowed his brow. "Eliza, how could you have known?"

"I should have."

"Oh, of course you should have, seeing as you have this amazing ability to see into the future." Wellington shook his head. "It was an unsolved case, buried in the Archives and, yes, forgotten. It would have remained so . . ." And his voice trailed off.

"Go on, Books," she insisted.

Wellington felt a tightness in his throat. "I'd rather not."

"You were doing so well trying to make me feel better, I'm sure, but the truth is—"

"That the reach of the Phoenix Society is far greater than we may realise it. Agent Thorne would have suffered the same fate if he had shown a recovery from his condition." He stared at her through the heavy, awkward silence. "Now we must focus on the matters at hand. In particular, this initiation weekend."

"Already thinking of that, Books." Eliza topped off her tea from the pot. "I have associates on the way who will be assisting us in what I'm assuming is your plan."

Wellington gave a short laugh. "You have no idea what my plan is, Miss Braun."

She grinned at him. "You are intending for us to be there for the initiation, aren't you? Inside surveillance, disguised as—no wait, let me guess—servant staff, or possibly delivery men as there will be a grand turnout for this weekend, yes?"

A burn tingled across Wellington's cheeks.

"Yes, Welly, very textbook. A ha'penny to you for remembering so well the basics of your Ministry training. However, what will we discover about this company of ne'er-do-wells while we are scrubbing dishes, mopping floors, and changing bedsheets?" Eliza cast a glance away from him on hearing the door open, and her smile softened immediately. "While I do not claim to be a perfect field agent, I do have a penchant for finding information in the most unconventional of manners."

With a thunder of small footsteps, a powerful odour of sweat, muck, and other less attractive human scents assailed Wellington's nostrils; and when two children entered, his eyes watered fiercely. When the remaining five ran into the parlour, Wellington made for a window. He was thankful Eliza, her own face rather pale, was also joining him in ushering in fresh air. One of the creatures looked to be nine or ten while another could pass for fifteen; their weathered skin, however, attempted to rob them of their youthful looks. All except a little girl who looked like a sweet cherub in desperate need of a good wash down. In fact, all they seemed to have in their possession, along with the threadbare clothes on their backs, was a vibrant, youthful energy, optimistic even in their dismal existence.

"Boys! And Serena!" Eliza called, openly recoiling at their collective bouquet. None of the children took offence. "What have I told you about bathing?"

"That it's something we should do?" the youngest boy asked.

The oldest lad shrugged, "Sorry about that, Miss Eliza. I know what we promised and all . . ."

She crooked an eyebrow. "And the rest of you lot?"

All of the children looked at the floor. The little girl—Serena, Eliza had called her—shuffled her feet, sticking her bottom lip out in a pout. She seemed heartbroken.

"So I see." Eliza nodded curtly. "Well then, hot baths for the lot of you . . . after breakfast this morning. You're going to need your strength. So go on, tuck in."

The children could not have moved faster if crushers were on their heels. They had scooted themselves up to the table when Alice reappeared with more platters of piping-hot eggs, porridge, bacon, kippers, kedgeree, and toast. Eliza smiled, her eyes twinkling slightly as she watched the street urchins wait for their plates to arrive before them.

"Remember, don't eat too fast lest you make yourselves sick," she said.

"Yes, mum," they answered in muffled unison, their cheeks already stuffed with food.

The little girl forced down her mouthful before the others, and said, "Miss Eliza mum, may I go first with a bath once my breakfast's all done?"

"Certainly you may, Serena."

The child lightly chewed the lip that was displayed in her earlier pout, and then asked, "Can I have my bath with them roses like yours?"

The boys chuckled, but were quickly silenced by a look from Eliza.

"I'll have Alice prepare the bath accordingly."

Wellington looked at the agent, perplexed.

Eliza shrugged. "It's a touch of hero worship."

He was about to speak when a subtle waving of a hand and a slow headshake held his words at bay. Whatever she was up to, these urchins were part of her plan.

"Oi!" another boy exclaimed, his mouth full of bread and marmalade. " 'Oo's the toff?"

Wellington raised an eyebrow, both to the child and Eliza's stifling a laugh. He frowned, hoping her plan would begin sooner than later.

"This is Wellington Books, Esquire. He is my . . ." She considered him for a moment, and then continued, ". . . my new partner. We are working on a rather tricky puzzle."

"Saving the world again, Miss Eliza?" the elder boy asked.

"Perhaps, Christopher. I'm hoping you and the lads will be able to answer the call of Queen and Country."

"Yes, mum," chirped the youngest boy before slurping down the rest of his tea.

"Mr. Books," Eliza motioned to the children, "these brave subjects of the Queen are the Ministry Seven, my eyes and ears on the streets of London."

"As well as your chamber pots, by the collected whiff of them," Wellington snipped.

"Oi," barked a lad next to Christopher, "come over 'ere and say that! I'll knock yer blimmin' teeth in!"

Eliza inclined her head to one side. "And Liam could do so, I assure you." She looked back to the boy and motioned him to resume his seat. "Mr. Books has a few names I want you all to hear." She then turned to Wellington and asked, "Would you mind reading off the names of the couples we just heard about?"

Wellington looked between them, his mind spinning. What was this woman up to? He cleared his throat and read off the Phoenix Society's candidates, his brow furrowing more with each one.

"All right," she began, "out of those four couples, who would you all consider to be the thickest?"

Without looking up from their food, the Ministry Seven replied in unison, "The St. Johns."

Eliza looked over at Wellington for a moment and then asked, "Are you sure—"

"Coo, mum," replied a skinny lad who, while filthy, managed to have the most brilliant blond hair Wellington had ever seen. "That couple makes Alice's porridge here look like chicken broth."

She bent at the knees to get closer to the boy, bringing herself to his eye level. "Now, Colin, why do you say that?"

"Trust me, mum," Christopher said, his mouth now twisted into a wry grin. "It's no exaggeration. If the St. Johns are out, it's a good day for us."

"Here now," Colin piped in, seemingly enjoying the attention. His smile widened as he returned back to his host. "We had them picked for right marks and so we went to liberates them of the lady's purse. I make the grab but my fingers do brush the lady's wrist. She turns on me and I knows I's a gonna'."

Eliza nodded. "Indeed."

"I'm supposed to try and make for the catch," Christopher said, "when the lady says 'Well now, fancy that, lad. I has a purse like that!' Then the bloke turns about and I's expects him to grab at Colin and take him to the peelers. He looks at the purse and then at Colin, and then says 'Well, now, I say, you can't have the purse without the matching gloves, son, so here.' He then hands Colin a few quid so he can go and buy the gloves. 'Don't keep your mum waiting, lad.' And they left Colin there, standing with the purse and the quid in his hands."

"Sounds as if you were just lucky," Eliza said.

"Tell him how many times, Colin," prodded Christopher.

"Three times." Colin said, "Each time, I was in a hurry and the like. Just saw the purse, went for it, and didn't realise it was the same couple. As God and St. Peter are my witness, each time, we had the same words. The very same."

Wellington scoffed. "Good Lord, that is thick! They must be extremely well-off to attract the Phoenix Society."

"Right then," Eliza said with a nod to Alice. "Ministry Seven, your country calls. I have a job for you."

Everyone paused in their wolfing down of food, and smiled to one another. All except for Serena who continued to stare at Eliza with wide-eyed admiration. From the elation in all their faces, it was going to be an exciting day for them.

"All thickness aside, this one is going to be tricky, but don't worry," she said as Alice returned to the parlour, "I'll make this worth your while."

Alice cradled in her arms a wide, flat box that opened with a soft creak. Wellington felt his eyes pop wide at the sight of the diamond necklace catching the light filtering into the atrium. With a slight shrug, Eliza presented the stunning creation to Christopher.

"What's the game then?" Christopher asked.

Eliza tipped her head to one side and then smiled, "Blind Man's Bluff?"

"Blind Man's Bluff?" asked Colin through a mouthful of pastry. "Nah, peelers will see right through that. Three Blind—"

"—Mice isn't right for the St. Johns," interjected the little girl, her expression now shrewd and impeccably sharp. "Sorry, Miss Eliza mum, but if this is a game of Who's Your Father? I'm thinking we're going to need something a touch more . . ."

"Sophisticated," interrupted Eliza. "You're absolutely right, Serena."

That acknowledgement made the little girl as radiant as the sunlight dappling the atrium's tiles.

Wellington found himself completely void. "Pardon me, but while I wait for your charming Comedy of Errors to conclude, I think I'm going to help myself to a fresh pot of tea."

A huff caused him to start. "You stay right there, gov!" insisted Alice, her legs giving a few quick puffs as she headed for the kitchen. "I'll have the kettle on straightaway." She made no complaint that this was the *third* pot of the morning.

Eliza's mouth opened as if she were about to correct Alice again, but Liam's words cut the silence quick. "Oi, I think the toff is onto something."

"I beg your pardon!" Wellington spluttered.

"Wha . . . ?" Christopher's eyes went back and forth between Colin and Wellington. "You can't be serious, Liam? The Comedy of Errors? It's been a while."

The soft laugh grabbed everyone's attention. Eliza rested her hands on her hips, considering Wellington as she said, "If what I have heard tell, the Comedy of Errors was even before my time. Makes it all the better."

"Wow," another boy whispered before saying to Liam,

"if Comedy of Errors was before mum's time, that makes it—"

"Another word from you, Callum," Eliza warned without looking at him, "and I promise you'll get the same rose-scented bath as Serena."

The little girl giggled.

"That's gonna get complicated, mum," Christopher said, his expression was wary and uncertain.

"An admirable bluff, Christopher," Eliza said, smirking slightly, "but the compensation you have already pocketed should very well cover the risk."

"She's got you there, Chrissy," sniggered Colin.

Christopher hissed at his compatriot, but his sharp turn caused the jewelry to clatter in his coat. The younger was absolutely right.

The whistle from the kitchen caused Wellington to straighten his stance, his hands lightly brushing the wrinkles from his trousers. "You lot have me at a loss, but I have a fresh cup of tea on the way so I honestly don't care. Miss Braun, when you are done holding class, perhaps we can—"

"Welly, the Comedy of Errors is a confidence game where the Ministry Seven here will carefully and cleverly plant stolen merchandise in the St. Johns' home, and then, with thespian skills rivaling the performers of the London Opera, will mistake the St. Johns for their ringleaders. While they are detained by the Constable, the evidence and eyewitnesses will mount high enough that the St. Johns will be detained for all the weekend, while you and I pose as the St. Johns at their scheduled appointment."

"Miss Braun," Wellington raised one hand, "the St. Johns will most likely call their solicitors and slip as quickly out of jail as these urchins get them in it."

"We are detaining a couple hand-selected for joining a secret society—a secret society that take their desire to stay secret very seriously, as we have recorded here. Do you think the St. Johns, socially challenged as they are, will complain? To anyone?"

Wellington opened his mouth to speak, paused, and then cleared his throat. "Good point, Miss Braun."

"So, Ministry Seven, do we have an accord?"

"I like it when you talk all fancy like that, mum," chuckled Colin.

"When do you need it done, Miss Eliza?" Liam asked.

"Before lunch, hence the big breakfast." Christopher gave a nod to Eliza. "Well done. Now finish up, and Alice will see *to your baths*." All of them groaned in protest. Eliza continued, "At one o'clock, I'll expect you back here with proper announcement cards and, as you're loading up their apartments, keep an eye out for this emblem. Books?"

Wellington flipped through the journal and came across a sketch he had made of the Phoenix Society emblem. The children gave it a hard look and then turned back to Eliza.

"If you find anything bearing that, bring it to us."

"As it is on your word, Miss Eliza," Christopher stated, "it's done."

"Excellent. We will see you here promptly at one. Now finish your breakfast." Eliza looked over to Wellington. "Shall we?"

Wellington blinked. "Shall we what?"

"Work. You know, Welly? The Archives? Keeping up appearances and all that?"

He blinked again. That's right. It was Friday morning. "Oh, well, yes."

"I'll even make you a fresh cup of tea at the Ministry."

Wellington rolled his eyes. "Lovely."

As they walked to the door, he cast a glance over to his shoulder.

"The Ministry Seven?" He shook his head ruefully. "I suppose I do not need to list how many protocols and regulations you have violated just in *giving* them any such name!"

"Sometimes, Welly, when an agent is in the field—particularly when the field is the Great City herself—you need to break convention. The Ministry Seven are very good at what they do. They have provided Harry and myself with fabulous intelligence. We gave them that name so that they might feel included. A part of the great machine that is the Ministry of Peculiar Occurrences."

"But Ministry Seven?" Wellington exclaimed. "Miss Braun, the Ministry would hardly endorse—"

The impossible woman actually wagged her finger at him. "They are *my* sources and do outstanding reconnaissance for your Queen and Country. Besides—there is never a situation that diamonds can't fix." She clicked her tongue suddenly, as if remembering something. "I would have liked to introduce you to all of them. I missed the twins. Those two are so bloody quiet. That is what makes them so good at slipping into impenetrable hideouts, you know."

He could see in her eyes she would brook no further argument on the children—he would have to learn to pick his battles. "Which reminds me," Wellington began as he opened the door for Eliza. "That necklace. Where did you ever get a treasure like that?"

"Assignment in Egypt." She sighed heavily. "Raj. He was a lovely man: dark skinned, finely toned muscles, and such romance. And from the gifts he bestowed upon me, he found me rather charming, too."

"Do the *Ministry Seven* know about Raj and your other exploits for Queen and Country, Miss Braun?"

"Oh Welly, I am not that foolish. They are a fine resource and I tell them enough but not so much that they are in any danger. They know they are serving the Crown in their own way when they assist me in cases."

Wellington clicked his tongue in disapproval, feeling his neck growing tender from so much head shaking.

"Besides, the children are not privy to all my secrets," she said with a wry grin, "as you were this morning."

"That is quite enough, Miss Braun," Wellington said, his cheeks burning as he waved for a cab. "I cannot be held accountable for your lack of modesty. I am an English gentleman, raised as such, and you do seem to want to take advantage of that."

"I see," she replied curtly, accepting Wellington's hand as he assisted her into the hansom, "and here I was, worried your gentlemanly sensitivities would be tested on seeing those six battle scars across my back."

"Seven."

Eliza looked back at him, her eyebrow crooked. "Precisely."

Wellington paused, and then lifted himself into the hansom. This was a bad omen for the weekend ahead of them.

INTERLUDE

In Which a Mysterious Woman of Past Transgressions Shows No Honour Amongst Thieves

The sound of silverware scraping against a porcelain plate was the only sound to interrupt Sophia's dinner. Her lifestyle was one of perilous pursuits and outcomes, but the payment assured her of living well and boarding in places that guaranteed many amenities. One of the most appealing for a woman of her profession: silence. Even in the bustling city of London, there were corners of the great city that knew luxury and solitude. Two things most assuredly in her top three favourite things in life.

She enjoyed the mutton served at this establishment. It was, perhaps, the finest dinner she had ever enjoyed. Not as succulent as lamb, mutton could still, with proper spices, sauces, preparation, and cooking times and temperatures, melt in your mouth.

This was such a recipe. Each bite improved on the previous one. And after the week she had endured, this was a well-earned, well-deserved reward. From this corner of her suite, her eyes able to sweep across and take in all of the spacious lodgings, she savoured her late dinner, allowing herself a precious moment to relax.

However, her next bite was interrupted by the sudden rattling of windowpanes. It could have been the wind, had weather conditions not been so still all day long. Sophia shook her head in disgust and cleaned the fork of her dinner before setting it to one side. Dabbing the corners of her mouth with the napkin, she rose, crossed to the offending window and unlocked it. She then reached underneath the windowsill and retrieved a small box she herself had placed there. She considered its lid adornment—a bird in flight emerging from a field of fire—before turning the tiny sculpture four times. Sophia glanced out of the window, paused, and turned the figurine an additional two times before gently placing the box on the sill against the break between the two windows. It played a soft, gentle song as the bird slowly rotated. The curtain she drew closed effectively deadened the music box's tune. She was thankful for that. At first she found music from such boxes charming, but on a fourth refrain, music boxes became something of a grating noise created by a brass comb scraping against a cylinder.

The knock came next. She had expected it to be more forceful.

Her skirts rustled as she crossed the room, the fabric surrendering to silence on stopping by the coat rack where she retrieved her cape. With a final look at her ensemble, just to be certain she was presentable, she opened the door to reveal her contact. *Previous* contact would have been a more precise description, but this unannounced appointment was hardly unexpected. Particularly after the previous evening's events.

"*Mademoiselle*," he said, his natural baritone so very pleasing to her ears.

Pity he was speaking French. He was well aware of how much she detested that language.

"So formal, Alexander," she chided, masking her distaste for his chosen tongue. She craned her neck to see the four men, all similarly attired, watching him and listening intently.

He motioned to her cape. "Going somewhere at this late hour?"

"Actually, yes," she stated. "I have business to tend to."

"Indeed," he said, closing in on her. He seemed to relish being so forward. "You do."

Sophia nodded and took a step back, motioning to her parlour. "Would you and your associates care to come in then? No need to cause a scene in the hallway."

"*Merci*," Alexander said, motioning for the others to follow him into the suite. "I would imagine you would be done with causing scenes for quite some time."

She smiled. "So you heard?"

"We have contacts at the newspapers that includes opera critics."

"And is that how you found me? Your network of contacts?"

"Oh no," he said, his smile wide. "I know your taste in lodgings, remember?"

Yes, Sophia did remember. She also remembered how in this very parlour he tried to charm his way into her bed while briefing her on his private airship's travel times. That attempt to mix their business with his pleasure she had found quite comical.

"It was remiss of me to forget that." Her reply was tinged with the tiniest of laughs.

Her door's lock sounded like a whip crack. She watched Alexander's associates turn away from the door and lock a steely gaze on her. In the light of her apartments she now got a better look at her contact's associates, and regretted it. Two of the men flanking him looked as if they had come from an evening of boxing. Apparently, they had lost.

"I can spare you some time, Alexander," she stated, pushing back the folds of her cape, "but only a few moments, and then I must be on my way. What brings you and your companions here to my lodgings tonight?"

"The Lord of the Manor sent me," he said, his tone a touch louder now that they were in closed quarters.

Sophia rolled her eyes. "The Lord of the Manor? I swear, I do not know why you bother to follow that *pezzo di merda*."

Alexander's glance over his shoulder kept his four compatriots still. He switched his attention to the cuffs of his black overcoat, adjusting them meticulously as he spoke. "*Mademoiselle*," he said with a grin, "if you show such disdain for the Lord of the Manor, why do you continue to work for the House?"

"You know the old saying, concerning fools and money," she retorted. "If fools wish to spend their money upon my person, I will not object. He was foolish to underestimate the opposition."

Alexander crooked an eyebrow. "And just how much do you know of the opposition?"

"A branch of your Monarch's government, it would seem, has been thwarting your organisation's agenda of late. I think that is enough to know of your enemy." She laughed as she returned to her dinner in the far corner of the suite. She took her wine in hand and spoke as she turned to the men in black. "You have employed me on a variety of operations, all of them successful as the goals were crystal clear. At least for me. One target. Eliminate. Disappear. Very little room for error.

"This time, you ask of me to bring back my target *alive*. This target, so my orientation led me to believe, was nothing more than a librarian for a ministry of your Crown's government. It was my own research that enlightened me on this ministry, or at least what little is known about them. What I did find out is they are the only people who have ever stood in your way, Alexander. They are, judging by the very encounters you've had with them, resourceful, insightful, and most of all, tenacious." She finished the wine and gingerly placed the empty glass on a small end table by a settee. "Did you really expect they would simply let the keeper of their secrets disappear without a trace?"

She felt a tiny rush of elation at watching his jaw twitch. Alexander's henchmen, for the lack of a better term, were standing in identical poses; and as they were all wearing fashionable black suits—and a good thing their shared tailor could work wonders with black lest they appeared to be a small convention of undertakers—Alexander and his hired thugs popped out against the cheerful, bright surroundings of her parlour as cutouts. She crossed to Alexander's right and smiled widely. Now she could see all of them.

"Perhaps it was a . . ." he paused, looking over his shoulder once again at the minion closest to him, and then continued, ". . . miscalculation on the part of the Lord of the Manor."

"Miscalculation?" She laughed. "You exposed your base of operations in Antartica!"

"We can rebuild."

"Not if they are watching Antarctica now."

Alexander's frown deepened. "It is a big place."

"And as you build, your construction will create disturbances that will appear far too rhythmic to be dismissed as tremors." She clicked her tongue, sighing with feigned remorse. "Your esteemed House have tipped their hand, my dear."

"Be that as it may," and he stepped forward, his grin somewhat unsettling, "your job remains unfinished."

How she hated surprises. "I beg your pardon?"

"The House of Usher hired you to obtain the Ministry's Archivist," he replied, his grin now a very satisfied smile. "As far as we are concerned, you are still on our payroll."

She nodded. "Apart from the attempt at Charing Cross, did you try again?" His reply was silence. Suddenly his associates' injuries made perfect sense to her. She looked at the fresh-faced gent by the door. "*Signor*, it was most fortunate for you that your dance card was engaged that day." Her eyes flicked back to Alexander. "My condolences for the loss of your man. Hopefully, he was not a blood relation."

"*Mademoiselle*, if you please," Alexander said, motioning to the door.

Her eyes narrowed. "Really? Well, Alexander, as far as *I* am concerned, the job was completed the moment I delivered him to your Antarctic base."

"The job was to deliver the archivist, alive, to the House of Usher." He gave a light shrug, spreading his arms wide. "The House of Usher is still waiting."

"English may be my second language, but you believe that is enough for you to best me in a game of semantics?" She took a moment to gather her wits, and then continued in a calmer tone. "I delivered him. You lost him. This matter is strictly your concern and," she said, motioning to the injured associates, "it would seem that while your House staff is proving ineffective, their confidence levels have hardly abated." She sighed and said, "*Se all'inizio non hai successo, ritenta ancora.*"

"The Lord of the Manor insists you return to our employment immediately."

On those words, the two bandaged thugs stepped forward.

How sweet.

She then heard the music box, the tune now playing in a key a note higher than before. The final refrain.

Alexander went to speak, but the small explosion from the concealed window caused him to start. The scream from outside was drowned out by a successive ringing of metal against metal, and then Sophia's hands shot out from underneath her half-cloak. The gear wheels split into two after passing Alexander. Two lodged in throats and a third buried itself deep in the chest of another henchmen. The last man tending to the door had a moment's luck as the lethal disc embedded itself in his shoulder. (She thought he had moved a step to the left, and chastised herself for not compensating.) His luck lasted only a moment as a bullet entered from underneath his jaw.

Her second pistol was trained on Alexander's forehead.

She kept him rooted to the floor as she approached, her thumb pulling back the pistol's hammer.

"We were discussing semantics," she said, her voice still steady and charming—as if she were serving him Amaretto at her villa.

"Now, now, *Signora* . . ." He chuckled, his eyes never leaving the end of her pistol.

Italian. Finally.

"Alexander," she cooed, her accent giving her disdain an even harder edge, "I am so sorry our business has come to this impasse."

"I do think you should take a moment to reconsider your course of action—"

She raised one eyebrow. "Says the man on the dangerous end of a gun."

"Are you certain you wish to dismiss the House so quickly, considering your compensation in the past?"

"You think I am acting rashly? Look around you." She sighed, her weapon showing no signs of faltering. "The House has been outbid."

He lowered his hands slowly, "*Signora*, think of your reputa—"

When the bullet struck his forehead, it snapped his head back, not lifting him off his feet but sending him back a couple of steps.

He had just started to fall when she strode over to the singed curtains. Sophia turned her face away as she parted them, airing out the acrid smoke from the token courtesy of her current employer. While the glass had merely cracked, it had been the heavy metal windowpanes that had blown outward, knocking the Usher associate on her ledge off balance. She looked down to the city street to see his twisted corpse. The would-be assassin would have most likely crept into her suite and dispatched her while she slept or some similar setting where she would find herself in a rare moment of vulnerability. The House of Usher could not be faulted for their valiant efforts.

In the distance the shrill of a policeman's whistle sounded. Soon enough, Scotland Yard would be pounding into the hotel. She needed to leave now.

Her bags waited by the door. She placed the dark hat on her head and secured its ribbons underneath her chin. In the mirror she glanced at the table where she had been enjoying her dinner. Her mouth watered slightly.

It was such a shame that she would leave this particular hotel. The chef here was truly a master.

CHAPTER TWENTY

In Which Eliza Braun Is Introduced to Britain's Upper Class and Finds Herself Beyond Words

Eliza loved New Zealand, and she hoped after a few years of exile her past transgressions would be forgiven or forgotten so that she could return there. She loved the wild landscape and even wilder mix of people—yet there was one accomplishment that her beloved outpost of the Empire did lack—one thing it could not possibly do as well as Old Blighty.

The Britons for all their pretensions knew how to build fabulous country houses. As they drove up in the fine carriage hired especially for this weekend, Eliza tried not to crane her neck and stare too obviously at the Havelock estate. It was a hard building to ignore, spread across the low hill in all its baroque glory. Hundreds of windows gleamed in the late afternoon sun as they clattered up the tree-lined avenue. Domed towers crowned both the west and east wings, looming over the surrounding spread of topiary gardens. It was the kind of place she had read about as a child, never imagining that her life would allow her to actually see one; but while this was hardly her first palace, considering her travels, there was a classic splendour about the Havelock estate.

"Now Miss Braun," Wellington intruded, somewhat thankfully, into her recollections. "We will have to tread carefully here."

Eliza sighed and dropped back into the swaying carriage seat. "You certainly know how to destroy a moment, Welly." *Thank you.*

Sometimes he couldn't contain his wince at her nickname for him. It was why she persisted in using it. The twist of his lips actually gave his handsome face something of a different character; perhaps a man he might have been in other circumstances.

"We're intruding upon a secret society with possible overtones of hedonistic natures."

Eliza smiled sweetly. "Sounds like fun."

"Miss Braun," he snipped, "what I mean to say is you will want to blunt your colonial edge, just a bit." She crooked an eyebrow at him, earning her a nervous throat clearing. "If we are to appear as a well-to-do couple, you will have to adopt a more . . ." He swallowed. Eliza lifted both eyebrows now, her look one of patience and sincere curiousity. " . . . subservient nature."

"Welly," she said, putting every bit of contempt behind the nickname, "I think I have a bit of experience in this sort of thing. Been around the block a few times." A few more times than you.

His mouth opened, but then he immediately sat back in his own seat. It seemed he thought better of whatever reply he was going to make.

Eliza ran her critical eye over him. He was wearing a very fine Savile Row suit, but with the aristocracy it was all about the little details. She fished in her valise and pulled out a small box.

Wellington eyed it with obvious suspicion, but before he could complain, Eliza raised one hand. "You are indeed in possession of a Gieves and Company suit, Welly, but you are rather lacking in one respect." She tugged her partner's wrist over onto his lap, and swiftly removed his rather pedestrian brass cuff links. She then produced from the box an exquisite silver and mother-of-pearl set which she proceeded to add to Wellington's ensemble.

"Who this time?" Wellington grumbled, though he did not tug back his arm. "A baron of a Germanic province? Or perhaps a member of the Czar's inner court?"

"A marquis, if you are curious," she replied sweetly. "They look better on you, however." Now on the other cuff, she crooked a single brow as she said, "As we are talking of maintaining appearances, what of the Ministry? I think I've spent far too much time around you, but I have my concerns about the Old Man being onto us."

"That is precisely why I have our absence for the afternoon taken care of. Provided he does not spend more than three hours at a time in a surprise visit to the Archives, we should be fine."

"Three hours, Welly?" She shook her head. "I don't know . . ."

"Miss Braun, it was all the time we could afford if we wished to arrive here at a fashionable time for the weekend."

"Perhaps. Let's just hope Doctor Sound does not get an urge to research the House of Usher during the weekend. And there!" she said with a nod before settling back into her seat. "Yes, they look far better on you."

Obviously disarmed by her compliment, Wellington said nothing more. As they followed the gravel path around a huge fountain with satyrs and nymphs cavorting in the spray, Eliza noticed that there was no modesty taken by their creator—interesting and possibly telling.

Wellington had not noted it—too busy glaring at her. When he finally broke the silence, his tone with her was different. He sounded colder. Angry perhaps? "We only have the barest clue what we are stepping into, and if these people discover that we are not initiates into their vile club, things could get . . ."

"Sticky?" She knew she was smirking.

"Uncomfortable." Wellington adjusted his very stiff, very proper collar. "Remember, this is reconnaissance. Identify the perpetrators, discover their intentions, and find evidence we can present to Doctor Sound . . . without appearing as if we have broken the rules."

Eliza bit her lip at that. *It is all about what the textbooks tell you, isn't it, Welly?* Perhaps that was an easy attitude to nurture down in the Archives.

While Wellington obviously deemed their Director as the be-all and end-all of Ministry wisdom, Eliza's time in the field made her of a far different opinion. Doctor Sound's obsession over the elusive House of Usher sometimes blinded him to other things, an irony that did not escape her when it concerned her previous partner. A good example of Sound's failure in objectivity, in seeing beyond his own personal agenda, sat in front of her: Wellington Books, Esquire. Both the Archivist and these unresolved cases were abandoned down in the basement. Skilled as she was, it was Books who enabled their escape from the Antarctica stronghold. It was also Books who made the connections to Harry's case and the Phoenix Society. What was this intelligent, intuitive man doing, wasting away in the Archives? This was the kind of detective reasoning that was needed—ye gods, *imperative*—in the field!

Then she recalled their flight from the Antarctic fortress and their incredible chase through Charing Cross. This irrational fear of guns was Books' one unavoidable weakness and this fear could prove problematic for her if their fortune turned this weekend. She tried to imagine herself descending into hostile situations with Agent Wellington Books, armed only with a combination-locked journal, covering her back. Even for her, that was—

A cloud passed before the sun, and Havelock Manor suddenly appeared far more imposing, if not menacing, the closer they drew.

Wellington fixed her with a stare. "I cannot believe I am about to do this," he barked. "What have you gotten me into, woman?"

She inclined her head to one side. *What have* I *gotten* you *into?* She looked at the manor once again, and fought back the instinct to call out to the driver, ordering the carriage back to London. This was for Harry; but if she slipped in any way during the weekend, both of them could end up in Bedlam, or dead.

Instead of bursting the Archivist's bubble, she smoothed her skirt. They were far more sedately attired than their moment of glory at the opera, but still wearing fashions of the upper class. That was after all what Havelock and his guests were expecting. The grey tweed jacket and matching skirt was still worn over a corset cinched in tight, perhaps more than day fashion required. To go with it Eliza had chosen a more discreet display of wealth: a single ruby around her neck, to catch the eye of men and draw them to her curves.

They rolled up to the cascade of stairs, and footmen scurried out to open the door. Eliza took one of their offered hands and stepped down onto the white gravel.

"Try not to gawp," Wellington blurted.

A swell of indignation began to build in her chest. *What the hell is he on about?* She had *not* been gawping—she'd been to palaces from India to France and had never "gawped" in any of them. What she was doing was assessing the lay of the land. Windows made her nervous—too many vantage points for snipers. However if they played their cards right, they wouldn't have to worry about it.

The only Joker in the deck right now: Wellington Books. Untrained in the field. Completely textbook. Hardly ready for covert work. She would have turned around to tell him so, had not the figure of a gentleman appeared at the stairs. Like a demure and obedient wife, Eliza took Wellington's arm, her eyes never leaving his face. Eliza hoped it appeared as that of a doting wife, perhaps a newlywed.

"You must be St. John." The voice was immediately familiar: Bartholemew Devane, the one whom she had only glimpsed but whose odious manner was imprinted on her memory like an oil stain.

The man's dark eyes raked over Eliza, assessing her worth before passing on to her "husband." Wellington shook the man's hand. "Yes, and you are . . . ?"

"Lord Bartholomew Devane." Eliza's grip tightened even further, but Wellington made no reaction to it. Instead he handed across the letter of introduction that the boys had liberated from the real St. Johns' lodgings. The roll of beautiful vellum had been held in place by a wax seal embossed with a rampant phoenix. Christopher had outdone himself noticing such a tiny detail.

Eliza had been in such a hurry she'd not dared try to read the contents of the letter. The conversation from the opera house had assured them that Havelock and his cronies had never met the St. Johns—however there was always a danger that some little detail was contained in the letter that would reveal them. She wasn't holding her breath, but she suddenly became aware of the *pounamu* pistols pressing against the small of her back where they were once more hidden.

When he crumpled the paper in one fist and tucked into a pocket, she began to think that indeed they might just pull this off.

Devane took a few deep puffs of the cigarette hanging indolently from his fingertips. "Glad to find you're an honest Englishman. I was worried Havelock was thinking about letting in damn continental aristos or, even worse, *colonials*."

Eliza's heart sank—just when she thought she'd got used to the bigotry, it slapped her in the face one more time. Hell's bells, this was about to get awkward.

Wellington laughed, harsh and sharp, an echo of Bartholomew. "I should hope not. The last thing I would expect would be having this weekend sullied with that manner of company." Then he turned to her, "May I introduce my wife, Hyacinth St. John. I should warn you, if she does not speak to you, she is not being rude. She is completely mute." Eliza's eyes widened, but Wellington took no notice. Over his shoulder he spoke to her in the same way a lord of the manor would speak to a faithful dog. "Hyacinth, show Lord Devane some respect, and do not embarrass me as you are prone to do."

She felt a sudden desire to shock everyone—particularly Wellington—playing off this ill-thought improvisation as some bawdy jest, but instead she stepped forward, eyes cast downward. Eliza curtseyed deeply, making sure her best attributes were visible. Her eyes never left the ground, but still she felt Devane's gaze on her. She then took two steps back, placing herself by Wellington's side once more.

The gruesome belly laugh Bartholomew released caused her skin to crawl. "Oh my, I think you have found yourself the perfect woman there, St. John." While she had prepared herself as an object to be admired, Eliza suddenly felt uncomfortable under Devane's inspection. If Wellington and she had really been married, she might have hoped her "husband" would challenge him to a duel, provided she didn't ram her new stiletto in the man's eyeball first.

"I think so," Wellington patted her hand as she smiled and snuggled close to him. "Well bred, attentive to any want, need, or desire of mine, and quiet as a mouse."

Eliza felt for the bundle of nerves near the elbow, a tactic from the Far East she had found fascinating as well as life saving. She applied a quick jolt of pressure there with her thumbnail. The wince from Wellington gave her quite a tingle of satisfaction.

Bartholomew, not noticing Wellington's sudden flinch, blew a long stream of smoke and his narrow lips twitched under his moustache. His leer was of epic proportions, the kind of suggestive inspection that the upper classes seemed to love indulging in, but would turn around and sneer at the lower classes for even daring to do so. Eliza now felt the Derringers strapped to her thighs. Instead of following what her primal instincts screamed to do, she continued playing her part.

A small dark-haired woman was standing at the steps waiting for them. Not a mark was visible on her, yet she had the demeanour of one that been beaten long and hard. Eliza was sure under that very modest grey dress there were bruises of all shapes and colors.

"My wife, Olivia," Devane jerked his head as if indicating to a piece of furniture. "Unfortunately not mute."

Yet not exactly a bubbling brook of conversation either. Her green eyes rose once, and she murmured, "Good afternoon."

"Once the flower of Hertfordshire," Devane went on, running his eyes over the slim form like she was some racehorse that had broken down on the track, "but the bloom quickly wore off. I've had three sons off her though, so not a total loss."

The hard knot in Eliza's throat would only be relieved by a howl of anger, but this was not the first time she'd come across this detestable nature. The Britons thought themselves so damn civilised, and yet denied half their population so much. The colonies Devane had spoken so dismissively of had given the vote to women two years ago. It was why Eliza loved frontier places most of all. No ancient conventions to fall back upon. Thanks to Wellington's impulsive character trait thrust upon her, she could not even offer Olivia words of feminine kindness.

This weekend Eliza would have to play the game of the submissive wife—and there could be no better template for it than Lady Olivia Devane.

Wellington broke her concentration momentarily with a show of aristocrat wit. "Nothing off Hyacinth yet," he said in a tone that almost perfectly mimicked Devane's, "but the ring is barely warm on her finger. I get to enjoy her for a while before putting her out to pasture."

"I am sure you do." The vile aristocrat blew a cloud of smoke and through it shot her a knowing smile.

Eliza returned a meek, demure smile, while in her mind she continued to ram Bartholomew's own nose into his skull. Her imagination also conjured Wellington on his knees, hog-tied next to Devane, watching the carnage . . . and knowing he was next.

"*Hyacinth!*" Wellington snapped, making Eliza start. "Stop with your incessant daydreaming *and come!*"

As soon as they found a moment, Eliza was going to have a word with Wellington's character choices.

Inside, the hall was full of the usual dark wooden paneling and dead creatures' heads hanging on the walls. Eliza hated such places; the feeling of sad, doomed eyes watching her everywhere was intense. People, evil people she had faced every day in her fieldwork were one thing—but animals were different. The killing of them merely for sport was something she found abhorrent.

Devane looked at them askance while his wife, much in the manner small creatures would hide from a predator, swiftly moved to a corner both dark and out of their way. "Well, I'll let you settle in. Our hosts won't be back until"—his eyes drifted to Eliza—"dinner." His peculiar emphasis on that last word made her stomach clench. His teeth flashed as he smiled. "I look forward to you seeing the dishes Havelock serves for dessert. He's well known for them."

Devane held out his hand and Olivia took it, but only by giving him just the tips of her fingers. Together they disappeared into what looked like the study.

The pain of clenching her teeth was the only thing Eliza concentrated on as a footman led them upstairs to their room, a pair of porters following in their wake bearing their cases. The footman opened a polished oak door, and there was their home for the weekend. She stood next to Wellington—as silent as his quick thinking had made her—taking in their luxurious country dwellings: a good-sized bedroom with a fine aspect over the garden, a four-poster bed with a large vanity at its foot, a collection of old masters on the walls, and a gramophone gleaming and new by the window.

"Dinner is in an hour," the servant, a tall and slightly imposing figure, informed them in deliberate, measured tones. Inclining his head for a moment, he silently exited, leaving them to their business.

Wellington's mouth opened, but she held up her finger in warning. Then once she had discerned the retreating footsteps of the manservant, Eliza spun on Wellington, grabbed him by the lapels, and—with a sigh of expectation and want—threw him onto the bed.

The wind went out of the Archivist, his eyes widened, and his mouth opened in shock; but before words could come out of him, Eliza pounced. She had the confused and somewhat overwhelmed Wellington pinned under her, and when she descended on him, he almost let out a scream, but a giggle burst out of him.

Eliza breathed easier, thankful Wellington was so ticklish.

She hissed in his ear, and her warning silenced him. "This time, *you* follow *my* lead, Welly. Most likely this room is observed. Just listen to me, and play along."

It was imperative he not wreck the moment. His hair was thick between her fingers as she yanked his head to one side and appeared to nibble on his neck. Underneath her the Archivist was struggling to find a place to put his hands. Finally he settled on her waist as she was straddling him.

She took the chance to hiss her anger into his skin. "Don't you think I have the skills to change my accent? Don't you think in all this time in the Ministry I have learned how to do that?" And then she sank her teeth into him, the "playful nip" a bit too hard to be playful.

His laugh became a sharp cry. "OW! Hyacinth, please—control yourself," Wellington said, rather louder than was required. Then he muttered against her hair, "I didn't . . . I'm so sorry I didn't think . . ."

"No, you did not!" Eliza took delight in grinding herself against him, a kind of savage repayment for effectively silencing her for their stay. "Improvisations like that could be the death of us. However, while I have been in worse situations, you may have done us both a favour." She nipped his ear for good measure, and was satisfied with his little yelp.

"How—how—how—" he whispered breathlessly. Eliza tugged on his hair to clear his head, but she was flattered at his reactions. "How so?" he finally wheezed into her ear.

Eliza sat up, remaining straddled across her "husband." As she stripped off her coat and gloves, she let out a little low growl. If anyone spied upon them they would be in no doubt of the very passionate marriage the St. Johns shared. They would also be in for a show.

When she dropped back into his embrace, she found her anger dissipating. "Stupid toffs will be more likely to make mistakes in front of a 'cripple.' "

The headiness working through Eliza caught her by surprise. House spies be damned—she had to stop. It was so easy to pretend, particularly with Harry, like this; but they knew as partners where limits were, considering their Budapest operation had almost strayed too far into the heat of the moment. Harry had recognised that, and brought the deception to the end.

Wellington, as she felt between her legs, had gone well passed his restraints and was on the verge of swooning.

For a moment she and Wellington looked at each other directly, the tips of their noses brushing. The look on his face, particularly in his eyes, was betrayal. Eliza blinked, feeling a tightness in her throat. She wanted to hold him close now, cry in his shoulder, and let him know—

Eliza scrambled to grab Wellington but her fingers grazed the fabric of his suit just before she bounced off the edge of the bed. She then crashed against the floor, her head rapping its hard wood so violently that stars exploded before her.

"Damnation, woman," his voice was a little unsteady, but

he was putting enough venom and contempt into his tenor to compensate for it.

She heard him get to his feet, but when he came around the bed, Eliza actually found herself scrambling back from him. Her fingers itched. She needed a Derringer now.

"Do that again, and I'll make sure your punishment is *most* appropriate." His eyes were cold, empty. The Archivist was gone. This man was a stranger to her. "Now if you are finished, we should prepare for dinner." He turned to the basin of water at the vanity. "My evening wear, Hyacinth."

Eliza scrambled back to her feet and just stared at Wellington as he splashed his face. Their eyes met in the reflection of the mirror, and it was he that looked on the verge of tears now.

Sorry, he mouthed.

Eliza had never been so happy to see Welly. She tweaked his nose and shot him a playful wink. No, this wasn't her first time in the field, but it was his; and bless the man, he was trying. She busied herself flinging open their luggage. Her own fingers were trembling, partially due to Wellington's erratic behaviour, but also from her own shortness of breath, the prickle of heat in her skin. Yes, perhaps she had enjoyed that erotic deception too much and Welly's reaction was needed to bring them back into the seriousness of their situation.

Wellington held up one of the gowns she had brought with her, the low V-neck and floating white sleeves causing him to look at Eliza askance. "Do you think this is the wisest thing to wear in unknown company?"

Now there's my little Welly, she thought playfully. With a wicked smile, Eliza produced a dinner jacket cut in the latest fashion.

The Archivist cleared his throat. After examining the offering, he raised an eyebrow. "Hyacinth, I was not aware that you knew my measurements so well."

It was probably a good thing that she couldn't use her

voice or she might have said any number of saucy replies to that.

Instead she turned around and gestured to her lacings. When she felt no aid forthcoming, she glared at him over her shoulder. This really wouldn't do. Especially since he'd loosened her well enough when she'd been drunk.

Finally, on catching Eliza's silent plea for assistance, Wellington began tugging and pulling at her. He certainly wouldn't make much of decent lady's maid.

Eliza slipped behind the painted Chinese screen and quickly stripped off the rest of her clothes. She knew pushing Wellington any further would have consequences and she needed him razor sharp. However, she also needed to get dressed for the evening. His sense of modesty would have to adapt. Stepping out with only the row of tiny buttons at the back of the dress undone, she again presented her back.

"I confess," Wellington whispered, pulling the lacings tight, "the use of your femininity as a weapon I find deeply disturbing. Tread . . ." he hissed into her ear with each tug, ". . . with . . . caution."

With a sigh, Eliza contemplated that surprising revelation. Not that it was surprising in itself, just that he had expressed it.

With a stare too long to be complimentary but also not as menacing as moments before, Wellington gathered up his evening suit and disappeared behind the screen to dress as well. With parts of her still tingling from their roll on the bed, Eliza felt a temptation to peek—but decided there were some mysteries she should not investigate just yet. Besides, she had rattled him (and herself) enough tonight already.

With Wellington slipping into his tailored evening wear, Eliza tended to one other piece of housekeeping. She moved to the walls and began carefully and silently examining them.

Snap. Snap. Snap.

A fingertip inspection found no watching holes, which were always a danger in an old house like this.

Snap! Snap! Snap!

Behind the paintings, underneath the bed, in or around small room fixtures, her eyes searched for wires or contraptions akin to Wellington's impressive auralscope.

"*Hyacinth!*" Wellington snapped.

The exquisite vase Eliza had been inspecting danced in her hand and then stopped when she regained her grip on it. She held the vase up as if to hurl it at him, and that was when she realised he was only half dressed, his shirt showing off more flesh she had ever seen from him.

This must be serious.

"I was trying to be polite and not call upon you like my hunting hound"—but he was gesturing wildly to the gramophone by the window, his face not cross but a bit pale—"but if I must, I shall. Fetch my cuff links."

He then mouthed a word Eliza couldn't make sense of. On his third, exasperated try, she finally recognised it as *auralscope*, and she understood. Gramophones were conspicuous displays of wealth. It was one reason behind the purchase of hers. They were still new and quite the statement of one's status. As she came closer to this gramophone, though, her senses prickled. Its base was all wrong. There was something odd about it, but she could not place her finger on exactly what it was.

"Did you look over there?" Wellington asked from behind the Chinese screen, holding out Eliza's baldrick of bladed weapons. "Well, keep looking."

She nodded in approval as she took the leather sash from him. Wellington was a fast learner.

Drawing her favourite Elsener knife, Eliza pried the side off the luxurious, ornate device and peered in. To her it looked a collection of clockwork, chassis, and gears, much like her own gramophone; but then her eyes caught sight of the rotating cylinder tucked within the array. The gramophone was not cranked, but still the cylinder rotated, and that was when she saw the thin wire that ran out of the gramophone and into the wall. *Well done, Welly.*

No sooner had she thought that commendation, Wellington Thornhill Books stepped out from behind the screens and stopped before the room's tiny fireplace, as if waiting for her approval.

She gave a light giggle and then produced a cylinder from the gramophone's stand. When the strains of "Love's Old Sweet Song" began to fill the room, she crossed over to him and smiled brightly. "An ingenious place to hide a recording device, but naturally it has its problems," she said. "While the music plays we can talk, as long as we keep our voices low."

He gave a sigh of relief, and then took a step back. He adjusted his glasses and stood to his full height. "Will I do, Mrs. St. John? Am I a suitable escort for you this evening?"

Eliza circled him and took full advantage of his discomfort. It struck her as rather amusing that she, a daughter of the colonies, should be called on to judge such a paragon of British aristocracy. Though she did not say it, he looked rather fine—better than such craven company deserved.

She did however step up to him and adjust his cravat. Straightening out the lines in the jacket was next. A very wifely thing to do, but she didn't stop doing it.

"I believe you shall," Eliza replied, glad of the opportunity to talk freely, "and now I can breathe a little easier."

"I'm sor—"

"We will just have to make the best of it, Welly. We can 'talk' later about this. Good then?"

Wellington held out his arm. "Well then, Mrs. St. John, shall we go down to dinner?"

She smiled brightly in return, feeling her pulse beginning to race with the thrill of the pursuit. "Indeed—let's!"

CHAPTER TWENTY-ONE

In Which a Remarkable Dinner Is Served

Succulent scents tickled both their noses. Even Eliza in her mute guise could still make an appreciative sound as the aroma of what was promising to be a lovely night of dining wafted up to them. From the second floor of the mansion, voices could be heard mingling, their laughter flitting through the hallways and foyers of the manor. It was all very proper, all very civilised.

Wellington glanced at his "perfect wife," as Bartholomew referred to her, and he felt a tightness in his chest. Her performance in the bedroom had been undignified, but he was aware that his own foolishness had bought her to it. Pressed against him so intimately, she immediately had the advantage as every logical thought had flown out of his mind. Now, with his wits and faculties back under his control, he understood there would be more to come.

Tonight they must share a bed.

She was so many things. Passionate. Unapologetic. Something he wasn't. Was that why he was suddenly here, outside of the Archives, taking risks he would have never dreamt of doing? Wellington then heard his father's voice in his mind, and saw the image of him shaking his head ruefully.

"I am disappointed in you, Wellington, to be engaging in such common behaviours."

That's it, Wellington thought to himself. *Just keep talking. I'm going to need that.*

Abruptly he felt a grasp on his forearm and the corridor around him disappeared suddenly. Once again she had yanked him around, but thankfully this time into a cupboard. He spun about to see Eliza close the door and then turn to face him.

"All right, Books, out with it," she whispered harshly.

"What?" he snapped back.

"You have a look on your face that isn't exactly instilling me with confidence. We are supposed to be rich fools."

"Yes, and you're supposed to be mute. Even with the whispering, you are taking a risk in completely blowing our cover."

"That, while it should be my concern, is not what puts me ill at ease." Her brilliant eyes bored through him. "It's you. Can you do this?"

"What makes you think I can't?"

"You may have the training, but you are not a field agent—and right now, my life rests in your hands."

He could feel his blood surging as he bit back, "So you don't particularly care for the turning of tables?"

"Not when the agent in question is about to take the reins on a covert assignment with only basic field training under his belt."

Wellington sneered as he leaned in close, the humiliation she had dished out to him in the bedroom now firing his anger. "Your confidence in me is overwhelming." She opened her mouth to reply, but he continued. "Eliza, if you must know, I am terrified, but right now I am trying to assume a role and you are *not* helping. If we are to play this couple and if we are about to descend into the lion's den, I have to become this persona completely. This means you do not question me or my judgement—do you understand?"

Eliza's eyes narrowed, but slowly she nodded.

A firm hand, Wellington, is what the common folk need.

His father's voice. His focus. Wellington swallowed, the pain in his throat causing him to start. "Good. Now please be quiet until we are safe in our rooms, if you please."

For a moment, they stood in the silence of the cupboard, and then Eliza, with a deep breath, cast her eyes down.

"Better," he whispered.

Wellington cracked the door open and looked up and down the corridor. With a nod over his shoulder, the two continued their way down to the main dining hall.

A few heads turned to watch Wellington and Eliza enter the room; and while he was well aware of Eliza's fashion and its intent to display her "wares" as she put it, he didn't like how quite a few men were allowing their gaze to linger on her. Suddenly he was aware of his skin against the fabric of his shirt. He wasn't nervous. Anything but. Wellington was well into his part now. He focused on the quick exchange between him and Eliza in the drawing room . . .

Respectable society. These are your people, Wellington Books, the familiar voice assured him.

"Richard!" the voice called out happily.

Wellington almost missed the greeting, but an unseen nudge from the woman at his side silenced the memory. He could feel the smile on his face. It seemed to shoot pain throughout his entire body.

"Ah, Lord Devane," he accepted the gentleman's hand, regardless of the screaming urge to recoil.

"Bartholomew, please," his eyes immediately jumped to Eliza, and the smile widened. "And here she is, the delicious Hyacinth St. John. You are looking very healthy tonight," he said, motioning to her breasts as if they were fashion accessories.

"I am proud of my possessions," Wellington replied as he gestured for a butler to approach. He took two champagne glasses from the tray and offered one to Eliza. Without raising her eyes up to join his own, she took the glass and waited. "This one, a diamond in the rough, but so worth the effort."

Wellington snapped his fingers. Eliza took a sip of the champagne.

"Oh, well done," Bartholomew said.

Wellington winked at him. "You should see some of the tricks I've taught her." Hearing himself speak those words made him queasy, but he quickly took a mouthful of champagne. The bubbles calmed him a bit.

"Would you care to join us? We're sitting closer to the head of the table."

"Well, I don't think that would be quite fair to the rest of the initiates," Wellington said, looking around them. The room was filling up quickly now, and from the glimpse of staff moving silently from the back passages to the adjacent dining hall, it was nearly dinner. "Are you allowed—"

Bam-bam!

Her boot heel striking the floor was loud enough to halt the parlour's conversation, but seconds later the din had returned to its previous level. Bartholomew looked at Eliza for a moment, a moment far too long to be comfortable, and then back to Wellington.

"You must forgive Hyacinth." Wellington sighed.

"Must I?"

"Yes, although she is mute, that does not mean she lacks a voice. Two raps usually means no, so now we play our little parlour game." Wellington then motioned around them. "How apropos." Finishing off the champagne, Wellington turned to Eliza. "Eyes up, Hyacinth."

Her eyes rose to meet his own. They revealed nothing.

This was when Wellington went cold. He was expecting to find that fire normally seen in Eliza's gaze to be a raging inferno—instead, there was a vacant stare, as if she were simply a clockwork automaton.

That reminded him . . .

The intricate pattern of the flute in his hand seemed to call him back. He blinked. How long had he been standing there? Had the dinner bell rung?

Eliza, his obedient pet, was still standing before him, a vacant stare returning his own gaze.

"Hyacinth," he began, his tone firm, "are you attempting to protest my declining Lord Devane's invitation to sit with him?"

Softer now, Eliza's heel struck the dark wood underfoot. Once.

"I see." Wellington gave a nod and then spoke over his shoulder, his eyes never leaving Eliza's. "She knows how much this weekend means to me."

Her heel struck the floor once.

"And I think," Wellington began, his eyes narrowing on Eliza's. She blinked and then looked down, like a child caught stealing cookies from the tin just before dinner. "Bartholomew, if I do not accept your invitation, I think my Hyacinth here will be quite cross with me."

Again, her heel rapped the wood.

"The invitation is open, Richard." And as if on cue, a bell chimed lightly. "Please," Bartholomew said, motioning to the dining room.

The din seemed only to rise in volume as they entered the long dining hall. It was easy to single out the initiates as they were gawking at the décor of the room. Down to the brilliant silverware and impressive ice sculpture that served as the table's centrepiece, this was promising to be an elegant evening, herald to a fantastic weekend in the country. While many of the initiates lingered on the Phoenix Society crest stretching across the opposite wall, Wellington found himself drawn to the many portraits. These, he deduced, must have been past members of the Phoenix Society. Some of the faces he recognised from British history, Guy Fawkes being one of the more prominent paintings in the collection. Captain James Cook. Sir Thomas More. King Richard III.

Interestingly, the wall was absent of Ferdinand Magellan. In fact, the entire wall was devoid of any foreigner.

"But I was so certain," he muttered.

"Certain of what, old boy?"

Wellington blinked, casting a quick glance at Eliza who was still playing the part of the obedient pet. He was now regretting that bit of improvisation.

"Oh my apologies, I was just noticing the—"

"Rogues Gallery, yes," Bartholomew said, his eyes seeming to sparkle with pride. "A fine history we have in the Society." He continued as they took their seats, "I wouldn't worry, old boy. The history is not that important in gaining entrance here."

"What is important here?" Wellington asked.

"The future." He glanced at Eliza, and then he returned to Wellington. "What matters to the Society is the future and how were are to shape it."

Lobster salad was placed before them as wine filled their glasses. Underneath the table, Wellington felt a light pat on his thigh.

Nicely done, Welly, he caught in her covert grin.

Olivia Devane entered and walked the length of the table, smiling to everyone she passed. Her radiance diminished with each step. By the time she reached their chairs, all pleasantries had faded from her face.

"Husband," she said, giving a light curtsey, as would a servant bestow to the manor lord.

"Olivia," he replied, his eyes never leaving his salad. "How go arrangements?"

"Oh, it will be lovely as always," she said pleasantly.

"And your niece?"

Lady Devane was already of a fair complexion, but she suddenly looked ashen, as if she were a ghost that now haunted the dining room. Still, even with her pallid looks, Wellington found her a truly striking woman. While the men ogled over Eliza and her bountiful chest, Olivia—perhaps not as endowed as his partner—could not be denied for her own slender figure or alluring qualities. Her skin was flawless. Her eyes, dark pools one could easily lose themselves in. Wellington blinked, catching himself staring. Maybe that was acceptable to these men, but not to him.

Then he looked around the table. *None* of the men regarded her. At all. Why?

"Constance is here, yes. I'm a little concerned as to how much I had—"

"Will she be joining us or no?"

Olivia cleared her throat. "She doesn't want to disappoint her Uncle Barty."

The smile across Lord Devane's face chilled Wellington.

"How sweet." Bartholomew took another bite of his salad, and then observed, "You're not eating, Richard."

He was staring again. "Forgive me, Bartholomew. I suppose I was distracted by your wife."

That was when Devane paused, set his fork down, and then reached for his wine. "Were you now?"

"Well, of course," he replied with a whimsical lilt to his words. "I can appreciate beautiful things in this world, can't I?"

Wellington cast a glance to Lady Olivia who remained still in her chair, hands crossed over her lap. The woman's eyes were shut, their lids pressing against each other so tight they were causing her brow to furrow. He caught the slightest tremble from one of her loose curls. Her nostrils flared lightly at the precise, controlled breathing she was now practising.

That was when he noticed the silence from around the table.

"Richard, you are a potential, so I do not expect you to know any better," Bartholomew said, the wineglass touching his lips for a moment before he continued, "and I must admit, I am flattered by your compliments to my wife. So I must like you a great deal." With another sip of the brilliant gold drink, he set down his glass. "Just understand this about me: I cherish all my possessions."

Wellington understood. In that moment, he understood all too well.

"A shame you got to her first," he added, leaning forward and giving Olivia a wink.

He knew she wouldn't see it, but it wasn't for her benefit. Bartholomew grew red, and Wellington readied himself for the challenge of pistols at dawn; but the challenge would not be issued—at least, not right now—as the double doors opened. The man was greeted with soft applause from the table. Wellington watched the stocky gentleman flash a smile that charmed everyone in the room, save for himself and the woman at his side. The man motioned for everyone to stop with the adulation, although it was obvious that the modesty was feigned. He absently stroked his thick handlebar moustache with the side of his index finger as he made his way opposite of where they sat.

Wellington cast a sideways look to Eliza. She watched the man, her fingers absently tapping the handle of a steak knife as he approached the seat at the head of the table.

"So," Wellington whispered, "that's him, is it? Doctor Deveraux Havelock?"

Bartholomew's anger seemed to abate for the time being. "You know his work?"

"Call me a great admirer," Wellington replied, "particularly for his standards."

One of the servants pulled back Havelock's chair, then a fresh plate was set before him, his glass filled, and they returned to their places facing the walls, their eyes watching the curved, polished butler's mirrors hanging in front of them.

Havelock cast a quick glance over his shoulder, seemingly unhappy with the impeccable service provided. He reached into his pocket, noted the time with his watch, and then proceeded to his dinner.

Wellington leaned forward to speak to the lord of the manor, but Bartholomew's hand gently pushed him back. "Easy, old boy. That's not how things work here."

"What do you mean?"

"While the conversation at the dinner table is all well and

good, you do not engage Doctor Havelock. He might engage you, and regardless if you have a slab of filet or a spoonful of mousse in your mouth, you would best respond. Until then, it is wise if you do not interrupt the man's dinner."

He cast a glance to the head of the table. "Does the good doctor always linger a course behind the rest of the dinner party?"

Bartholomew gave a soft chuckle. "A sharp eye you have there, old boy." He cleared his mouth with a quick sip of wine. "He prefers to observe the people around him on the first night. I would not be surprised if he has already eaten, and this is more for show."

A soft chime sounded, and staff appeared with meticulous timing. They cleared away the plates and presented the main course in short order. The smell of the venison hit Wellington before he actually recognised it. Immediately he was awash in memory—the kind of childhood memories he would really rather not have.

So he sat as still as the rest of the guests, while the servants piled their plates with meat, root vegetables, and gravy.

Devane obviously knew his superior well, for indeed Doctor Havelock was nursing his glass of wine. His dinner remained untouched.

"I must admit, Richard," Bartholomew chimed in suddenly, "you hardly seem the type for our club."

Wellington paused, his fork halfway to his mouth. Carefully, he lowered it back to the plate. "I beg your pardon, Bartholomew?"

"A man of your backgrounds. Rather pedestrian. Not what I would necessarily consider prime candidate material for the Society."

"Because I am in textiles?" Wellington muttered.

"It's not as if you are into ironworks, munitions, or something more . . ." Bartholomew's voice trailed off, something akin to a sneer forming on his face, ". . . aggressive."

"I see." Wellington nodded, his hand reaching for his

wineglass. He did not remember when it was refilled. "And tell me, just how many soldiers charge on the battlefield stark naked?" The fork was now back in his hand and, once again, Wellington was enjoying a lovely dinner. After a few bites, he dabbed at his mouth and added, "In my line of industry, everyone needs clothing. Both sides, if you must know. To me, warfare is not a matter of politics or ideology, but colour, fashion, and fabrics." *Now*, he thought, *time to place this cad in check.* "So long as the respective warring factions are doing their part to weed out the runts, thin the herd, whatever you wish to call it, I will make sure they are properly clothed."

That caused both shadows to either side of him to stop.

"So you hold no loyalty to any one side in your business then, is that what you're saying, old boy?"

"What I'm saying is, let the so-called heirs to the government and the great unwashed masses tend to one another. If they want to whittle their own numbers down while making a tidy profit in the process, why would I care? My pursuits—including personal ones outside of my humble textile mills—will remain funded." Wellington finished off a spear of asparagus, dabbed at his mouth and then took a sip of his wine. He found the silence around him assuring. "I do not believe in a government that fails us, only in the ideals of what our society was based upon."

Wellington realised in the moments that seemed to slink past that he was truly beginning to appreciate this fine dinner.

"You, Richard, are a man full of surprises."

He finally turned to Devane. If it were anywhere else, he would have insisted on meeting him in a boxing ring. Queensbury Rules, naturally.

"You have no idea, Lord Devane," he replied quietly.

Plates were cleared and dessert—a delightful-looking Neapolitan Ice—was presented before everyone. Wellington enjoyed the tingle against his tongue, subduing it only a bit with a sip of water. He looked to Eliza who happened to be staring at Havelock at that moment. Wellington followed her gaze; and as he had been at the beginning of the dinner, Havelock was still drinking what appeared to be his first glass of wine for the evening. The Society's leader continued to watch silently from his grand throne at the head of the table.

When their eyes met, Wellington felt a sweat form on his back. *Now what do I do?*

Havelock's eyebrow went up in a curious arch as did the curl of his lips. The salute with his glass was warm, charming, and sincere.

Wellington gave a slight nod, returning the smile, and then he turned his eyes back to the dessert. In his peripheral vision, he could see Eliza had already finished her own plate.

"He likes you," Devane whispered. "And his approval did not go without notice."

Wellington glanced up from his dessert and observed the other couples, those without the lapel pin of the Phoenix Society on their person, coldly staring at him.

"Well played, old boy," Bartholomew whispered again.

I have no bloody idea what I did.

Wellington's growing panic slipped away at the sudden ringing of crystal. The conversation diminished, and all attention was now at the head of the table, on the Head Master of the Phoenix Society. Two butlers from the wall had turned and were moving his chair free of the table. Before Havelock stood, one servant cleared his place setting while the other stood by the chair, waiting. The doctor gave the second servant a dismissive wave as the first disappeared into the kitchens.

After a few minutes of silence, of taking all of them in, his voice filled the hall. He did not need to raise his voice. The acoustics of where he stood carried his commanding presence to them all. "My Brothers, welcome Initiates, and you that serve and tend to Us, welcome to First Night."

From behind him, Wellington heard Eliza take a long,

deep breath. "*You that serve and tend to Us.*" Miss Braun was more modern than even the most militant suffragist, so no doubt that phrasing crept under her craw.

"I am so looking forward to meeting you, those who wish to join our most hallowed ranks. While I am sure we will get to know one another better, I cannot impress upon you that this weekend is more than simply good company, fine sport, and refined diversions. This weekend, we will test the very reasons you are here, for the invitation to join us is not to be given—nor taken—lightly. We are not some common Gentlemen's Club where the order of business is merely sipping brandy, smoking cigars, and complaining about the state of the Empire. Ours is an elite brethren dedicated to fundamentals that have been, of late, falling by the wayside. Something we cannot—nor should not—tolerate." He paused, looking at the initiates for a moment. His face, dark and hard, suddenly radiated with a pleasant warmth rivaling a hearth in the middle of a Downing Street pub. "This is not to say we do not enjoy our cigars, brandy, or other such pleasures."

The Society's men chuckled while its women silently rose from the table and filed out of the room. The initiates looked to one another and then to Doctor Havelock who answered their unasked queries with a simple shake of his head.

"We will get to know one another. We will make our final choices. We will also enjoy ourselves and remember what makes us who we are here in the Phoenix Society. Have no doubt. Just as a reminder to you all, we have hunting on the morrow for the gentlemen. Ladies, if you care to accompany your menfolk, we are more than happy to oblige, provided you understand we are not ones who believe shooting is a proper sport for a lady. As far as the Society is concerned, those in the Suffrage Movement can continue to do just that—suffer."

Another sharp breath to his left, and Wellington didn't have to look behind him to know Eliza was close to her cracking point.

"So," Havelock said, his face brightening as he tapped his goblet with his spoon three times, "with the close of dinner, I would like to invite the ladies to join the Brethren's wives and companions for an after-dinner social. For your pleasure."

As he spoke, the male servants moved to the wall behind Wellington, Eliza, and their side of the table. By the time Havelock had finished speaking, the servants were turning ornate wheels that were built into these walls. The vines and leaf patterns along them made these valves appear less as pressure releases and more as actual room décor. The subtle hiss was joined first by the soft rumbling of the wall's center partition of the wall moving upward like a massive plaster curtain. Both of these sounds were joined by a cacophony of moans, groans, and audible gasps until finally the hydraulics of the wall went silent.

The moans, groans and gasps, however, continued.

Many of the women were still in their corsets and bloomers but some were completely naked, their legs either open for an interested partner or embracing another woman as their mouths kissed and tasted each other. The erotic display was a continuously changing mass of flesh, of femininity intertwined and hungrily taking pleasure from whomever was willing to share with the group.

Wellington winced at how suddenly dry his throat was. He looked over to Eliza, and he swallowed again. Her eyebrow was crooked sharply, seeming to mimic the smirk on her face.

"Ladies, you may feel free to strip here and join the others. If you are more modest, feel free to change into a morning robe provided upstairs in your suites." Havelock tipped his head back, his smile full of pride. "No need to rush. Our ladies possess amazing stamina."

A pair of women, with a nod from their men, rose from the table and started unlacing their evening wear. They had not even crossed the threshold when two women, like silent naiads emerging from a thicket of wanton desire, greeted them with hungry kisses, their hands working at their complicated garments while pulling them closer to the pile.

Without looking, Wellington reached over to Eliza and slapped his hand across hers, stopping her from untying the top bow of her corset.

"Gentlemen," Havelock said, his eyes back to the table, his demeanour nonchalant even with the music of laughter, gasps, and groans from the other room, "feel free to partake after port and cigars in the main study."

The brethren and initiates all nodded in agreement and, one by one, rose to enjoy a nightcap. Wellington noted on a few of the "gentlemen's" faces that it would be the most *brief* of nightcaps.

Particularly for the man talking to him. "So, old boy, how silent is your lovely lady here?"

"I said she is mute," Wellington said, his voice practically dripping with pride and lechery, "not silent, and most assuredly not quiet."

"Well, I do hope she will be joining us later." He pointed to a striking young girl, her platinum-blonde hair spilling behind her as her back arched. Her eyes were screwed tight as she cried out, her tiny, firm breasts quivering ever so slightly as another woman's mouth drew a moan from her. "That is Constance. This is her first weekend at the Society, with Uncle Barty as her guardian. If she is up for it after I am through with her, I can make an introduction."

He hoped his face was as calm and placid as his voice. "That would be very kind." Wellington turned to Eliza. "Come along, Hyacinth. If you wish to partake, I think we should have you change into a morning robe. I do know how you enjoy yourself. Might as well make your changing quick and effortless."

Keeping his eyes trained on the doorway, Wellington led Eliza back into the main foyer and upstairs to their suite.

CHAPTER TWENTY-TWO

In Which Mr. and Mrs. St. John Have Their First Argument

The click of the door closing was far louder than Wellington expected. This time he was ready for Eliza when she grabbed hold of him again.

"You that serve and tend to Us," Eliza pressed her anger into his hair, mimicking Havelock's voice and cadence.

She pushed him away, gave him a lustful pant that did *not* reflect what she conveyed in her face, strode over to the gramophone, picked one of the musical cylinders without even regarding what it was, and shoved it into its cradle. Wellington winced slightly at the force Eliza exerted. The fact the gramophone was intact when she returned to him was a real credit to its craftsmanship.

Eliza's mouth opened, no doubt to loose a barrage of bottled-up insults, but she froze on hearing the dainty, cheerful notes erupting from the brass bells.

Never mind the why and wherefore,
Love can level ranks, and therefore,
Though his lordship's station's mighty,
Though stupendous be his brain,

Though her tastes are mean and flighty
And her fortune poor and plain . . .

"Well now, Eliza, you certainly know how to set a mood," Wellington said, staring at the gramophone. "I cannot be held responsible for my actions when a lovely lady uses Gilbert and Sullivan as backdrop to her lovemaking."

Eliza turned away from the music. After a deep breath, she found her voice. "As far as the Society is concerned, those in the Suffrage Movement can continue to do just that . . ." Wellington was actually surprised at how calm she was. "Pommy bastard! If only Kate Sheppard were here . . ."

"If she were," Wellington retorted, grabbing her by the arms and throwing her to the wall. His fingers quickly loosened her dress. "I don't think she would be in such a hurry to join the festivities downstairs."

Eliza, over one shoulder, smiled as sweetly as a milkmaid. "One thing you learn on assignment: When you're in the field, sometimes you have to surrender a scruple or two," she said with a certain level of malice.

"From the looks of it I would have to surrender quite a few." Wellington replied, feeling his own temperature rise.

"Oh, for the love of God, Queen, and Empire, don't be such a prude. When in Rome, love as the Romans do. Just su—"

"Please do *not* finish that very common statement," he growled. "Might I remind you that we are not on assignment, but working a clandestine operation far from the parameters, or dare I say the protection, of the Ministry?"

"Dare?" Eliza turned to face him, her eyes unreadable in the near dark, but he could hear clearly her undertone. He was suddenly very glad she was unarmed. "You have been more daring than I, Welly. First, there was the 'mute' attribute, completely tying my hands so I have the devil's own time trying to communicate with you. Then there is your immersion into the role of Richard St. John which has been terrifying to watch. *No one* is that good of an actor."

"I'm not acting." Wellington shifted uncomfortably.

Eliza tipped her head to one side, her brow furrowing. "Beg your pardon?"

"Miss Braun, these are—" Wellington took a moment, winced at a memory that flashed before him, and then continued. "These wretches are the reason I joined the Ministry. My family is quite well off and my father was all about bringing up his family within proper society . . .

"I'm not saying he would approve of this sort of hedonistic behaviour. What I am saying however is that the fundamentals of the Phoenix Society—what we heard at the Opera House and what we heard tonight—are all that I was brought up on. I had to make you subservient, and that appeared to me as the best option at hand. And had you been allowed to speak, your rather independent approach to things would have jeopardized any chance of getting close to Doctor Havelock, something that—at least according to Devane—I may have taken a step towards. As I said before making you mute was a snap decision and one I should have talked with you about. As far as my transformation into this role . . ."

Eliza held up one hand. "I can see you have issues with these sorts of people, Wellington, but now is not the time to open up that particular wound and examine it. I know neither of us thought I would to end up in the Archives, and neither of us imagined ending up here. But we are here now, so very close to the answers Harry lost his life to discover. We can't afford to falter."

"I am *not* faltering," Wellington hissed through clenched teeth. He cast a nervous glance to the gramophone before continuing. "I am merely making you aware of my particular point of view before we go any further."

His colleague's mouth opened a couple of times, and then she took a seat to sit on the bed. She smiled in earnest, "Why goodness me, Wellington, are you starting to act like my partner, and not someone I dragged along on this adventure?"

He tugged on the edges of his jacket, considering his next words very carefully. "Miss Braun, may I point out that at any particular moment in this whole mad mess, I could have stopped you. I could have walked away. I could have informed Doctor Sound about what you were doing. I think the fact that I am here right now, and took none of those options, should count for something."

She folded her hands in her lap, and nodded seriously. For once there was no sign of her rather cutting wit. "That's a fine point, Wellington, and one I should have appreciated earlier. I'm sorry."

Such sincerity was deeply confusing, but then she went and righted the matter by chuckling. "Besides the fact that you've been doing all the talking, and we have yet to be rumbled, is practically a mandate from heaven. So I say we have to trust each other, rely on each other, work together, or . . ."

"We die," he finished. Both of them paused, sizing up the space between them like two combative cats.

Then, after a moment a slow smile spread on Eliza's lips.

"Then I best get dressed," she murmured. "They will miss me." She slipped behind the screen with something that almost might have been called meekness.

There was a moment where Gilbert and Sullivan seemed deafening, and Wellington found his skin tingling with dread and anticipation. He could not—nor should not—allow this. When she appeared again he was struck by how magnificent she looked. Even with just a plain red robe of fine satin, Eliza made it her own. Every instinct in Wellington told him to stop her, but one look at her determined face as she strode to the door convinced him he should keep his peace.

"I trust you." Wellington sat on the corner of the bed where she had so recently been, however when her hand touched the handle he found himself leaping to his feet. He went over to the gramophone and silenced the cheerful musical. "Do enjoy yourself, Hyacinth. Remember you carry my family name."

Just be careful, Wellington mouthed. *Please*.

Eliza placed a finger up to her lips and winked. She mouthed in silent reply, *Don't wait up*, and then was gone.

Wellington, now feeling the oppressive silence of the room, removed his shoes and climbed into bed. As he leaned back he stared at the intricate patternwork of the ceiling, trying to lose himself in it. It was quite beautiful. Such detail, beauty, and love had been put into the manor. Perhaps as much love and care as had gone into his childhood home; the fine estate that his mother had created. For a moment, he could hear her playing Schubert downstairs, and smell the lavender of her perfume wrap around him. Strange how childhood memories haunted him in this moment where his partner was putting herself in so much physical and moral danger.

He knew why. His mother had been like Eliza—brave, beautiful, and rash. But for all of that it hadn't saved her. She'd been killed when her horse had thrown her at a hunt. She had refused to believe she couldn't jump that last impossible hedgerow—at least that was the story. Wellington had only been ten, and with her passing all joy went out of the house.

She would have undoubtedly liked Eliza. They would have got on. His father—that was another story. He probably would have set the dogs on the unrepentant colonial.

Wellington sighed, rolled over, and punched the pillow a few times. It was indeed easy to channel his father here. This was his natural environment. In fact, the Archivist would have not been surprised to see his grizzled, bitter face appear round a corner—but Howard Books never left the manor now. It was one small mercy for which his son was always grateful.

Wellington really wanted to remain awake for his partner's sake, but already he felt consciousness slip away from him, and it was a relief not to think about his father—it was bad enough to draw on his teachings. He didn't need his voice in his head any more than was absolutely necessary. What he did need was sleep. Whether he wanted it or not in that moment, it found him.

CHAPTER TWENTY-THREE

Where Miss Braun Breaks Her Silence in the Midnight Hour and Mr. Books Rejects a Perfectly Good Pistol at Dawn

It was certainly a vigorous evening's entertainment. Eliza pulled her robe around her, and shut the heavy oak door. She was used to ducking out of parties early, and those she had left to the orgy were so wrapped in the hedonism they had created they wouldn't notice she was gone. By her calculations, she had titillated the right number of people, helped a few others out of their clothes, and yet somehow managed to maintain most of her virtue.

Well, at least on this occasion.

It shouldn't really have mattered, but something of Wellington's disapproval during the orgy had altered her plans for the night. She was hoping to enamour one—or several—of the society during the orgy; despite the prickly nature of their relationship, she found herself caring what Welly thought. On her descent, she decided tonight would simply be an introduction for herself. Nothing more.

She had stayed long enough to make an impression—unlike a certain other person.

An initiate's wife whom whispers had identified as Dahlia Fairbanks had cut out far earlier than Eliza, and it had most certainly been noticed. Particularly by Lord Devane. Eliza climbed the stairs, more than ready to find some sleep, when she heard sobbing from a room down the hall. A quick examination showed that the Fairbankses' door was ajar. Eliza padded down the hall, and pushed it all the way open.

Dahlia was quite the sight. The poor thing's corset was askew, her dark hair undone, and when she turned and looked at her late night caller, her green eyes were swimming in tears. "I . . ." She shook her head, her bottom lip quivering as she said, "I don't know why I'm here."

Eliza took a deeper look into Dahlia Fairbanks' eyes, and a chill stole through her.

She strode the short distance and gave the foolish woman a sharp slap across the face. The retort of the blow echoed around the bedroom, even as Dahlia's hand flew to her cheek. Before she could recover, Eliza was already placing a cylinder into the gramophone. Once the cheery strains of "Daisy Belle," crooned by Katie Lawrence, filled the room, Eliza resorted to what had made her such an outstanding field agent in Doctor Sound's assessments: her snap decisions.

"I don't know who you are, but I know for a fact you are not Lady Dahlia Fairbanks."

The tiny woman gaped at her, a result of two shocks in such quick succession. Finally she managed to stutter, "They . . . they said you were mute."

"Congratulations," Eliza said snippily in return. "Now that we both know each other's secrets, we can be honest. Who are you?"

The other woman swallowed, gathering a little of her bravery around her. "Who are you?"

Eliza leaned in, blocking out the sole flickering gaslight, "I'll tell you who I am: I am the other hen in the fox's den. In other words, I am the only person you can trust."

"Molly," the other choked out, "I'm a journalist from the

Tribune." She blinked, and then her pathetic manner grew even more sheepish. "Well, more like a proofreader; but I'm just needing a chance . . ."

Eliza tilted her head back, and hissed, "Spectacular—just what this weekend needs—amateurs!" She looked over her shoulder at the door, making sure it was shut tight, and then narrowed her gaze back on Molly. "Your 'husband' then, I assume, is the one who put you up to this?"

"That's Fred, yes. Fred Abbot."

No, not him! "Fred Abbot as in the *Tribune*'s columnist that indulges in criticisms against industrial barons, bankers, and the other Imperial elite?"

"Yes," and Molly actually giggled. "One of the benefits of being a writer is a degree of anonymity. People know your work, but wouldn't know you if they were standing right next to you. Fred is my mentor at the *Tribune*."

"Lucky you," Eliza snapped.

"Fred and I heard there were some wild goings-on here. We managed to bribe the real Fairbankses, and—"

"Molly dear, I could barely give a toss about how you got here. I need to know what you've done *since* being here." She took a long deep breath. "For example, while your fellow journalist seems to be fully partaking of dessert—you are here, sobbing in your room."

"But you stepped out early too," Molly muttered, making Eliza realise she couldn't be more than twenty. She sounded like an overindulged child who had been caught snogging the stable boy.

"The difference being, I did enough to make them remember I was there—before they devolved into *mindless* debauchery." Eliza sighed. "I think you and your prolific partner should leave immediately. This is far more dangerous than you can know."

Molly swallowed, and tried to gather some semblance of professionalism. "It's only a bit of hanky panky, they just—"

Eliza leaned over the woman and glared at her. "It is far

more than just that. These people are responsible for a score of murders. Do you think a secret society not caring a jot over the lives of women and children would stop themselves from polishing off a couple of journalists?"

She held Molly's gaze for a long moment, and then asked. "Do you believe me?"

Her tone was stern, very like the one she'd heard Harry use often in the field. It seemed to work, because Molly nodded and her voice came out with a discernable quaver in it. "Y—yes . . ."

"Good, now please tell me you haven't been talking amongst yourselves about your real profession."

Molly blushed, and Eliza's heart sank.

"Let me hazard a guess. Upon your arrival, you came up here to your room, jumped up and down on the bed and shouted, 'Yes, yes, we made it inside the secret society!' "

Again Molly didn't answer, but the agent didn't need her to.

"Well"—she pointed to the still jauntily playing gramophone—"unfortunately for you, this contains a listening device—so you really had better get out of here. Bugger your belongings. Find your partner. And run. Now."

The journalist brushed tears out of her eyes and nodded. "Yes, yes, perhaps that is best."

Eliza felt a twinge of empathy. Once she'd been this young, and someone had taken her under her wing. She found herself giving the younger woman a hug. "It'll be all right, Molly. Just get out tonight and don't look back."

The poor thing was quite unsuited to deception, because she actually sobbed into Eliza's shoulder. Instinct took hold; and Eliza patted Molly's back gently, rocking her back and forth, murmuring words her own mother had once used on her.

Eliza then pushed Molly away, and gave her the lightest of shakes. "So you'll wait for your partner, and then get out of here?"

The younger woman nodded and Eliza made for the

door. She heard Molly whisper to her, "Thank you, whoever you are."

Eliza could still hear the operatic groans of the Phoenix Society flitting up from downstairs. Perhaps it was the outpouring of emotion from Molly the Journalist that gave her a pang of conscience for Constance, Devane's niece. The young girl had pulled Eliza close and kissed her, hard and hungrily. Eliza had to quash the urge to wrench herself free of the erotic greeting. Constance's tongue tasted heavy of laudanum. It was when Devane lost himself in the fresh pleasures of his niece that Eliza made her exit. Had she tarried a heartbeat longer, she would have most assuredly been his next prey.

The downward spiral, Harry's mates had called this. After watching a demonstration of what the Queen was suggesting would become the RIA, the Royal Imperial Aerocorps, Harry and she joined at the airfield's pub two dapper gents still wearing the grime and soot from their aeroriders. They had talked about the "downward spiral" which was a term used for when one of their craft failed, and both pilot and gunner would be trapped by incredible forces that would pin them to their seats, and their world would spiral into nothingness.

That was what she was feeling now. The downward spiral. Wellington, Constance. Molly. This was a descent into madness, and now she—not Harry—had to be the stalwart lighthouse providing a beacon of hope. Molly had a chance, slim at best but still a chance. Constance? The poor girl would probably find solace in the laudanum, no doubt supplied by Auntie Olivia.

Wellington, she thought as she reached her door. *What about Wellington?*

She remembered asking one of Harry's flyboy mates, "So how do you pull out of a downward spiral?"

He had laughed and answered, "You ride the spiral and hope God grants you a miracle."

Eliza could still feel the spinning even after she found

her bed. Next to her, Wellington slept. She felt a new pang in her heart now, this one more selfish and needy. She needed a man's embrace. She wanted Harry more than ever, of course; but that was an opportunity lost. Now, all she had was Wellington Books. A man of the very elite that they had infiltrated. An agent completely void of field experience. A man that seemed immune to her charms. And yet, if he were to simply roll over and hold her, keep her safe, that would make everything better.

A rumble escaped from the figure slumbering far away from her.

Eliza covered her eyes.

Yes, this was the downward spiral. She would ride it out, and she—Eliza Braun, not God on high—would see them all through.

As she slipped towards exhausted sleep, she held onto that belief. Wellington's snoring should have kept her awake, but instead she felt the darkness slip around her. The darkness, and a dreadful sense of vertigo. Eliza spared a fleeting thought, perhaps it was a prayer, for her dreams to be merciful. It had been a full day, and rest—not an evening of worst situations and failing those who counted on her—was what she needed. If she did face such dreams, then her evening would be far from over.

Instead she became acutely aware of sunlight and the bed trembling underneath her. Eliza was now being awakened by Wellington Books. It only felt as scant moments, but there it was: morning. She had made it through the night.

Her eyes flicked open, and she could make through the blur of receding sleep her partner slipping behind the screen to get dressed.

Oh so modest, Mr. Books, she thought to herself, *even if we spent the night under the same sheets!*

The space between the two of them in the grand bed would have been difficult to explain to any early morning maid. Even Wellington had been unable to deny the sensible necessity of sharing a bed.

It wasn't what was worrying her however. Eliza instead found herself wondering what he thought had happened the previous evening. He was most likely imagining far worse than the reality. Assumption or no, Eliza felt resentment swell in her. She would be damned if it would fall upon *her* to relieve him of his notions.

Let him think her a strumpet if he liked. It was of no matter to her.

Wasn't it?

Regardless of Wellington's cast aspersions, she knew she had done a good thing last night. The foolish journalists would be on their way back to London, and it mattered little what they ended up writing. By the time any of that happened, she and Wellington would have closed the case.

If her acting skills had passed muster, then Mr. and Mrs. St. John would be found acceptable to this vile little secret society. With a sigh, Eliza rolled over, turning her back to the screen where Wellington was still carrying on his charade of manners. He was so stuck in his ways, and yet proving remarkably adept in his role. That gave her pause, and at the same time intrigued her.

Shoving back the bedclothes from around her shoulders, she peered around. Today was the hunting party, and Eliza was determined to keep playing the role Wellington had pushed her into. A gun in her hands though—that was going to prove to be a challenge. Especially with the person who had ordered Harry's killing only a bullet away from her.

Wellington emerged from the shadow of the screen, dressed in green tweed, his short pant legs tucked into long worsted socks. The morning light gleamed in his beard and for a second he looked like one of those silhouettes that hung on the wall of every middle-class family: a model of English normality. It was obvious that he wasn't aware she was awake. It was a skill Eliza had learned back home, and had proved one of the skills necessary for survival at school.

So it gave her some time to observe Wellington tiptoeing around the room. This moment where he did not know he was being watched was charming—he appeared genuinely relaxed, even as he stood at the dresser and adjusted his cravat. Curious, considering the situation they were in.

From under her eyelashes Eliza conducted an experiment. When she groaned softly, as if she was waking and rolled over in the bed, Wellington immediately snapped upright. Could it be that he was intimidated by women—or was it just her?

She sat up in bed, in what she considered a modest linen shift, but his gaze darted away as if she were stark naked. It wasn't as if she was even backlit by the sun, and most men would have taken the chance to see as much as possible. Harry certainly had at every opportunity.

No. She told herself. *Don't think about Harry—not yet.*

Wellington adjusted his shirt collar and looked at her in the mirror with some evident suspicion. Then he went to the gramophone and put on some early-morning music to mask their pending argument. Of course it had to be an argument regardless if the refrain of "The Moon Has Risen Her Lamp Above" served as their score.

"I'm sorry about last night, Miss Braun." He coloured slightly. "Training never covered that sort of situation."

Her lips twitched. "It's all right—one's first orgy is always a bit of a challenge."

Should she tell him that was her first too? Eliza had been in plenty of interesting situations, but never one of such . . . breadth. If it had been Harry at her side—well, things might have been different. The spasm of pain, of lost possibilities and choices made, went deep at that thought. Life had taught Eliza Braun about loss, but apparently its sting was not lessened at all by experience.

He cleared his throat. "I was concerned about that Devane chap. He was practically slavering to . . ." He paused to find a civilized word for it. "Well, I just didn't think it was necessary for you to go through that. Our good Queen would not demand that of a lady."

Indeed, the idea of that pervert's hands on her made Eliza

feel ill—luckily Devane had been too busy with his wife's niece. Still it would have been educational to see Wellington Books unleashed. In the midst of passion often the true nature of a person was revealed.

It would have to remain another mystery for another day. Slipping out of bed, she padded to the window and looked out. A beautiful clear day—perfect for all sorts of nefarious activities. With a series of stretches, which once again Books avoided looking directly at, Eliza prepared herself for the day. The bruises from previous adventures in London were fading, but she realistically expected them to be replaced with new ones before the end of the weekend.

"This had better work," she said moving behind the screen in deference to his sensibilities. "I had a rather nice offer of dinner at the Ritz for tonight."

"Who with?"

"No one you know, Welly. Some of us do have lives outside the Ministry." She poured a chilly bowl of water from the pitcher and washed herself quickly. She stepped into short petticoats and then into a light corset. Eliza backed away from the screens, towards Wellington. "Now be a dear and do me up?"

This time he did not hesitate. "It seems to me you are taking some enjoyment in getting me to act as your lady's maid," he said tartly, while pulling her stays firmly.

"You have promise," Eliza replied. "But you will have to best Alice in a knife fight to take her place."

Despite the situation, Wellington Books chuckled. "I will leave it to her then—I think your maid is too formidable for me."

She remained silent on her earlier observations. Wellington had his own inner grit that she believed, would indeed give her fearsome young Alice a run for her money.

"Right then," she slipped on a long green wool skirt over the top of her petticoats and buttoned on a cotton shirt and tailored jacket. "Let's just start anew and do our best to fit in."

Eliza produced from underneath their bed one of their suitcases, pulled from it a long leather satchel, and then unfurled said satchel as one would a tablecloth. Displayed before them in all their glory and menace were the weapons she'd brought with her. Trusting their hosts with supplying them firearms would have been a very foolish move and perhaps a fatal one. A gun could be rigged to misfire at an important moment. She cleaned and checked the pair of hunting rifles with as much precision as one born to the task would. Wellington did not help or offer to—which she admired. Most men would have been emasculated by her proficiency, but he was content to keep clear of something he knew nothing about.

Once she was done with her inventory check, Eliza turned to him. "What you have here are two Sharpe 92s. What every gentleman will be shooting next year—that ought to impress. However, they are not our only armaments." With a smooth gesture, she flipped up the long tweed jacket she wore to show him the *pounamu*-handled pistols. In hunting attire there was far more room to conceal them than in a damned evening dress. They fitted neatly in the small of her back, and as long as Bartholomew kept his hands to himself, there would be no reason why anyone would suspect anything.

And yet—she should not be the only one armed. After all, if they got separated, the Archivist needed some chance of defending himself. He couldn't know how hard it was for her, but she flicked out one of her treasured pistols and offered it to him.

He looked at her. "I have explained my position on guns, Miss Braun."

Damn stubborn man! Swallowing her anger, she reholstered the weapon and with another flick of her hand, she pulled out two stilettos from the inside lining of her jacket. These were not as fine as the two she had lost at the opera but were sturdier. She prided herself on learning from her lessons. She was also generous.

"Then this should be more your speed, Welly." He looked down at the offered knife as if she were presenting him with a rabbit that had been run over by a carriage wheel and sat by the side of the road for days. Eliza was mildly offended, but somehow not surprised.

"I don't think so."

Now he was being completely foolish. "Come on, Welly!" She fixed him with her most steely gaze. "You need to be able to take care of yourself. This is not a stroll through Hyde Park on a crisp spring day. We're in amongst tigers here. Think of what they did to Harry."

His lips pursed a little as he sized up her determination, and then he took one of the knives. It slipped from his fingers and would have hit the floor if Eliza hadn't caught it. Wellington smiled, but she wasn't letting him off that easy. Fishing out a sheath from her open suitcase, she slipped the knife within it and handed the now safer blade back to him.

"I confess, Miss Braun. The last time I used a knife it was on a goose at Christmas. And even then I cut myself."

Eliza patted his arm. "Then let us regard this token as an emergency plan—one we hope you never have to use. Now then"—she shoved one of the rifles into his hands—"have you ever been hunting before?" Wellington would at least have to pretend to know how to fire.

The look he shot her over the top of his glasses was amused as he examined the gun—and most definitely now was not the time for him to be amused.

"I see how this is," Eliza snatched the rifle out of his hands. "Leave it to me."

"And if . . ."—the Archivist cleared his throat—"If a similar situation to last night's occurs again?"

With a squeeze of his arm, she looked him straight in the eye. "This time, neither of us can flinch. Neither of us!"

His curt nod was the only answer she would accept. Yet, they could not afford to be grim. As they walked downstairs, past the gilt-framed pictures and hanging heads of animals mounted to the wall, Eliza readjusted her face into a pleasing smile.

"Come on, Welly," she hissed to him, giving his arm a yank. "Try not to look like you're going to the gallows."

The smile he plastered on would have put the actors of Drury Lane to shame. *Again with those talents of yours, Wellington*, Eliza thought to herself, and immediately was reminded of Harry.

No, she would *not* make those same mistakes again.

INTERLUDE

In Which Doctor Sound Investigates His Employees' Work Habits and Indulges in His Own Pursuits

Tick . . . tock . . . tick . . . tock . . .

A simple thing, a clock. Granted, take such a simple thing apart—be it a fob from a waistcoat or Big Ben itself—and, it is not nearly so simple. Gears. Cogs. Springs. So many elements that come together, fit into place, and then the element of Time is broken down to measurements of seconds, minutes, and hours. Amazing, and yet so futile to try and keep track of it.

Doctor Basil Sound unlaced his fingers and turned his attention to the calendar on the wall. Days. Months. Years. He smiled as he fixed his gaze on the current date, and then the compulsion, once again, struck him. The creak of the chair reminded him that he was no longer the man of this particular age. Not anymore. The prime he knew in his twenties and thirties was in the past, after all. Now he had the gait and the sparse hairstyle of experience, wisdom, and knowledge.

That was the perception, anyway.

Tick . . . tock . . . tick . . . tock . . .

Damnable clock, he thought. What was the fascination Man nursed to track Time, to reduce something so incredible to measurements that children learnt in school?

Doctor Sound removed his pocket watch and popped open the cover. His eyes went back and forth between the fob and the mantelpiece. *It's running slow*, he thought, crossing the room to remedy the inaccuracy. After opening the glass pane protecting the timepiece's face. Doctor Sound moved the minute hand forward by two minutes. If only it were true that Time could slow down, that with a gesture its current could be easily altered. Currents carried power, and Time's power was unmistakable. No, Time's current could not be manipulated so, but it was still a current like water; and those currents could be channeled, their power focused and applied to situations at hand. That was after all how the Ministry was powered.

Double-checking that the timepieces were calibrated properly, Doctor Sound gathered his satchel and, with one final look at its contents, fastened its latches tight. A last glance at the day on the calendar confirmed that indeed it was Saturday, meaning he had the entire office to himself. The lift would be as it was this morning: his.

He closed the lift's gate tight and brought its Chadburn all the way to "Archives" which began the descent. The motors and winches slowly eased him to the very bottom of the building, the gate revealing a tiny stone corridor that ended at a heavy iron hatch. After a long, low groan from the door, the silence accompanying Doctor Sound was peppered by the perpetual hum of the Ministry's generators and his own footfalls.

He paused on the stone staircase. Both agents were absent, and then he chided himself for expecting them to be present as it was the weekend. He searched his mind on when he last talked to them, a discussion that he meant to follow up, but failed to do so on account of his own agenda for today.

He thought back to the previous day's news—most of it

about a terrible production of Verdi's *Macbeth* which he had not bothered to skim. Like Eliza Braun he had no love of caterwauling of Italian divas so reading the critics' venom over a night at the opera hardly interested him. What he was looking for, much to his relief, was notably absent. No unexplained riots in the streets. No buildings decimated. Nothing in the papers to implicate them. Their own desks, though, looked as they had when he had prodded them about the shenanigans in Charing Cross.

He continued down the steps, his eyes studying the shared desk. Everything appeared to be exactly as they—

"No-no-no, Agent Braun," a familiar voice echoed. "You're cataloguing by name, when you need to start with the date first."

Another familiar voice chimed in with, "Very well, Agent Books, would you please be so kind as to explain it to me, once again?"

Considering the hollow sound of their voices, the conversation originated from the far end of the Archives. Tightening his grip on the satchel, Doctor Sound crept forward. If they were to see him, his agenda would have to dramatically change. *Perhaps*, he thought, *I could always address the Charing Cross matter again. That would explain why I chose to come in on a Saturday.*

"Once again," came Books' voice, "we deduce the unsolved case's year and group it by year. Once we have grouped the years, we will then go back and group them by individual dates of that particular year, and finally, we will alphabetise them based on the month they appear in the case header."

From the top of the stone staircase, Doctor Sound could make out a pair of shimmering shadows moving back and forth within the Archives' crypt.

"To think I am giving you a weekend for all this," Braun huffed.

"Miss Braun, look at the amount of cases here. Do you really think it will be tended to in just *one* weekend?"

Admirable, Doctor Sound thought with a smile. *Also, the best of distractions for Agent Braun.*

Turning away from the stone stairwell leading to the forgotten cases, Doctor Sound reached into his coat and pulled out the pair of keys needed for this hatch. He slipped each key into its respective hole and then simultaneously turned them towards each other. He then spun the massive wheel to the left until it locked. The dull *thunk* boomed through the Archives, making him freeze. Doctor Sound held his breath and looked over his shoulder.

"Welly?" she asked.

"Miss Braun, please!"

"Sorry, Agent Books. Now, *Welly*, where does this trinket go?"

"They do teach reading in the colonies, yes?" Doctor Sound managed to stifle a laugh. He was impressed that Books was managing to hold his own against the feisty lass. "What does the tag say?"

With a soft exhale, Doctor Sound turned the keys away from each other. The hatch's lock released with a hiss that made him pause again—just in case his hardworking employees heard it. He watched as the sapphire luminescence from the Restricted Area reached past him, extending his shadow even further. Still, Books and Braun worked diligently in the depths of the Archives, far from the glow and the undulating hum, which now greeted him. He looked into the light for a moment and then back in the direction of his agents. They were still talking. Or was it bickering?

"Why yes, you've got it!" Books laughed. "By George, I think you've got it."

"Books"—and that warning made even Doctor Sound pause—"if you ever say *You've got it. By George, I think you've got it* to me again, I promise you all the fires of hell and the tortures of Beelzebub will pale in comparison to five minutes with me and a teaspoon. Are we clear?"

Doctor Sound realised he was holding his breath again. He needed them to break this silence.

"Crystal, Agent Braun."

Talking. Bickering. So long as they are not listening, he thought. Doctor Sound removed the two keys from the hatch and placed his satchel on the other side of the threshold. He gave one final look towards the crypt, slipped the keys back into his pocket, and then stepped through the hatch.

He turned back to secure it behind him, and that was when he felt the hair on the back of his neck stand.

Movement. He was sure of it. Someone else—not Agents Books or Braun—was down here in the Archives.

He narrowed his eyes, peering into the stacks. Perhaps his more-than-overactive, fertile imagination was playing tricks with him again. Having Books and Braun so close must have unnerved him more than he cared to admit. It was Saturday, after all. Why were they not elsewhere? He was surprised Agent Braun, for one, was not enjoying a weekend's retreat in the country somewhere with some dapper, handsome beau. Maybe Wellington Books was blunting that edge of hers. A bit.

"And now?"

"Now, we go alphabetical," Books answered. "One step at a time, Miss Braun. That's the way."

Again, Doctor Sound leaned toward the Archives. He waited, but all was still. Apart from the Archivists in the crypt, the Director was alone.

Time to go.

His hand touched the breast of his coat, where he had returned the keys. Assured, Doctor Sound gave the valves inside the entrance several turns. With a steady hiss the heavy iron hatch slowly closed, devouring him with the low hum, the warm blue light, and what remained locked within the Ministry's Restricted Area.

CHAPTER TWENTY-FOUR

In Which Our Dashing Duo Do a Spot of Hunting and Discover What the Phoenix Society's Favourite Sport Truly Is

Below, in the marble floor atrium, the people from the night before were gathered once again. They were quite different from the last glimpses Eliza had of them. Naked and leering the Phoenix Society and their initiates indulged in behaviours baudier than most drinking songs, dirty limericks, and music hall revues she had known. Now in the light of a new day, they had reverted back to all their pompous nature, the previous evening a distant memory, best forgotten. That was another thing British aristocracy did well—and one thing Eliza's New Zealand sensibilities could not stand: arrogance.

She had seen the destruction it could wreak on "the little people" below them. The Ministry, despite its promises to Queen and Country, was the great leveler. Harry had believed that they were the advocate for the people without a voice. He had died for that belief. And if it came to it, so would she.

The servants were also dressed for hunting, and Eliza

contemplated what secrets they might be privy to. They were standing stone-faced, lining the hallway like emotionless statues.

When Bartholomew Devane looked at her, lust written in every line of his face, she smiled sweetly. Even in the brilliance of a breathtaking day, the man sent an unsettling shiver underneath her skin. His poor wife also glanced up, but hers was the look akin to the house servants. Other ladies were twittering like a flock of disturbed birds, but Olivia Devane stood apart. Her hands held each other, as if they could give her comfort. Eliza recognised those gestures, those fruitless gestures.

"St. John," Bartholomew bellowed, "Lord, why is your wife dressed for the hunt? Most of the ladies are spending the day at proper pursuits—embroidery and some such."

Perhaps, it was a good thing Wellington had cast her in the role of mute because she had to bite the inside of her cheek from saying something very cutting at this point. Her "husband" waited until they were free of the mansion's entranceway and standing next to the great bombast before giving his reply in a far more civilised tone. "Mrs. St. John is also my valet. She enjoys taking care of my needs, and because of her affliction she is also more trustworthy than a mere servant."

Eliza's jaw twitched, and she stomped against the floor once.

Bartholomew's eyes gleamed. "Oh I do like your style, old boy. You must be in my party today."

He then turned to his wife as he took a drag off his cigarette, the disappointment on his face clear as the cerulean blue outside, and then puffed smoke into the poor woman's face. "See Olivia, you should learn from St. John's wife. Get yourself a skill—or perhaps just learn to shut up and stay as such."

If there were any accusations to be leveled at Olivia it was not that she was a chatterbox. As the men drifted away, Eliza reached out and lightly touched the poor woman's shoulder. It was a show of solidarity that she shouldn't have really given, yet she felt the other flinch.

At least with her husband out on the hunt Olivia would have a moment's peace. Eliza knew that if she had been in her place, she would have cracked. The crack would have happened with Devane's neck, and it would have been a *clean* break.

The crowd, including a handful of women, moved outside with servant dutifully following in their wake.

"A lovely day," came the voice behind everyone, "Just capital for sport, wouldn't you all agree, my Brethren?"

Everyone turned in unison to see Doctor Havelock standing on the steps of his manor. His smile reflected the warmth of the morning sun, while his eyes twinkled with a jovial benevolence. The Society members all called out felicitations as he continued down the steps of his home to where everyone was collected.

"And you, Initiates, I take it you all rested well?" Havelock asked, his eyes moving from gentleman to gentleman.

When Havelock saw Eliza alongside Wellington and Devane, his head cocked to one side. His feet crunched in the fine gravel, and he hooked his thumbs in his vest pockets as he walked over to their party.

"The church mouse," Doctor Havelock began, his expression as cool as the southern ice cap while considering Eliza, "but not so quiet the previous evening. Quite the erotic songbird you are." Havelock turned to the other ladies present. "Do take your cue from this one. Limit your fine conversation this morning, as this is a gentlemen's outing, yes?"

The men all laughed on cue while Eliza blushed and looked away. Havelock gave a soft chuckle to Wellington, and then drew them over to the other initiates.

"Stay close to me, St. John," Bartholomew whispered, giving him a friendly wink.

The Pembrokes appeared refreshed and a picture of prime English upbringing, ready for a morning's hunt. The Collins, on the other hand, looked tired. Eliza recalled Angelique partaking in the night's revels with great zeal, her husband watching her with keen interest. Presently, they were summoning up fortitude and smiles.

It was like being in school again. They so wanted to fit in, to be selected as the teacher's favourite.

Her eyes casually passed over the party. The Fairbankses were nowhere to be seen. No one would have noticed, but Eliza let out a long, silent exhale. She felt herself pulling free of the previous night's downward spiral.

"We have a lovely morning ahead of us," Havelock said to all of them, "and it promises to be a smashing afternoon. Enjoy the sport, everyone."

They were quickly divided into groups an initiate paired up with one or two Brethren. It would have been preferable for her and Wellington to be in the party containing Havelock, had Havelock joined a party. Instead, he inexplicably returned to the manor, choosing not to sully his day shooting with jostling initiates.

However, as he had promised, Bartholomew arranged for them to head off with him.

In the distance, mist was just beginning to lift off the dark green hills. The air was sharp and clear, very unlike London. Truly, a beautiful day—and normally the prospect of hunting would have lifted her spirits. However, the present company sullied the occasion. The guests and their accompanying trail of servants spread out over the hills, while beaters, who had been out hours before, worked their way through the low brush to scare up pheasants.

While Wellington chatted with Bartholomew and took little sips from a fine silver hipflask, Eliza prepared his weapons. A grim-faced valet was doing the same for the vile aristocrat. The man revealed nothing in his expression or action, and did not spare a word to her. Very well trained, these servants of Havelock. The working class on this estate either lived in fear of their lives, or were just as committed to the goals of their master. Presently, she had no way of finding out.

Shots popped and cracked down the line as birds leapt from the brush and swept away in great arch in the bright blue sky above them. A glance told Eliza that Wellington was nervous as hell as shots worked their way towards them. She gave him a nudge and handed him a different weapon, one that was not loaded. The colour in his face started to recede, but a jerk of her head and his eyes lit up.

Another flock of pheasant sprung out in front of their little group, and Wellington stepped forward, raising his rifle. He looked as if he was about to draw a bead on the fowl, when he gasped and pointed to the right. "Doctor Havelock?" he called.

Devane was certainly of the nervous, stupid sort, because he spun around as if an assassin was leaping at him. In that split second, Eliza cocked the rifle cradled in her arms, placed the primed rifle's barrel on Wellington's shoulder, and fired twice, the hammers both striking close to Wellington's ear. As two birds tumbled and Wellington's once-confident stance wavered, Eliza handed him the smoking gun and snatched the empty one from his grasp.

"Bloody hell," Devane turned back. His face was bright red. "What do you think you were doing, old boy?"

"I'M SORRY!" Wellington bellowed.

"You called out to Doctor Havelock when he was nowhere in sight!"

"NO, I'VE NOT SEEN BANGKOK AT NIGHT! I HEAR IT'S LOVELY!"

His brow furrowed, and Eliza saw the man's grip tighten across the butt of his own rifle. "I can respect an opportunist, to be certain. But a cad?"

Eliza felt a stinging sensation in her neck. She hoped he didn't notice her flinch. *He* was calling her partner a cad?

Wellington massaged his ear canal for a moment and then mimicked yawning, shaking his head with a quick exhale that caused his lips to flutter audibly. "Sorry about that, Lord Devane, but I had forgotten that my hearing is quite sensitive to loud noises. I wear cotton wadding in the factories so that my hearing rema—"

"Stuff your hearing, St. John, and explain yourself!"

Straightening up to the challenge, Wellington once again displayed his disturbing ability to blend in with this vile crowd. He laughed up boorishly. " Oh, I see, you are at odds with me for the distraction? Well now, Lord Devane, I ask you where has there been true honour on the field of battle? This is an initiation, after all. Everything we do is a test, isn't it?"

"That's as may be, St. John, but—"

"And you have a Major as one of the candidates? I'm certain he will bag two quail with little to no effort. How do I compete against that sort of skill? Ingenuity."

Devane glared at him, but there was a grudging tone of admiration in his voice. "Clever solution, old boy."

Wellington shot back a wink. "I have my moments."

For the remainder of the afternoon, Lord Devane took measure (and from what Eliza saw, pride) in shouldering Wellington out of the way every time a brace of pheasant rose from the undergrowth. Yes, it was—after all—an initiation for Wellington, and assuredly everything was a test. Her bagging had shown Wellington's "skill" enough for him to irritate Devane. This may not have been the most ideal situation Eliza would have wished for, seeing as she wanted Wellington to shine. However, the spiteful part of her was thrilled. She liked annoying Bartholomew Devane.

The tall, imposing butler who had been tending to Doctor Havelock the previous night slowly traversed over the rolling hills of the estate, tapping a small, handheld gong. The parties followed the servant to a flat clearing where the help had laid out a very fine feast on a series of tables. Eliza's status as valet to her "husband" had neatly relegated her to servant status, an unexpected advantage in intelligence gathering that she would begrudgingly need to thank Wellington for. She was able to circulate through the crowd of men dining on sandwiches and scotch without notice.

Unfortunately none of the conversations were particularly worthy of note, mostly about the current sport, the delectable entertainment of First Night, or the appalling state of the Empire, usual topics for a gathering of men.

The gong that had called them all together rang softly once more. Eliza finished off her flute of champagne and callously set it aside for the servants to tend to. *All part of the façade*, she tried to assure herself, though it gave her little comfort. The company was now adjourning for the afternoon's entertainment; but as Eliza returned to where the Devane party waited, their collected numbers seemed smaller. She paused, looking at the parties spreading out.

"Hyacinth," Wellington barked, "unless what you have forgotten is tantamount to the Holy Grail, do get a move on!"

All part of the façade, she seethed, and this time the mantra gave her less comfort.

After an hour, the beaters had not lifted any more birds from the underbrush and even Lord Devane lowered his gun. He lit a freshly rolled cigarette and scanned the scene. It seemed that every party was enduring the same luck, and small hipflasks were in evidence as the hunters waited for more game to be driven towards them.

"Damned fine woman, your wife, St. John." His look raked up Eliza, as if she were a display at a museum. "I can understand you not wanting her available for everyone at last night's entertainment. Once you're a member though, she will be considered part of the Society, to be shared accordingly."

Wellington touched her face, running down Eliza's cheek in the kind of proprietary fashion she would have barely allowed in her lovers. "We are still just getting to know each other, you see, so I wholeheartedly admit my selfishness. Once we are all joined up though, I suppose I will have to learn to share."

Their companion took another long puff. "Now just a moment, old boy. You're not part of the Society. Yet. But if you would care to have a champion within the ranks, I would be more than happy to speak on your behalf, in exchange for a sampling of this fine dish." His head jerked towards the wood at their backs. "If I weren't such a gentleman perhaps I would suggest"—his grin widened—"a little outdoor adventure—but as per the previous evening, I would prefer to have her wholly naked." Devane's eyes jumped back to Wellington. "I say this completely with respect, old boy. She's a fine creature."

Eliza imagined smashing the butt of the rifle into that leering face—thinking about it hard helped her stop from actually doing it.

Wellington chuckled, but his reply was cut off. Devane gave a curt nod to his manservant, and his cigarette was exchanged for a primed shotgun. "No time for that now, I'm afraid," he gasped, his voice now overcome with elation as the gun raised.

Eliza's impulses lifted her own rifle, but Wellington moved with unexpected grace, catching the barrel of her shotgun before it could return Devane's threat. He now brandished the weapon, his eyes silently assuring her *I'll have to manage.* Both Wellington and Eliza whirled around in the direction in which Devane was walking. Whatever could have produced such excitement in him could not be a good thing.

Their fears were validated on hearing the scream. Time stretched around that terrible moment. The Fairbankses—or the journalists Eliza knew were masquerading as Harold and Dahlia Fairbanks—were scrambling through the low scrub, keeping a pace Eliza was familiar with. It was not to be mistaken—this was the all-out flight for life. She would have opened fire on the hunters regarding the imposters as sport, had she been armed. However, it was all happening too fast. Observation was easy, reaction lagged far behind.

The Brethren and the Society candidates were taking shots at them. From design or chance, the pair were running in a zigzag pattern, stumbling and falling over the uneven, unfamiliar ground.

Molly screamed a choking, horrified scream for mercy and survival as Fred tugged her after him. Eliza's throat constricted. Molly and Fred weren't lucky, and the Brethren weren't poor shots.

Bartholomew had already lazily raised his rifle, tracked their progress with a measured horizontal movement of the barrel. Then he fired twice. Two shots, two perfectly measured shots. Molly dropped, immediately followed by Fred. One was, mercifully, a headshot, but Eliza's stomach rolled on hearing a thrashing around in the underbrush, accompanied by a hard, high-pitched hacking cough. Molly was choking on her own blood. Eliza recognised in the woman's throes the sign that she now had a hole in her throat. She was dying by inches.

"Now *that* is proper sport!" Devane erupted. He himself was ecstatic. "Care to finish her off, old boy?" he asked Wellington.

"Forgive me, Bartholomew," Eliza heard Wellington's voice but she could not look away from the carnage. She couldn't have been more than twenty. "I prefer to kill on the first shot."

Devane's laughter turned into a disgusted moan. "Oh I say, Hewitt," he said over his shoulder, holding out the spent shotgun, "Please take care of that pathetic creature."

"Very good, sir," the man replied, replacing Devane's weapon with his still-lit cigarette.

Hewitt casually checked a pistol and then strode off into the bush. Even from their distance, the three of them could see Molly's white dress twitching, and smeared with the crimson strokes of a mad artist.

Eliza felt the vertigo creep in. Molly was in the same outfit from last night. Wellington and Eliza stood very still, watching Hewitt close the distance. She couldn't breathe, suspended above the situation in horror.

Their companion savoured another long drag and looked at them through the smoke. "Journalists. Not the right sorts at all—and hardly proper putting on a pretense as they did.

Havelock saw it at once. We do not tolerate deception, old boy."

There was the confirmation: this Phoenix Society was far more than just a modern Hellfire Club. Eliza moved imperceptibly closer to Wellington. Against a group armed with long-range weapons she and the Archivist would only be marginally more likely to escape—

The pop of the pistol rang out over the grounds. Eliza did not flinch. Neither did Wellington. She might not have shown any outward sign, but inwardly she made a promise to Molly: There would be a reckoning. By the time she and Wellington walked away from this place there would be justice for all those the Phoenix Society had crushed beneath their feet so thoughtlessly. Obviously Molly had not let on about the other two hens in the den, but that was cold comfort. It was going to be impossible for Eliza to forget her face.

Wellington considered her then twisted his mouth into a smirk. "And here I thought the Phoenix Society was lax on their standards. So nice to know that discipline is so well maintained." His arm locked around Eliza, pulling her in close. She could feel his anger in his grasp, but still he kept the illusion. "And that you're a fine shot."

"Thank you, old boy." Devane shook his head. "A bit disappointed in you, though."

Eliza's grip tightened on his arm but Wellington merely replied with, "I don't finish what others start, Lord Devane, and I wouldn't have missed."

"Excellent shooting, Barty!" Havelock called, walking from the direction of the manor. His smile was as broad and charming as a shark's. "But what happened with the woman?"

"I could have imbibed too much brandy throughout the morning." Devane shrugged, his eyes never leaving Wellington. "I will endeavour to do better next time."

"So you should," he chided. Havelock turned to Wellington and Eliza, his eyes still nurturing their earlier look of jollity. "The Fairbankses were journalists, we discovered.

They were looking to pen an article on private clubs, like ours. We just couldn't have that."

"Certainly not, Doctor Havelock," Devane agreed quickly.

"Now," Havelock said, smiling, "how about a bite to eat?"

"As long as the entree has nothing to do with what Lord Devane just brought down." Wellington chuckled.

While Eliza watched Devane join in with the laughter, Havelock did not. His face remained as chill as stone. "We're not in the colonies, St. John. We are a civilised society." He adjusted his collar. "We will have them stuffed and mounted for display."

By the tone of his voice it was hard to judge if he was joking or not. Either way Eliza decided that at tonight's dinner they had indeed better play whatever game was required of them.

CHAPTER TWENTY-FIVE

Wherein Doctor Havelock Displays His Work and an Unexpected Guest Makes a Fashionable Entrance

Apart from the Fairbankses, something was notably absent from the dinner party that night. It was an identical setting as the First Night celebration, but Wellington sensed something was off. Quite off. There was no mention of the couple, but he did not believe it was out of respect for their memory. It was fear. Fear of association with them. Fear of becoming *like* them. Uttering their names could have at best meant a black mark against any chances of initiation; and considering how the Fairbankses were dealt with, any reasons for repercussion were to be avoided.

Wellington wondered how huge of a black mark it would have been if Havelock knew he had thrown up in the toilet on returning from the hunt.

Eliza had remained by his side, amazingly enough. He did not understand why she continued to gently rub his back as he gagged and heaved. Surely this would provide hours of amusement for her on returning to the Archives.

With every spasm, with every painful retching ripped

from his throat, she had sat by him, palm gently pressing into his back, making long, slow circles. "*It's all right,*" she'd whispered to him, again and again. Had he the voice, Wellington would have wanted to scream, *No, it is not all right. We watched a couple gunned down like foxes at the hunt. How is that all right?*

Instead, he continued to vomit until there was nothing left in his stomach. He didn't remember leaving the bathroom or passing out on the bed. When he stirred, he was under the covers, Eliza asleep on the chaise longue. The sun was setting. It was a picturesque moment of tranquility that screamed for a photographer. At least that was how it appeared in that moment of heavy silence.

He needed to wash his mouth out, brush his teeth, and prepare for the night's revels.

"*It's all right,*" he kept hearing Eliza whisper.

"*Perhaps the colonial is, for once, correct,*" came the voice of his father when he emerged from the water closet. "*Perhaps those people were not right for this circle. Nothing wrong with separating those who are from those who are not.*"

"What?" Eliza had asked, noting his reflection in the mirror.

"*Common woman,*" his father seethed in Wellington's mind. "*Making sacrifices for Queen and Country, she calls it? The trollop enjoyed herself the previous night, I have no doubt.*"

"It's nothing."

"Books, if you are not up for—"

"I said it's nothing. Therefore, it is *nothing.*" His contempt even surprised him. He snatched up a brush and began working on his hair. "Do not question me, Miss Braun—otherwise, you never will trust me," he said, setting the brush aside and tugging at his vest.

Seconds slipped away. The silence, Wellington considered, had been oppressive.

"Stay with me, Wellington," she had told him. "There is a time and a place to lose yourself in a part—"

"*How dare this woman address you in such a fashion*," hissed his father.

"—and there will be those times you will need to remain cognisant of who you are and whom you trust. Do we understand each other, Books?"

Wellington remained silent, his eyes fixed into the mirror.

"Agent Books?"

There was something soothing about the repetitive grooming.

"Do we have an understanding?"

"Yes," he finally answered. "Indeed we do."

Wellington really didn't understand. He didn't understand why someone would choose to do field work. The Archives made sense to him. Logistics. Facts. Deduction.

Not this.

There was a specific kind of person that engaged in covert intelligence. He understood the type usually to be detached and distant. They were talented people. That, he would never question.

"*No need to muck about with the soldiers in the trenches*," his father would scoff.

With a final, long look to each other, Wellington and Eliza had discarded their own demeanors for their St. John personas; and now once more, they were in the dining room, enjoying a lovely dinner.

However, there was no avoiding the two vacant places at the table, and everyone heeded the warning in their own way.

The initiates were now taking careful stock of one another. The Pembrokes particularly were keeping their distance—from everyone. It must have been his military training, assessing the very real threat surrounding him and his wife. With children to consider, they must have changed their priority to surviving the weekend. Nathaniel Pembroke, on locking eyes with Wellington, sized him up. Had the man been holding a pistol, Wellington would have felt an urge to dive for cover.

The other remaining couple, the Collinses, appeared nervous. Barnabus was sweating, while Angelique's pallid complexion against her white evening dress gave her the semblance of a wraith. Both of them were looking quickly to either side of them, desperate to keep up the appearance of eager, willing initiates.

Wellington glanced at Eliza; her eyes were still downcast.

"I say, St. John," came a voice next to him.

Wellington dabbed at his mouth with his napkin before answering, "Lord Devane."

"Tosh, man, you know to call me Bartholomew. Why the formal—" Then he paused, and gave a soft "Ah," accompanied with a bright, knowing smile. "I wouldn't worry, old boy, about your running for the spot. You are making many around here sit up and take notice."

"Am I now?"

"Quite," he assured Wellington. "Apart from your delightful wife, you are showing good character. The right fit for our Society."

"Well then," Wellington said, giving a slight exhale. "I assume then that means my brains will remain in my head."

Devane chuckled. "We have standards and traditions, old boy. You have to understand."

"I do—though I do find your initiation rituals a bit—incontrovertible."

Devane nodded. "They have to be. When you hear what Havelock has to say tonight, you will understand fully."

"I look forward to it," Wellington replied as calmly as he could, casting a quick glance to the head of the table.

Doctor Havelock, this time, had been waiting for everyone, his face warm and pleasant with no trace of remorse from the afternoon's grizzly judgement passed on the journalists. He now enjoyed the first course with everyone, even through the tension in the air. Wellington then cast his eyes around the dining room, and that's when he noticed the additional space. Was it on account of the missing couple? No. The gaslight was catching the butler's mirrors in the walls. The gaslight caught the curved fixtures as there were no servants standing by them. Behind Havelock's throne, where servants would have been, was a pair of brass obelisks, rising up waist high to the only servant present in the room. Their appetizer had been served and the first round of wine had been poured; but now, only the imposing butler always within Havelock's call was present. The servant was as still as the two obelisks.

"Good evening, Brethren and Initiates all," Havelock spoke, silencing everyone. "I know that my presence here, and my current outburst, is not characteristic to those of you who know me well; but to you, my Brethren, when have I ever been known for convention?"

The laughter was polite, perhaps touched with a hint of apprehension.

"I am here for a simple indulgence: to see your reactions." Havelock turned to his butler. "Pearson, you may begin."

The lone butler turned to one of the obelisks, reaching behind it to lift a lever fixed in its back, Pearson's efforts providing mild amusement for some of the ladies in the room. Once the lever locked into the upright position, silvery-pearl jets erupted from vents on either side. The loud, accompanying hiss evoked gasps from the ladies, but the screams of surprise and horror came when metal plates slid back and skeletal arms and legs comprised of gears, pistons, and struts extended from the casing. By the time the obelisk's top rotated and transformed into an angular face accented by eye sockets and a mouth-shaped grill that glowed with a gaseous, deep emerald light, Pearson had locked the lever on the second obelisk.

Havelock took in the reactions of shock and terror with all the delight of a child on Christmas morning.

Wellington struggled to keep an eye on their quarry, but

he himself found the new devices far too enticing. He could feel the cool exterior he had worked so hard to build evaporating; but the more the automatons took form, the less Wellington cared.

When they moved of their own accord, he felt himself straighten slightly, a surge of joy in his chest. These creations were simply magnificent! He thought he heard a gasp come from Eliza, but a moment later he realised that it was from his own mouth.

Then his eyes happened to meet Havelock's. The man was staring at *him*, and his smile widened. He gave Wellington a compatriot's nod. *You understand*, the simple gesture conveyed. Havelock kept his gaze on Wellington until the eight-foot automatons flanked him.

"I give you tonight's attendants, my friends. I give you the future," he announced, sounding like a father announcing the birth of his child. "The future that the Society has dreamed for so long, they will bring to fruition. But before that reality comes to pass—"

His finger flipped a single switch on the closest "attendant's" wrist, and the green glow from inside its brass cranium surged for a moment. Havelock repeated the gesture on the other automaton, and both stomped out of the room with a strange grace that came unexpected concerning their imposing build and height.

"—dinner first? Please, everyone, return to your seats."

Once again, a lovely meal of greens, poultry, and lamb, and fine wine that never seemed to end, was served. It was all as delightful as the previous evening, yet the serenity and civility of the proceedings were continuously broken when the ominous mechanical monsters would slowly tread into the dining room. Astoundingly, the automatons were able to handle the tasks of tending to the dinner party's needs with the same efficiency as the house staff. Any delay based on their size seemed to be taken into account.

There was also the look of the automatons themselves. One or two of the Brethren's wives—and even a few of the

Society's men—grew pale when the things leaned in to serve. Conversation couples shared would cease abruptly as a metallic arm extended between them in order to replenish their wine. Wellington found it curious that while the house servants were regarded as appliances for the privileged, these mechanised manservants were more so. They were not alive, sentient, or in any way possessing consciousness. No egos to bruise. No fragility or vulnerabilities. If they had a particularly bad day, you could send them in for repair. These automatons *were* appliances.

One advantage the now apparently outdated house staff still possessed over this modern convenience: their invisibility. It was easy for the upper class to dismiss or ignore the working class. An apparatus of hydraulics, brass cylinders, pumps, and spinning gears provided a greater challenge to ignore, particularly when said apparatus reached between you and your wife to fill the glasses.

Dash it all, Wellington thought as he dabbed the corners of his mouth. Then he turned towards the head of the table where Havelock watched his creations' clockwork ballet with glee. "Doctor Havelock, a word if you please?"

All conversation ceased. In the distant corner of his eye Wellington could see Bartholomew, now almost as ashen as his wife. Not even Eliza's gentle touch on his thigh caused him to start. The die had been cast, and this was his opportunity. This was his area of expertise.

Havelock's smile eased a bit, a bushy eyebrow crooking ever so silently. "You have a question, St. John?"

"Yes, Doctor," Wellington replied. "I am compelled to ask—how?"

Now Eliza's fingers squeezed his knee, none too gently either. Wellington reached for his glass of wine, downed it in a rather ungentlemanly display, and then replaced it on the table. His hand slipped under the table afterward, resting on top of Eliza's—trying to communicate assurance—even though his head was spinning slightly after partaking of the drink so quickly.

With a soft hiss, the metallic arm extended into the space between him and Havelock. Wellington kept his gaze locked with the man; his own knowing smile never faltering as his glass was refilled and the automaton stepped back to its neutral position.

Wellington inclined his head forward, the slight gesture earning him a few soft gasps from the ladies of the table. It was a silent repeat of the question. *How?*

Havelock's own smile widened once more. He began to laugh, his own eyes twinkling at Wellington's initiative. He waved a finger at him, "For a man in the textiles industry, Richard, you seem quite taken by the sciences."

Wellington grinned, noting with a quick glance how Bartholomew's once pallid complexion was now scarlet. "To keep a factory running, one must have machines. To keep the factory running efficiently, it is good to know how these machines work. To keep the factory profitable, it is essential to know how to improve upon the current technologies."

"So you get your hands dirty, do you?"

"On occasion, yes." Wellington heard someone snort at the other end of the table. "But while others are tending to their managers when mills encounter mechanical failure, I am solving matters and improving upon the situation."

"Fascinating," Havelock whispered with reverence, casting a glance down the table. A throat cleared, and then he continued. "Do you have any patents pending on these advancements?"

"Do you?" Wellington shot back. Eliza's grip tightened further on his leg, but he remained steady. "Why, Doctor Havelock, would I want to share my advantages with the world?" He reached for the wine, swirled it slightly in the glass, sampled its bouquet, and added, "Not yet. When I am ready to sell the company, then I will sell my ideas to the highest bidder. Not before. When the world is ready. When *I* am ready."

"That sounds like good business sense," Havelock replied.

"But, Doctor, you are evading the question." Wellington took a sip of his wine.

"Under the table," their host said with a smile.

Wellington removed his hand from Eliza's and felt the table's unseen surface. He chuckled, causing the men to scoot away and crane down to look underneath the table as well. Wellington's fingers traced the heated coils to various points of the table, making certain not to touch the copper for too long. The coils all led to what felt like large metal plates. One was wide enough to cover where his plate was while another was located just underneath his wineglass.

"Your heating element?"

"The manor was built on the site of a geothermal fissure, a rather large one as a matter of fact." Havelock fixed him with a satisfied smirk. "It provides ample power for the pressure pads built into the table, the wireless that the *Mechamen* are in constant contact with, and the plumbing here in the house."

Wellington nodded in approval. "So when the weight on the table changes—the plate itself, the setting, or the amount of wine in one's glass—your wireless sends commands to the—"

"Mechamen," he said, his pride quite powerful.

"Mechamen," Wellington repeated, nodding slowly as he looked about the table. "But to calibrate the movements and timing to fill a glass or—"

A memory from the previous night struck him. It had been a fleeting moment, the tiniest of details that could have easily been overlooked, falling into place as the Mechamen stood in waiting, their gears and cogs ticking rhythmically as would a metronome.

Wellington beamed. "That is ingenious."

"Thank you, Richard," Havelock stated.

Wellington looked around him. While Devane's own gaze remained dark and malicious, the Brethren and Initiates stared at him. Some appeared curious. Others impatient.

"Did you notice how Doctor Havelock kept an eye on the time with his house staff?" he asked the table. "He was not timing their performance, but merely noting the timing of their actions, watching for consistencies, and it was the average mean of their performance times he used to set the internal clocks of the Mechamen." Wellington raised his glass to Doctor Havelock. "Bravo, Doctor."

He simply raised a hand in response, perhaps an attempt at modesty? "Tosh, I am no artist."

"These Mechamen are brilliant," Wellington retorted. "An incredible achievement."

"Oh, Richard," Havelock rose slowly from his table. "What you have seen—" He then took his eyes to everyone at the table, "What you all have seen is merely the tip of the iceberg, that which is visible. You have no idea what lurks underneath the surface."

That was the verbal cue to the one human servant in attendance, Pearson, who started turning the ornate valve set in the wall. As he was the only one there, he had to weave past the Mechamen to the opposite valve which also hissed as he released the pressure. The wall, as it had the previous evening, slid back, revealing not a collection of intertwined bodies but several targets. Standing inside two archery targets secured to bails of hay were bamboo representations of men—men dressed in what appeared to be uniforms of the British Empire. Wellington glanced to Pembroke who showed no revulsion or distaste. In fact, his mouth seemed to twitch into the lightest of grins.

"Allow me to demonstrate," Havelock said, motioning to his manservant to tend to his creations, "the full potential of my Mechamen."

Pearson now went to each automaton and threw the small switch within their forearms from the far right to the far left. He then wasted no time excusing himself from the room with extra long strides as the giants began emitting a soft whine, a whine that grew louder with each second. The luminescent mist that filled their faceplates turned from deep green to a deep red, their internal whine now subsiding to the ticking sound of their cogs at double their earlier pace. Their arms snapped downward, and the panels covering certain gearworks started turning and sliding up and back, making room for a pair of cylinders sliding out of the shoulders' chassis. When these new features locked into place, Wellington felt his throat tighten. The cold, icy demeanour fell to the wayside as he slapped Eliza on the shoulder and then plugged his ears with his fingers. Without question Eliza did the same.

When the Mechamen moved this time, the floor trembled, the ceiling and wall chandeliers tinkled. Dinner guests recoiled even though the brass leviathans did not even look in their respective directions. They were now taking positions within the ballroom, their prearranged targets far on the other side of it. The Mechamen's arms swung up and then bent at a hinge where a man's elbow would be. With a sharp, loud sting of metal, the arms again locked fast.

That was when the cylinders started spinning.

If any of the women were screaming, their caterwauling was drowned out by the gunfire. The Gatling guns were obviously smaller than even the army had; but the noise was far louder in the small space. Bullet shells bounced and sprayed everywhere as the Mechamen let fly against the archery targets. Once the structures holding them in place collapsed, the bamboo figures were next. They did not remain standing for long as the guns tore through the durable wood as if it were tissue paper.

Then the flames protruding from the arms of the Mechamen vanished. The roar of artillery had ceased. The smoke surrounding them hung heavily, its scent causing the ladies—all save Eliza—to cover their mouths with their husbands' kerchiefs. The ballroom's chandelier remained intact, but the display's sound had knocked out a few panes of glass from the bay windows. Everyone started as the Mechamen suddenly stood up to their full height, their arms slowly extending outward and then lowering to their sides.

Their faceplates still radiated red, but the glow was much softer now.

Wellington and Eliza lowered their fingers and shared a glance with each other.

"Good God," Bartholomew said, "these things are—"

"Merely the beginning," interrupted Havelock.

"Incredible," came another voice. "Doctor Havelock, this is truly an amazing achievement on your part."

"Thank you, Charles," he beamed in reply, "but I certainly cannot take all the credit for it. I needed a good weapons master to consult with me on these Mechamen."

Havelock then turned to the doorway, and that was when Wellington saw Pearson there, waiting dutifully. How long had he been there? When this tall butler moved, he was as silent as the softest whisper. Pearson gave a single nod, and then motioned in the direction of the foyer.

"Imagine my surprise when that master was, in actuality, a *mistress*." He chuckled.

The woman entering the room brought smiles to the faces of the men. She possessed a bosom rivaling Eliza's, however, the ebony evening dress she wore made her appear menacing and yet ethereal. Wellington swallowed, feeling the sudden dryness in his throat; and with all the wine he had drunk he was now in desperate need of a water closet. Certainly he knew her—how could he forget *her*?

A sharp laugh tore his gaze away from the woman in black. Devane was not making any attempt to hide his contempt for this new arrival, even with Olivia stepping closer to him. Lady Devane looked as if she might faint. His arm around her was the first sign of affection he had displayed for his wife since arriving to the estate. This woman, at least to the Devane household, was some sort of common ground.

Then came the sound of a breath—someone taking a long, deep breath. Wellington turned to Eliza, and was surprised to find she looked ready to go on a rampage. She motioned with her eyes to the newcomer, her jaw tightening as she was no doubt fighting to unleash some savage battle cry.

Wellington furrowed his brow. He understood his reaction, but not hers.

"Brethren, those who serve, and welcome Initiates," Havelock began, "may I introduce *Signora* Sophia del Morte, a woman of many talents who does serve the Phoenix Society admirably."

"Good Doctor," she cooed, her Italian accent seeming to steal the men's breaths quite easily, much to the chagrin of their accompanying wives. "You flatter me. I work for the Society so admirably because you, my dear Doctor, pay me so admirably."

The laughter was generous from the assembled party, all except for the Devanes who remained silent.

"I believe you know most of the assembled here," Havelock said, motioning to everyone.

"I do," she said, bestowing a pleasant smile to those she made eye contact with.

There was no escape. None whatsoever.

"Wellington!" she cooed, walking slowly towards him, the Society giving her a wide berth. "I had no idea you would be here! If I did I would have worn my hair as on the day we first met."

The only one not quiet was the chortling Bartholomew Devane. "You daft dago," he spat. "What are you on about? Are you saying you know Richard St. John of Wessex? Seeing as all you wear is black, I doubt if you are a frequent patron of the textile industry."

Good Lord, Wellington thought, *but you are thick, Devane.*

"Eloquent as always, Lord Devane, but still not so bright," she mocked as she now stood in front of Wellington. "Ladies and gentlemen, I wonder if you have been formerly introduced to *Signor* Wellington Books, Esquire, humble servant to the Queen, Country, and Empire."

"I beg your pardon?" Devane asked, his mirth slipping away.

"Another client asked me to retrieve this rather knowledgeable man, for whatever reason. I did not know or care. Perhaps the only mark I have been asked to bring back alive." She smiled, apparently indulging in a memory. "So, I enjoyed myself," she teased, brushing the tip of his nose.

When Wellington flinched, her eyes then landed on Eliza. "And *signorina*! So good to see you again. I have not enjoyed such an entertaining opponent before—surely, worthy of a repeat performance."

Now it was Doctor Havelock's voice. "Wait a moment. St. John's wife—"

"Good Doctor, I do not know what these people have told you," she said, slowly backing away from them both, "but from what I know of Wellington and how that woman fights, I would say without question or challenge you all have been spending the weekend with a pair of British spies."

The clicks that rose into the air were not from the Mechamen, but from the pistols that appeared suddenly in Eliza's hands. The gentlemen of the Society, however, possessed the wherewithal to make concealed weapons part of the dress code for the evening dinner party. Some of the guns were reminiscent of Eliza's vanity pistols while others were simple deadly weapons. Wellington's eyes widened slightly at three of the Brethren's wives also sporting tiny Derringer pistols, their stance and hold of the miniature firearms just as steady as Eliza's.

Once silence fell over the group again, Wellington and Eliza looked around them, taking stock of the barrels that all held within them their final fate.

"Right then," Eliza spoke, startling everyone save for Wellington and Sophia. "I have two pistols, twelve bullets total. Who wants to be first to die?" She continued to retrain her pistols on members of the Society. When she brought one gun around to Sophia, Eliza went still as she promised the woman, "I have one specially set aside for you though. Have no worry."

"My God, you can talk!" Bartholomew gasped.

"That's right, mate," she bit back, all the pride of New

Zealand behind her words. "Thought you'd find my accent too damn alluring to resist."

Havelock took a step forward, his eyes trained on Wellington. His face revealed nothing.

"Well now," Wellington began, "this is truly an awkward spot. However, I will say that this has been a delightful evening. Fine wine. Fantastic food. An impressive display of the applied sciences. Truly inspiring. So if you all do not mind—"

Wellington then pushed through the crash of gears, returned to the table, pulled at his chair, and sat back down.

"Books," Eliza said, her eyes and guns flicking from man to man, "what the hell are you doing?"

"Miss Braun," he said over his shoulder, paying no mind to the gauntlet he passed. "I am educated enough to assess the danger and know we are unequivocally—as the working class would say—*buggered*." Wellington then spread his napkin across his lap. "So, if these are to be my last few moments upon God's Earth, I intend to conclude this evening properly."

Pearson remained in the doorway, his eyes going from Havelock to the sole man at the table, and then back to his master again. Wellington gave the servant an impatient nod of his own, and that indication was enough to bring the butler by his side.

"Coffee and dessert, sir?"

"Yes," Wellington replied, adjusting the cuffs of his tuxedo. "That would be lovely."

CHAPTER TWENTY-SIX

Wherein Our Daring Duo Find Themselves in a Spot of Trouble

"I must say"—Eliza leaned back against the dank wall and looked around her tiny cell—"this estate is most well appointed."

Wellington, slumped in his adjoining accommodation, propped his arms on his knees and crooked one eyebrow. "This was not quite the place I had intended our evening to end."

"I would hope not." She shivered, wishing that their captors had not seen fit to strip her to her underclothes. "I would have much rather ended up with some sex and cigars." She did not point out that she felt incredibly vulnerable without her concealed knives and pistols.

Wellington got up, shrugged off his jacket and passed it through the bars. Eliza stared at him, but he shook it in a commanding way—perhaps a holdover from the role he'd taken to so easily. So she took it. It did little to keep off the cold of their underground prison, but she appreciated the gesture. At least he would feel he did everything he could to gallantly protect his partner in the field.

A pang of longing shot through her—huddling together

for warmth would have been preferable. That would have provided far more comfort than his evening coat. Instead she settled down next to Wellington, a few scant inches apart so they could whisper to each other through the bars, rather than pronouncing their feelings to anyone who might be eavesdropping.

Beyond their cells was a rather threatening room, open and within sight of all the cells here. Eliza eyed the display of torture devices hung on the wall there. A long narrow table the ideal length to spread a body across stood in full view—that would have been as much a coincidence as how this place was designed to be so visible to any and all detainees of the Society. Havelock obviously believed such interrogations should have audiences, be it the other prisoners or his own people, as was apparent from the two burly armed servants just beyond their locked doors. It was truly the full medieval treatment here at Havelock Manor and, judging by some suspicious marks next to a large hook in the wall, the Master of the House was a regular practitioner.

"Well, this is quite the pickle." Eliza sighed, breaking the silence. "But I've been in worse. Harry and I once were locked in the Duke of—"

"At present," Wellington broke in, "I do not feel like being regaled with your past exploits with the daring Harrison Thorne."

"Really? So what do you feel like doing then, Wellington? Because they searched me rather thoroughly, so lock picking is not an option. If there is something more fun you had in mind, I guess we can work around the bars . . ."

The Archivists blushed, opened his mouth a couple of times, readjusted his glasses, and then grudgingly loosed his words. "You're not making this easy. I have a confession to make."

The tone of his voice made her nervous. "I hope you're not going to profess undying love for me—because I don't think things are quite *that* bad," she quipped.

Nothing but silence.

"It's all right." Eliza dared to slide a hand through the bars to gingerly take hold of the Archivist's shoulder. "They took all my weapons along with my lock picks, so you can tell me anything."

A long ragged breath, and then it all came out in a rush. "It was her, Miss Braun. It was *her*!" His hands were clenched into fists, and his whole body shook. "*Signora* Sophia del Morte was the woman who lured me into the House of Usher's trap."

"Oh." Eliza bit her lip, and for once she was unable to think of anything to say.

"Yes, 'oh,'" Wellington snapped, jerking away from her consoling touch. He leapt to his feet and began to pace the tiny cell with more anger than Eliza had ever seen him display before. "That woman . . . that *vixen* who seduced me so easily is apparently working for these scoundrels!"

"She is a professional," she offered. "You have to realise that you are—"

"—just an Archivist?" He whirled around and glared at her through his glasses. The light down here was so minimal that they obscured his eyes, but she imagined they were blazing. "Eliza, I am still a trained agent. I should have known!"

"That may be true, but you are first and foremost a man."

Wellington's head tipped to one side. "What on earth is that supposed to mean?"

"She is a very beautiful woman—well trained to manipulate the male . . ."

"Well," he crossed his arms, "so are you and yet I have managed to avoid your charms."

He was so angry that he didn't realise he just paid her a sideways compliment. Eliza laughed. She was genuinely amused. "To be fair I haven't been turning them on to you." She fixed him with a level gaze. "Believe me, Mr. Wellington Books, Esquire, you would know if I was."

The silence stretched out painfully.

"Now," she got to her feet and stood in front of him, "Are you going to be able to act like an agent in Her Majesty's Service and put your injured pride behind you?"

A small muscle in his jaw twitched.

"Please, Wellington." She wrapped her hands around the bars and tried to wrench his attention away from his humiliation. "If I can put aside what they did to Harry, then you can do this."

"I suppose," he muttered, pressing where the upper-breast pocket of his coat would have been, had he not offered it to her.

Eliza furrowed her brow, noticing the gesture. The same gesture. Again and again. "Did they punch you in the chest or something when searching you?"

"I beg your pardon?" he asked. He glanced at where his hand was, looked at Eliza now wearing his coat, and flexed his fingers nervously. "Oh. Oh . . . well, ah . . . yes . . ."

Yes, he might possess the training of an agent, but he was hardly that. He had no ability whatsoever to conceal anything. Eliza glowered at him. "Go on, Welly. Out with it!"

"They . . ." He reached through the bars, and peeled back one of his coat's lapels. "They took it."

She loathed guessing games. "They took *what*?"

His shoulders sagged as he motioned to the coat she now wore. "My journal."

Eliza narrowed her gaze on him for an instant and then followed his eyes to his jacket's inside lining, now torn and open. The lining within flapped open. Once upon a time that had been a pocket.

She looked at him in horror. "You had . . ." While it did make sense, considering his habits, his interests, and who he was, something was eluding her comprehension of it all. ". . . that journal, the one with the combination lock? That journal . . ."

"My memoirs." Wellington brushed his hair back with his fingers, his eyes screwed shut as he continued. "Things I researched for the Ministry, my thoughts on Doctor Sound, on the various agents I worked alongside, my own life, my own musings. It's all in there."

Of course it was all there. He had the blasted eyesore with him constantly! So, if his life was in there . . .

"What about sensitive Ministry intelligence?"

His eyes met hers and Eliza went pale.

"Doctor Sound . . . ?"

"He knows about it," he conceded. "It's policy, after all. If you keep a casebook, a notepad, or even a personal journal, it must be registered with the Ministry in case of death, abduction, or loss of faculties. Upon retirement—" Wellington looked around them both, "—provided you live that long, your memoirs would be passed through inspection and then returned to you upon approval. Do any of you field agents bother to learn Ministry regulations?"

Only now did she fully grasp her original orders back in Antarctica.

The clamour at their respective cells caused them both to start. With a low groan, the cell doors swung back, and henchmen entered armed with what appeared to be smaller versions of the Mechamen's Gatling guns. They compensated for the large packs covering their backs, and were not hindered in the least by the tubes that snaked around their forearms and attached themselves to the mini-Gatlings.

Wellington was staring at them in mute fascination. Eliza was beginning to recognise another weakness of her partner's: a love for the gadgets. Through the bars, she jabbed him in the shoulder.

However her own thoughts scattered as, adjusting the cuffs of a very smart after-dinner jacket, Bartholomew Devane entered her cell with Pearson as a second shadow, carrying an assortment of restraints, blades, and devices that she immediately recognised.

Eliza considered the rather imposing phallus on Pearson's tray, nodded, and snapped her gaze back on Devane. "Thank God. Had you come into the cell alone undoing your trousers I thought it would be torture."

"Witty little tart, aren't you?" he said. He sounded thirsty, and she knew what he was truly craving. Yet he enjoyed stretching the moment a little as he spoke over his shoulder. "Books, is it?" he asked, making her partner jump. "Wellington Books? My attendant here will escort you to see the good doctor."

"Doctor Havelock?" Wellington asked.

"The very same. He wants a word with you."

Devane nodded to Pearson who, with a small bow, went from Eliza's cell to Wellington's, training a *pounamu*-decorated pistol on the Archivist.

"I thought you would enjoy the notion of your partner taken down with one of your own bullets." Devane sneered. "I wouldn't keep the old man waiting."

Wellington looked to Eliza, his eyes pausing at the tray by Devane before reaching hers.

"It's all right, Books," she assured him, fully aware of what would be coming next. It was the risk all agents took, and extra incentive in excelling at the job and avoiding capture.

With a hesitant nod, Wellington raised his hands and made his way for the corridor.

"Be seeing you, old boy." When Wellington reached Eliza's open door, Devane added, "And rest assured, I don't plan to be gentle with the delightful Miss Braun here. I'll be doing what you plainly aren't man enough to do."

Wellington stiffened, but the soft throat-clearing from Pearson kept him still. With a final look to Eliza, he continued out to the passageway.

"Sentry?"

"Yessah?" the soldier barked, stomping his foot hard against the stone floor.

"You are relieved. So's your man in Books' cell. Assume your post at the main entry." A sinister darkness flickered in Devane's gaze. "Outside."

The man looked at Eliza for a moment, then snapped his eyes front. "But, sah, I must—"

"Do as I say," Devane interjected. "I have my own key. I have the means to leave once I am done with her."

Eliza refused to flinch, even when he leered salaciously at her.

"Sah?" the soldier asked again.

"Both of you are relieved." It was no longer a command. It was a warning.

The head sentry gave a nod to the other soldier and both lowered their mini-Gatlings and disappeared into the outer corridor, the door to the detaining area groaning shut. Its large lock catching echoed faintly over the sentries' heavy steps.

"As Doctor Havelock desired some chitchat with your man, Books, he suggested I spend a little quality time with you. A fair trade."

She could not have really expected the perverted Devane to remain upstairs when the woman he'd been eyeing since her arrival Friday afternoon was conveniently locked up below.

"Trade?"

"I wanted to immediately put a bullet between your man's eyes. As it is in the Society, I do not tolerate deception." Devane already had slipped his fine jacket free, and was now working on his collar.

Eliza straightened her spine and waited for him to come for her. He would have to come for her.

That would be his first mistake.

CHAPTER TWENTY-SEVEN

Finally the Greatness Wellington Books so Rightly Deserves Is Thrust upon Him

The depths of the chasm opened before them, and Wellington felt the heat wrap itself around him as he drew closer to the massive structure of metal, coils, and cylinders. The main silo reached down into the depths of what could only be the geothermal fissure that Doctor Havelock spoke of during dinner. Around him, gauges read pressure, monitored temperature, and rerouted heat from boiler to boiler. Scientists called out numbers to one another, referenced notations, and nodded as they continued to switch their attentions between the difference engines in front of them and the metallic giant reaching out in every direction. Wellington could also make out smaller boilers that, he theorised, were dedicated to specific rooms of the manor or perhaps different areas of this underground facility. The behemoth looming over all of them was the main reactor, the heart of this subterranean hideout.

"Impressive, isn't it?" the voice asked, ripping Wellington's eyes away from the main boiler to the man walking towards him. Doctor Havelock was dabbing at his forehead, but he appeared to be a man appreciative of the sweat earned when working towards a goal. Wellington could see that in his smile. He himself knew that smile.

"*Take note, Wellington,*" he could hear his father in his head. "*This is a man of fine character.*"

"The actual silo does not do justice to its inside workings. We built the structure in stages, and it was finally completed nearly a year ago."

"A year ago?" Wellington looked around at the scientists all working diligently, one of them adjusting valves and lightly chewing his bottom lip as he did so. "Are your colleagues—"

"These gentlemen are not my colleagues," Havelock said, his voice touched with annoyance. "They are competent minds that share my own visions, but they are not my equals—An equal would have mastered this design much sooner than this."

Wellington nodded. "So if you are the designer, what of this machine's chief engineer?"

"Ah, yes." Havelock sighed. After a moment of respect, he continued, "Sadly, we had a parting of ways with that Brother a few months ago. Nearly seven months ago, in fact."

"I see," Wellington said. "And when this Brother parted company with you—did he burn bridges as well?"

"You could say that," Havelock said, casting a glance at one of the gauges and slowly, gently, adjusting its accompanying valve.

"And what was his crime against the Phoenix Society?"

"Well, it seems that when his creation exceeded expectation, he desired to take his plans elsewhere for further investment and development. I would not allow it, at least not until we had carried out our First Phase. Well, it seems that Brother Finnes did not care to wait. We were informed of his extending offers to curious investors, and we took matters into our own hands."

"The Society is quite thorough in covering their tracks," Wellington conceded. "You've been doing so for centuries, it seems."

"Yes, and I'm certain that being an Archivist you are passionate of the past, but I am more concerned with the future, Mister Books, or do you prefer Wellington?" Havelock finally looked up. "I want to know about the future, and if I can figure you into it."

The Archivist blinked. After a few moments, he realised he was staring. In this stunned silence, Wellington hoped he hadn't been standing there with jaw hanging open.

"Forgive me, Doctor Havelock," he finally said. Suddenly, the heat of the crevasse and the monstrous generator in front of him were no longer a concern. "You have me at a disadvantage."

"How so?"

"I am your prisoner here. The rather ill-mannered treatment from your guards and the ruining of a perfectly good dinner jacket can attest to that," he grumbled.

"No more ill-mannered than you and that common woman Braun sneaking into our hallowed halls under false pretenses." Havelock's tone now had an edge of sharpness to it.

Wellington went to retort, but he did have him there.

"Oh, perhaps you could argue 'for Queen and Country' and some such rubbish, but the fact you had to resort to such underhanded tactics? Disgraceful."

"Perhaps," Wellington said, "but considering your own callous regard for human life or your blatant disrespect to the Crown, it would seem that—"

"We are both utter cads," muttered Havelock.

He gave a curt nod. "Apparently."

"Cads but with very different agendas." Havelock motioned with his hand back towards the entrance and, with Pearson well in eyesight, continued as they walked. "Your own agenda, so I gather, is the preservation of the Empire. My agenda, however, is not as so far off from your own. Mine concerns the Empire as well, but I am more committed to returning it to its rightful place in the world."

"Restoring some of the faded glory, as it were?"

Wellington meant for the question to be a slight, but

Havelock was quick to answer with, "Exactly. At one time we were more than just a tiny speck of land in the Atlantic. We were the dominating influence of this planet. We were not just the major power of the world—we *were* the world, the very heart and soul of civilisation! To accomplish what we in the Phoenix Society stand for, Mister Books, we must work in shadow and take risks that the Crown ignore. And considering your field of excellence, you of all people must know how seats of power regard risks. Inspiration cannot nor should not be cast aside so easily."

The drive and determination in his voice made Wellington turn to look at him. Doctor Deveraux Havelock nursed in his eyes a fire that he had once nurtured in the seminars the Archivist had attended, before the scientist and visionary became the "brilliant recluse" amongst academic circles. Wellington had been impressed with the good doctor's conclusions and theories, but many of them were far too radical or—more to the point—dangerous for science to begin practising.

What Wellington would not admit, even to himself, was how inspirational, how infectious, the man's words were. Sometimes, yes, risk had to be taken in order to push Man forward. It was risk that drove Man out of the caves to evolve, out of the shipyards of Spain to discover the lands across the seas, and away from the Earth itself in order to master the skies in airships.

Seeing this passion up close, however, was intoxicating. "And you want me to be a part of this grand vision of Britannia's future?"

Havelock looked at Wellington and waved his finger at him, his mouth curling back into a positively wicked grin. "Oh now, do not be so humble or modest. I saw the wonder in your eyes when the Mechamen first appeared. That was not your put-upon persona, but true awe. You were impressed by their craftsmanship, their engineering. Then, on seeing their armament, you were completely enraptured."

A heat rose under Wellington's collar. Yes. Havelock had

him dead to rights: the Mechamen were stunning masterpieces of engineering.

"There is no shame in it, Books," he said, motioning ahead of them. "In fact, it was such a refreshing change to see it. Do you know how many of my Brethren claim to admire and respect my work? While I'm sure they do, in their own simple way, they do not understand it. But you?" He nodded and led the way into another alcove where a gentle breeze chilled the perspiration on Wellington's skin. "I saw a deep understanding, a true comprehension of what I was attempting to accomplish."

"Attempting?" Wellington laughed. "Doctor Havelock, I think you mean *succeeded*, do you not?"

His host stopped and smiled, his expression gloating. "As I surmised." He shook his head. "Please do not insult me with masking your admiration, Books. It is hardly complimentary of my labours."

With a soft chuckle, Havelock continued to a table where a Mechaman laid, the chest plate removed as if work were being done on it. "The servants here are excellent workers, but even their supervisors lack an appreciation for what I have done here."

Wellington's eyes ran the length of the brass soldier open before them. "Is this one the prototype?"

"No, this particular Mark I just does not seem to function properly. It came off the line and cannot seem to continue basic automaton functions."

The words stole his breath for a moment. Wellington sized up the Mechaman and then asked, "You say this came off the line?"

"Yes," Havelock replied, slipping on a pair of thick, rubber gloves. "Assembly line one level down."

He nodded. When he licked his lips, Wellington was surprised, considering the humidity of the other alcove, at how dry they were. "And this model is number . . . ?"

Havelock placed two fingers at the crown of the Mechaman and read, "Twenty-seven."

"Twenty-seven," he repeated. "Of how many?"

It appeared as if Havelock, his hands raised before him, was intending to perform surgery on the automaton; but he paused and motioned behind Wellington before reaching into the metallic chest cavity.

Wellington walked to the edge of the platform, and gripped the railing tight as his eyes took in the cavern floor below. He tried to count the brass obelisks that stood in ranks, but their numbers continued on and on, filling the visible cavern floor that spread open before him. Hundreds on hundreds *on hundreds* of Mechamen, all quiet for the time being. Waiting.

Wellington doubted they were going to be serving dinner, once activated.

"Quite the sight isn't it?" Havelock gestured to him from the workbench, "but I intended for you to see this, actually."

Tearing himself away from the vista of Mechamen, Wellington returned to his host's side. The contraption before him matched the breadth of Havelock's chest, egg-shaped and comprised of a solid pistons, various rotors, and belts—many belts.

"Not really sure why the engine isn't working. This one starts, but I fail to grasp why it cannot continue running."

"Seizing up, is it?" Wellington asked, moving the lantern closer.

"Exactly."

"Are its belts tight enough? Without proper torque, you will fail to get the pistons moving."

Havelock removed his gloves and then slid a large parchment closer to Wellington. "If you wish to take a closer look at how things are connected, please do."

The engine, by design, should have been running. With a flathead screwdriver, Wellington tested the belts' tautness; all of them seemed to be giving plenty of tension against their crankshaft.

"Can you vouch for the elasticity of this—" Wellington's brow furrowed. "This isn't rubber."

"No," Havelock said gently, "it's what I would call the personal touch to the Mark I Mechamen."

His concentration went from schematics to device, then back to schematics. This contraption was absolutely inspired: complex in its construction, but very simple in its design and ability to be reproduced on an assembly line.

"I take it," Wellington began, reaching inside the motor and adjusting a screw, "that you have a shift working down here? Or were these Mechamen assembled at the same plant where your generator was fabricated?"

"Many of my workers do come from that plant. While I did have a falling out with that particular Brother, his workers remained valuable assets. Quite skilled they are. In particular, the children."

He closed his eyes, feeling his jaw tighten. "I see. And your workers are presently . . . ?"

"Oh dear God, Books, I am not an idiot." Havelock smiled coldly. "They will not be in until Monday. Sunday is the Lord's Day for the working class, and it keeps them in their place."

Wellington resumed his work, continuing minute adjustments. "It would appear," he said, turning the screwdriver slightly, "that whichever child you had assigned to this engine, misunderstood the precision involved and secured your flywheel too tight. These screws are so snug that your mechanics cannot run. I think—" And with a final nod, Wellington straightened up. "Yes, that should do it."

Havelock considered Wellington for a moment and then reached around the motor, taking a firm grip on a small knob. With a sharp twist, the motor hummed to life, the gears and turbines spinning up and then settling into a constant, comfortable rhythm.

"And you are an Archivist?" Havelock asked.

"A man needs his hobbies out of office," Wellington replied with a shrug.

"Indeed."

They watched the motor for a few moments, Wellington's

eyes moving between the "heart's" schematics and the final creation itself.

Wellington felt a tightness form in his throat. "These belts, Doctor Havelock, that are assisting this motor—you called them 'the personal touch' to these Mechamen."

"I did, Mister Books."

His eyes closed, a bitterness forming in the back of his throat as he reached his conclusion. "But not *your* personal touch?"

"You are a perceptive man, Mister Books. May I call you Wellington?"

One body had been gutted, or perhaps a more accurate description in Harrison Thorne's casebook was that most of the muscular system had been removed. Another corpse was completely drained of blood.

"Human tissue?"

"More muscle and sinew, Wellington. Consider it for a moment—a renewable source of elasticity, durable, and impressive in the amount of weight and tension it can stand. Granted, you have to lubricate it with the appropriate substance, maintain a constant temperature for said substance which the Mechamen can do quite aptly . . ."

Wellington cleared his throat. "So," his voice trembled, "the bones?"

"A failed experiment, I am afraid," Havelock said, his voice sounding as if he had just dropped an egg on to the kitchen floor. "It stood to reason that if the muscles and blood were the missing key, what could we accomplish employing a true skeletal frame to the Mark I?" He turned off the motor, and placed his hand on the clockwork heart, lightly thrumming his fingers on top of it. "I had no idea bones were so fragile."

What Wellington had begun to think of as ingenuity was now revealed as an abomination. A strange dizziness threatened to overtake him when Havelock snapped him to a terrifying state of sobriety.

"And considering the amount of undesirables cluttering

the streets of London, our supply of raw materials is virtually inexhaustible—and the much cheaper option."

Wellington took in a deep breath. He knew he was not just noticing a strange scent that faintly reminded him of a crematorium. That would have been too coincidental. He gave a slight nod and then tore his gaze away from one of the heart's belts and fixed it instead on Havelock. It appeared the doctor had been staring at him for some time.

"Perhaps I am unorthodox in my research. Perhaps my ends are so abhorrent that they cannot justify their means. While the Society knows what I am capable of, you, Wellington, *appreciate* what I do. I have spent so long looking for a like mind."

"I see," he said, the sweat now lightly tickling the back of his neck.

Havelock grinned. "This use of undesirables as spare parts may seem a bit barbarous to an outsider, I must concur, but this bold move was essential to advance the project as well as continue the ideals of the Society. We are dedicated to the betterment and preservation of the Empire. This would mean dramatic measures to keep its numbers in check.

"And this is where you are needed, Wellington. A mind such as yours is not only a benefit to the Society, but a treasure to me. Currently, my confidant is, as I'm sure you have surmised, Lord Devane."

"I was uncertain if—"

Wellington was going to politely insinuate that Devane was merely the sycophant found in every group, but Havelock cut him off with, "The man is a complete and utter dolt. Yes, he serves me well. Yes, he has some influence in the right circles. But he is a complete bombast. He understands the spoils of war, but that is not what I need. I need a confidant that understands what goes into the preparation for battle. You, as an Archivist with a passion for logistics, respect this kind of preparation."

He cleared his throat. "I suppose I do."

"That is why you have caught my attentions, young Wellington Books. This is a very good thing for you. While I do admire your tenacity for whatever clandestine organisation you serve, please remember—as long as I remain interested in you, you and Miss Braun remain alive. Regard that as incentive in your joining our Society."

"But from what it seems, Doctor Havelock, I have a place in your order. My partner, Miss Braun, does not."

"Oh I'm sure we'll find a place for her, somewhere." He chuckled and said with a wry smile, "There's always tending to the needs of our Brethren. A few restraints, and she will serve us quite admirably."

"Doctor Havelock," Wellington began, "what you have shared with me in confidence is most . . ." *Terrifying? Monstrous? Delusional?* Instead, he chose ". . . impressive—I will not deny that. But if I fully comprehend what you are asking of me, I am going to have to decline your most gracious offer. You would have me betray that which I have sworn an oath to. Simply swearing another to the Phoenix Society would carry little merit—how would you ever believe me?"

Havelock's face darkened, but his eyes betrayed a flicker of respect. The kind, Wellington surmised, bestowed on an opponent, just before the first pawn moves.

"A pity," he sighed. "I had high hopes."

"I am a realist," Wellington cleared his throat. "I was dead the moment you brought me down here." The doctor's head tipped to one side, but Wellington shook his own as if contradicting an unsaid compliment. "You knew my name, of course, from the lovely *signora*—but my partner's name? I can only assume you've read my journal."

"There is only so much you can read in a half hour's time."

"Naturally," Wellington said with a slight nod. "But you've read enough to know my character."

Havelock nodded. "Perhaps I was hoping to appeal to your curiousity, but it seems I overestimated your intellect."

"No," Wellington returned gently. "You underestimated my ethics." He extended his hand. "Thank you, again, Doctor Havelock. I would now very much like to return to my cell. I left my partner with a right bastard."

"Pearson," Havelock called over Wellington's shoulder. He glanced at the extended hand and turned away from it, replacing his thick work gloves. "Rather charming—your sense of nobility for a common strumpet."

Wellington's jaw clenched at such a label, but he managed to speak relatively calmly. "Oh, it's not Miss Braun I am concerned about," he said, turning to face the gun-wielding butler. They had just reached the gangway leading back to the detention block when he stopped and faced Havelock again. "And I would recommend jumping to the final few entries of my journal. Eliza D. Braun may be a host of many things, but 'common' she is not."

Wellington placed his hands in his pockets, turned, and resumed the walk back to his cell, whispering to himself the best countdown he could estimate.

CHAPTER TWENTY-EIGHT

In Which Miss Braun Displays Her Skills and Mr. Books' Journal Comes in Handy

Devane's smile was that of a shark, and whatever was to come Eliza was glad that Wellington would not be there to see it.

In too many nations, in too many hairy situations, Eliza had felt that particular predatory look directed at her. It would have been too much to hope for a clean death.

He pulled up a stool and looked at her hard—drawing out the moment he had promised her. Devane's eyes raked over her, the kind of examination Columbus might have leveled upon America—sizing up what he could get out of it.

"I am so glad you are not, in fact, silent." His voice was low and conversational, while his eyes remained fixed. "I prefer my women at least to be able to scream."

Eliza tilted her head and returned the same smile, "I doubt that anything you could do to me would make me scream. Amuse, perhaps. Laugh? Most likely."

That slight won her a raised eyebrow. "Oh, I am going to enjoy this. It has been a very long time since I have found a little kitty with some fight in her."

"You really must visit New Zealand then—we have suffragists there that would love to be alone in a room with you." Her survival instinct was kicking in, telling her to keep him talking, while she examined the room for something to give her advantage. The image of what the two Kates would do to this foul creature, though, provided some comfort.

"The colonies?" Devane made a face as if he'd just smelt something rancid under his nose. "Damned if I would do any such thing!"

"Oh, come along now, Barty," she taunted, her voice dipping into its lower register as she let Wellington's coat fall to the cell floor, "are you, presumably one of the finest examples of British breeding, afraid of us wee savages?" Eliza then nodded, experiencing a revelation. "Or are you afraid of not measuring up to the colonials—brave enough, bold enough, and possessing far bigger balls than you—who did what you were incapable of doing: dare the unknown."

The smile faded.

"Ah well then." She sighed, shaking her head ruefully, "A shame you cannot measure up to New Zealand's standards. Must be why that striking wife of yours is as skittish as a frightened kitten. She's afraid people will find out about your shortcomings."

The stool clattered behind him as he bolted to his feet, his face scarlet, the muscles tightening in his neck. The speed at which he had snatched up the scalpel was impressive. He now pointed the instrument at her, and in the cell's dim light it still managed to glint.

"I am too much of a man for her," he hissed. "I am a man of many appetites."

"Really, Barty?" she sneered. "I'm sure all the East End whores tell you that, provided you slip them an extra ha'penny or two?" All she needed was for him to take another step closer or even throw the scalpel at her. "I wonder how much of a bawdy jest is made at your expense at the pubs of London?"

She could see his face twitch slightly. He was almost hers.

"Holding back on New Zealand, Barty?" Eliza purred, undoing one of the ties between her breasts.

The muslin parted slightly, revealing their curves to him. Merely shifting her stance, she knew, would give him a delightful glimpse of what her chemise concealed. Her new stance would also provide her more solid footing.

Her whisper seemed to fill the entire detention area. "What are you waiting for?"

His laughter robbed Eliza of her own smile. Devane might be a shark, but he was not a stupid one. "I have heard about your peculiar talents, you little minx—so I think I will have to decline your offer."

He had something else planned and Eliza was fairly sure it involved the scalpel and other assorted instruments on the tray now in front of him.

Devane unwrapped a bundle lying next to the other devices. Her other *pounamu* pistol, various knives, and lock picks were spread out before her, like accoutrements for surgery.

"Quite an arsenal for a well-bred lady of"—he let out a little sneering laugh—"New Zealand."

"I like to keep ahead of fashion," Eliza replied, aching to have her hand wrapped around just one of those items. "If you are confused as to how they work I would be so pleased to give you a demonstration."

Devane grinned. "Oh, I am sure you would, but again I must decline the offer, with regret."

Eliza could feel her cocksure, devil-may-care front begin to slip as inside she trembled at a memory. She had spent some nightmarish weeks in the Kaiser's cells, the pet project of the dungeon's interrogator. They had not broken her, but it was not an experience she wished to revisit. Devane's perusal of his implements, though, brought those fears back with haunting clarity.

Devane, however, was not a professional like the Kaiser's man. *This is personal, Eliza*, she assured herself. "So am I to assume it will be this, then—torture, then a bit of necrophilia, just so I don't reveal your problems—"

Her insult stopped short when she caught the flare in his eyes, not of anger but of wanton desire. Her gaze traveled down and she realised that the movement in his trousers had only grown as they talked. "By the gods," she snapped, "You're *enjoying* this—you *want* me to insult you?"

Devane let out a little strangled sigh, as if he had been found out.

Eliza suddenly found herself at the end of a rather troublesome conundrum: if she surrendered, he would just help himself, but he would get his jollies if she struggled. *Bloody wonderful*, she thought.

No, her mother had not bred a shrinking violet; and with this perverted pom the pride and the honor of New Zealand and its women were Eliza's to defend—none of these known for their meekness. She would not be a victim, and neither would she grant her opposition's fantasies. One man would not get the better of her.

Devane must have caught that flash in her own eyes. He took up the remaining *pounamu* pistol of hers, and lost himself in its detail.

Even at this moment Eliza still cherished those gifts. She would be damned if she were to take a bullet from her own guns.

Her captor's hand tightened on the pistol. "I don't doubt if you were to reach any of these quaint contraptions, you would dispatch me with all speed. That is why, to get to them, you will need to get past me."

The morning's hunt had revealed Devane as a crack shot. She could never close the current distance without Devane stopping her. Two steps closer and she would have a better chance. Three steps and he was hers.

His free hand reached across to the tray and hooked a pair of cuffs. With a light clatter, he tossed them at her feet. "A little insurance." He tucked the keys into his pocket, "I like a challenge but not that much. A chap must learn to protect himself."

Eliza looked at the restraints at her feet with careful consideration. Then she looked up, "You know, a lady prefers diamonds . . ."

That, he found funny. "As if *you* are a lady?" He aimed the pistol down a little. "I could just shoot you in the gut. It's a painful way to die, but you'd be alive long enough to enjoy my attentions."

Devane would do it too. Considering what she knew of him, blood was probably just one more in an expansive list of perversions.

Taking her time, Eliza picked up the cuffs and snapped them shut on each of her wrists as he instructed. She quickly ran through her memory of what the Kates had taught her, the different scenarios they had run through. The elder Kate, her hair neatly coiffed, instructed her in three different ways to incapacitate a man while hands were tied. None of the situations practiced back home had ever resembled one like this. Eliza glanced at the bench out of the corner of her eye. He was unlikely to let her get close enough.

Devane, on seeing her secured as she was, wasted no more time and closed the distance on her, slipping across the cell as silently as an owl would descend on a field mouse. He lifted her chin up with the *pounamu* pistol's muzzle, forcing her gaze into his. The cool kiss of Eliza's own gun against her jugular was not a pleasant sensation.

Using the short chain between the cuffs as a makeshift leash he tugged her over to the wall to take advantage of a "convenient" hook overhead. When he hoisted her by the cuffs with his free arm onto the hook, she felt her arms and sides stretch. Eliza would be forced to stand on tiptoes to take the tension off her shoulders.

At least she now had an idea of Devane's strength. To lift her like that and still keep her at gunpoint? Strong *and* coordinated. This just kept getting better and better.

Satisfied that she was helpless, her tormentor took a step

back, tracing her jaw with the barrel of her gun as he spoke. "Now my sweet little morsel from the colonies," he said shuddering lightly as he let the barrel of her gun slink down to trace the exposed curve of her left breast, "I'll give you an education in proper English manners."

"I thought it was all about being a gentleman," Eliza commented, covertly eyeing up if the bench was close enough for her to reach if she swung her legs out.

He drew closer, caressing her check with his breath. "I can be a gentleman when required." Devane let his eyes rake over her as if she were a Christmas present and he a very naughty boy who had crept down to enjoy an early unwrapping. "But for a little savage like yourself I think something more primitive is called for."

He pulled apart his shirt, his eyes remaining fixed on Eliza's neckline as he backed up to the tray. Taking his time, Devane set down her pistol and picked up the scalpel again.

She knew his sort—the kind that needed to see blood as well as inflict pain.

Suddenly, he was on her. His hand clamped around Eliza's neck, forcing her to keep eye contact. "I wonder if ladies of the colonies taste different from the ladies bred here."

She felt the sting of the scalpel against her arm, and she felt a trickle of blood run down her arm. That didn't repulse her.

The feel of Devane's tongue against her skin did.

His tongue was lapping up the blood, and on reaching the small wound he suckled lightly. With him so close to her, Eliza could feel his erection pressing against her.

With a delighted gasp, he pulled away from her arm, grabbed Eliza's hair, and tugged hard. Her surprised wince was enough for Devane to shove his tongue into her mouth. She could taste traces of her blood on his tongue, smell the sweat on his skin, and he pressed himself even closer to her. The harder he pulled on her hair, the harder he kissed. His moans were sickening, even more sickening than the feel of his hand cupping her breast through the muslin of her undergarments, his forefinger and thumb teasing her nipple.

That was the mistake she was hoping for.

Devane had kept his eyes all weekend on Eliza's breasts, but his eyes should have been on other parts of her anatomy—her arms, in particular. Naturally modest gentlewomen of the Empire did not possess upper body strength worth noting, confining themselves to proper activities like embroidery and flower arranging. Eliza D. Braun considered herself blessed that she had never been modest nor proper. She had spent a great of time in the exercise facilities of the Ministry of Peculiar Occurrences. And then there was her youth in New Zealand where the Maori had taught her to fight, not just to win, but to survive.

Eliza brought her teeth together, trapping Devane's thick tongue in her mouth. He screamed, louder still when she lifted herself by the arms. She bit down even harder, and Devane finally released her. That was when she trapped his neck between her calves, one across the nape, the other across his throat. With her legs locking him in a vise grip, she pulled him closer, using his frame as leverage to unhook herself from the wall. She held on to the hook with her hands and pushed him back with a hard, swift kick to the face.

Devane had just righted himself when a serviceable two-fisted uppercut lifted him off his feet. Eliza couldn't be sure, but it was quite possible she'd broken his nose. All for the good—the intense pain of it would hopefully keep him pliable for the next few minutes.

Her cuffed hands now looped around his throat, and—just to emphasise this spectacular turn of events—Eliza quickly snatched up another blade from Devane's tray and pressed its sharp point tight against his jugular.

"One move," she hissed into his ear, "and I'll give you another mouth to leer out of."

When he made to reply Eliza jerked the chain around his neck tight. "Did I say I wanted you to speak? Shut it!"

The clatter of the corridor's hatch unlocked and groaned

open. Wellington appeared, staring wide-eyed at her with an equally wide-eyed but better-armed Pearson at his back. The tall man swiftly leveled Eliza's second pistol straight at the back of the Archivist's head, creating just the scenario Eliza did not wanted to be stuck in.

This was going to take some balls of steel, as Second Kate would have said.

Devane squawked when Eliza jammed the knife harder against his neck and a trickle of blood began to stain his shirt. "Tell your man there to drop my gun, get cozy in a cell, or I make him unemployed."

The valet's gaze flickered to the aristocrat—yes, that had indeed hit home.

"Never," Devane bluffed. "He'll blow your partner's brains all over this room if you do."

Eliza laughed, sounding cruel and icy even in her own ears. "Oh that's priceless. You think I give a toss about him?"

She half-expected Wellington to look as if she had hit him in the face with a brick with such a comment, but he took no notice. He was whispering to himself. Whispering . . . numbers?

"He's your partner," the valet growled. She watched her pistol push harder into the back of Wellington's skull, making him wince.

Still, the Archivist's counting remained constant.

Eliza in turn yanked her prisoner tighter against her. "He was the only toff the agency could find at short notice. And considering that git kept me silent and obedient all weekend—do you feel like gambling that I even remotely like him?"

A taut instant passed, with valet and master sharing a somewhat panicked look. That was when a huge sound echoed down the rock corridors of the prison, and then another rumble—this one far louder that the first one. The concussion shook the prison then shook as if it were a piggybank and a giant child was demanding the last farthing from it. Wellington and Pearson lurched forward. Chunks of rock fell from above them. One of the empty cells buckled. In the confusion, Eliza gave Devane a quick twist with her chain, throwing him against the bars of her cell.

Alarms blared. There were shouts outside, some of them orders and others screams of panic. "If only I had time to really work on you," she hissed in Devane's ear before slamming his head into the cell bars again.

"Miss Braun!" Wellington grunted, trying to roll the large butler off. Pearson had been rendered unconscious thanks to a fist-sized rock connecting with the back of his skull, so the butler's head told her. "A little assistance now would be quite grand, don't you think?" the Archivist wheezed.

Fishing the key out of Devane's pocket, she freed herself, slipped back into Wellington's jacket, and reclaimed her armaments. Outside there was plenty of chaos unfolding. If they were very lucky, amidst the klaxons and damage crews, there might be smoke to go with it.

"Damn fine timing," she grunted through gnashed teeth as she lifted while Wellington pushed at Pearson. "It's too much to hope for a shock team I suppose."

"I would have warned you about the blast," he gasped, once Pearson was off him, "but I lost count somewhere in the tunnel and had to start again. They opened my journal without the combination, and . . . well, it is too complicated to get into now, but without the proper sequence, the whole things turns into—"

"A bomb?" Eliza's eyebrows shot up. "A man after my own heart. You kept an incendiary device within reach this whole time?"

Wellington adjusted his glasses. "That wasn't its *primary* purpose."

Laughter burbled out of Eliza. "Oh, you are such the Don! We could have used something like that to stop the carriage, incapacitate the Italian—or a hundred other things!"

"But it's my *journal!*" Wellington protested, "I didn't want to blow it up."

That was the mark of a true archivist, she supposed, but she wasn't going to mourn the loss of some papers when it could have been them.

"There are the carbon copies in my desk I suppose," he muttered, "But it will take some time to—"

Eliza reunited her *pounamu* pistols with each other and then tapped Wellington on the forehead. "I think we can sort out your journal issues later—say, when we are safely back in the Archives?"

"Ah yes, good point." Wellington adjusted his collar and straightened slightly. "So it is your pair of pistols against all those guards and a madman?"

"Looks to be about the size of it."

"And we have no Ministry backup, and no escape plan whatsoever?"

"Let me think on that . . ." she said, pulling back the pistols' hammers. "No, none of those to speak of."

"So we're going to have to stop Havelock alone then, while trying to escape with our lives and any hard intelligence we can gather?"

"Yes, Books."

"Do you have a plan?"

"Working on one," she replied brightly. "Be a dear and get the door, will you? My hands are full."

CHAPTER TWENTY-NINE

Wherein Our Heroes Face Inner Demons

The earth didn't just rumble underneath them—it rumbled *around* them. Wellington countered his sudden stumble with a push against the rock wall, and he continued forward into the faltering light. When a pair of gaslight spheres exploded above him, he took stock of the various devices he'd seen within Havelock's workshop. Then there was the lower level where the dormant Mechamen stood to take into account. The smaller boilers surrounding the main would also be a matter of concern. These explosions, he surmised, simply would not stop until everything was either consumed by fire or buried under earth and rock.

One spark. That's all it would take. And yet instead of heeding the words of a trained field agent, a woman with an extensive background in explosives, here he was leading a charge back into the belly of the beast, back towards the generator cavern that *at any moment* would become Havelock's Inferno.

"Books! I say, Books! We do not appear to be heading for an exit!" Eliza sounded more than a little concerned.

But this was the right way. This was the path he had walked with Havelock, where they discussed the future, and what a beautiful future. So full of possibilities . . .

His feet skidded against the stone floor as he recognised the alcove. The shudder passing through the rock and Eliza Braun colliding with him knocked him to one side, but she caught him by the forearm and pulled him back upright.

"Stopping, at present, is ill advised," she shouted.

"This way," he said, yanking her after him into the tiny tunnel.

The floor underfoot changed from earth and rock to a metal grating, and Wellington was, once more, overlooking the Mechamen's assembly line. His eyes darted over the tables.

And by the glow of a distant explosion, he saw them. They were still there.

He quickly folded up the parchments, catching glances of the Mark I schematics and its related weaponry. It then struck him that, unlike his earlier visit where only the heart-engine plans were open, every last schematic, strangely enough, had been unfurled.

His eyes went wide at the last plan in the pile. *Of course*, he thought, *it made perfect sense, after all.*

"Wellington . . ."

The echo of Eliza's voice snapped him back. She had been leaning over the railing all this time, lost in shock at what stood before her. "Look at them. So many . . ."

Wellington shoved his dinner jacket down off her shoulders, grabbed her corset, and pulled. Hard. He pressed his knee against the small of her back and he tugged again, giving himself just enough of a gap to shove the plans secure between her corset and her back.

When he released her, she spun around and slapped him hard.

"Miss Braun!"

"You're lucky you're my partner," she snapped. "Or that would have earned you a punch!"

With a groan, Wellington pushed her ahead of him. "Come on!"

Their footsteps rang hard against the platform until the explosion ripped through the assembly line. For a moment, it smothered all other sounds—including his own heartbeat. Then the platform buckled and slipped away from underneath them.

Wellington heard Eliza's scream as a vague buzz in his ringing ears. "Jump, Welly!"

She landed hard in the tunnel leading out. At least Wellington assumed that. His own footing had not been as sure as Eliza's. His reaching hands slapped hard against the gangway, and his curled fingers caught like claws into the platform's metallic weave. He chose not to look down for the heat enveloping him was assurance enough of a fire raging underneath his feet.

"Eliza!" he cried out. "Perchance, are you there?"

"I have to be," came the reply and the welcome feeling of hands wrapping around his wrists. "Otherwise, no one would be available to save your arse, now would they?"

He knew he should have regarded the grunting she gave on hefting him as most unladylike, but he reconsidered, as this remarkable show of strength lifted him high enough to swing a leg onto the platform. With a gasp of his own, Wellington pulled himself up onto its remains, and then blindly reached out ahead of him.

Eliza grabbed his forearm and yanked him close to her. "The first time was for Queen and Country. This time, we're off the clock." She gave him a rakish wink. "You owe me. Now, this time, Welly, *you* follow *me*."

They were back in the catacombs, Eliza leading the way, until another explosion rocked them off their feet. The rumbling, however, seemed to only grow more intense.

"Cave in!" Wellington pushed Eliza to the ground and covered her body with his.

The smell of earth filled his nostrils as the chamber began to collapse upon itself. He tightened his hold on Eliza as the rumble grew to a roar. Wellington gave a few hard coughs but thanked God that, yes, he could still find air.

Above him, pieces of the ceiling broke free. "Ow . . . Ow . . . Ow . . . Ow . . ." he complained as fist-sized stones struck hard against his back.

And then the rumbling subsided. Smaller rocks and pebbles still fell around them, only to disappear into shadow and dust. Mercifully Wellington felt nothing broken, and they managed to land clear of the newly-formed wall. Wellington could still see light from the Mechamen factory through a dusty brown haze that thickened with each passing second.

"Welly," came a muffled voice from underneath him, "I think the cave-in has ceased for the moment—you can get off me now."

"Ah, yes." Wellington wheezed as they clambered to their feet. "Quite."

The stillness was short-lived as another treamour rippled through the soles of their shoes.

"Back the way we came," she said, pulling him into a run that matched her own. "Our only way out now." They passed through a pair of junctions before Eliza asked between gasps, "Just how potent was that journal of yours?"

"I never did quite calculate how much of the ink was combustible, or its reaction with the leather's natural oils, or attempt an accurate—"

They froze in their escape as two shadows disturbed the haze. Her *pounamu* pistols were up and firing, and both soldiers dropped. Of course they weren't alone down here. Now they had more than cave-ins and explosions to concern themselves with.

As Eliza checked bullets, disarmed corpses, and removed supply belts, she spoke over her shoulder, "So the explosion's potency was based on how much ink was between the pages, you say?"

"Oh yes, that was the idea behind the device. A portable munitions dump, as it were."

She chortled, grabbing the rifle and doing a final pat down of the soldier's body. "That must have been some read."

Eliza had another pair of pistols in the belt now slung over her shoulder, added to her own *pounamu* pistols holstered in a belt cinched around her waist. She gripped the rifle, priming it to fire; and between both belt's various pouches were plenty of shells and bullets. Their chances had just improved exponentially.

A pistol remained in a dead man's grasp. Her focus flicked back and forth several times from it to Wellington.

"I could always carry it for you," he offered.

"Damn it all," she spat before continuing on.

They followed the drone of generators struggling to continue their work, the masterpiece of Havelock's devising futily defying the destruction that ripped at the manor's foundations. Both of them shielded their eyes from the glare and flames; but through the ripples of heat, another walkway could be seen hugging the cavern wall.

"Move fast!" Eliza said, gripping the Martini-Henry with both hands. "Let's hope the good doctor was a talented architect as well as an engineer!"

Ignoring the shuddering underfoot, Wellington and Eliza pushed forward through the massive boiler room, their eyes never leaving the stairwell that reached up to safety and freedom. Wellington wanted to rest. His lungs burned, and he was so bloody hot, but any hesitation on his part was countered by Eliza's insistence.

They had just managed to reach the first gangway when a horrific roar from the cavern's mouth caused their escape staircase to shake and then list. It could not have been more than two degrees Wellington calculated, but they both felt it.

"Climb!" he urged. The exit was only another two landings away. They could make it. "Climb!"

"Yes, yes," Eliza fired back, "I get the idea!"

They now skipped every other step, and Wellington felt his legs protesting. His breath was coming in short gasps.

At the top of the stairwell, Wellington heaved open the iron hatch, shoving Eliza in before him. His own foot crossed the threshold when a loud grating echoed in the crevasse. The stairwell was no longer keeping its hold within the rock. As it began to fall, another sound reached Wellington's ears: the low groan of iron under immense pressure. Superheated water collected in the smaller boilers was now attempting to send its collected power somewhere—*anywhere*—but there were no scientists or attendants at the valves to manage it. Through walls of steam and smoke though he could see those very scientists and attendants. They were no longer manning their stations. They were trying to find a way out.

Wellington pulled himself back into the relative coolness of this new chamber where he had sent his partner, and slammed shut the iron hatch. He heard and felt a dull thud from the other side of it, soon followed by the rapid clattering of metal. Welts the size of Wellington's palm appeared across the iron door, and he stumbled back, holding his breath.

The boilers had now successfully undergone their transformation from engineering miracles to bombs. Their time was now entirely borrowed and accruing interest quickly.

Wellington looked around him. Where was Eliza? There was only one way out of this antechamber; and as his own heartbeat calmed, he could now hear what sounded like a rifle being fed shells. He left the muffled destruction of Havelock's Mechamen factory behind him, and emerged into the light of another open cavern, not as deep underground as the main reactor room but still as open and vast.

He looked down to see Eliza loading a final shell into her rifle, her back pressed hard against a wide stalagmite. "Well, that was a close—"

Her hand dug into his vest and shirt and yanked him down to the rock floor. The bullets came next, tearing away at the cave wall where he had been standing an instant before.

The treamour coming through the ground was quick and

sharp, so intense that it nearly lifted Wellington. Then it came again. And again. He knew these treamours were not aftershocks. They were deliberate. Rhythmic. Something large—*very* large—was causing it.

He didn't have long to wait. Wellington could now see it—well, most of it. He craned his neck up and up, but the very top of this Mechaman still remained hidden. While it stood only a third as tall as Big Ben, it looked sturdy enough to take down the landmark. It was an identical build to the smaller, faster Mark I, but this larger version carried a driver inside of its head, or perhaps two. Wellington could not be certain, having only glanced at the plans before stuffing them into Eliza's corset.

Peeking around the stalagmite that served as his shield, Wellington could now see more of where their escape had led them. This large cave outfitted with metal scaffoldings and cranes would have looked more appropriate in a shipyard than underneath a country estate. At the feet of this metallic leviathan walked a modest front line of five infantrymen wearing the same portable Gatling they had seen on their cell masters.

"Lucky us." Eliza said. "We found the armoury."

"And Doctor Havelock's other experiment, it would seem."

She slipped her finger around the rifle trigger. "His *other* experiment?"

"The Mechamen, he referred to as the Mark I. When I was gathering up the schematics from his workshop, I glimpsed at the plans for these monsters: the Mark IIs."

A second pair of poundings could be felt. They had two giants bearing down on them now. Eliza splayed her fingers across the rifle and took in a deep breath. "You didn't happen to glimpse at any vulnerable points on this Mark II, did you?"

Wellington stared back at her blankly.

"It was worth the asking." She cast a glance at a pistol

lying idly beside her. It was one of the tricks from Basic Field Training: always keep a reserve on the ground just in case. "Are you sure I can't convince you to pick up a weapon?"

"*Go on, lad, pull the trigger,*" scolded his father. "*Every proper gentleman knows how to shoot!*"

His mouth opened to reply, but Eliza was already shaking her head. "Well, mate, if you decide to change your mind, do let me know—preferably before we are both killed!"

She leaned out from their hiding place, firing off shot after shot. Two of the soldiers fell, but Wellington could also hear the shouts of reinforcements moving in to pin them down.

The clatter of a spent rifle sounded but not before the telltale popping from a pair of pistols. Then came the whine, reminiscent of the Mark I's demonstration. He did recall in his "quick glance" at the Mark II's armament that it did include Gatlings of a larger, more imposing make than standard. He heard less and less as the whine grew louder and louder until the cavern erupted with gunfire that tore away at their natural defenses. The stalagmites, though, withstood the onslaught of bullets, but these rocks would not be able to shield them from the Mark II for long.

It was a strange time to be thinking of his father, and yet this might be the last time he had a chance. "*You are embarrassing me, Wellington,*" he had said, loading the pistol with a sneer. "*When I was your age, I had already taken down my first stag. Now get on with it!*"

Eliza's head jerked back sharply, and Wellington's father vanished as she stumbled back and fell hard against the rock floor.

"*Eliza!*" Wellington, shouting her name over the gunfire, leapt across the tiny clearing between them and crouched low by her side.

Gingerly he turned her head towards him to examine the head wound. There was so much blood. Far too much for his liking, at first glance. The bullet had—much to his relief—only grazed her temple. The fall and head bump had knocked her out.

"*Wellington Books, you are no son of mine.*" The Mark II Gatlings were spinning up again, but he could only hear the gentle autumn wind of his family's estate. "*Pull the trigger.*"

He had wanted to explain to Eliza why. There was a very good reason Wellington didn't care for guns. It went well beyond his father's passion for them.

The stalagmite exploded around them. On a third assault, there would be nowhere for them to hide.

When he took up her pistols, he smiled at how their grips were still warm. He studied the tiki, the one he had seen in Antarctica in detail now. A Hei-Hei, for those who were calculating, cunning, and committed to a cause. He found the charm comforting then. He still found it so.

Wellington turned back to his fallen comrade. *Not dead*, he reassured himself. *Just resting*. She looked quite striking, so peaceful. *She called me her partner.*

Wellington pulled back the hammers of the two pistols. "Stay here, Eliza. I'll be but a moment."

When he stepped free of the rock's protection, there was the slightest tinge of sulfur to the air he drew into his lungs. He saw the two foot soldiers in full detail, and felled them before they paused in their slow advance. The pair behind them were armed with Gatlings, but to compensate for the extra armament, their collarbones and heads were unprotected and in the open. Again, Wellington fired Eliza's pistols and both men dropped.

Three more infantry were charging him, screaming wildly, their bayonet-strapped rifles thrust forward. Wellington could see in the third soldier's face recognition that their shock tactic had backfired when the bullet drove through his helmet and into his skull. It had been the same quick, surprising death for the other two, as well.

A single shot lightly prickled Wellington's face with dirt

and rock. Glancing at a fresh hole in the nearby stalagmite before ducking behind it, Wellington checked his weapons. One pistol had two bullets remaining. The other had three. When the sniper's next shot bit into his hiding place, Wellington leaned his head away from the impact point. He quickly considered the delay between shots, the echo, and the angle at which the bullets removed the rock. His eyes swept around him to stop at the dead soldier he had just dispatched, his rifle lying idly out of reach, and presumably loaded and primed.

The earth trembled underneath him. Another boiler had exploded. "*Tick-tock, Welly,*" he heard Eliza chide.

He stepped out of his hiding place, firing as he moved for the rifle. On his last shot, his heel struck it. Wellington turned, slipping his foot underneath its block and giving it a quick heft. The rifle rose up to his chest where he grabbed, turned, aimed, and fired. The sniper toppled from his hiding place.

Filling the cavern was a low groan of metal joints moving. A hiss of hydraulics and the pounding of massive feet shook the ground under Wellington. The Mark II towering over him had started its turn in his direction, and behind the leviathan another one was powering up.

This would be a far trickier shot and perhaps not as accurate as he would prefer. Not accurate, but not impossible either. The viewport that the Mark II pilots used to see through was a necessity. Along with visibility, it also allowed for air to circulate, lest humans inside would suffocate from their own expended breath. This viewport, sadly, was a vulnerability that Doctor Havelock had to allow if he wanted this dream realised.

Wellington shouldered his rifle, and then paused. His eyes narrowed on the Mark II behind the one closing on him. It was definitely more of a challenge, reliant on circumstances, but would kill two birds with one stone. Or shot, considering present settings.

Reacquiring the viewport of the second Mechaman, Wellington fired two shots. The massive automaton continued forward. He fired again. On the fourth shot, its arms lowered with a long, sudden hiss but the Mechaman still lumbered forward. It made no effort to avoid massive breastplates waiting to be riveted onto other Mark IIs. The plates were suspended high over the assembly line by chains, massive iron works that Wellington had hoped would slow down the second Mechaman. His gamble, however, was not playing to his favour. He then heard the whine of a Gatling reaching its peak, preparing to mow him down.

What he did not consider were these breastplates swinging wildly behind both automatons. Their heavy chains could no longer compensate for the uneven weight distribution, and began snapping like rope. One plate swung wildly into the back of the charging Mark II, helping it along its way into the first Mechaman. The toppling monsters and their great cannons roared in protest, spraying ordnance in every direction. Wellington dashed for Eliza and dragged her back into the safety of the tiny alcove where they had entered from, and stayed low as the Mechamen's Gatlings continued to fire.

Following what felt like a long, languid fall, rivets immediately failed to contain the explosion of the Mark II's internal gyroscopes. After the rumble of rock against metal subsided, Wellington looked over his point of cover. Both Mark IIs' engines were still attempting to run their massive legs but the imposing war machines appeared as helpless as overturned turtles.

No reinforcements came. All that could be seen and heard were alarms, fire, steam, smoke, and a shower of mason work from the estate's foundation.

Wellington looked down at the sleeping Eliza. In the protective alcove of stone, he discarded all of her weaponry, save for the *pounamu* pistols which he replaced in their adopted holsters.

This weekend, she had chosen to forgo her Ministry-issue

corset as it would have clashed dreadfully with her evening wear. For her keen sense of fashion, he was quite grateful.

"Time to go, Eliza," he grunted, hauling her into a Fireman's lift over his shoulder.

CHAPTER THIRTY

Wherein Our Heroes Endure Perdition's Flames

With every step his legs ached, and with every breath the air grew more toxic with smoke and acrid chemicals. The fire was indeed spreading now to the other Mark II Mechamen—it would only be a matter of time before this den of iniquity would be claimed by appropriate fires of hell.

The lift Wellington saw to his left would be a risk, but there were no stairs in sight. There was very little to consider: either die of smoke inhalation while searching for stairs, or chance the lift's cable system failing and sending them plummeting to their deaths. The latter would at least be quick. He tried to push back both scenarios to the furthest recesses of his brain as he threw the winch forward without bothering to close the gate. Their lift shook as if it were a child's kaleidoscope, but still the cables remained taut and the pulleys continued their painfully slow ascent to the main estate.

They were halfway up the shaft when the explosion erupted from the floor below. Wellington moved away from the open back of the cab just as the wall of smoke, flame, and heat slipped around them as would a claw of some great beast reaching in vain to pull them back. The underground facility of the Phoenix Society was giving way to the destruction, and still the winches—with their grinding protestations and snapping cables—pulled them higher.

Light struck his face; and by the time his eyes adjusted, he understood what was behind the screams and shouts assailing him. The manor above ground was also gripped by pandemonium. Servants appeared like rats on a sinking ship, running for the nearest exit, but not before helping themselves to anything that was not bolted or nailed down. Some of the more loyal house staff attempted to preserve the manor's integrity by struggling with the opportunists, or that was what Wellington convinced himself the odd skirmishes were all about. He watched a diminutive kitchen maid grab a small knife from a table setting and drive it into the eye socket of a stable boy. A butler, his wig awry, wrestled with an old man on the stairs, apparently for a pair of fine candlesticks.

Wellington had no time to intervene—he had to even the score and save Eliza.

His reminder of what little time remained came in the form of a long, menacing creak of wood and metal accented by a gentle tinkling of crystal against crystal. Like a ship in a storm, the manor *listed*. The angle was getting steeper with each of his steps. The failure of the manor's foundations was imminent. Shifting Eliza's limp body on his shoulders, Wellington pressed onward towards the main entrance.

Plaster and moulding rained down on them. Servants and weekend guests cried out in panic and blind terror, all of them succumbing to an instinct that transcended class barriers: the survival instict. Perhaps Wellington's expectations had been too high. The Phoenix Society preached a return to propriety and good English values, but he felt none of it as one of the Brethren, a man he recognised from across his place at dinner, shoved him out of the way, knocking both of them into a nearby wall. With a grunt, Wellington regained his balance.

It was odd that he heard it, but clear as fine crystal, a bird call cut through the mayhem. He followed the chirping,

Eliza growing heavier with each step, until finally the haze of Havelock's crumbling estate surrendered to sunlight. Wellington could see the outside world, and it appeared to be a bright, picturesque day in the country. *How lovely*, he thought quickly, just as a chunk of moulding fell in front of him. He could also see, waiting in the sunlight, a collection of carriages, tethered mares stomping impatiently and frothing at the mouth. He took in another deep breath—they were nearly there!

The light fixture just above him on the wall exploded. He knew it had not shattered from the stress of the unstable mansion. It had been a single pistol shot.

Wellington turned to see their assailant covered in soot, blood, and earth. Bartholomew Devane, provided he lived through this, would never again be the dashing gentleman he fancied himself to be. The entire right side of his face was covered in gore, much of it dried and clinging to flesh that had been caressed by fire. The arm not holding the pistol hung mangled by his side. Still, even in his condition, the man-thing smiled; and that normally cold, predatory smile of Devane's was even less attractive now.

"Leaving so soon, old boy?" His voice had also been ravaged by the destruction of Havelock's underground lair. It was grating, rough, and painful to Wellington's ears. He wondered how hard it was on Devane. Or was he relishing in his agony? "I was denied by your partner there but a moment ago. She seems to be in a far more agreeable state at present."

The manor suddenly jostled as if something had struck it. They both fought to keep their balance when Wellington felt a sharp pain in his foot. He looked down in alarm as a hot stinging sensation wrapped around his right foot. He couldn't move it. Something *underneath* his right foot was holding him there.

With a desperate, agonizing tug, Wellington yanked his foot free, fighting the knee's wish to sink to the floor. He was still standing, but now the stinging rippled up his right leg.

A spoke, belonging to a cog Wellington guessed would have to be the size of his head, protruded through the floorboard where he had been. Its dark tip was now decorated with his blood. Then he saw another wheel protruding in front of Devane. Another two behind him. At various spots across the cherrywood floor, gears, cogs, and what appeared to be the outer hatch to a boiler all cracked through.

"For the love of God, Devane, look around you!" Wellington shouted, his legs starting to tremble slightly. In the corner of his eye, he could see a tea tray begin to roll on its own accord. "The main boiler has to be reaching critical at any moment, and the manor's foundation is failing. Perhaps you would you care to indulge in this melodramatic moment of revenge outside?"

Over the sounds of silverware jangling and wall fixtures falling, Wellington still heard the hammer of Devane's pistol locking into a firing position. "Here will do just fine, although I might just enjoy myself with your 'blushing bride' there on the lawn. Being a colonist, she probably fancies herself an outdoors type."

"Enough, Devane! The Phoenix is dying! It is—"

"It will be over," he interjected, "in just a bullet or two."

Wellington closed his eyes tight. He wouldn't blame Eliza for dragging him out of the Archives. She'd been right. She had been right all this time. Wellington would not regret it. This had been one ripping good time.

Thank you, Eliza. I'm sorry.

The shot rang out sharp and loud, and he flinched slightly at the air rushing out of him. Wellington waited for more pain to come, for the feeling of blood cooling on his skin, for the impact against the floor, and for the despair that would consume him at seeing Eliza dragged outside by Lord Devane for his own concupiscent whims.

None of it came.

Opening one eye, Wellington saw Devane there, his arm still outstretched, the pistol still in his grasp. He opened his second eye when tiny crimson droplets fell free from Devane's lips. The sidearm fell, but Devane was not done. Wellington could see awareness in the man's face. Devane knew he had been shot, but by whom? He turned to the adjoining corridor from where it had come.

Olivia Devane's arm was steady, as was her hand. The pistol firm in her grasp was primed and ready again, but she was hesitating. She said nothing as she closed the distance.

"Darling," he gurgled as he stretched his good arm out to her. "Come to me. A farewell kiss, for all the lovely memor—"

The second shot pushed him backwards tripping over one of the protruding cogs, sending him with a hard crash to the floor. Wellington assumed revenge was behind the other three shots Olivia put into him, regardless of the fact he was most assuredly dead.

"Come along, Lady Devane!" Wellington shouted, adjusting Eliza again as the mansion gave what surely must be its dying shudder.

"You don't understand." Olivia was free, but her eyes were vacant. "I have one bullet remaining." She pulled the hammer back. "Mustn't let it go to waste."

He never got the opportunity to protest as the barrel slipped into her mouth. The back of her head decorated the painting behind her with a splatter of deep red, textured with flesh, hair, and bone. The painting had been an original from the Realist movement. That irony did not escape Wellington.

With the pain of his foot driving him on and keeping him alert and aware, he growled and made for the open door of the Havelock estate, now leaning ten degrees to its left. His feet struggled against stone torn from the sagging mansion, but still he kept going, Eliza across his neck and shoulders threatening to take him down. He did not stop after he cleared the manor's entrance. He did not stop when he heard the brick, stone, and wood crumble, groan, and tear. He did not stop when his feet were digging into the gravel and rocks of the causeway. Even when his own cries and the gentle crunching underfoot yielded to the deafening explosion, Wellington Books kept moving.

He finally collapsed at a grove just off the causeway. Here the grass was thick and soft, and it cushioned Eliza when he fell. Catching his breath, Wellington forced his gaze back to where the manor stood and watched with morbid fascination as the earth opened and devoured Havelock Manor and any trace of the Phoenix Society.

INTERLUDE

In Which Our Beautiful Assassin Is Taught a Lesson

If Sophia's arms and legs weren't bound, she would have kicked herself for being so damn sloppy—not just once but twice.

The first time was shortly after she'd been congratulating herself for so easily liberating the schematics from Havelock's laboratory. She had just been about to make her unhurried exit when the explosion knocked her off her feet. The world tilted, but Sophia had been able to see from where the angry flames licked beyond the door frame that there had been a catastrophic failure in Reactor Room Number Three.

Inglesi, she had sworn in her jostled head. *Questi Inglesi son Stronzi!* Those idiots had apparently not paid close-enough attention to the gauges, and it was so easy to turn a boiler into a bomb. After gathering up her plans for the Mark III, she had ascended the closest stairs.

Upon reaching the manor level, she had frozen at the madness unfolding before her. Members of the Phoenix Society were making mad dashes for the door, the husbands pulling at their wives or companions, both of which were struggling with their luggage. It seemed their lives were worth as much as their wardrobe. Around them were servants like vultures around the carrion, picking at whatever meat they could grab.

She had paused for a moment to enjoy the spectacle.

That indulgence cost her as an explosion had rocked the house so hard, the grand chandelier in the room she was harbouring herself in had crashed to the floor and then rolled to one side, trapping her in what had been her safe corner. The fixture looked so delicate when hanging from the ceiling, but its intricate build and significant weight had made it difficult to leverage herself against. A dull bang from underneath her feet popped her off the floor. Sophia managed to get a sure hold on the chandelier and work herself free of her corner. Once clear of her deathtrap, she had assured herself the Mark III plans were still tucked inside her bodice before making a hasty retreat.

It had been one minor mistake—and she had survived it. It remained to be seen if she would survive the second.

Back in her hotel, Sophia had indulged in one of the establishment's best vintages. Perhaps the Phoenix had returned to the ashes, but she had escaped with most of her payment from them for services rendered and now with the schematics for at least one quaint device worth a coin or two to her *other* employer.

Perhaps the Mark III could serve as her finale, she'd thought, her farewell to the cloak-and-dagger world. This contraption would be her ticket to a more quiet life of luxury.

She usually took only a single glass of wine, but with this unexpected boon she was going to risk a little and enjoy the bottle. Besides, it was Italian, and it would have been a crime to let such a delicious nectar from her home go to waste.

It was during her fourth glass that the door's lock shattered. The dark figure entered her room and did not wait to survey the surroundings, did not pause, never stopped in moving through the room. Whether her hesitation was due to shock or her inability it did not matter. It was still hesitation.

Sophia had known she would never reach her pistols in time, so she had thrust her arm out, triggering the gauntlet covering her forearm, launching a pair of her lethal cogs.

The tall man had dodged them as if they were stones thrown by a child.

Locking her other arm forward, she had extended the stiletto, tearing the blouse cuff as she did. She had moved to charge him, but the tall man's arms had slipped inside her own, knocking away her gauntlets with soft metal clangs of his own.

He had been far too close for an opponent to be, and when his forearm caught her on the chin she had felt the hard, cold brass concealed underneath his evening coat. The second blow across her brow ushered in the darkness, darkness that prevailed to her awakening.

Dropping her guard in a hotel? Being carried like laundry?! These were the mistakes of an amateur, like those House of Usher idiots.

Could this be their revenge, she thought quickly, *for Alexander and his men?* Could the House of Usher have tracked her once more, and were now saving their reputation? In her profession, dissatisfied clientele would sometimes turn colleagues against one another.

But this man was not a colleague. Quite frankly, she had no idea who or what this man was. No man or woman in her field moved liked that.

The binds holding her wrists loosened and then slipped free. She was however still blindfolded.

A sharp hiss of steam caused her to start, but then the deadly silence returned.

Sophia ripped the blindfold free. When her eyes adjusted to the glow of gaslight, she saw in a moment just who her captor was.

She hadn't been sloppy after all—she had been outclassed.

"*Bona Sera, Signora Sophia del Morte*," the voice wheezed, his mechanised tones concluding with a soft puff from some unseen engine. She wondered absently if his condition was in fact necessary or simply part of some theatrical disguise. "It is such a relief to see that you did not suffer the fate of Havelock Manor. That would have been too . . . convenient . . . for you."

"*Signor*," she began, the alcohol's effect now quashed by the fear uncoiling in her stomach. "I know what you expected of me, but I cannot be held responsi—"

"Just because I greet you politely," the cloaked man interjected, "does not mean you have leave to beg for your life and slander those who are not here to defend themselves!"

The door flew open behind her, and a shadowed figure kicked a disheveled, pathetic excuse of a gentleman into the light. The newcomer, removing the sack from his head, revealed himself as the tattered and unkempt Doctor Deveraux Havelock, scientific visionary and leader of the fallen Phoenix Society. Despite the conspicuous stubble on his face, and the numerous cuts and abrasions, he still carried the bearing of a man not used to being challenged. When he heard the hiss from his host's breathing apparatus, he licked his lips. Havelock's breathing slowed, and he drew himself to his full height. It was the same demeanour as he had used with her, and no doubt with his now dead Society.

Sophia concealed a smirk. It seemed that tonight would be their trial; but this time Havelock would be standing under someone else's rule.

"Now then," the voice wheezed, "let the slander commence."

"Slander?" Havelock laughed. "Hardly slander, considering how this dago tart failed in her office."

"*Va-fanculo, Bastardo, Figlio di buttana, Ingrassatto!*" Sophia spat. "I fail in nothing!"

"So that is what you call your evening at *Macbeth*—a success?"

"*Macbeth* would have never happened had you not insisted on discretion! I would have dispatched that English spy otherwise."

"We had to rein you in, following that massacre in Charing Cross . . . and at your hotel!" he retorted. "Your methods were attracting attention we most assuredly didn't need."

"So that is why you refused to allow me to complete the job? Send house servants to kill the nurse, eh? *Stupidi Inglesi!*"

"Damn you, woman, I will not tolerate your excuses for incompetence!"

"There was no talk of government agents," she bit back. "I do the job I was hired for. Agents of your English Queen—*that* will cost you."

"Government agents that you recognised, and *still* did not put down. Even when they were presented on a plate in front of you!"

"Government agents that you *invited* into your own *manor*, and unveiled our projects to as if you were proud mother showing off babies!"

"You daft bint, had you dispatched them in my ballroom like a proper assassin, I do believe the Phoenix Society would be continuing on a schedule that pleases his lordsh—"

"Enough!" called the cloaked judge and jury seated before them.

Havelock's hand lowered back to his side. Breaking the silence were the occasional pops of air and steam coming from their master. That, and Sophia muttering "*Testa di Cazzo, ti ammazzo.*"

"*Signora*," the shadows beckoned, "come closer."

Sophia's stomach churned, not out of excitement or desire but out of sheer terror. The fear had uncoiled fully, and all that wine was catching up with her.

"I am saddened by this turn of events, my dear." He sighed, which resembled the wheezing his voice naturally made. "We were doing so well and had such high hopes."

From behind her, she heard the faintest ring of what her

ear recognised was sharpened metal. Could she escape? For all she knew, this man was an invalid and Havelock would provide a fine shield, if needed.

"Doctor Havelock is quite correct in that you did fail us all in recognising government agents and not performing what is expected of you." She could see a shadow move. Was his head shaking? "I suppose we will need to be more clear in what we expect from our own."

She let out a tiny cry on hearing the blade cut into flesh, and that was when her bladder failed her—just a little.

The blade rang again in her ears as it slipped free. Havelock never made a sound, not even a final gasp, as the blade entered the side of his neck and lanced his trachea. He collapsed before her, his blood pooling around his head and her feet. Sophia flinched at the smell of her own urine mixing with the tang of blood.

Yet why would this offend her? She knew Death. He was a familiar companion. This was her chosen profession, after all. Yet she felt herself recoil, watching the blood flow through and over Havelock's fingers, bloody fingers that tried with feeble, futile gestures to close the wound and then claw at her dress. The great mind behind the Phoenix Society reminded her of nothing more than a beached fish.

Sophia had seen worse. Far worse. What was so terrifying about this then?

I am afraid, she thought quickly. *These people are better than me. They can kill me at any time.*

"I will have Pearson issue you a new contract that will, with unmistakable clarity, outline what we expect of you in the future, *Signora* del Morte," the master said, intermittent hisses punctuating his raspy, tinny words. "You are the finest in your office, and that has won you my attentions."

"*Si*," Sophia agreed. She wiped the smallest beads of sweat from her lip. "What about Wellington Books and his partner, *Signor*?" she asked. "I can take care of them straightaway."

The shadows moved as if his head tilted up to consider

the moon overhead, a moon that only he could see through the walls of this windowless room. "No. Not at the moment. Their deaths might bring the Ministry's attention to us. We are not yet ready for that." After a pause, he spoke again, his tone lighter. "So, my dear *Signora* del Morte, we have an accord, do we?"

She nodded vigorously.

"Excellent," he replied. " I believe this new contract will make clear what I expect from you."

"Thank you, *Signor*."

The metallic hand reached out of the darkness and wrapped around her throat. The cool brass fingers that hoisted Sophia off the ground were twice as thick as a normal man's appendages, so she could feel the slightest stretching in her neck. She could hear steam venting angrily, as if the room were now filled with cobras warning of a pending death strike. The heat around her rose and those moving shadows now puller her closer. Her own hands grabbed the large mechanical wrist—not in an attempt to struggle but for leverage. She tried to lift herself up to alleviate the stretching of her neck. Sophia managed a few precious gasps just before coming to a stop.

From the darkness, a malicious ruby eye flared, its glow cutting through the void. "I expect you will not fail me again."

She felt a cold rush of air on her skin, followed by her impact against the far wall. Her breaths were ragged as were her coughs, and the gentle rubbing of her tender neck did little to ease the pain. The hand that had held her so effortlessly now threw down a trinket for her. She gathered up the strange square ring. Much like the House of Usher and the Phoenix Society, he had a mark, but it was simple as opposed to heraldic. She lost herself in the symbol, her curiosity as to why he chose something so elementary. "A symbol of our new agreement that you will soon understand," the metallic voice boomed, "but for now wear it at all times as a display of your loyalty."

Without question Sophia slipped it on her finger, though she knew this was far more serious than even a wedding ring. She shivered.

The brass arm now motioned down to Havelock. "Pearson, make sure the good doctor here is unrecognisable so that even if he is found by the scavengers he is not identified. And then see the lovely *Signora* to her new apartments, if you please. The contract can wait until tomorrow."

"Very good, sir," the tall man replied as he stepped into the light.

"And have the lovely *Signora* attend upon your duties tonight. As you bested her so easily this evening, I believe she has a great deal to learn from you." With that, the cloaked master melted into the shadows of the room, disappearing completely this time.

Sophia pulled her knees up to her chest as Pearson, the trusted head butler of Havelock Manor, removed a long hunting knife from its sheath at the small of his back, ready to set about his charge.

And by the soft glow of gaslight, Sophia watched. She watched, and learned.

CHAPTER THIRTY-ONE

Wherein Doctor Sound Is Regaled with an Exciting Tale of a Weekend in the Country

Tick . . . tock . . . tick . . . tock . . .

"Now this is exceptional work. You have come far, I must say." Doctor Sound continued reading. "Your earlier reports—I found them difficult to muddle through. This is a vast improvement."

Tick . . . tock . . . tick . . . tock . . .

"This is also not quite what I expected, particularly from you. When I read in the papers about the unfortunate accident in the country, I immediately suspected the mayhem and chaos behind it to have been helped along. A failure of the estate's foundations on account of geothermal instabilities? Not what I would think, at first."

"No, sir," Wellington Books replied, "I still found myself unable to believe it all as I was also busy assisting Agent Braun usher the innocents to safety."

Tick . . . tock . . . tick . . . tock . . .

Damnable clock, Wellington thought to himself. He was already nervous enough about this meeting with Doctor Sound. That clock was *not* helping.

It would have been far easier to attempt concealing their

extracurricular activities from the Ministry head had the Fire Brigade, Scotland Yard, and various newspaper reporters not so rapidly appeared on the scene of what remained of Havelock Manor. Eliza had been spirited away to a hospital while Wellington found himself sequestered with all the other survivors after his own wounds had been treated.

So it was to Scotland Yard that Wellington had been forced to reveal his credentials and true identity. This was also necessary in order to make certain alongside charges of treason to the Crown those survivors in league with the Phoenix Society were held accountable for the deaths of the journalists, Doctor Christopher Smith, and Agent Harrison Thorne. He also knew in that moment, as the Collinses protested their arrest and the Pembrokes loosed a final glare on him, that justice would come with a price: an interrogation with Doctor Sound.

After Eliza had awakened in the hospital, she and Wellington quickly compared notes. He could see the question in her eyes. She was wondering whether or not he would truly go through with this. Would he back her up, or would he return to his ways of the Archives? Would he stick to the facts, and keep things accurate and clinical to the last letter, to the final number?

"And just so we are all clear on what you and Braun are reporting," Sound's voice bought him back to the here and now, "you two were in the Archives for the weekend when you encountered a geothermal anomaly?"

"Yes, sir." Wellington cleared his throat and began their hastily constructed tissue of lies. "Throughout the weekend, we were having problems with the Archives' analytical engine—its computation times were inconsistent."

Sound gave a chortle. "Well now, that sounds like a problem I would defer to Research and Design. They do keep us operational in all manners, you know?"

He could feel the hair on the nape of his neck prickle. With a deep breath, Wellington forced a smile and said, "As you know, sir, I do like being self-sufficient within the Archives. Furthermore, Research and Design have so much on their plate to begin with."

Add to that they are complete and utter tossers.

"Agent Braun and I, in investigating the Archives' difference engine, discovered severe fluctuations coming from the Ministry's generators"—Wellington shifted in his seat, peering over his spectacles as he suddenly added to his recollections—"which reminds me, Doctor, the moisture level of the Archives is still a concern of mine. I know I have sent to your office several communiqués concerning the matter, and I feel it should be addressed and made a priori—"

"Yes, Books, I am well aware of the matter. Please," Doctor Sound said, gently gesturing with his hand. "Continue."

He had probably sacrificed an opportunity to really change things in the Archives but Wellington needed that diversion. *It will make your meeting feel more genuine to the Old Man*, Eliza had told him. He could see it in the Ministry Director's eyes: Eliza, once again, was right.

The Archivist gave a slight shrug and, as requested, continued. "Well, I had the engine run a few possible scenarios as to why performance would suffer."

"Just a moment, Books," interrupted Sound, "you had the computation device that was acting faulty run a computation to analyse what would make it faulty?"

"A self-repairing diagnostic, as it were, yes, Doctor." Wellington gave a little smile at his own ingenuity. Not in the concept, but in his storytelling. "It's a bit like noting your elbow is suddenly sore. You ask yourself 'How did that happen?' and I was doing this, only having the analytical engine ask itself that question."

"Well played, Books." Sound leaned forward, resting his forearms against the desk.

"Thank you, sir. The scenarios we ran—"

"*We* ran?"

"Well, sir, I was responsible for most of the computations. Agent Braun . . . watched."

Tick . . . tock . . . tick . . . tock.

He cleared his throat after a long, awkward moment, and resumed. "The computations all seemed to point towards a geothermal anomaly altering the salinity and temperature of the Thames by varying degrees, so we traced back the source of the fluctuations to the Havelock estate. When we asked to see the head of the house to inform him of the potential danger, we were immediately taken into their custody. That was when we discovered the nefarious plans of this secret organisation, whomever they were."

"The Phoenix Society," Doctor Sound responded flatly.

"Ah, yes, quite, sir. I think this Society panicked a bit when we revealed ourselves as members of a Ministry. Not that we named the Ministry, but that we served at the discretion of Her Majesty. It was Agent Braun's field training that managed to get us out of their dungeons; and I should add, sir, that could not have been timed better. Their experiments were disrupting natural pressure points in the cavern system underneath the Havelock estate. I ascertained it was only a matter of moments before their daring—but yes, sinister—plots provoked a calamity."

"Which it seems that they did." Doctor Sound's expression was revealing very little, making it impossible to tell if he was convinced by the yarn. "Now according to Braun's own report, they were creating some sort of mechanised soldiers?"

"Yes, christened Mechamen. The Mark IIs were these leviathans that were piloted by men, while the Mark Is were self-propelled. From what I gathered on the intelligence Agent Braun collected, it was a natural progression. The first model would be expendable automatons. Shock troops, as they would be produced in mass quantities from an assembly line. The second model would add the human element, creating unstoppable war machines."

He hoped he wasn't growing pale. The human element of Havelock's still haunted him. Instinct told him not to share it with the Ministry.

"Doctor, are you aware if the Ministry was able to locate any schematics or secure prototypes?"

"The evidence and technology, so it would seem, has been buried under rock and earth. It would take a large excavation to uncover those treasure troves, but something tells me you already knew that."

The twinkle in Sound's eye was less malicious than foreboding. It was as if the Director knew, Wellington thought quickly, that woven within his detailed report was a confidence scheme.

"I concluded as much, yes, sir." Wellington adjusted his cravat, and then motioned to the report. "Did a Ministry inspector find any evidence if the lord of the manor—Doctor Havelock, I think his name was—made it out alive or not?"

"Well, according to Campbell, the only bodies that were recovered that matched descriptions you and Braun provided were those of Lord Bartholomew Devane and his wife, Lady Devane. Doctor Havelock's body was not found." Sound closed the case report and slid it aside. His fingers tapped it idly, and then he looked back. "Seems to have been quite an amazing trip for you, Alice?"

Wellington's brow furrowed. "I'm sorry, sir?"

"Your trip through the Looking Glass?" he said, a slight chortle in his voice. "I daresay that the things you experienced outside the Archives were a bit like tumbling down the rabbit hole."

"I was grateful for my training."

"Tosh! You were grateful to have such an agent as resourceful as Eliza Braun by your side. It was quite an amazing set of circumstances you both found yourself in."

"Yes, sir." Wellington then chuckled. "I am beginning to wonder if trouble does not find Agent Braun as moths find flames in the night."

"I wonder the same thing as well, Books."

Silence, save for the *tick . . . tock . . . tick . . . tock . . .*

"Will that be all, sir?"

Doctor Sound tapped his fingertips together, his eyes never leaving the Archivist. "For the time being, yes."

With a small nod, Wellington stood with help from his cane and made for the door. The twinges sending jabs of pain up his leg told him his strides were wider than usual.

"How is the foot, Books?"

Wellington swallowed hard, and then turned to face Doctor Sound. "I'm on the mend, sir. Thank you."

"Good man." He then leaned back in his chair and asked, "Before you go, one more query: did Braun motivate you in any way to pursue these events that you two have reported?"

"I'm sorry, sir?"

"Agent Books, one of the forgotten cases down in your Archives directly involves Harrison Thorne, her former partner. Were you aware of this?"

"Of the forgotten case, or that Former Agent Thorne was Agent Braun's partner?"

"Both."

Wellington suddenly noticed how warm Sound's office was. "I am cognisant of her history. I think the silence of the Archives makes her a bit nervous, to be honest with you. I was not aware of any particular case, forgotten or otherwise, that would motivate Agent Braun to operate outside of the Ministry's operational procedure." He then straightened up and crooked his eyebrow as he said, "And if I may speak my mind, Director, I do not think that she would be so cavalier as to jeopardize her already tenuous position here. She is in fact quite bright and most efficient."

"Really?" Now it was Doctor Sound's turn to raise an eyebrow. "You have learned all this after such a brief time working with her, have you?"

"I have, sir. Agent Braun may not be used to the lifestyle of an Archivist, but she is definitely not a hindrance to what I do. In fact, she is quite an asset. I may not have understood or appreciated the decision initially, but I do not mind so much now. We are . . ." Wellington paused. He didn't want to lie to the Director on this point. It meant a lot to him. ". . . getting to know each other."

"I see." Doctor Sound gave a curt nod, and turned his attention to another case file apparently awaiting his final inspection and approval. "Well then, good show in this unexpected weekend of excitement, Agent Books. That will be all."

Wellington was at the door when Sound stopped him once more with, "Speaking of the Ministry's pepperpot, is she still in the hospital?"

"Afraid not, sir. The doctor's had one day with her once she was conscious. She checked herself out the day after."

"Same as always then." Doctor Sound shook his head. "So where is she this morning?"

"Personal leave, sir. Just for this morning."

INTERLUDE

Where Agent Campbell Has a Most Distressing Meeting

The much-lamented Prince Albert might have been a self-important Hun, but he had known how to make things happen. He also might not have been the architect behind the Crystal Palace, but this Great Exhibition had been a brilliant concept. Quite impressive for one man.

Agent Bruce Campbell glanced up at the vaulted curved glass that towered above him. The Crystal Palace had first been built in Hyde Park, but then later moved to be a permanent exhibit on Sydenham Hill. For nearly fifty years it had remained the popular place to spend your free time in London. That was, if you liked your leisure time to be genteel and not involving booze.

In the heyday of Queen Victoria it must have been quite a marvel, but now, like Herself, it was starting to look decidedly shaky. Ever since Albert had been killed while tinkering with a boiler for another of his mad designs, she'd retreated from the world.

And yet they were all still loyal to the little rotund Empress of the world. Well, for the moment anyway. Such were the bitter thoughts of an agent preparing to betray his friends.

Bruce couldn't see Sussex anywhere, but the note he'd found slipped under his front door that morning had to be from him. The meeting place. The very stylish, polished handwriting on the card. Yes, it was most assuredly Sussex.

"This place is bloody huge," the agent grumbled to himself. However, he guessed that was part of the Privy Counsellor's plan: keep his "Ministry Mole" off balance. Not that he needed to worry on that score. Bruce had been pinned down by gunfire in hopeless situations and still felt more confident than he did now. He was certain Sussex would be less than amused with the recent turn of events.

Five more minutes, he promised himself, and then he'd head off and not respond to any more stupid notes. He was at least grateful that because it was a weekday there were not so many crowds.

The agent blindly turned into the Ninevah Court. One circuit. That would be all. Passing between the nearly twenty-foot-high human-headed bulls, he glanced up, and had to admit they remained impressive. Though he had actually seen the real thing in the deserts of Persia, the awe was dampened somewhat.

On the left was a picture of some long dead Assyrian ruler. The agent leaned forward to examine its details.

"Wonderful to see you educating yourself," Sussex quipped in Bruce's left ear.

"Bloody hell!" The agent couldn't help it. The explicative echoed in the chamber and several ladies spun around in horror. Their twittering was only silenced when Bruce flashed his smile and made an apologetic bow. It also gave him a second to take his heart out of his throat and jam it back into his chest. No one ever—ever—snuck up on him like that. Not the tribesmen of the steppe, not the Shuar headhunters of the Amazon, and most certainly not a bloody toff from England!

Yet Sussex had.

Bruce cocked his head. Something about Sussex was decidedly off, so he was going to have to watch his step for sure around him. He swallowed back his natural inclination to violence and merely nodded.

Sussex's smile was thin and cold as he stepped away, deeper into the Ninevah Court. Bruce had no choice but to follow. Further on, the Court was full of palm trees and quietly chatting ladies. Even though it was cool in here, Bruce could feel the back of his neck break out in a sweat.

Finally he couldn't take it anymore.

"Look, Your Grace . . . I need more time."

Sussex spun on his heel, "To do what exactly? I have given you plenty of time to prove yourself, Campbell. Instead this morning I find a report on my desk that the Ministry has uncovered some plot to bring down the Empire."

Bruce clenched his teeth lest he offend more ladies. Sussex, nearly nose to nose with him now, seemed itching for a fight. Unexpected for someone so highborn. Every muscle in the man's body was tense, and this toff looked ready to knock Bruce down or at least have a go at it. The Australian, however, felt his "Flight" not "Fight" impulses under Sussex's hard gaze. Those manicured hands were clenched into fists, the large thick ring on one hand threatening to make a fine mess of Bruce's pretty face. He might be an aristocrat but there was a coiled menace about him.

The moment drew out, and then Sussex seemed to get hold of himself. Finally he managed, "I confess, I am reconsidering my offer to you, Agent Campbell. The Ministry may have won a small reprieve in the affections of Her Majesty."

One look in those ice-chip blue eyes said that Sussex wasn't going to be put off. He would not stop, even in light of this development, until the Ministry went down in flames. Whatever the Fat Man had done to earn such enmity Bruce didn't hazard to guess—maybe Sound had been or was presently sticking it to his wife or something.

"With Sound back in the Queen's favour, I may need to

consider alternatives. Alternatives that keep you as part of the problem."

Sussex licked his lips. "My dear colonial, whatever will happen to your children?"

Now Bruce could feel the croc's teeth in his leg again, so he said the first thing that came to mind. "Sound is up to something. Something that he doesn't want anyone to know about."

The Privy Counsellor's eyes narrowed, a disturbing smile tugging at the corners of his mouth. "Admirable bluff, but I have read all the files on the Ministry—everything that there is to know. Enjoy the rest of the Palace, *mate*." And with the contempt still dripping off his salutation he turned to leave.

"Did you know about the Restricted Area?" Bruce asked, his voice loud enough to catch the tiniest of echoes. "In the Archives?"

That brought Sussex back to him. "Go on."

"I'm not sure what's in there," Bruce muttered, feeling a strange swelling of remorse fill his belly. "I asked around, as discreetly as I could, but no one seems to know." His voice then dropped to a whisper. "I saw him go in there. He disappeared behind the door, and then a moment later he came out. There was fresh snow on his shoulders.

"A private project? Wonderful!" Sussex tilted his head back looking up at the towering frescos. "Do you know your history, Campbell?"

The abrupt change of topic sent the agent's head reeling. He shrugged. "Never been much for that sort of thing."

Sussex gestured upwards. "Two thousand years ago, the Kings of Assyria had the world in the palm of their hand. They were the masters, but they also made a fatal mistake. They became complacent. Their Empire ceased moving forward—it stagnated." He straightened. "And I have no intention of ours going the same way."

Bruce kept his face unmoving. Whatever Sussex was talking about, he'd left the agent far behind. Best to just listen.

"No, our time will not end with the demise of Victoria. We will endure, provided we have nothing to detract us."

The Privy Counsellor returned his focus on Bruce. "Get inside that Restricted Area and find out what Sound is hiding. Once I know that, I can decide how best to proceed."

"How the bloody hell am I supposed to do that?" Bruce opened his mouth to give the protest a voice but then snapped his jaw shut. Sussex had given his charge.

"Right-o then," Bruce muttered. "I'll do my best."

"You will," Sussex assured him, "but just in case, why don't you buy yourself a little memento at the gift shop—something to take back to Australia. Just in case." Then he turned and strode away, leaving Bruce standing there.

Sussex had him right where he wanted. Backing out now would reveal his complicity to Sound and end a lifestyle far more magnificent than what waited for him back home.

Everything relied on finding out exactly what was behind that great iron door. And Bruce could only hope it would be enough to bring Sound and the Ministry down.

When the agent turned and wandered out of the Crystal Palace, he felt as lonely as Judas—with not even twelve pieces of silver to comfort him. And he might not know much of The Bible, but he knew how that story went.

CHAPTER THIRTY-TWO

In Which Miss Braun Says Goodbye and Wellington Books Discovers the Shrew Is Far from Tamed

It should always be raining when one is standing in a graveyard crying over the headstone of a friend. London, however, was being her usual contrary self with not even a cloud in the sky and the kind of heat that might be found in the tropics. In short, hardly the best weather to be wearing black.

The children who stood around her had tried so hard to tidy up for this visit—though their clean clothes were hardly tailored for them and were mismatched in colour. Probably stolen. Regardless of their ill-fitting attire or the means in which they had acquired it, it was the gesture that mattered. All of the Ministry Seven were around her, and very proud to be asked to accompany her to the graveyard.

Eliza readjusted her black veil over the bandage across her temple and stared down at the fresh grave. "They buried him so quickly."

"Always do from Bedlam," Christopher piped up, stuffing his hands into his pockets, "At least the doctor shelled out for a proper grave, so he didn't end up dumped out the back with all the rest of 'em."

Eliza flinched at his rough assessment, but knew it was true. She wiped away more tears and managed to stifle a sob.

Serena's little hand slipped into hers. "I'll miss the lollies he'd bring us." The eight-year-old, who had taken some care to do her hair up, started to cry. Her tears left little track marks in their wake, revealing that maybe she hadn't been all that successful at getting the grime from her face. Eliza pulled her close and let the distraught girl sob into her side. She petted Serena's head and looked down at the fine granite headstone.

HARRISON THORNE,
FELL IN SERVICE TO HIS COUNTRY.
LOVED AND MISSED BY ALL.

I wonder what they would put on mine, she thought, and the idea chilled her. She'd always imagined being buried back home. As much as she enjoyed her work, she craved New Zealand. *Aotearoa.* She missed her hills, the Pacific, the great green forests, and her people.

"He was a good sort, Miss Eliza," Colin's voice jerked her out of her reverie as he snuggled in on her other side. For once she was positive he wasn't going to be helping himself to what was in her purse.

It was hard for the children, but not in ways that the pampered darlings of the upper classes would understand. The Ministry Seven were used to death all around them, in horrible and offhand ways. What they were not used to was outward displays of grief—when Eliza had started crying some hidden well of their own emotion had cracked open. It was also difficult for the Seven as Harry had regarded them as part of the team.

Eliza felt her breath taken away with the gentlest of sobs as the silent twins, Jonathan and Jeremy, placed two roses by the gravestone. For the children, they had lost a friend; and that was an emotion hard to contain.

All except for Christopher: as a tough young man he would not allow any tears to fall.

"Yes," Eliza finally whispered, "Harry was a good man."

She had been dwelling on those days in Paris since waking up in the hospital. The image of Harry's laughing face on their boat ride along the Seine was painful. Would things have been different if instead of turning away from the moment he had leaned in to kiss her? Would he have not pursued those missing women if he had her instead? Might she have, in fact, been with him that night? Maybe he wouldn't be lying in a cold grave if she had.

She swallowed hard and then brushed tears from her eyes with the back of her hand. "Children, I hope you remember something—if you ever have a chance to be happy, pursue it. Without hesitation."

"You mean like when a mark has this nice dangling pocket watch?" Eric, who at ten years old was probably the best pick-pocket in the East End, looked up at her with wide disbelieving eyes. "'Course we'd go for that, quick smart-like." The others were looking up at her, their expressions so confused that Eliza found words jamming in her throat.

She went to explain but thought better of it. Their chances of finding happiness were probably as impossible as her own. "Never mind." She ruffled the red-headed boy's hair, "Silly old Mum is just feeling a bit soft today is all. You'd best be off back home."

They crowded around her, giving her a rough hug that wasn't entirely sweet-smelling but was well meant and well received. They had come because she was sad and Harry had been kind to them: they had certainly not been expecting compensation. It didn't matter. She wouldn't be able to sleep tonight if she imagined them without a roof or food.

"Here, Christopher," she slipped him a handful of coins, "I don't want this wasted on gin."

"Can we get some ices on the way back, mum? It's awful

hot." The older boy being polite meant a lot to Eliza—it happened so very rarely.

"Very well then, but the rest must go on hot meals for all of you tonight."

"Yes, mum!" They loved to call her that, and Eliza didn't do anything to dissuade them. The Ministry Seven were different from the other urchins on the street. They had hope. They had her.

Eliza watched them run out of the graveyard, leaping over the lower headstones and running around the tall obelisks, easily forgetting the grief as only children with the prospect of a treat ahead could do. Unfortunately the possibility of a cool refreshment on this baking day would not do the same for her.

Yet, she too had to move on. Eliza undid the Cheshire Cat locket from around her neck, and placed it carefully on top of the new slice of granite. For a moment she rested her hand there. "We did it Harry—*you* did it. Rest now."

She tilted her head up, looking at the clear blue sky. Faith was something she once had; but if there was a God, then she hoped Harry would be in heaven, flirting up a storm with the angels.

"I'll never forget Paris, Harry," she added, kissing her trembling fingertips and touching the headstone again. "Never."

Eliza turned and walked slowly back to the gates. Her eyes flicked over the headstones as she passed. Unfortunately Harry's name was not the only one she recognised. This was where many agents of the Ministry ended their days. It wasn't like there was some delightful seaside cottage in the South of France where her sort of person retired; mostly what they got was a fine piece of lawn and a reasonably priced granite headstone.

And there he was—standing underneath the gates of the cemetery, just as he had outside Bedlam. Wellington Thornhill Books was dressed in a charcoal grey suit, complete with matching bowler hat and tinted spectacles to ward off the day's glare. With the assistance of a silver-topped, ebony cane, he stood up to his full height to greet her. He was dressed very smartly for a work day. Not that he was ever anything but dapper—yet today he appeared to have taken special care.

"Welly!" she called, and though he did not wince at the shortening of his name, she did see him roll his eyes behind the darkened lenses. Eliza had begun addressing him that way to get under his skin, but now she was quite fond of it. Her pace quickened until she was beside him. "You could have come in, you know." Eliza flipped up the fine layers of her veil and found she still had a smile in her.

"Quite all right, Miss Braun," Wellington replied, tipping his hat to her. "It didn't seem appropriate to intrude as you said your goodbyes." He paused, glanced down at his feet and then held something out to her. It was something quite unexpected.

Two white roses, with a spray of lily of the valley. As Eliza stood still in shock, Wellington tried pinning the little offering to her jacket.

"I know it isn't a necklace of diamonds, but I thought you'd like it." Wellington stabbed himself at least once before securing it on her lapel. "And it is far more appropriate for a gift between partners. An urchin was selling them on a street corner, and I thought it would bring you . . . a bit of cheer."

Eliza glanced down at the flowers. He mustn't be aware of their meaning. The Archivist was not one for the gentle arts, more intrigued by steam and clockwork, than something as mundane as the language of flowers.

Trust. Sweetness. I am worthy of you.

A far more appropriate gift between partners, indeed.

Instead she bit her lip, concentrating on what she was sure of: while she had mourned Harry, Wellington had been giving the account of their actions at the Havelock estate.

"I came straightaway, after my meeting with the Director, so I have not check—"

"Per your instructions, I dismantled the phantasmagoria. It is boxed up and concealed in the crypt alongside a few other dead cases. No one will notice it."

He nodded. "Ah, good. Well then . . ." Wellington cleared his throat and peered over his glasses. "Per my instructions?"

"To the letter." Eliza gave a chuckle. "I did watch it for a minute or two before dismantling it. Quite a clever gadget you had there, Welly. Nicely done." Her head tipped to one side. "Is that why you came out here, straightaway?"

Gripping his cane's silver top and rapping the sidewalk lightly, he finally said, "I came to escort you home."

The shear ridiculousness of that statement and his arm extending outward would have made her laugh out loud only a few weeks before. Things however had changed. Rather than bristling at her partner's attempt at gallantry, Eliza took his offered elbow. "That would be lovely, Mr. Books."

Together they turned and began walking down the street, under the trees that offered some shade from the relentless heat.

At the corner a penny ice truck had just rolled to a stop and was already surrounded by the laughing Ministry Seven. The low three-wheeled transport was not much bigger than a velocipede, but the little barrow it towed behind sprouted a collection of pipes, valves, and even an exhaust that would shower the children with a cool blast of air and snow. The children, the Ministry Seven and others gathering swiftly, all roared with delight as the brief semblance of a distant winter swept across their skin. Along with the magical display of misplaced seasons, the barrow sported a delightful miniature calliope—its jaunty music kept time with the clockwork that clicked at a steady pace. The music, the children's laughter, and the vendor's pleasant demeanour were a delight to Eliza's somewhat battered soul.

"Ingenious," Wellington remarked with a child-like wonder. "The exhaust not only allows for a circumventing of excessive pressure, but it also works as a guarantee for the coolness of the barrow's contents."

Eliza shook her head at Wellington's analytical assessment. "It is also quite fun for the children."

His brow furrowed, and then he looked back at the sounds of the children's cheer. "Oh yes, I suppose it is."

"Wellington Thornhill Books," she scolded, "I worry that you may be a hopeless cause."

"Really?" He stopped for a moment, considered the truck, and then sniffed. "Would a penny ice restore your faith?"

Eliza's mouth twisted into a wry grin and she tugged on his arm. "It's a start."

They watched as Serena jumped up and down until Christopher handed over her scoop of cool goodness. Simple pleasures were so easy to supply to the children—maybe that was why Eliza enjoyed doing it so much.

"You know," she mused, "I have very little recollection of what happened in the cellars of the Havelock house. I really have no idea how we made it out alive."

"You were magnificent," Wellington assured her, "Quite the most miraculous thing I have ever seen. I am only sorry you cannot recall it, what with the knock on the head and all."

She gingerly touched the spot. "Well, it's the training I suppose—it just kicks in when you need it most." Eliza shot him a sly look, "Nice to know that the adventure ended as it began, with me saving your arse once more."

As soon as the words were out of her mouth they felt . . . *wrong.* The gap in her memory was not only annoying but also frustrating. *Something* had happened, and her instinct said she could never have stopped all those men, let alone the Mechamen Mark IIs. If Books knew cataloguing, then she knew combat—and as he would have said, something was severely misfiled.

But this was Wellington Thornhill Books, Esquire, a man obsessed with the facts, illustrated brilliantly just a moment ago. What he recounted to her, and no doubt to Doctor Sound, was certainly consistent with what she would do in a situation like that. The only problem here was she couldn't remember a bloody thing. That had never happened to her before in the field. Yet the Archivist would never tell a tale that fantastic.

Would he?

Up ahead the Seven had finished their fun with the penny ice man—though if she were him Eliza might have checked his pockets before letting them go. The boys all waved to their "mum" as they crossed the street, but little Serena was far too engrossed in her treat for any of that.

When they reached the truck, still playing its cheery tune, Wellington slipped his hand into his pocket and surprised Eliza by ordering one *each* of the little scoops of ice.

It was indeed bliss to have something so cool in her mouth. They walked on for a little bit without saying anything, simply enjoying the treat.

Eventually Wellington broke the silence. "I imagine you are wondering how my interview with the Director went . . ."

"Not really," Eliza replied, unbuttoning the top two buttons on her rather severe collar.

The Archivist blinked. "But don't you want to know—"

"Wellington," Eliza stopped and held him still by one wrist, "There is only one thing I want to know."

He cleared his throat. "And what is that?"

"Do we still have our jobs?"

"Certainly," Wellington tilted his head. "Doctor Sound was quite—"

Eliza pressed one finger against his slightly chilly lips, "Then that is all I need. As long as we have the Ministry and the Archives I am quite content."

He stood there, her finger resting against his skin, and Eliza smiled sweetly at him before removing it.

"You are?" He was genuinely taken aback.

"Indeed."

"But . . . but what about your fieldwork, all that black powder and excitement you said you missed so much?"

And Eliza did laugh then. "My dear, sweet Welly—what we just went through was more than enough to satisfy even my"—she paused and grinned somewhat devilishly—"base instincts." With another lick of her ice she enjoyed the effect of her surprising statement.

When he was befuddled the Archivist was far handsomer than he realised. It was part of his charm. Kicking the damned skirts out from around her legs, Eliza turned and walked away, leaving the Archivist in her wake.

No footsteps followed after, but he did call out. "And the Cases in the back room, you'll let those be, won't you?"

Eliza thought of what they had achieved together. She didn't know what had happened after she'd been knocked out, but she suspected that Wellington was not telling her the whole truth, and that meant he had acquitted himself admirably. Eliza could live with the small concealments—she had plenty of her own after all.

"For now, Wellington," she replied lightly over her shoulder. "Until something else takes my fancy."

"Miss Braun?" he asked, gently at first. Wellington was still rooted where she had left him. She wondered if the penny ice was melting across his hand. She suspected it was. When his voice called again, there was a hint of panic in it. "*Miss Braun?!*"

Eliza didn't need to turn around to know what his expression would be. She increased her stride, feeling a smile spread across her face.